George Allan

Cursed

George Allan England

Cursed

1st Edition | ISBN: 978-3-75234-365-6

Place of Publication: Frankfurt am Main, Germany

Year of Publication: 2020

Outlook Verlag GmbH, Germany.

Reproduction of the original.

CURSED

BY

GEORGE ALLAN ENGLAND

CHAPTER I

AT BATU KAWAN

Slashed across the copper bowl of sunset, the jagged silhouette of tawny-shouldered mountains, fringed with areca-palms in black fretwork against the swift-fading glow, divided the tropic sky. Above, day yet lingered. Below, night's dim shroud, here and there spangled with glow-lights still or moving, had already folded earth in its obscurity.

Down from that mountain crest the descending slopes fell through grove and plantation to the drowned paddy-fields and to the miasmatic swamps, brooded by settling mists like thin, white breath of ghosts that in this Malay land all men gave faith to.

Nearer still, it reached the squalid *campong* of Batu Kawan. Batu Kawan, huddled in filth, disorder and disease between the steaming arsenical green of the lowlands and the muddy idleness of the boat-jammed Timbago River. Batu Kawan, whence the New Bedford clipper-ship, *Silver Fleece*, should have sailed two hours ago on the high tide, this 18th day of February, 1868. Batu Kawan, pestilent, malodorous, sinister, swarming with easy life, hemmed round with easier death.

William Scurlock, mate, was looking townward, leaning with crossed arms on rail. The umber smudge of half-light in the sky, fading over the torn edge of the mountains, revealed something of his blond bigness, freckled, weather-bitten, with close-cropped hair, a scarred jaw and hard teeth that gripped his cutty-pipe in bulldog fashion.

Scurlock seemed to be engaged with inward visionings, rather than outward. The occasional come-and-go of some dim figure in the waist of the ship, the fan-tan game of four or five Malay seamen—for the *Silver Fleece* carried a checkerboard crew, white, yellow and brown—as they squatted on their hunkers under the vague blur of a lantern just forward of the mainmast, and the hiccoughing stridor of an accordion in the fo'c's'le, roused in him no reaction.

Nor, as he lolled there under the awning, did he appear to take heed of the mud-clogged river with its jumble of sampans and house-boats, or of the thatched huts and tiled *godowns* past which the colorful swarm of Oriental life was idling along the bund. This stewing caldron of heat, haze, odors, dusk where fruit-bats staggered against the appearing stars said nothing whatever to the mate. All he could see in it was inefficiency, delay and loss.

Not all its wizardry of gleaming lights in hut and shop, its firefly paper lanterns, its murmuring strangeness could weigh against the vexing fact that his ship had missed the tide, and that—though her full cargo of tea, rattan, tapioca, cacao and opium was under hatches—she still lay made fast to the bamboo mooring-piles. What could offset the annoyance that Captain Alpheus Briggs, ashore on business of his own, was still delaying the vital business of working downstream on the ebb?

"Devil of a cap'n!" grumbled Scurlock. He spat moodily into the dark waters, and sucked at his pipe. "Ain't it enough for him to have put in a hundred boxes of raw opium, which is liable to land us all in hell, without stealin' a nigger wench an' now drinkin' samshu, ashore? Trouble comin'—mutiny an' murder an' damnation with trimmin's, or I'm no Gloucester man!"

Savagely he growled in his deep throat. Scurlock disapproved of Batu Kawan and of all its works, especially of its women and its raw rice-whisky. The East grated on his taut nerves. Vague singing in huts and the twangle of musically discordant strings set his teeth on edge. He hated the smells of the place, all seemingly compounded of curry and spices and mud and smoke of wood fires, through which the perfumes of strange fruits and heavy flowers drifted insistently.

The voices of mothers calling their naked little ones within their doors, lest Mambang Kuning, the yellow devil who dwells in the dusk, should snatch them, jarred upon his evil temper. So, too, the monotonous *tunk-tunk-tunk* of metal-workers' hammers in some unseen place; the snuffling grunt of carabaos wallowing in the mud-swale beyond the guava clump, up-stream; the nasal chatter of gharry-drivers and Kling boatmen; the whining sing-song of Malay pedlers with shouldered poles, whence swung baskets of sugar-cane and mangosteens. Scurlock abominated all that shuffling, chattering tangle of dark, half-clad life. The gorge of his trim, efficient, New England soul rose up against it, in hot scorn.

"Damn the Straits!" he grumbled, passing his hand over his forehead, sweaty in the breathless heat. "An' damn Briggs, too! It's my last voyage East, by joycus!"

Which was, indeed, the living truth, though by no means as Scurlock meant or understood it.

A plaintive hail from the rough brick coping of the bund drew his atrabilious attention. The mate saw that a brown, beardless fellow was making gestures at him. A lantern on the quarterdeck flung unsteady rays upon the Malay's nakedness, complete save for the breech-clout through which a kris was thrust. In his left hand he gripped a loose-woven coir bag, heavily full.

His left held out, on open palm, three or four shining globules. Scurlock viewed with resentment the lean, grinning face, lips reddened and teeth jet-black by reason of long years of chewing lime and betel.

"Turtle egg, sar, sellum piecee cheap," crooned the Malay. "Buyum turtle egg, sar?"

Scurlock's answer was to bend, reach for a piece of holystone in a bucket by the rail, and catapult it at the vagabond who had made so bold as to interrupt his musings. The Malay swung aside; the holystone crunched into the sack of eggs and slid to earth.

The screaming curse of the barbarian hardly crossed the rail ahead of the flung kris. The wavy, poisoned blade flickered, spinning. Scurlock stooped away; the fraction of an eyewink later would have done his life's business very neatly. Into the mizzen-mast drove the kris, and quivered there.

Scurlock turned, strode to it and plucked it out, swearing in his rage. The Malays at fan-tan by the gleam of the slush-light under the awning grew silent. Their fantastic little cards, of gaudy hue, dropped unheeded; for they had heard the name of Ratna Mutnu Manikam, god who brings death. Wherefore they shuddered, and turned scared faces aft; and some touched heart and forehead, warding off the curse.

Back to the rail, kris in hand, ran Scurlock.

"*Juldi*, you!" he shouted, with an oath unprintable. "Top your broom, you black swine—skip, before I come ashore an'split you! *Juldi jao!*"

The Malay hesitated. Scurlock, flinging "*Sur!*" at him, which in the *lingua franca* denominates a swine, started for the gangway. Silently the Malay faded into the little fringe of brown and yellow folk that had already gathered; and so he vanished. Scurlock was already setting foot upon the gangway that led slantwise down to the bund, when through the quickly coagulating street-crowd an eddy, developing, made visible by the vague light a large head covered with a topi hat wrapped in a pugree. Powerful shoulders and huge elbows, by no means chary of smashing right and left against the naked ribs, cleared a passage, amid grunts and gasps of pain; and once or twice the big man's fists swung effectively, by way of make-weight.

Then to William Scurlock's sight appeared a tall, heavy-set figure, rather dandified, in raw yellow bamboo silk and with very neatly polished boots that seemed to scorn the mud of Batu Kawan. A first glance recorded black brows of great luxuriance, a jungle of black beard contrasting sharply with a face reddened by wind, weather and hard liquor, and, in the V of a half-opened shirt, a corded neck and hairy chest molded on lines of the young Hercules.

4

This man would be going on for twenty-eight or so. Fists, eyes and jaw all lusted battle.

Alpheus Briggs, captain and part owner of the *Silver Fleece*, had returned.

CHAPTER II

ALPHEUS BRIGGS, BUCKO

For a moment, Briggs and Scurlock confronted each other, separated by the length of the gangway. Between them stretched silence; though on the bund a cackle and chatter of natives offended the night. Then Captain Briggs got sight of the kris. That sufficed, just as anything would have sufficed. He put his two huge, hairy fists on his hips; his neck swelled with rage born of samshu and a temper by nature the devil's own; he bellowed in a formidable roar:

"Drop that knife, Mr. Scurlock! What's the matter with you, sir?"

A wise mate would have obeyed, with never one word of answer. But Mr. Scurlock was very angry, and what very angry man was ever wise? He stammered, in a burst of rage:

"I—a Malay son of a pup—he hove it at me, an' I—"

"Hove it at you, did he, sir?"

"Yes, an'—"

Tigerish with drunken ferocity, Briggs sprang up the plank. A single, right-hand drive to the jaw felled Scurlock. The kris jangled away and came to rest as Scurlock sprawled along the planking.

"*Sir*, Mr. Scurlock!" fulminated Briggs—though not even in this blind passion did he forget sea-etiquette, the true-bred Yankee captain's "touch of the aft" in dealing with an officer. No verbal abuse; just the swinging fists now ready to knock Scurlock flat again, should he attempt to rise. "Say *sir* to me, Mr. Scurlock, or I'll teach you how!"

"Sir," mumbled the mate, half dazed. He struggled to a sitting posture, blinking up with eyes of hate at the taut-muscled young giant who towered over him, eager for another blow.

"All right, Mr. Scurlock, and don't forget I got a handle to my name, next time you speak to me. If any man, fore or aft, wants any o' my fist, let him leave off *sir*, to me!"

He kicked Scurlock heavily in the ribs, so that the breath went grunting from him; then reached down a gorilla-paw, dragged him up by the collar and flung him staggering into the arms of "Chips," the clipper's carpenter— Gascar, his name was—who had just come up the quarterdeck companion.

Other faces appeared: Bevans, the steward, and Prass, the bo'sun. Furiously Briggs confronted them all.

"Understand me?" he shouted, swaying a little as he stood there with eager fists. "Where's Mr. Wansley?"

"Asleep, sir," answered Bevans. Wansley, second-mate, was indeed dead to the world in his berth. Most of the work of stowing cargo had fallen on him, for in the old clippers a second-mate's life hardly outranked a dog's.

"What right has Mr. Wansley to be sleeping?" vociferated the captain, lashing himself into hotter rage. "By God, you're all a lot of lazy, loafing, impudent swine!"

One smash of the fist and Bevans went staggering toward the forward companion ladder, near the foot of which a little knot of seamen, white, brown and yellow, had gathered in cheerful expectation of seeing murder done.

Briggs balanced himself, a strange figure in his dandified silk and polished boots, with his topi hat awry, head thrust forward, brows scowling, massive neck swollen with rage and drink. Under the smudgy gleam of the lantern on the mizzen, his crimson face, muffled in jetty beard, and the evil-glowering eyes of him made a picture of wrath.

Briggs stooped, snatched up the kris that lay close by his feet, and with a hard-muscled arm whistled its keen edge through air.

"I'll keep order on my ship," he blared, passionately, "and if I can't do it with my fists, by God, I'll do it with this! The first man that loosens his tongue, I'll split him like a herring!"

"Captain Briggs, just a moment, sir!" exclaimed a voice at his left. A short, well-knit figure in blue, advancing out of the shadows, 'round the aft companion, laid a hand on the drunken brute's arm.

"You keep out of this, doctor!" cried Briggs. "They're a mutinous, black lot o' dogs that need lickin', and I'm the man to give it to 'em!"

"Yes, yes, sir, of course," Dr. Filhiol soothed the beast. "But as the ship's physician, let me advise you to go to your cabin, sir. The heat and humidity are extremely bad. There's danger of apoplexy, sir, if you let these fellows excite you. You aren't going to give them the satisfaction of seeing you drop dead, are you, captain?"

Thrown off his course by this new idea, Briggs peered, blinked, pushed back his topi and scratched his thick, close-curling poll. Then all at once he nodded, emphatically.

"Right you are, doctor!" he cried, his mood swiftly changing. "I'll go. They shan't murder me—not yet, much as they'd like to!"

"Well spoken, sir. You're a man of sense, sir—rare sense. And on a night like this—"

"The devil's own night!" spat Briggs. "God, the breath sticks in my throat!" With thick, violent fingers he ripped at his shirt, baring his breast.

"Captain Briggs!" exclaimed Scurlock, now on his feet again. "Listen to a word, sir, please."

"What the damnation now, sir?"

"We've lost the tide, sir. The comprador sent word aboard at four bells, he couldn't hold his sampan men much longer. We should be standin' downstream now, sir." Scurlock spoke with white, shaking lips, rubbing his smitten jaw. Hate, scorn, rage grappled in his soul with his invincible New England sense of duty, of efficiency, of getting the ship's work done. "If they're goin' to tow us down to-night, by joycus, sir, we've got to get under way, and be quick about it!"

Briggs dandled the kris. Its wavy blade, grooved to hold the dried curaré-poison that need do no more than scratch to kill, flung out vagrant high-lights in the gloom.

"For two cents I'd gut you, Mr. Scurlock," he retorted. "*I'm* master of this ship, and she'll sail when *I'm* ready, sir, not before!"

"Captain, they're only trying to badger-draw you," whispered Filhiol in the bucko's ear. "A man of your intelligence will beat them at their own game." Right well the doctor knew the futility of trying to get anything forward till the captain's rage and liquor should have died. "Let these dogs bark, sir, if they will. You and I are men of education. I propose a quiet drink or two, sir, and then a bit of sleep—"

"What the devil do you mean by that, sir?" flared Briggs, turning on him. "You mean I'm not able to take my ship out of this devil's ditch, to-night?"

"Farthest from my thought, captain," laughed the doctor. "Of course you can, sir, if you want to. But this mutinous scum is trying to force your hand. You're not the man to let them."

"I should say *not!*" swaggered the captain, with a blasphemy, while low-voiced murmurs ran among the men,—dim, half glimpsed figures by the mizzen, or in the waist. "Not much! Come, doctor!"

He lurched aft, still swinging the kris. Ardently Filhiol prayed he might gash himself therewith, but the devil guards his own. With savage grimace at

Scurlock, the physician whispered: "Name o' God, man, let him be!" Then, at a discreet distance, he followed Briggs.

Scurlock nodded, with murder in his eyes. Gascar and Bevans murmured words that must remain unwritten. Under the awning at the foot of the forward companion, white men from the fo'c'sle and Malays from the deck-house buzzed in divers tongues. Briggs, the while, was about to enter the after companion when to his irate ear the sound of a droning chant, somewhere ashore, came mingled with the dull thudding of a drum, monotonous, irritating as fever pulses in the brain of a sick man.

Briggs swerved to the starboard quarter rail and smote it mightily with his fist, as with bloodshot eyes he peered down at the smoky, lantern-glowing confusion of the bund.

"The damned Malays!" he shouted. "They've started another of their infernal sing-songs! If I could lay hands on that son of a whelp—"

He shook the kris madly at a little group about a blazing flare; in the midst squatted an itinerant ballad-singer. Tapping both heads of a small, barrel-like drum, the singer whined on and on, with intonations wholly maddening to the captain.

For a moment Briggs glared down at this scene, which to his fuddled senses seemed a challenge direct, especially devil-sent to harry him.

"Look at that now, doctor, will you?" Briggs flung out his powerful left hand toward the singer. "Want to bet I can't throw this knife through the black dog?"

He balanced the kris, ready for action, and with wicked eyes gauged the throw. Filhiol raised a disparaging hand.

"Don't waste a splendid curio on the dog, captain," smiled he, masking fear with indifference. Should Briggs so much as nick one of the Malays with that envenomed blade, Filhiol knew to a certainty that with fire and sword Batu Kawan would take complete vengeance. He knew that before morning no white man would draw life's breath aboard the *Silver Fleece*. "You've got a wonderful curio there, sir. Don't lose it, for a mere nothing."

"Curio? What the devil do *I* care for Malay junk?" retorted Briggs, thick-tongued and bestial. "The only place I'd like to see this toothpick would be stickin' out of that swine's ribs!"

"Ah, but you don't realize the value of the knife, sir," wheedled Filhiol. "It's an extraordinarily fine piece of steel, captain, and the carving of the lotus bud on the handle is a little masterpiece. I'd like it for my collection." He paused, struck by inspiration. "I'll play you for the knife, sir. Let's have that drink we were speaking of, and then a few hands of poker. I'll play you anything I've got—my watch, my instrument case, my wages for the voyage, whatever you like—against that kris. Is that a go?"

"Sheer off!" mocked Briggs, raising the blade. The doctor's eye judged distance. He would grapple, if it came to that. But still he held to craft:

"This is the first time, captain, I ever knew you to be afraid of a good gamble."

"Afraid? Me, afraid?" shouted the drunken man. "I'll make you eat those words, sir! The knife against your pay!"

"Done!" said the doctor, stretching out his hand. Briggs took it in a grip that gritted the bones of Filhiol, then for a moment stood blinking, dazed, hiccoughing once or twice. His purpose, vacillant, once more was drawn to the singer. He laughed, with a maudlin catch of the breath.

"*Does* that gibberish mean anything, doctor?" asked he.

"Never mind, sir," answered Filhiol. "We've got a game to play, and—"

"Not just yet, sir! That damned native may be laying a curse on me, for all I know. Mr. Scurlock!" he suddenly shouted forward.

"Aye, aye, sir," answered the mate's voice, through the gloom.

"Send me a Malay—one that can talk United States!"

"Yes, sir!" And Scurlock was heard in converse with the brown men in the waist. Over the rail the captain leaned, staring at the singer and the crowd, the smoky torches, the confused crawling of life in Batu Kawan; and as he stared, he muttered to himself, and twisted at his beard with his left hand—his right still gripped the kris.

"You damned, outrageous blackguard!" the doctor thought. "If I ever get you into your cabin, God curse me if I don't throw enough opium into you to keep you quiet till we're a hundred miles at sea!"

Came the barefoot slatting of a Malay, *pad-pad-padding* aft, and the sound of a soft-voiced: "Captain Briggs, sar?"

"You the man that Mr. Scurlock sent?" demanded Briggs.

"Yas, sar."

"All right. Listen to that fellow down there—the one that's singing!" Briggs laid a hand on the Malay, jerked him to the rail and pointed a thick, angry finger. "Tell me what he's sayin'! Understand?"

"Yas, sar."

The Malay put both lean, brown hands on the rail, squinted his gray eyes, impassive as a Buddha's, and gave attentive ear. To him arose the droning words of the long-drawn, musical cadences:

Arang itou dibasouh dengan ayer
Mawar sakalipoun tiada akan poutih.

Satahoun houdjan di langit ayer latout masakan tawar?

Sebab tiada tahon menari dikatakan tembad.

Tabour bidjian diatas tasik tiada akan toumbounh—

On, on wailed the chant. At last the Malay shook his head, shrugged thin shoulders under his cotton shirt, and cast an uneasy glance at Briggs, looming black-bearded and angry at his side.

"Well, what's it all about?" demanded the captain, thudding a fist on the rail. "Sayin' anythin' about me, or the *Silver Fleece*? If he is—"

"No, sar. Nothin' so, sar."

"Well, what?"

"He sing about wicked things. About sin. He say—"

"*What* does he say, you cinder from the Pit?"

"He say, you take coal, wash him long time, in water of roses, coal never get white. Sin always stay. He say, rain fall long time, one year, ocean never get fresh water. Always salty water. Sin always stay. He say one small piece indigo fall in one jar of goat-milk, spoil all milk, make all milk blue. One sin last all life, always." The Malay paused, trying to muster his paucity of English. Briggs shook him roughly, bidding him go on, or suffer harm.

"He say if sky will go to fall down, no man can hold him up. Sin always fall down. He say, good seed on land, him grow. Good seed on ocean, him never grow. He say—"

"That'll do! Stow your jaw, now!"

"Yas, sar."

"Get out—go forrard!"

The Malay salaamed, departed. Briggs hailed him again.

"Hey, you!"

"Yes, sar?" answered the brown fellow, wheeling.

"What's your name—if pigs have names?"

"Mahmud Baba, sar," the Malay still replied with outward calm. Yet to call a follower of the Prophet "pig" could not by any invention of the mind have been surpassed in the vocabulary of death-inviting insult.

"My Mud Baby, eh? Good name—that's a slick one!" And Briggs roared into a laugh of drunken discord. He saw not that the Malay face was twitching; he saw not the stained teeth in grimaces of sudden hate. Gloom veiled this. "I'll remember that," he went on. "My Mud Baby. Well now, Mud Baby, back to your sty!"

"Captain Briggs," the doctor put in, fair desperate to get this brute below-decks ere blood should flow. "Captain, if you were as anxious as I am for a good stiff game of poker and a stiffer drink, you wouldn't be wasting your breath on Malay rubbish. Shall we mix a toddy for the first one?"

"Good idea, sir!" Briggs answered, his eyes brightening. He clapped Filhiol on the shoulder, so that the man reeled toward the after-companion.

Down the stairway they went, the doctor cursing under his breath, Briggs clumping heavily, singing a snatch of low ribaldry from a Bombay gambling-hell. They entered the cabin. To them, as the door closed, still droned the voice of the minstrel on the bund:

Sebab tiada tahon menari dikatakan tembad,
Tabour bidjian diatas tasik tiada akan toumbounh.

One drop of indigo spoils the whole jar of milk;
Seed sown upon the ocean never grows.

CHAPTER III

SCURLOCK GOES ASHORE

Sweltering though the cabin was, it seemed to Dr. Filhiol a blessèd haven of refuge from the probabilities of grevious harm that menaced, without. With a deep breath of relief he saw Briggs lay the kris on the cabin table. Himself, he sat down at that table, and while Briggs stood there half-grinning with white teeth through black beard, took up the knife.

He studied it, noting its keen, double edge, its polished steel, the deft carving of the lotus-bud handle. Then, as he laid it down, he offered:

"It's a genuine antique. I'll go you a month's wages against it."

"You'll do nothin' of the kind, sir!" ejaculated Briggs, and took it up again. "The voyage, you said, and it's that or nothing!"

The doctor bit his close-razored lip. Then he nodded. Filhiol was shrewd, and sober; Briggs, rash and drunk. Yes, for the sake of getting that cursed knife out of the captain's hands, Filhiol would accept.

"Put it out of harm's way, sir, and let's deal the cards," said he. "It's poisoned. We don't want it where we might get scratched, by accident."

"Poisoned, sir?" demanded Briggs, running a horny thumb along the point. His brows wrinkled, inquisitively. No fear showed in that splendidly male, lawless, unconquered face.

"For God's sake, captain, put that devilish thing away!" exclaimed the doctor, feigning to shudder; though all the while a secret hope was whispering:

"Heaven send that he may cut himself!" Aloud he said: "I'll play no game, sir, with that kris in sight. Put it in your locker, captain, and set out the drink. My throat's afire!"

"Poisoned, eh?" grunted the captain again, still with drunken obstinacy testing the edge. "All damned nonsense, sir. After that's been run into the Oregon pine of my mizzen, a couple of inches—"

"There's still enough left to put you in a shotted hammock, sir, if you cut yourself," the doctor insisted. "But it's your own affair. If you choose to have Mr. Scurlock take the *Silver Fleece* back to Long Wharf, Boston, while you rot in Motomolo Straits—"

With a blasphemy, Briggs strode to his locker. The doctor smiled cannily as Briggs flung open the locker, tossed in the kris and, taking a square-shouldered bottle, returned to the table. This bottle the captain thumped down on the table, under the lamp-gleam.

"Best Old Jamaica," boasted he. "Best is none too good, when I win my doctor's entire pay. For it's as good as mine already, and you can lay to that!"

Speaking, he worried out the cork. He sniffed at the bottle, blinked, peered wonderingly at the label, and sniffed again.

"Hell's bells!" roared Briggs, flaring into sudden passion.

"What's the matter, sir?"

"Old Jamaica!" vociferated the captain. "It *was* Old Jamaica, but now smell o' that, will you?"

Filhiol sniffed, tentatively. In a second he knew some one had been tampering with the liquor, substituting low-grade spirits for Brigg's choicest treasure; but he merely shrugged his shoulders, with:

"It seems like very good rum, sir. Come, let's mix our grog and get the cards."

"Good rum!" gibed Briggs. "Some thieving son of Satan has been at my Jamaica, and has been fillin' the square-face up with hog-slop, or I never sailed blue water! *Look* at the stuff now, will you?"

He spilled out half a glass of the liquor, tasted it, spat it upon the floor. Then he dashed the glass violently to the boards, crashing it to flying shards and spattering the rum all about. In a bull-like roar he shouted:

"Boy! You, there, boy!"

A moment, and one of the doors leading off the main cabin opened, on the port side. A pale, slim boy appeared and advanced into the cabin, blinking up with fear at the black-bearded vision of wrath.

"Yes, sir? What is it, sir?" asked he, in a scared voice.

Briggs dealt him a cuff that sent him reeling. The captain's huge hand, swinging back, overset the bottle, that gurgled out its life-blood.

"What *is* it?" shouted Briggs. "You got the impudence to ask me what it is? I'll learn you to step livelier when I call, you whelp! Come here!"

"Yes, sir," quavered the boy. Shaking, he sidled nearer. "What—what do you want, sir?"

"What do I *want*?" the captain howled; while Filhiol, suddenly pale with a rage that shook his heart, pressed lips hard together, lest some word escape them. "You swab! Catechisin' me, are you? Askin' *me* what I want, eh? If I had a rope's-end here I'd show you! Get out, now. Go, tell Mr. Scurlock I want him. Jump!"

The lad ducked another blow, ran to the cabin-door and sprang for the stairs. Ill-fortune ran at his side. He missed footing, sprawled headlong up the companion stairway.

With a shout of exultation, Briggs caught up from a corner a long, smooth stick, with a polished knob carved from a root—one of the clubs known in the Straits as "Penang-lawyers," by reason of their efficacy in settling disputes. He grabbed the writhing boy, now frantically trying to scrabble up the stairs, in a clutch that almost crunched the frail shoulder bones. Up the companion he dragged him—the boy screaming with terror of death—and hurled him out on deck, fair against the wheel.

The boy collapsed in a limp, groaning heap. Briggs laughed wildly, and, brandishing the Penang-lawyer, advanced out upon the dim-lit planking.

An arm thrust him back.

"You ain't goin' to hit that there boy!" shouted a voice—William Scurlock's. "Not while I'm alive, you ain't!"

A wrench and the club flew over the rail. It splashed in the dark, slow waters of the Timbago.

Briggs gulped. He whirled, both fists knotted. Then, swift as a cobra, he sprang and struck.

Scurlock dodged. The captain's fist, finding no mark, drove against one of the spokes of the wheel with a crash that split the hickory. As Briggs had never cursed before, now he cursed. For a second or two he nursed his damaged hand.

The brief respite sufficed. Scurlock snatched up the boy. He started forward, just as the doctor appeared at the top of the companion.

"Captain Briggs, sir!" cried Filhiol, in a shaking voice. Still he was hoping against hope to keep the peace. "Are you hurt, sir?"

"To hell with you!" roared Briggs, now forgetting sea-etiquette—surest indication of the extremity of his drunken passion. He lurched after the retreating Scurlock. "Back, here, you bloody swine! Drop that brat, and I'll show you who's boss!"

Scurlock laughed mockingly and quickened his stride. Mad with the rage that kills, Briggs pursued, a huge, lunging figure of malevolence and hate. Before he could lay grips on Scurlock, the mate wheeled. He let the fainting boy slide down on deck, whipped out a clasp-knife, snicked open the blade. Holding it low, to rip upward, he confronted Briggs under the glimmer of the mizzen-lantern.

Now this was raw mutiny, and a hanging matter if Scurlock drew one drop of the captain's blood. But that Scurlock cared nothing for the noose was very plain to see. Even the crimson rage of Briggs saw death knocking at the doors of his life. Barehanded, he could not close for battle. He recoiled, his bloodshot eyes shuttling for some handy weapon.

"Damn you, if I had that kris—" he panted.

"But you ain't, you lousy bucko!" mocked Scurlock. "An' you turn your back on me, to go for it, if you dare!"

Briggs sprang for the rail. He snatched at a belaying-pin, with wicked blasphemies. The pin stuck, a moment. He wrenched it clear, and wheeled— too late.

Already Scurlock had snatched up the boy again. Already he was at the gangway. Down it he leaped, to the bund. With the unconscious boy still in the crook of his left arm, he shoved into the scatter of idling natives. Then he turned, raised a fist of quivering hatred, and flung his defiance toward the vague, yellow-clad figure now hesitating at the top of the gangway, pin in hand:

"I'm through with you, you rum-soaked hellbender! He's through, too, the boy is. We'll take our chances with the Malays an' the plague."

Scurlock's voice, rising out of the softly-lit tropic evening, died suddenly.

"Come back, Mr. Scurlock, and bring that boy!" cried the doctor, from the rail.

"I've got nothin' against you, sir," answered Scurlock. "But against *him*. God! If I come back, it'll only be to cut his black heart out an' throw it to the sharks. We're done!"

A moment Briggs stood drunkenly peering, half minded to pursue, to match his belaying-pin against the mate's dirk. Gurgling in his throat—for excess of rage had closed upon all speech—he panted, with froth upon his black beard, while dim figures along the rail and on shore waited great deeds. Then all at once he laughed—a horrible, deep-throated laugh, rising, swelling to mighty and bestial merriment; the laugh of a gorilla, made man.

"The Malays and the plague," he thickly stammered. "—He's said it—let 'em go! They're good as dead already, and hell take 'em!"

He swung on his heel, then strode back unsteadily to the companion.

16

Down it he lunged. Still laughing, he burst into the heat and reek of the cabin.

"Come on, doctor," cried he, "our cards, our cards!"

CHAPTER IV

THE CURSE OF NENEK KABAYAN

"He'll steal no more of my Old Jamaica," exulted Briggs, flinging himself into a chair by the table. "And that sniveling boy will give me no more of his infernal lip! Skunks!" He picked up the bottle, still containing a little rum, and poured a gulp of liquor down his throat. "On my own ship!"

"Where are the cards, sir?" asked Filhiol. His voice, quivering, was hardly audible.

"Petty game," burst out the captain, "no good. Make it a real one, and I'll go you!"

"What do you mean, sir?"

"Stakes worth playin' for! Man-size stakes! You got money in Boston, sir. Some fifteen thousand. I'll play you for that, plus your wages this voyage!"

"Against what, sir?"

"Against my share of the ship's cargo, and my share of the *Silver Fleece*, herself. And if I scuttle her, as scuttle her I may, in case the insurance money foots bigger than the ship's worth and the cargo, I stake that money, too!"

The doctor pondered a moment, while Briggs pressed a hand to his thick neck, redly swollen with heat and rum. Suddenly the captain broke out again:

"That's an A1 gamble for you, sir. When I land my West Coast natives at San Felipe, and slip my opium into Boston, there won't be a shipmaster walk up State Street that will be better fixed than I'll be."

"Bring out the cards, sir," answered the doctor. "But the kris goes in as part of the wager?"

"Yes, damn it, and I'll be generous," slavered Briggs. He jerked open the table drawer and fetched out a well-thumbed pack of cards, which he flung on the green cloth. "I'll put up a stake that'd make any man's mouth water, sir, if he *is* a man! Though maybe you're not, bein' only a sawbones!"

"What's that, sir?"

"The yellow wench asleep in my berth—Kuala Pahang!"

"Done!" exclaimed Filhiol, humoring the ruffian to all possible limits, till liquor and heat should have overcome him.

"Deal the cards, sir!" cried Briggs. "I may be a bucko, and I may be drunk to-night, but I know a man when I see one. I'm not too drunk to add your wages and your savin's to my plunder. Deal the cards!"

Filhiol had just fallen to shuffling the pasteboards when a groan, from behind the door of the captain's private cabin, arrested his hand. Frowning, he swung around. In his tensing hand the cards bent almost double.

Briggs buffeted him upon the shoulder, with huge merriment.

"*She's* not dead yet, is she?" exulted he. "No, no, not yet. Even though everybody in this devil's hole claims the wenches will die first, before they'll be a white man's darlin'." His speech had become so thick as to be hardly speech at all. "All infernal liars, sawbones! She's been here already two days, Topsy has. An' is she dead yet? Not very! No, nor not goin' to die, neither, an' you can lay to that! Nor get away from me. Not while I'm alive, an' master o' the *Silver Fleece!*"

The doctor's jaw set so hard that his tanned skin whitened over the maxillary muscles. Very vividly Filhiol still perceived the danger of general mutiny, of mass-attack from Batu Kawan, of fire and sword impending before the clipper could be got down-river and away. Come all that might, he must cling to Briggs, warily, humoringly.

After all, what was one native girl, more or less? The doctor shuffled the cards again, and dealt, under the raw light of the swinging-lamp. A louder cry from the girl turned Briggs around.

"Damnation!" he blared, starting up. "If the wench gets to howling, she'll raise the town. I'm goin' to shut her jaw, and shut it hard!"

"Quite right, sir," assented the doctor, though his deep eyes glowed with murder. "But, why not get under way, at once, drop down the river to-night, anchor inside Ulu Salama bar till—"

Briggs interrupted him with a boisterous laugh.

"Even Reuben Ranzo, the tailor," he gibed, "could give you points on navigation!" He stared at Filhiol a moment, his face darkening; then added harshly: "You stick to your pills and powders, Mr. Filhiol, or there'll be trouble. I won't have anybody tryin' to boss. Now, I'm not goin' to tell you twice!"

For three heartbeats their eyes met. The doctor's had become injected with blood. His face had assumed an animal expression. Briggs snapped his thick fingers under the physician's nose, then turned with an oath and strode to his cabin door. He snatched it open, and stood there a moment peering in, his face deep-lined in a mask of vicious rage.

"Captain Briggs!"

The doctor's voice brought the ruffian about with a sharp turn.

"*You* mutinous, too?" shouted he, swinging his shoulders, loose, hulking, under the yellow silk of his jacket.

"By no means, sir. As a personal favor to me, however, I'm asking you not to strike that girl." The doctor's voice was shaking; yet still he sat there at the table, holding his cards in a quivering hand.

"You look out for your own skin, sawbones!" Briggs menaced. "The woman's mine to do with as I please, an' it's nobody's damn business, you lay to that! I'll love her or beat her or throw her to the sharks, as I see fit. So now you hear me, an' I warn you proper, stand clear o' me, or watch out for squalls!"

Into the cabin he lunged, just as another door, opening, disclosed a sleepy-eyed, yellow-haired young man—Mr. Wansley, second-mate of the devil-ship. Wansley stared, and the doctor stood up with doubled fists, as they heard the sound of blows from within, then shriller cries, ending in a kind of gurgle—then silence.

The doctor gripped both hands together, striving to hold himself. The life of every white man aboard now depended absolutely on seeing this thing through without starting mutiny and war.

"Get back in your cabin, Mr. Wansley, for God's sake!" he exclaimed, "or go on deck! The captain's crazy drunk. If he sees you here, there'll be hell to pay. Get out, quick!"

Wansley grasped the situation and made a speedy exit up the after-companion, just ahead of Briggs's return. The captain banged his cabin door, and staggered back to the table. He dusted his palms one against the other.

"The black she-dog won't whine again, for *one* while," he grinned with white teeth through his mat of beard. "That's the only way to teach 'em their lesson!" He clenched both fists, turning them, admiring them under the lamp-light. "Great pacifiers, eh, sawbones? *I* tell you! Beat a dog an' a woman, an' you can't go far off your course. So now I'll deal the cards, an' win every cent you've got!"

"The cards are dealt, sir," answered Filhiol, chalky to the lips.

"Yes, an' you've been here with 'em, all alone!" retorted the captain. "No, sir, that won't go. Fresh deal—here, I'll do it!"

He gathered the dealt hands and unsteadily began shuffling, while the doctor, teeth set in lip, swallowed the affront. Some of the cards escaped the drunken brute's thick fingers; two or three dropped to the floor.

"Pick 'em up, sir," directed Briggs. "No captain of my stamp bends his back before another man—an' besides, I know you'd be glad to knife me, while I was down!"

Filhiol made no answer. He merely obeyed, and handed the cards to Briggs, who was about to deal, when all at once his hands arrested their motion. His eyes fixed themselves in an incredulous, widening stare, at the forward cabin door. His massive jaw dropped. A sound escaped his throat, but no word came.

The doctor spun his chair around. He, too, beheld a singular apparition; though how it could have got there—unless collusion had been at work among the Malays in the waist—seemed hard to understand.

So silently the door had slid, that the coming of the aged native woman had made no sound. Aged she seemed, incredibly old, wizen, dried; though with these people who can tell of age? The dim light revealed her barefooted, clad in a short, gaudily-striped skirt, a tight-wrapped body-cloth that bound her shrunken breast. Coins dangled from her ears; her straight black hair was drawn back flatly; her lips, reddened with lime and betel, showed black, sharp-filed teeth in a horrible snarl of hatred.

Silent, a strange yellow ghostlike thing, she crept nearer. Briggs sprang up, snatched the rum-bottle by its neck and waited, quivering. Right well he knew the woman—old Dengan Jouga, mother of Kuala, his prey.

For the first time in years unnerved, he stood there. Had she rushed in at him, screamed, vociferated, clawed with hooked talons, beaten at him with skinny fists, he would have knocked her senseless, dragged her on deck and flung her to the bund; but this cold, silent, beady-eyed approach took all his sails aback.

Only for a moment, however. Briggs was none of your impressionable men, the less so when in drink.

"Get out!" he shouted, brandishing the bottle. "Out o' this, or by God—"

The door, opening again, disclosed the agitated face of Texel, a foremast hand.

"Cap'n Briggs, sir!" exclaimed this wight, touching his cap, "one o' the Malays says *she*, there, has got news o' Mr. Scurlock an' the boy, sir, that you'll want to hear. He's out here now, the Malay is. Will I tell him to come in?"

"I could have you flogged, you scum, for darin' to come into my cabin till you're called," shouted Briggs. "But send the pig in!"

The bottle lowered, as Briggs peered frowning at the silent hag. Uncanny, this stillness was. Tempests, hurricanes of passion and of hate would have quite suited him; but the old Malay crone, standing there half-way to the table, the light glinting from her deep coal-black eyes, her withered hands clutching each other across her wasted body, disconcerted even his bull-like crassness.

The seaman turned and whistled. At once, a Malay slid noiselessly in, salaamed and stood waiting. Texel, nervously fingering the cap he held in his hands, lingered by the door.

"Oh, it's you again, Mud Baby, is it?" cried the bucko. "What's the news Dengan Jouga has for me? Tell her to hand it over an' then clear out! Savvy?"

"Captain, sahib, sar," stammered Mahmud, almost gray with fear, every lean limb aquiver with the most extraordinary panic. "She says Mr. Scurlock, an' boy, him prisoner. You give up girl, Kuala Pahang. No givem—"

The sentence ended in a quick stroke of the Malay's forefinger across the windpipe, a whistling sound.

Briggs stared and swore. The doctor laid a hand on his arm.

"Checkmated, sir," said he. "The old woman wins."

"Like hell!" roared the captain. "I don't know what the devil she's talkin' about. If Scurlock an' the boy get their fool throats cut, it's their own fault. They're bein' punished for mutiny. No girl here, at all! You, Mud Baby, tell that to old Jezebel!"

Mahmud nodded, and slid into a sing-song chatter. The woman gave ear, all the while watching Briggs with the unwinking gaze of a snake. She flung back a few crisp words at Mahmud.

"Well, what now?" demanded Briggs.

"She say, you lie, captain, sar!"

"I *lie*, do I?" vociferated the bucko. He heaved the bottle aloft and would have struck the hag full force, had not the doctor caught his arm, and held it fast.

"My God, captain!" cried Filhiol, gusty with rage and fear. "You want mutiny? Want the whole damned town swarming over us, with torch and kris?"

Briggs tried to fling him off, but the doctor clung, in desperation. Mahmud Baba wailed:

"No, no, captain! No touch her! She very bad luck—she Nenek Kabayan!"

"What the devil do *I* care?" roared Briggs, staggering as he struggled with the doctor. "She's got to get out o' my cabin, or by—"

"She's a witch-woman!" shouted Filhiol, clinging fast. "That means a witch, Nenek Kabayan does. If you strike her, they'll tear your heart out!"

Mahmud, in the extremity of his terror, clasped thin, brown hands, groveled, clutching at the captain's knees. Briggs kicked him away like a dog.

"Get out, you an' everybody!" he bellowed. "Doctor, I'll lay you in irons for this. Into the lazaret you go, so help me!"

The witch-woman, raising crooked claws against him, hurled shrill curses at Briggs—wild, unintelligible things, in a wail so penetrantly heart-shaking, that even the captain's bull-like rage shuddered.

From the floor, Mahmud raised appealing hands.

"She say, give girl or she make *orang onto* kill everybody!" cried the Malay. "*Orang onto*, bad ghost! She say she make *sabali*—sacrifice—of everybody on ship." His voice broke, raw, in a frenzy of terror. "She say Vishnu lay curse on us, dead men come out of graves, be wolves, be tigers —*menjelma kramat*—follow us everywhere!"

"Shut your jaw, idiot!" shouted Briggs, but in a tone less brutal. The man was shaken. Not all his bluster could blink that fact. The doctor loosed his arm; Briggs did not raise the bottle, now, to strike. On and on wailed Mahmud:

"She say *chandra wasi*, birds of ocean foam, poison us, an' Zemrud, him what keep life, leave us. She say blind face in sky watch you, cap'n, sahib, an' laugh, an' you want to die, but you not die. She say you' life be more poison than *katchubong* flowers—she say evil seed grow in you' heart, all life long— she say somethin' you love, cap'n, sar, somethin' you love more than you' life, sometime die, an' you die then but still you not die! She say—"

Briggs chewed and spat a curse and, turning to the table, sat down heavily there. Astonished, Filhiol stared at him. Never had he seen the captain in this mood. A wild attack, assault, even murder, would not have surprised the doctor; but this strange quietude surpassed belief. Filhiol leaned over Briggs, as he sat there sagging, staring at the witch-woman still in furious tirade.

"Captain," he whispered, "you're going to give up the girl, of course?

You're going to save Mr. Scurlock and the boy, and keep this shriveled monkey of a witch from raising the town against us?"

Briggs only shook his head.

"No," he answered, in a strange, weary voice. "She can't have her, an' that's flat. I don't give a damn for the deserters, an' if it comes to a fight, we got our signal-cannon an' enough small-arms to make it hot for all the natives between here an' hell. The girl's plump as a young porpoise, an' she's mine, an' I'm going to keep her; you can lay to that!"

Mahmud, still stammering crude translation of the witch-woman's imprecations, crawled to Briggs's feet. Briggs kicked the man away, once more, and burst into a jangle of laughter.

"Get 'em all out o' here, sawbones," said he, his head sagging. The life seemed to have departed from him. "I'm tired of all this hullabaloo." He opened his table drawer and drew out an army revolver. "Three minutes for you to get 'em all out, doctor, or I begin shootin'."

In the redness of his eye, bleared with drink and rage, Filhiol read cold murder. He dragged Mahmud up, and herded him, with Texel and the now silent witch-woman, out the forward cabin door.

"*You* get out, too!" mouthed the captain, dully. "I'll have no sawbones sneakin' and spyin' on my honeymoon. Get out, afore I break you in ways your books don't tell you how to fix!"

The doctor gave him one silent look. Then, very tight-lipped, he issued out beneath the awning, where among the Malays a whispering buzz of talk was forward.

As he wearily climbed the companion ladder, he heard the bolt go home, in the cabin door. A dull, strange laugh reached his ears, with mumbled words.

"God save us, now!" prayed Filhiol, for the first time in twenty years. "God save and keep us, now!"

CHAPTER V

THE MALAY FLEET OF WAR

Dawn, leaping out of Motomolo Strait, flinging its gold-wrought, crimson mantle over an oily sea that ached with crawling color, found the clipper ship, whereon rested the curse of old Dengan Jouga, set fast and fair on the sandspit of Ula Salama, eight miles off the mouth of the Timbago River.

Fair and fast she lay there, on a tide very near low ebb, so that two hours or such a matter would float her again; but in two hours much can happen and much was destined to.

At the taffrail, looking landward where the sand-dunes of the river met the sea, and where tamarisk and mangrove-thickets and pandan-clumps lay dark against the amethyst-hazed horizon, Dr. Filhiol and Mr. Wansley—now first mate of the *Silver Fleece*, with Prass installed as second—were holding moody speech.

"As luck goes," the doctor was growling, "this voyage outclasses anything I've ever known. This puts the climax on—this Scurlock matter, and the yellow girl, *and* going aground."

"We did the best we could, sir," affirmed Wansley, hands deep in jacket pockets. "With just tops'ls an' fores'ls on her—"

"Oh, I'm not criticising your navigation, Mr. Wansley," the doctor interrupted. "The old man, of course, is the only one who knows the bars, and we didn't dare wait for him to wake up. Yes, you did very well indeed. If you'd been carrying full canvas, you'd have sprung her butts, when she struck, and maybe lost a stick or two. Perhaps there's no great harm done, after all, if we can hold this damned crew."

Thus hopefully the doctor spoke, under the long, level shafts of day breaking along the gold and purple waters that further off to sea blended into pale greens and lovely opalescences. But his eyes, turning now and then towards the ship's waist, and his ear, keen to pick up a more than usual chatter down there under the weather-yellowed awnings, belied his words.

Now, things were making that the doctor knew not of; things that, had he known them, would have very swiftly translated his dull anxieties into active fears. For down the mud-laden river, whose turbid flood tinged Motomolo Strait with coffee five miles at sea, a fleet of motley craft was even now very purposefully making way.

This fleet was sailing with platted bamboo-mats bellying on the morning breeze, with loose-stepped masts and curiously tangled rattan cordage; or, in part, was pulling down-stream with carven oars and paddles backed by the strength of well-oiled brown and yellow arms.

A fleet it was, laden to the topmost carving of its gunwales with deadly hate of the white men. A fleet hastily swept together by the threats, promises and curses of old Dengan Jouga, the witch-woman. A rescue fleet, for the salvation of the yellow girl—a fleet grim either to take her back to Batu Kawan, or else to leave the charred ribs of the *Silver Fleece* smoldering on Ulu Salama bar as a funeral pyre over the bones of every hated *orang puti*, white man, that trod her cursèd decks.

Nineteen boats in all there were; seven sail-driven, twelve thrust along with oars and paddles cunningly fashioned from teak and *tiu* wood. These nineteen boats carried close on three hundred fighting men, many of them head-hunters lured by the prospect of a white man's head to give their sweethearts.

A sinister and motley crew, indeed; some of chief's rank, clad in rare feather cloaks, but for the most part boasting no garment save the *de rigueur* breech-clout. Among them rowed no less than eight or ten Mohammedan *amok* fanatics, who had sworn on the beard of the Prophet to take a Frank dog's life or else to die—in either event surely destined for paradise and the houris' arms. And one of these fanatics was the turtle-egg seller, with special hopes in mind which for the present cannot be divulged.

Under the leadership of Dengan Jouga and a lean, painted *pawang*, or medicine-man, the war fleet crawled downstream. Spears, axes, stone and iron maces with ornate hafts bristled in all the long war-canoes, high-prowed and gaudy with flaring colors. Blow-guns, too, were there, carrying venomed darts, and krises by the score—wavy-edged blades, heavy and long, that, driven by a sinewed arm, would slice through a man's neck as if it had been *ghee*, or melted butter; would open a man's body broad to the light of day; or, slashing downward, split him from crown to collar bone.

The morning shafts of sun glinted, too, on gun-barrels—old flintlock muzzle-loaders, with a few antique East India Company's rifles that in some obscure channels of trade had worked their way up the east coast of the Malay Peninsula to Batu Kawan. Some bowmen had long arrows wrapped in oil-soaked cotton pledgets. Such fire-balls, shot into the sun-dried canvas of the clipper, might go far towards leaving her bones ableach on Ulu Salama.

Nor was this all. More formidable still was a small, brass cannon, securely lashed in the bows of a seagoing proa, its lateen sail all patched with brown and blue; a proa manned by fifty chosen warriors, and carrying the medicine man and Dengan Jouga herself. True, the Malays had only a scant dozen charges for their ordnance, but if they could catch the hull of the *Silver Fleece* between wind and water, as she careened on the bar, they might so riddle her that the up-coming tide would pour her full of brine.

Down the fever-smelling river, steaming with heat and purple haze under the mounting sun, the war-fleet drove, between lush banks now crowded with sandal and angsana-trees all clustered with their lolling, yellow blooms, now mere thickets where apes and screaming parrots rioted amid snarled labyrinths of lianas, now sinking into swamps choked with bamboo and lalang grass.

In some occasional pool, pink lotus-blossoms contrasted with fragrant charm against the vivid, unhealthy green of marsh and forest. And, louder than the crooning war-songs that unevenly drifted on the shimmering air, the loomlike whir of myriad trumpeter-beetles blurred the waiting day whose open eye shrank not from what must be.

Here, there, a fisherman's hut extended its crazy platform out over the sullen waters. From such platforms, yellow-brown folk with braided top-knots shouted words of good augury to the on-toiling warriors. Naked, pot-bellied children stood and stared in awe. Flea-tormented curs barked dolefully. And from such fisher-boats, as lay anchored in the stream, rose shouts of joy. For, in the mysterious way of the Orient, the news of the great, black deed done by the devil-captain, Briggs Sahib, had already run all down the Timbago.

Thus the war-fleet labored downward to the sea, coming [towards the hour that a landsman would call eight o'clock,] to salt water. Withered Dengan Jouga, crouching snake-eyed in the proa, caught sight of the long, turquoise line that marked the freedom of the open.

She pointed a skinny arm, flung a word at Akan Mawar, the medicine man, and clutched more tightly the thin-bladed knife which—so all had sworn to her—she, and only she, should plunge into the heart of the black-bearded devil. Silently she waited, as the seascape broadened. The sunlight, sparkling on that watery plain, dazzled her eyes like the shimmer of powdered glass, but still she peered, eager to catch a glimpse of the *Silver Fleece*. Her betel-reddened lips moved again. She whispered:

"My daughter I shall have. His blood, his blood I shall have, even though he flee from me *diatas angin*, beyond the back of the wind! King Surana, who reigns in the watery depths, will give him to me. Even though he flee through the Silken Sea, at the end of the world, I shall have his blood! *Tuan Allah poonia krajah!* It is the work of the Almighty."

"Tuan Allah poonia krajah!" echoed old Akan Mawar; and other voices raised the supplication. Back drifted the words from boat to boat; the whole river murmured with confused echoes: *"Tuan Allah poonia krajah!"*

Now silence fell again, but for the lipping of cleft waters at many prows, the dip of oars, the little whispering swirl of eddies where paddles lifted. Bright-yellow sands, here and there gleaming pearl-white with millions of turtle-eggs, extended seaward from the river-mouth, pointing like a dagger of menace at Ulu Salama bar eight miles to sea; the bar that Alpheus Briggs so easily could have left to starboard, had he not been sleeping off the fumes of samshu in the cabin with Kuala Pahang.

Cries from the proa and the war-canoes echoed across the waters. No longer could savagery repress its rage. Already, far and dim through the set of haze that brooded over Motomolo Strait, dimming the liquid light of morning, eyes of eager hate had seen a distant speck. A tiny blot it was, against the golden welter on the eastern horizon; a blot whence rose fine-pricked masts and useless sails.

And spontaneously there rose an antiphonal *pantun*, or song of war. Up from the fleet it broke, under the shrill lead of the hag, now standing with clenched, skinny fists raised high. She wailed:

Adapoun pipit itou sama pipit djouga!

Others answered. A drum of bamboo, headed with snake-skin, began to throb.

Dan yang enggang itou sama enggang djouga!

As the echoes died, again rose the witch-woman's voice, piercing, resonant:

Bourga sedap dispakey!

The others then:

Layou—dibouang![1]

The song continued, intoned by the witch-woman with choral responses from the fighting men. From lament it passed to savage threats of death by torture and by nameless mutilations. Maces began to clatter on shields, krises to glint in sunlight, severed heads of enemies to wave aloft on spears.

And out over the liquid rainbow surface of the strait rolled a long echo, blent of war-cries, shouts of vengeance, the booming of snake-skin drums— defiance of the human wolf-pack now giving wild tongue.

Dr. Filhiol and Mr. Wansley stopped in their speech and raised peering eyes landward, as some faint verberation of the war-shout drifted down upon them. The doctor's brows drew to a frown; he narrowed his keen eyes toward the line of hot, damp hills. Mr. Wansley pushed back his cap and scratched his head. Together they stood at the rail, not yet glimpsing the war-fleet which still moved in partial concealment along the wooded shore.

Into their silence, a harsh, liquor-roughened voice broke suddenly:

"Empty staring for empty brains! Nothin' better to do than look your eyes out at the worst coast, so help me, God ever made?"

Neither answered. Mr. Wansley surveyed in silence the hulking, disordered figure now coming forward from the after companion. The doctor drew a cigar from his waistcoat pocket and lighted it. Complete silence greeted Briggs—silence through which the vague turmoil trembling across the mother-of-pearl iridescence of the strait still reached the *Silver Fleece*.

CHAPTER VI

COUNCIL OF WAR

A moment the two men eyed the captain. Malay voices sounded under the awning. Forward, a laugh drifted on the heat-shimmering air. Briggs cursed, and still came on.

A sorry spectacle he made, tousled, bleary-eyed, with pain-contracted forehead where the devil's own headache was driving spikes. Right hand showed lacerations, from having struck the wheel. Heavy shoulders sagged, head drooped. Angrily he blinked, his mood to have torn up the world and spat upon the fragments in very spite.

"Well, lost your tongues, have you?" he snarled. "I'm used to being answered on my own ship. You, Mr. Wansley, would do better reading your 'Bow-ditch' than loafing. And you, doctor, I want you to mix me a stiff powder for the damnedest headache that ever tangled my top-hamper. I've had a drink or two, maybe three, already this morning. But that does no good. Fix me up something strong. Come, stir a stump, sir! I'm going to be obeyed on my own ship!"

"Yes, sir," answered the doctor, keeping his tongue between his teeth, as the saying is. He started aft, followed by Wansley. Briggs burst out again:

"Insubordination, mutiny—that's all I get, this voyage!" His fists swung, aching for a target. "Look what's happened! Against my orders you, Mr. Wansley, try to take the *Fleece* to sea. And run her aground! By God, sir, I could have you disrated for that! I'd put you in irons for the rest of the voyage if I didn't need you on deck. Understand me, sir?"

"Yes, sir," answered Wansley, with exceeding meekness. Briggs was about to flare out at him again, and might very well have come to fist-work, when a hard, round little concussion, bowling seaward, struck his ear.

At sound of the shot, the captain swung on his heel, gripped the rail and stared shoreward.

"What the hell is *that*?" demanded he, unable to conceal a sudden fear that had stabbed through the thrice-dyed blackness of his venom.

"I rather think, sir," answered Filhiol, blowing a ribbon of smoke on the still morning air, "it's trouble brewing. By Jove, sir—see that, will you?"

His hand directed the captain's reddened eyes far across the strait toward the coastal hills, palm-crowded. Vaguely the captain saw a long, dim line. At its forward end, just a speck against the greenery, a triangle of other color was creeping on. Briggs knew it for the high sail of a proa.

"H-m!" he grunted. Under the bushy blackness of his brows he stared with blood-injected eyes. His muscles tautened. Suddenly he commanded:

"Mr. Wansley, my glass, sir!"

The doctor pursed anxious lips as Wansley departed toward the companion.

"Trouble, sir?" asked he.

"I'll tell you when there's trouble! How can I hear anythin', with your damned jaw-tackle always busy?"

The doctor shut up, clamwise, and leaned elbows on the rail, and so they stood there, each peering, each listening, each thinking his own thoughts.

Mr. Wansley's return, brass telescope in hand, broke both lines of reflection. Briggs snatched the glass, yearning to knock Wansley flat, as he might have done a cabin-boy. Wansley peered at him with bitter malevolence.

"You hell-devil!" muttered he. "You've murdered two of us already, an' like as not you'll murder all of us before you're done. If the sharks had you this minute—"

"By the Judas priest!" ejaculated Briggs, glass at eye. He swung it left and right. "Now you lubberly sons of swabs *have* got me on a lee-shore with all anchors draggin'!"

"What is it, sir?" demanded Filhiol, calmly.

"What *is* it?" roared the captain, neck and face scarlet. "After you help run the *Silver Fleece* on Ulu Salama bar, where that damned war-party can close in on her, you ask me what it is! Holy Jeremiah!"

"See here, Captain Briggs." The doctor's voice cut incisively. "If that's a war-party, we've got no time to waste in abuse. Please let me use that glass and see for myself."

"Use nothing!" shouted Briggs. "What? Call me a liar, do you? I tell you it *is* a war-party with five—eight—twelve—well, about sixteen boats and a proa, I make it; and you stand there and call me a liar!"

"I call you nothing, sir," retorted the physician, his face impassive. In spite of anger, Filhiol comprehended that he and Briggs represented the best brain-power on the clipper. Under the urge of peril these two must temporarily sink all differences and stand together. "You say there's a war-party coming out. I place myself at your orders."

"Same here, sir," put in Mr. Wansley. "What's to be done, sir?" Urgent peril had stifled the fires of hate.

"Call Mr. Prass and Mr. Crevay," answered the captain, sobered. "You, doctor, mix me up that powder, quick. Here, I'll go with you. You've got to stop this damned headache of mine! Look lively, Mr. Wansley! Get Bevans, too, and Gascar!"

In five minutes the war-council was under way on the after-deck. Already the doctor's drug had begun to loosen the bands of pain constricting the captain's brow. Something of Briggs's normal fighting energy was returning. The situation was already coming under his strong hand.

Careful inspection through the glass confirmed the opinion that a formidable war-fleet was headed toward Ulu Salama bar. The far, vague sound of chanting and of drums clinched matters.

"We've got to meet 'em with all we've got," said Briggs, squinting through the tube. "There's a few hundred o' the devils. Our game is to keep 'em from closing in. If they board us—well, they aren't goin' to, that's all."

"I don't like the look o' things forrard, sir," put in Crevay, now bo'sun of the clipper, filling the position that Prass had vacated in becoming second mate. "Them Malays, sir—"

"That's the hell of it, I know," said Briggs. He spoke rationally, sobered into human decency. "If we had a straight white crew, we could laugh at the whole o' Batu Kawan. But our own natives are liable to run *amok*."

"We'd better iron the worst of 'em, sir, an' clap hatches on 'em," suggested Crevay. "There's seventeen white men of us, an' twenty natives. If we had more whites, I'd say shoot the whole damn lot o' Malays an' chuck 'em over to the sharks while there's time!" His face was deep-lined, cruel almost as the captain's.

Silence followed. Gascar nodded approval, Bevans went a trifle pale, and Wansley shook his head. Prass turned his quid and spat over the rail; the doctor glanced forward, squinting with eyes of calculation. Under the brightening sun, each face revealed the varying thoughts that lay in each man's heart. Filhiol was first to speak.

"Those Malays are valuable to us," said he. "They make excellent hostages, if properly restrained in the hold. But we can't have them at large."

"We can, and must, all of 'em!" snapped Briggs. His eye had cleared and once more swept up the situation with that virile intelligence which long had made him a leader of men. His nostrils widened, breathing the air of battle. His chest, expanding, seemed a barrier against weakness, indecision. The shadow of death had blotted out the madness of his orgy. He stood there at the rail, erect, square-jawed, a man once more. A man that even those who most bitterly hated him now had to respect and to obey.

"We need 'em all," he repeated, with the resonance of hard decision. "We're short-handed as it is. We need every man-jack of them, but not to fight. They won't fight for us. We daren't put so much as a clasp-knife in their murderin' hands. But they can work for us, and, by the Judas priest, they shall! Our pistols can hold 'em to it. Work, sweat, damn 'em—sweat the yellow devils, as they never sweat before!"

"How so, captain?" asked the doctor.

"It'll be an hour before that fleet lays alongside. There's a good chance we can kedge off this damned bar. Twenty natives at the poop capstan, with you, Mr. Bevans—and I guess I'll let the doctor lend a hand, too—standing over 'em with cold lead—that's the game." Briggs laughed discordantly. "How's your nerve, Mr. Bevans? All right, sir?"

Sea-etiquette was returning. Confidence brightened.

"Nerve, sir? All right!"

"Ever shoot a man dead in his tracks?"

"I have, sir."

"Good! Then you'll do!" Briggs slapped Bevans on the shoulder. "I'll put you and the doctor in charge of the natives. First one that raises a hand off a capstan-bar, drill him through the head. Understand?"

"Yes, sir," said Bevans. The doctor nodded.

"That's settled! To work! We won't want the natives at large, though, till we get the kedge over. We'll keep 'em in the 'midships deck-house for a while yet. Doctor, you stand at the break and shoot the first son of a hound that sticks his nose out. Mr. Wansley, muster all the white men aft for instructions. Mr. Prass, take what men you need and get up all the arms and ammunition. First thing, get out that stand of rifles in my cabin. Here's two keys. One is my private locker-key, and the other the key to the arms-locker. In my locker you'll find a kris. In the other, three revolvers. Bring those." The captain's words came crisp, sharp, decisive. "Bring up the six navy cutlasses from the rack in the cabin. Mr. Gascar will help you. Mr. Gascar, how many axes have you got in your carpenter's chest?"

"Four, sir, and an adz."

"Bring 'em all. Tell the cook to boil every drop of water he's got room for on the galley range. Get the marline spikes from the bo'sun's locker and lay 'em handy. Cast loose the signal-gun lashed down there on the main deck. We'll haul that up and mount it at the taffrail. God! If they want war, they'll get it, the black scuts!"

"We're short of round-shot for the gun, sir," said "Chips." "I misdoubt there's a dozen rounds."

"No matter. Solid shot isn't much good for this work. Get all the bolts, nuts and screws from your shop—all the old iron junk you can ram down her throat. How's powder?"

"Plenty, sir."

"Good! We've got powder enough, men enough and guts enough. To your work. Mr. Crevay!"

"Yes, sir?" A lank, bony man, Crevay, with fiery locks and a slashed cheek where a dirk had once ripped deep. An ex-navy man he, and of fighting blood.

"I'm goin' to have you serve the gun when ready. You and any men you pick," the captain told him, while the others departed each on his own errand, tensely, yet without haste or fear. "Meanwhile, I'll put you in charge of kedgin' us off. Cast loose and rig the kedge-anchor, lower it away from that davy there to the long-boat, and sink it about a hundred fathom off the starb'd quarter. With twenty Malays at the capstan-bars, we ought to start the *Fleece*. If not, we'll shift cargo from forrard. Look alive, sir!"

"Yes, sir!" And Crevay, too, departed, filled with the energy that comes to every man when treated like a man and given a man's work to do.

As by a miracle, the spirit of the *Silver Fleece* had changed. Discipline had all come back with a rush; the battling blood had risen. No longer, for the moment, were the captain's heavy crimes and misdemeanors held against him. Briggs stood for authority, defense in face of the peril of death. His powerful body and stern spirit formed a rallying-point for every white man aboard. And even those who had most poisonously grisled in their hearts against the man, now ran loyally to do his bidding.

Forgotten was the cause of all this peril—the stealing of Kuala Pahang, in drunken lust. Forgotten the barbarities that had driven Mr. Scurlock and the boy ashore. Forgotten the brutal cynicism that had refused to buy their liberty at the price of giving up the girl. Of all these barbarities, no memory seemed now to survive. The deadly menace of twenty Malays already growling in the waist of the ship, and of the slow-advancing line of war-canoes, banished every thought save one—battle!

Once more Captain Alpheus Briggs had proved himself, in time of crisis, a man; more than a man—a master of men.

Thus, now, swift preparations had begun to play the game of war in which no quarter would be asked or given.

CHAPTER VII

BEFORE THE BATTLE

Strenuous activities leaped into being, aboard the stranded clipper ship.

All the Malays were herded in the deck-house, informed that they were sons of swine and that the first one who showed a face on deck, till wanted, would be shot dead. The doctor, with a revolver ready for business, added weight to this information.

Under the orders of Mr. Wansley, all the white sailors came trooping aft. Noisily and profanely they came, making a holiday of the impending slaughter. A hard company they were, many in rags, for Briggs could never have been called other than conservative regarding credits from the slop-chest. Rum, however, he now promised them, and whatever loot they could garner from the Malay fleet; so they cheered him heartily. They, too, had all become his men.

Bad men they looked, and such as now were needed—three or four Liverpool guttersnipes, a Portuguese cut-throat from Fayal, a couple of Cayman wreckers, a French convict escaped from the penal ship at Marseilles, and the rest low-type American scum. For such was the reputation of Alpheus Briggs, all up and down the Seven Seas, that few first-class men ever willingly shipped with him before the mast.

Workers and fighters they were, though, every one. While black smoke began to emerge from the galley funnel, on the shimmering tropic air, as the cook stuffed oily rags and oil-soaked wood under all the coppers that his range would hold, divers lines of preparation swiftly developed.

Already some were casting loose the lashings of the signal-gun and rigging tackle to hoist the rust-red old four-inch piece to the after-deck. Others fell to work with Mr. Crevay, rigging the kedge-anchor or lowering away the long-boat. Another gang leaped to the task of getting above-decks all the rifles, cutlasses, powder, ball-shot and iron junk, the axes and revolvers; of loading everything, even of laying belaying-pins handy as a last line of hand-to-hand weapons.

Briggs supervised all details, even to the arming of each man with the butchering-tool he claimed to be most expert with. The best were given the rifles; to those of lesser skill was left the cutlass work. A gun crew of two men was picked to serve the cannon with Mr. Crevay. Three were detailed to help the cook carry boiling water.

"Mr. Bevans will stand over the natives at the capstan," directed Briggs. "And you, doctor, will act in your medical capacity when we get into action. If hard-driven, you can be useful with the kris, eh? Quite in your line, sir; quite in your line."

Briggs smiled expansively. All his evil humors had departed. The foretaste of battle had shaken him clean out of his black moods. His genius for organizing, for leading men, seemed to have expanded him to heroic proportions. In his deep, black eyes, the poise of his head, the hard, glad expression of his full-blooded, black-bearded face, one saw eager virility that ran with joy to meet the test of strength, and that exulted in a day's work of blood.

A heroic figure he, indeed—thewed like a bull; with sunlight on face and open, corded neck; deep-chested, coatless now, the sleeves of his pongee shirt rolled up to herculean elbows. Some vague perception crossed the doctor's mind that here, indeed, stood an anomaly, a man centuries out of time and place, surely a throwback to some distant pirate strain of the long-vanished past.

Imagination could twist a scarlet kerchief 'round that crisp-curling hair, knot a sash about the captain's waist, draw high boots up to his powerful knees. Imagination could transport him to the coasts of Mexico long, long ago; imagination could run the Jolly Roger to the masthead—and there, in Captain Briggs, merchant-ship master of the year 1868, once more find kith and kin of Blackbeard, Kidd, Morgan, England, and all others of the company of gentlemen rovers in roistering days.

Something of this the doctor seemed to understand. Yet, as he turned his glance a moment to the line of war-craft now more plainly visible across the shimmering nacre of the strait, he said, raising his voice a trifle by reason of the various shouts, cries and diverse noises blending confusedly, and now quite obliterating all sounds from the war fleet:

"You know what those canoes are coming after, of course."

"The girl! What of it?"

"And you know, sir, that old Dengan Jouga is bound to be aboard. There'll be a medicine man or two, as well."

"What the devil are you driving at?" demanded Briggs.

"That's a formidable combination, sir," continued the doctor. "We've got twenty Malays on board that will face hell-fire itself rather than see any harm befall a native *pawang* or a witch-woman. We'll never be able to hold them to any work. Each of them believes he can reach paradise by slaughtering a white man. In addition, he can avenge harm done to the old woman and the girl. Under those circumstances—"

"By God, sir, if I didn't need you, sir—"

"Under those circumstances, my original suggestion of holding them all under hatches, as hostages, has much to recommend it, if we come to a fight. But need we come to a fight? Need we, sir?"

"How the devil can we sheer off from it?"

"By giving up the girl, sir. Put her in one of the small boats with a few trade-dollars and trinkets for her dowry—which will effectually lustrate the girl, according to these people's ideas—and give her a pair of oars. She'll take care of herself all right. The war-fleet will turn around and go back, which will be very much better, sir, than slaughter. We've already lost two men, and —"

"And you're white-livered enough to stand there and advise taking no revenge for them?" interrupted Briggs, his voice gusty with sudden passion.

Briggs struck the rail with the flat of his palm, a blow that cracked like a pistol-shot; while the doctor, wholly unhorsed by this tilt from so unexpected an angle, could only stare.

"By the Judas priest, sir!" cried Briggs furiously. "That's enough to make a man want to cut you down where you stand, sir, you hear *me*? And if that yellow-bellied cowardice wasn't enough, you ask me to give up the girl—the girl that's cost me two men already—the girl that may yet cost me my ship and my own life! Well, by the Judas priest!"

"Don't risk your life and the ship for a native wench!" cut in the doctor with a rush of indignation. "There are wenches by the score, by the hundred, all up and down the Straits. You can buy a dozen, for a handful of coin. Wenches by the thousands—but only one *Silver Fleece*, sir!"

"Devilish lot you care about the *Fleece*!" snarled Briggs. "Or about anything but your own cowardly neck!"

"Captain Briggs, don't forget yourself!"

"Hell's bells! They shan't have that girl. Witch-women, medicine men or all the devils of the Pit shan't take her back. She's mine, I tell you, and before I'll let her go I'll throw her to the sharks myself. Sharks enough, and plenty— there's one now," he added, jerking his hand at a slow-moving, black triangle that was cutting a furrow off to starboard. "So I want to hear no more from you about the girl, and you can lay to that!"

He turned on his heel and strode aft, growling in his beard. The doctor, peering after him with smoldering eyes, felt his finger tighten on the trigger. One shot might do the business. It would mean death, of course, for himself. The courts would take their full penalty, all in due time; but it would save the ship and many white men's lives.

Nevertheless, the doctor did not raise his weapon. Discipline still held; the dominance of that black-bearded Hercules still viséed all opposition into impotence. With no more than a curse, the doctor turned back to his guard duty.

"Are you man or are you devil?" muttered Filhiol. "Good God, what *are* you?"

Already the defense of the *Silver Fleece* was nearly complete; and in the long-boat the kedge-anchor was being rowed away by four men under command of Mr. Crevay. The war-fleet had drawn much nearer, in a rough crescent to northwestward, its sails taut. Flashing water-jewels, swirled up from paddles, had become visible, under the now unclouded splendor of the sun. More and more distinctly the chanting and war-drums drifted in.

The off-shore breeze was urging the armada forward; the dip and swing of all those scores of paddles gave a sense of unrelenting power. But Briggs, hard, eager, seemed only welcoming battle as he stood calculating time and distance, armament and disposal of his forces, or, with an eye aloft at the clewed-up canvas, figured the tactics of kedging-off, of making sail if possible, and showing Batu Kawan's forces a clean pair of heels.

"Look lively with that anchor!" he shouted out across the sparkling waters. "Drop her in good holdin' ground, and lead that line aboard. The sooner we get our Malays sweatin' on the capstan, the better!"

"Aye, aye, sir," drifted back the voice of Crevay. And presently the splash of the anchor as the boat-crew tugged it over the stern, flung cascades of foam into the heat-quivering air.

The boat surged back bravely; the line was bent to the capstan, and Briggs ordered the Malays to the bars. Sullen they came, shuffling, grumbling strange words—lean, brown and yellow men in ragged cotton shirts and no shirts at all—as murderous a pack as ever padded in sandals or bare feet along white decks.

Among them slouched Mahmud Baba, who, like all the rest, shot a comprehending glance at the on-drawing fleet. Up the forward companion-ladder they swarmed, and aft to the capstan, with Briggs, the doctor and Wansley all three on a hair-trigger to let sunlight through the first who should so much as raise a hand of rebellion. And so they manned the capstan-bars, and so they fell a-heaving at the kedge-line, treading with slow, toilsome feet 'round and 'round on the hot planks, where—young as the morning was—the pitch had already softened.

"Come here, you *surkabutch!*" commanded the captain, summoning Mahmud Baba. "*Juldi, idherao!*"

The Malay came, gray with anger—for Briggs had, in hearing of all his fellows, called him "son of a pig," and a Mohammedan will kill you for calling him that, if he can. Nevertheless, Mahmud salaamed. Not now could he kill. Later, surely. He could afford to wait. The Frank must not call him son of a pig, and still live. Might not Allah even now be preparing vengeance, in that war-fleet? Mahmud salaamed again, and waited with half-closed eyes.

At the capstan the *thud-thud-thud* of twoscore trampling feet was already mingling with a croon of song, that soon would rise and strengthen, if not summarily suppressed, and drift out to meet the war-chant of the warrior blood-kin steadily approaching.

Click-click-click! the pawl and ratchet punctuated the rhythm of feet and song, as the hawser began to rise, dripping, from the sea. Briggs drew his revolver from his belt, and ground the muzzle fair against Mahmud's teeth.

"You tell those other *surkabutchas*," said he with cold menace, "that I'll have no singing. I'll have no noise to cover up your plotting and planning together. You'll all work in silence or you'll all be dead. Understand me?"

"Yas, sar."

"And you'll hang to the capstan-bars till we're free, no matter what happens. The first man that quits, goes to glory on the jump. Savvy?"

"Yas, sar." Mahmud's voice was low, submissive; but through the drooping lids a gleam shone forth that never came from sunlight or from sea.

"All right," growled Briggs, giving the revolver an extra shove. "Get to work! And if those other sons of pigs in the canoes board us, we white men will shoot down every last one o' *you* here. We'll take no chances of being knifed in the back. *You'll* all have gone to damnation before one o' *them* sets foot on my decks. You lay to that, my Mud Baby! Now, tell 'em all I've told you, and get it straight! *Jao!*"

Briggs struck Mahmud a head-cracking blow with the revolver just above the ear and sent him staggering back to the capstan. The song died, as Mahmud gulped out words that tumbled over each other with staccato vehemence.

"Get in there at the bars!" shouted Briggs. "Get to work, you, before I split you!"

Mahmud swung to place, and bent his back to labor, as his thin chest and skinny hands pushed at the bar beside his fellows.

And steadily the war-fleet drew in toward its prey.

CHAPTER VIII

PARLEY AND DEATH

In silence now the capstan turned. No Malays hummed or spoke. Only the grunting of their breath, oppressed by toil and the thrust of the bars, kept rough time with the slither of feet, the ratchet-click, the groaning creak of the cable straining through the chocks.

"Dig your toe-nails in, you black swine!" shouted Briggs. "The first one that—"

"Captain Briggs," the doctor interrupted, taking him by the arm, "I think the enemy's trying to communicate with us. See there?"

He pointed where the fleet had now ranged up to within about two miles. The mats of the proa and of the other sailing-canoes had crumpled down, the oars and paddles ceased their motion. The war-party seemed resting for deliberation. Only one boat was moving, a long canoe with an outrigger; and from this something white was slowly waving.

"Parley be damned!" cried Briggs. "The only parley I'll have with that pack of lousy beggars will be hot shot!"

"That canoe coming forward there, with the white flag up," Filhiol insisted, "means they want to powwow. It's quite likely a few dollars may settle the whole matter; or perhaps a little surplus hardware. Surely you'd rather part with something than risk losing your ship, sir?"

"I'll part with nothin', and I'll save my ship into the bargain," growled the captain. "There'll be no tribute paid, doctor. Good God! White men knucklin' under, to niggers? Never, sir—never!"

Savagely he spoke, but Filhiol detected intonations that rang not quite true. Again he urged: "A bargain's a bargain, black or white. Captain Light was as good a man as ever sailed the Straits, and *he* wasn't above diplomacy. He understood how to handle these people. Wanted a landing-place cleared, you remember. Couldn't hire a man-jack to work for him, so he loaded his brass cannon with trade-dollars and shot them into the jungle. The Malays cleared five acres, hunting for those dollars. These people can be handled, if you know how."

The captain, his heavy brows furrowed with a black frown, still peered at the on-drawing canoe. Silence came among all the white men at their fighting-stations or grouped near the captain.

"That's enough!" burst out Briggs. "Silence, sir! Mr. Gascar, fetch my glass!"

The doctor, very wise, held his tongue. Already he knew he was by way of winning his contention. Gascar brought the telescope from beside the after-companion housing, where Briggs had laid it. The captain thrust his revolver into his belt. In silence he studied the approaching canoe. Then he exclaimed: "This is damned strange! Dr. Filhiol!"

"Well, sir?"

"Take a look, and tell me what you see."

He passed the telescope to the doctor, who with keenest attention observed the boat, then said:

"White men on board that canoe. Two of them."

"That's what *I* thought, doctor. Must be Mr. Scurlock and the boy, eh?"

"Yes, sir. I think there's still time to trade the girl for them," the doctor eagerly exclaimed. A moment Briggs seemed pondering, while at the capstan the driven Malays—now reeking in a bath of sweat—still trod their grunting round.

"Captain, I beg of you—" the doctor began. Briggs raised a hand for silence.

"Don't waste your breath, sir, till we know what's what!" he commanded. "I'll parley, at any rate. We may be able to get that party on board here. If we can, the rest will be easy. And I'm as anxious to lay hands on those damned deserters o' mine as I was ever anxious for anything in my life. Stand to your arms, men! Mr. Bevans, be ready with that signal-gun to blow 'em out of the water if they start trouble. Mr. Gascar, fetch my speakin'-trumpet from the cabin. Bring up a sheet, too, from Scurlock's berth. That's the handiest flag o' truce we've got. Look alive now!"

"Aye, aye, sir," answered Gascar, and departed on his errand.

Silence fell, save for the toiling Malays, whose labors still were fruitless to do aught save slowly drag the kedge through the gleaming sand of the sea-bottom. Mr. Wansley muttered something to himself; the doctor fell nervously to pacing up and down; the others looked to their weapons.

From the fleet now drifted no sound of drums or chanting. In stillness lay the war-craft; in stillness the single canoe remained on watch, with only that tiny flicker of white to show its purpose. A kind of ominous hush brooded over sea and sky; but ever the tramp of feet at the capstan, and the panting breath of toil there rose on the superheated air.

Gascar returned, handed the trumpet to Briggs, and from the rail waved the sheet. After a minute the canoe once more advanced, with flashing paddles. Steadily the gun-crew kept it covered, ready at a word to shatter it. Along the rail the riflemen crouched. And still the little white flutter spoke of peace, if peace the captain could be persuaded into buying.

The glass now determined beyond question that Mr. Scurlock and the boy were on board. Briggs also made out old Dengan Jouga, the witch-woman, mother of the girl. His jaw clamped hard as he waited. He let the war-craft draw up to within a quarter-mile, then bade Gascar cease displaying the sheet, and through the speaking-trumpet shouted:

"That'll do now, Scurlock! Nigh enough! What's wanted?"

The paddlers ceased their work. The canoe drifted idly. Silence followed. Then a figure stood up—a figure now plainly recognizable in that bright glow as Mr. Scurlock. Faintly drifted in the voice of the former mate:

"Captain Briggs! For God's sake, listen to me! Let me come closer—let me talk with you!"

"You're close enough now, you damned mutineer!" retorted Briggs. "What d' you want? Spit it out, and be quick about it!"

Another silence, while the sound traveled to the canoe and while the answer came:

"I've got the boy with me. We're prisoners. If you don't give up that girl, an' pay somethin' for her, they're goin' to kill us both. They're goin' to cut our heads off, cap'n, and give 'em to the witch-woman, to hang outside her hut!"

"And a devilish good place for 'em, too!" roared Briggs, unmindful of surly looks and muttered words revealing some disintegration of the discipline at first so splendidly inspired. "I'll have no dealin's with you on such terms. Get back now—back, afore I sink you, where you lie!"

"See here, captain!" burst out Filhiol, his face white with a flame of passion. "I'm no mutineer, and I'm not refusing duty, but by God—"

"Silence, sir!" shouted Briggs. "I've got irons aboard for any man as sets himself against me!"

"Irons or no irons, I can't keep silent," the doctor persisted, while here and there a growl, a curse, should have told Briggs which way the spate of things had begun to flow. "That man, there, and that helpless boy—"

He choked, gulped, stammered in vain for words.

"They'll hang our heads up, and they'll burn the *Silver Fleece* and bootcher all hands," drifted in the far, slow cry of Mr. Scurlock. "They got three hundred men an' firearms, an' a brass cannon. An' if this party is beat, more will be raised. This is your last chance! For the girl an' a hundred trade-dollars they'll all quit and go home!"

"To hell with 'em!" shouted Briggs at the rail, his face swollen with hate and rage. "To hell with you, too! There'll be no such bargain struck so long as I got a deck to tread on, or a shot in my lockers! If they want the yellow she-dog, let 'em come an' take her! Now, stand off, there, afore I blow you to Davy Jones!"

"It's murder!" flared the doctor. "You men, here—officers of this ship—I call on you to witness this cold-blooded murder. Murder of a good man, and a harmless boy! By God, if you stand there and let him kill those two—"

Briggs flung up his revolver and covered the doctor with an aim the steadiness of which proved how unshaken was his nerve.

"Murder if you like," smiled he with cold malice, his white teeth glinting. "An' there'll be another one right here, if you don't put a stopper on that mutinous jaw of yours and get back to your post. That's my orders, and if you don't obey on shipboard, it's mutiny. Mutiny, sawbones, an' I can shoot you down, an' go free. I'm to windward o' the law. Now, get back to the capstan, afore I let daylight through you!"

Outplayed by tactics that put a sudden end to any opposition, the doctor ceded. The steady "O" of the revolver-muzzle paralyzed his tongue and numbed his arm. Had he felt that by a sudden shot he could have had even a reasonable chance of downing the captain, had he possessed any confidence of backing from enough of the others to have made mutiny a success, he would have risked his life—yes, gladly lost it—by coming to swift grips with the brute. But Filhiol knew the balance of power still lay against him. The majority, he sensed, still stood against him. Sullenly the doctor once more lagged aft.

From the canoe echoed voices, ever more loud and more excited. In the bow, Scurlock gesticulated. His supplications were audible, mingled with shouts and cries from the Malays. Added thereto were high-pitched screams from the boy—wild, shrill, nerve-breaking screams, like those of a wounded animal in terror.

"Oh, God, this is horrible!" groaned the doctor, white as paper. His teeth sank into his bleeding lip. He raised his revolver to send a bullet through the captain; but Crevay, with one swift blow, knocked the weapon jangling to the deck, and dealt Filhiol a blow that sent him reeling.

"Payne, and you, Deming, here!" commanded he, summoning a couple of foremast hands. They came to him. "Lock this man in his cabin. He's got a touch o' sun. Look alive, now!"

Together they laid hands on Filhiol, hustled him down the after-companion, flung him into his cabin and locked the door. Crevay, guarding the Malays at the capstan, muttered:

"Saved the idiot's life, anyhow. Good doctor; but as a man, what a damned, thundering fool!"

Unmindful of this side-play Briggs was watching the canoe. His face had become that of a devil glad of vengeance on two hated souls. He laughed again at Scurlock's up-flung arms, at his frantic shout:

"For the love o' God, captain, save us! If you don't give up that girl, they're goin' to kill us right away! You got to act quick, now, to save us!"

"Save yourselves, you renegades!" shouted Briggs, swollen with rage and hate. His laugh chilled the blood. "You said you'd chance it with the Malays afore you would with me. Well, take it, now, and to hell with you!"

"For God's sake, captain—"

Scurlock's last, wild appeal was suddenly strangled into silence. Another scream from the boy echoed over the water. The watchers got sight of a small figure that waved imploring arms. All at once this figure vanished, pulled down, with Scurlock, by shouting Malays.

The exact manner of the death of the two could not be told. All that the clipper's men could see was a sudden, confused struggle, that ended almost before it had begun. A few shouts drifted out over the clear waters. Then another long, rising shriek in the boy's treble, shuddered across the vacancy of sea and sky—a shriek that ended with sickening suddenness.

Some of the white men cursed audibly. Some faces went drawn and gray. A flurry of chatter broke out at the toiling capstan—not even Mr. Crevay's furious oaths and threats could immediately suppress it.

Briggs only laughed, horribly, his teeth glinting as he leaned on the rail and watched.

For a moment the canoe rocked in spite of its steadying outrigger, with the violence of the activities aboard it. Then up rose two long spears; spears topped with grisly, rounded objects. A rising chorus of yells, yells of rage, hate, defiance, spread abroad, echoed by louder shouts from the wide crescent of the fleet. And once again the drums began to pulse.

From the canoe, two formless things were thrown. Here, there, a shark-fin turned toward the place—a swirl of water.

Silence fell aboard the clipper. In that silence a slight grating sound, below, told Briggs the kedging had begun to show results. A glad sound, indeed, that grinding of the keel!

"By God, men!" he shouted, turning. "The forefoot's comin' free. Dig in, you swine! Men, when she clears, we'll box her off with the fores'l—we'll beat 'em yet!"

Once more allegiance knit itself to Briggs. Despite that double murder (as surely done by him as if his own hand had wielded the kris that had beheaded Mr. Scurlock and the boy), the drums and shoutings of the war-fleet, added to this new hope of getting clear of Ulu Salama, fired every white man's heart with sudden hope.

The growl that had begun to rise against Briggs died away.

"Mr. Crevay," he commanded, striding aft, "livelier there with those pigs! They're not doin' half a trick o' work!" Angrily he gestured at the sweat-bathed, panting men. "You, Lumbard, fetch me up a fathom o' rope. *I'll* give 'em a taste o' medicine that'll make 'em dig! And you, Mr. Bevans—how's the gun? All loaded with junk?"

"All ready, sir!"

Briggs turned to it. Out over the water he squinted, laying careful aim at the canoe where Scurlock and the boy had died.

The canoe had already begun retreating from the place now marked by a worrying swirl of waters where the gathering sharks held revel. Back towards the main fleet it was circling as the paddlemen—their naked, brown bodies gleaming with sunlight on the oil that would make them slippery as eels in case of close fighting—bent to their labor.

On the proa and the other sailing-canoes the mat sails had already been hauled up again. The proa was slowly lagging forward; and with it the battle-line, wide-flung.

Briggs once more assured his aim. He seized the lanyard, stepped back, and with a shout of: "Take this, you black scum!" jerked the cord.

The rusty old four-inch leaped against its lashings as it vomited half a bushel of heavy nuts, bolts, brass and iron junk in a roaring burst of smoke and flame.

Fortune favored. The canoe buckled, jumped half out of the water, and, broken fair in two, dissolved in a scattering flurry of débris. Screams echoed with horrible yells from the on-drawing fleet. Dark, moving things, the heads of swimmers already doomed by the fast-gathering sharks, jostled floating things that but a second before had been living men. The whole region near the canoe became a white-foaming thrash of struggle and of death.

"Come on, all o' you!" howled Briggs with the laughter of a blood-crazed devil. "We're ready, you *surkabutchas*! Ready for you all!"

With an animal-like scream of rage, a Malay sprang from the capstan-bar where he had been sweating. On Crevay he flung himself. A blade, snatched from the Malay's breech-clout, flicked high-lights as it plunged into Crevay's neck.

Whirled by a dozen warning yells, the captain spun. He caught sight of Crevay, already crumpling down on the hot deck: saw the reddened blade, the black-toothed grin of hate, the on-rush of the *amok* Malay.

Up flung his revolver. But already the leaping figure was upon him.

CHAPTER IX

ONSET OF BATTLE

The shot that Wansley fired, a chance shot hardly aimed at all, must have been guided by the finger of the captain's guardian genius. It crumpled the Malay, with strangely sprawling legs. Kill him it did not. But the bullet through his lower vertebræ left only his upper half alive.

With a grunt he crumpled to the hot deck, knife still clutched in skinny fist. Shouts echoed. Briggs stood aghast, with even his steel nerve jangling. The quivering Malay was a half-dead thing that still lived. He writhed with contorted face, dragging himself toward Briggs. The knife-blade clicked on the planking, like the clicking of his teeth that showed black through slavering lips.

"*Allah! il Allah!*" he gulped, heaving himself up on one hand, slashing with the other.

Why do men, in a crisis, so often do stupid, unaccountable things? Why did Briggs kick at him, with a roaring oath, instead of shooting? Briggs felt the bite of steel in his leg. That broke the numbing spell of unreason. The captain's pistol, at point-blank range, shattered the yellow man's skull. Blood, smeared with an ooze of brain, colored the stewing deck.

"*Allah! il Al—!*"

The cry ended in a choking gurgle on lips that drew into a horrible grin. And now completely dead even beyond the utmost lash of Islamic fanaticism, the Malay dropped face down. This time the captain's kick landed only on flesh and bone past any power of feeling.

At the capstan-bars it was touch-and-go. Crevay was down, groaning, his hands all slippery and crimson with the blood that seeped through his clutching fingers. For a moment, work slacked off. Wansley was shouting, with revolver leveled, his voice blaring above the cries, oaths, imprecations. Things came to the ragged edge of a rush, but white men ran in with rifles and cutlasses. Briggs flung himself aft, trailing blood.

Crazed with rage and the burn of that wound, he fired thrice. Malays sagged down, plunged screaming to the deck. The captain would have emptied his revolver into the pack, but Wansley snatched him by the arm.

"Hold on!" he shouted. "That's enough—we need 'em, sir!"

Prass, belaying-pin in hand, struck to right, to left. Yells of pain mingled with the tumult that drowned the ragged, ineffective spatter of firing from the war-fleet. The action was swift, decisive. In half a minute, the capstan was clicking again, faster than ever. Its labor-power, diminished by the loss of three men, was more than compensated by the fear of the survivors.

"Overboard with the swine!" shouted Briggs. "Overboard with 'em, to the sharks!"

"This here one ain't done for yet, sir," began Prass, pointing. "He's only —"

"Overboard, I said!" roared Briggs. "You'll go, too, by God, if you give me any lip!"

As men laid hands on the Malays to drag them to the rail, Briggs dropped on his knees beside Crevay. He pulled away the man's hands from the gaping neck-wound, whence the life was irretrievably spurting.

"Judas priest!" he stammered, for here was his right-hand man as good as dead. "Doctor! Where the devil is Mr. Filhiol?"

"In the cabin, sir," Prass answered.

"Cabin! Holy Lord! On deck with him!"

"Yes, sir."

"And tell him to bring his kit!"

Prass had already dived below. The doctor was haled up again, with his bag. A kind of hard exultation blazed in the captain's face. He seemed not to hear the shouts of war, the spattering fusillade from the canoes. His high-arched chest rose and fell, pantingly. His hands, reddened with the blood of Crevay, dripped horribly. Filhiol, hustled on deck, stared in amazement.

"A job for you, sir!" cried Briggs. "Prove yourself!"

Filhiol leaned over Crevay. But he made no move to open his kit-bag. One look had told him the truth.

The man, already unconscious, had grown waxen. His breathing had become a stertorous hiccough. The deck beneath him was terrible to look upon.

"No use, sir," said the doctor briefly. "He's gone."

"Do something!" blazed the captain. "Something!"

"For a dead man?" retorted Filhiol. As he spoke, even the hiccough ceased.

Briggs stared with eyes of rage. He got to his feet, hulking, savage, with swaying red fists.

"They've killed my best man," he snarled. "If we didn't need the dogs, we'd feed 'em all to the sharks, so help me!"

"You're wounded, sir!" the doctor cried, pointing at the blood-wet slash in the captain's trouser-leg.

"Oh, to hell with that!" Briggs retorted. "You, and you," he added, jabbing a finger at two sailors, "carry Mr. Crevay down to the cabin—then back to your rifles at the rail!"

They obeyed, their burden sagging limply. Already the dead and wounded Malays had been bundled over the rail. The fusillade from the war-canoes was strengthening, and the shouts had risen to a barbaric chorus. The patter of bullets and slugs into the sea or against the planking of the *Silver Fleece* formed a ragged accompaniment to the whine of missiles through the air. A few holes opened in the clipper's canvas. One of the men who had thrown the Malays overboard cursed suddenly and grabbed his left elbow, shattered.

"Take cover!" commanded Briggs. "Down, everybody, along the rail! Mr. Wansley, down with you and your men. Get down!"

Indifferent to all peril for himself, Briggs turned toward the companion.

"Captain," the doctor began again. "Your boot's full of blood. Let me bandage—"

Briggs flung a snarl at him and strode to the companion.

"Below, there!" he shouted.

"Aye, aye, sir!" rose the voice of one of the foremast hands.

"Get that wench up here! The yellow girl! Bring her up—an' look alive!"

"Captain," the doctor insisted, "I've got to do something for that gash in your leg. Not that I love you, but you're the only man that can save us. Sit down here, sir. You'll bleed to death where you stand!"

Something in Filhiol's tone, something in a certain giddiness that was already reaching for the captain's heart and brain, made him obey. He sat down shakily on deck beside the after-companion. In the midst of all that turmoil, all underlaid by the slow, grinding scrape of the keel on the sand-bar, the physician performed his duty.

With scissors, he shore away the cloth. A wicked slash, five or six inches long, stood redly revealed.

"*Tss! Tss!*" clucked Filhiol. "Lucky if it's not poisoned."

"Mr. Gascar!" shouted the captain. "Go below!" Briggs jerked a thumb downward at the cabin, whence sounds of a struggle, mingled with cries and animal-like snarls, had begun to proceed. "Bring up the jug o' rum you'll find in my locker. Serve it out to all hands. And, look you, if they need a lift with the girl, give it; but don't you kill that wench. I need her, alive! Understand?"

"Yes, sir," Gascar replied, and vanished down the companion. He reappeared with a jug and a tin cup.

"They're handlin' her all right, sir," he reported. "Have a drop, sir?"

"You're damned shoutin', I will!" And the captain reached for the cup. Gascar poured him a stiff drink. He gulped it and took another. "Now deal it out. There'll be plenty more when we've sunk the yellow devils!"

He got to his feet, scorning further care from Filhiol, and stood there wild and disheveled, with one leg of his trousers cut off at the knee and with his half-tied bandages already crimsoning.

"Rum for all hands, men!" he shouted. "And better than rum—my best wine, sherry, champagne—a bottle a head for you, when this shindy's over!"

Cheers rose unevenly. Gascar started on his round with the jug. Even the wounded men, such as could still raise their voices, shouted approval.

"Hold your fire, men," the captain ordered. "Let 'em close in—then blow 'em out o' the water!"

CHAPTER X

KUALA PAHANG

The doctor, presently finishing with Briggs, turned his attention to the other injured ones. At the top of the companion now stood the captain with wicked eyes, as up the ladder emerged the two seamen with the struggling, clawing tiger-cat of a girl.

The cruel beating the captain had given her the night before had not yet crushed her spirit. Neither had the sickness of the liquor he had forced her to drink. Bruised, spent, broken as she was, the spirit of battle still dwelt in the lithe barbarian. That her sharp nails had been busy to good effect was proved by the long, deep gashes on the faces and necks of both seamen. One had been bitten on the forearm. For all their strength, they proved hardly more than a match for her up the narrow, steep companion. Their blasphemies mingled with the girl's animal-like cries. Loudly roared the booming bass of the captain:

"Up with the she-dog! I'll teach her something—teach 'em all something, by the Judas priest! Up with her!"

They dragged her out on deck, up into all that shouting and firing, that turmoil and labor and blood. And as they brought her up a plume of smoke jetted from the bows of the proa. The morning air sparkled with the fire-flash of that ancient brass cannon. With a crashing shower of splinters, a section of the rail burst inward. Men sprawled, howling. But a greater tragedy—in the eyes of these sailormen—befell: for a billet of wood crashed the jug to bits, cascading the deck with good Medford. And, his hand paralyzed and tingling with the shock, Gascar remained staring at the jug-handle still in his grip and at the flowing rum on deck.

Howls of bitter rage broke from along the rail, and the rifles began crackling. The men, cheated of their drink, were getting out of hand.

"Cease firing, you!" screamed Briggs. "You'll fire when I command, and not before. Mr. Bevans! Loaded again?"

"All loaded, sir. Say when!"

"Not yet! Lay a good aim on the proa. We've got to blow her out o' the water!"

"Aye, aye, sir!" And Bevans patted the rusty old piece. "Leave that to me, sir!"

Briggs turned again to the struggling girl. A thin, evil smile drew at his lips. His face, under its bronze of tan, burned with infernal exultation.

"Now, my beauty," he mocked, "now I'll attend to you!"

For a moment he eyed Kuala Pahang. Under the clear, morning light, she looked a strange and wild creature indeed—golden-yellow of tint, with tangled black hair, and the eyes of a trapped tigress. Bruises wealed her naked arms and shoulders, souvenirs of the captain's club and fist. Her supple body was hardly concealed by her short skirt and by the tight Malay jacket binding her lithe waist and firm, young breast.

Briggs exulted over her, helpless and panting in the clutch of the two foremast-hands. "To the rail with her!" he ordered.

"What you goin' to do, sir?" asked one of the men, staring. "Heave her over?"

Briggs menaced him with clenched fist.

"None o' your damned business!" he shouted. "To the rail with her! Jump, afore I teach you how!"

They dragged her, screeching, to the starboard rail. All the time they had to hold those cat-clawed hands of hers. From side to side she flung herself, fighting every foot of the way. Briggs put back his head and laughed at the rare spectacle. Twice or thrice the sailors slipped in blood and rum upon the planking, and once Kuala Pahang all but jerked free from them. At the capstan, only the pistols of the three white guards held her kinsmen back from making a stampede rush; and not even the pistols could silence among them a menacing hum of rage that seethed and bubbled.

"Here, you!" shouted Briggs. "Mahmud Baba, you yellow cur, come here!"

Mahmud loosed his hold on the capstan-bar and in great anguish approached.

"Yas, sar?" whined he. The lean, brown form was trembling. The face had gone a jaundiced color. "I come, sar."

Briggs leveled his revolver at the Malay. Unmindful of the spattering bullets, he spoke with deliberation.

"Son of a saffron dog," said he, "you're going to tell this wench something for me!"

"Yas, sar. What piecee thing me tell?"

"You tell her that if the boats don't go back to land I'll heave her over the rail. I'll feed her to the sharks, by God! Alive, to the sharks—sharks, down there! Savvy?"

"Me savvy."

"And she's got to shout that to the canoes! She's got to shout it to 'em. Go on, now, tell her!"

Mahmud hesitated a moment, shuddered and grimaced. His eyes narrowed to slits. The captain poked the revolver into his ribs. Mahmud quivered. He fell into a sing-song patter of strange words with whining intonations. Suddenly he ceased.

The girl listened, her gleaming eyes fixed on Mahmud's face. A sudden question issued from her bruised, cut lips.

"What's she asking?" demanded Briggs.

"She ask where her mother, sar?"

"Tell her! Tell her I've shot the old she-devil to hell, and beyond! Tell her she'll get worse if she don't make the canoes stand off—worse, because the sharks will get her alive! Go on, you black scut o' misery, tell her!"

Mahmud spoke again. He flung a hand at the enveloping half-circle of the war-fleet. The nearest boats now were moving hardly a quarter-mile away. The gleam of krises and of spears twinkled in the sun. Little smoke-puffs all along the battle-front kept pace with the popping of gunfire. In the proa, oily brown devils were laboring to reload the brass cannon.

Mahmud's speech ended. The girl stiffened, with clenched hands. The sailors, holding her wrists, could feel the whipcord tension of her muscles.

"Tell her to shout to the proa there!" yelled the captain in white fury. "Either they stand off or over she goes—and you see for yourself there's sharks enough!"

Again Mahmud spoke. The girl grunted a monosyllable.

"What's that she says?" demanded Briggs.

"She say no, sar. She die, but she no tell her people."

"The hell you say!" roared the captain. He seized her neck in a huge, hairy paw, tightened his fingers till they bit into the yellow skin, and shook her violently.

"I'll break your damned, obstinate neck for you!" he cried, his face distorted. "Tell your people to go back! Tell 'em!"

Mahmud translated the order. The girl only laughed. Briggs knew himself beaten. In that sneering laugh of Kuala Pahang's echoed a world of maddening defiance. He loosened his hold, trying to think how he should master her. Another man grunted, by the rail, and slid to the deck, where a chance bullet had given him the long sleep.

Briggs whirled on Mahmud, squeezed his lean shoulder till the bones bent.

"*You* tell 'em!" he bellowed. "If she won't, you will!"

"Me, sar?" whined the Malay, shivering and fear-sick to the inner marrow. "Me tell so, they kill me!"

"If you don't, *I* will! Up with you now—both o' you, up, on the rail! Here, you men—up with 'em!"

They hoisted the girl, still impassive, to the rail, and held her there. The firing almost immediately died away. Mahmud tried to grovel at the captain's feet, wailing to Allah and the Prophet. Briggs flung him up, neck and crop. Mahmud grappled the after backstays and clung there, quivering.

"Go on, now, out with it!" snarled Briggs, his pistol at the Malay's back. "And make it loud, or the sharks will get you, too!"

Mahmud raised a bony arm, howled words that drifted out over the pearl-hued waters. Silence fell, along the ragged line of boats. In the bow of the proa a figure stood up, naked, gleaming with oil in the sunlight, which flicked a vivid, crimson spot of color from a nodding feather head-dress.

Back to the *Silver Fleece* floated a high-pitched question, fraught with a heavy toll of life and death. Mahmud answered. The figure waved a furious arm, and fire leaped from the brass cannon.

The shot went high, passing harmlessly over the clipper and ricochetting beyond. But at the same instant a carefully laid rifle, from a canoe, barked stridently. Mahmud coughed, crumpled and slid from the rail. He dropped plumb; and the shoal waters, clear-green over the bar, received him.

As he fell, Briggs struck the girl with a full drive of his trip-hammer fist. The blow broke the sailors' hold. It called no scream from Kuala Pahang. She fell, writhing, plunged in foam, rose, and with splendid energy struck out for the canoes.

Briggs leaned across the rail, as if no war-fleet had been lying in easy shot; and with hard fingers tugging at his big, black beard, watched the swimming girl, her lithe, yellow body gleaming through the water. Watched, too, the swift cutting of the sharks' fins toward her—the darting, black forms —the grim tragedy in that sudden, reddening whip of brine. Then he laughed, his teeth gleaming like wolves' teeth, as he heard her scream.

"Broke her silence at last, eh?" he sneered. "They got a yell out of the she-dog, the sharks did, even if I couldn't—eh?"

Along the rail, hard-bitten as the clipper's men were, oaths broke out, and mutterings. Work slackened at the capstan, and for the moment the guards forgot to drive their lathering slaves there.

"Great God, captain!" sounded the doctor's voice, as he looked up from a wounded man. "You've murdered us all!"

Briggs only laughed again and looked to his pistol.

"They're coming now, men," said he coolly. To his ears the high and rising tumult from the flotilla made music. The lust of war was in him. For a moment he peered intently at the paddlemen once more bending to their work; the brandished krises and long spears; the spattering of bullets all along the water.

"Let 'em come!" he cried, laughing once more. "With hot lead and boiling water and cold steel, I reckon we're ready for 'em. Steady's the word, boys! They're coming—give 'em hell!"

CHAPTER XI

HOME BOUND

Noon witnessed a strange scene in the Straits of Motomolo, a scene of agony and death.

Over the surface of the strait, inborne by the tide, extended a broad field of débris, of shattered planks, bamboos, platted sails.

In mid-scene, sunk on Ulu Salama bar only a few fathoms from where the *Silver Fleece* had lain, rested the dismantled wreck of the proa. The unpitying sun flooded that wreck—what was left of it after a powder-cask, fitted with fuse, had been hurled aboard by Captain Briggs himself. No living man remained aboard. On the high stern still projecting from the sea—the stern whence a thin waft of smoke still rose against the sky—a few broken, yellow bodies lay half consumed by fire, twisted and hideous.

Of the small canoes, not one remained. Such as had not been capsized and broken up, had lamely paddled back to shore with the few Malays who had survived the guns and cutlasses and brimming kettles of seething water. Corpses lay awash. The sharks no longer quarreled for them. Full-fed on the finest of eating, they hardly snouted at the remnants of the feast.

So much, then, for the enemy. And the *Silver Fleece*—what of her?

A mile to seaward flying a few rags of canvas, the wounded clipper was limping on, under a little slant of wind that gave her hardly steerageway. Her kedge cable had been chopped, her mizzen-topmast was down, and a raffle of spars, ropes and canvas littered her decks or had brought down the awnings, that smoldered where the fire-arrows had ignited them.

Her deck-houses showed the splintering effects of rifle and cannon-fire. Here, there, lay empty pails and coppers that had held boiling water. Along the rails and lying distorted on deck, dead men and wounded—white, brown and yellow—were sprawling. And there were wounds and mutilations and dead men still locked in grapples eloquent of fury—a red shambles on the planks once so whitely holystoned.

The litter of knives, krises, cutlasses and firearms told the story; told that some of the Malays had boarded the *Silver Fleece* and that none of these had got away.

The brassy noonday fervor, blazing from an unclouded sky, starkly revealed every detail. On the heavy air a mingled odor of smoke and blood drifted upward, as from a barbaric pyre to some unpitying and sanguinary god —perhaps already to the avenging god that old Dengan Jouga had called upon to curse the captain and his ship, "the Eyeless Face that waits above and laughs."

A doleful sound of groaning and cursing arose. Beside the windlass—deserted now, with part of the Malays dead and part under hatches—Gascar was feebly raising a hand to his bandaged head, as he lay there on his back. His eyes, open and staring, seemed to question the sun that cooked his bloodied face. A brown man, blind and aimless, was crawling on slippery red hands and knees, amidships; and as he crawled, he moaned monotonously. Two more, both white, were sitting with their backs against the deck-house. Neither spoke. One was past speech; the other, badly slashed about the shoulders, was groping in his pockets for tobacco; and, finding none, was feebly cursing.

Bevans, leaning against the taffrail, was binding his right forearm with strips torn from the shirt that hung on him in tatters. He was swearing mechanically, in a sing-song voice, as the blood seeped through each fresh turn of cotton.

From the fo'c's'le was issuing a confused sound. At the wheel stood a sailor, beside whom knelt the doctor. As this sailor grimly held the wheel, Filhiol was bandaging his thigh.

"It's the best I can do for you now, my man," the doctor was saying. "Others need me worse than you do."

A laugh from the companionway jangled on this scene of agony. There stood Alpheus Briggs, smearing his bearded lips with his hirsute paw—for once again he had been at the liquor below. He blinked about him, set both fists on his hips, and then flung an oath of all-comprehensive execration at sea and sky and ship.

"Well, anyhow, by the holy Jeremiah," he cried, with another laugh of barbaric merriment, "I've taught those yellow devils one good lesson!"

A shocking figure the captain made. All at once Prass came up from below and stood beside him. Mauled as Prass was, he seemed untouched by comparison with Briggs. The captain's presence affronted heaven and earth, with its gross ugliness of rags and dirt and wounds, above which his savage spirit seemed to rise indifferent, as if such trifles as mutilations lay beneath notice.

Across the captain's brow a gash oozed redly into his eye, puffy, discolored. As he smeared his forehead, his arm knotted into hard bunches.

His hairy breast was slit with slashes, too; his mop of beard had stiffened from a wound across his cheek. Nothing of his shirt remained, save a few tatters dangling from his tightly-drawn belt. His magnificent torso, muscled like an Atlas, was all grimed with sweat, blood, dirt. Save for his boots, nothing of his clothing remained intact; and the boots were sodden red.

Now as he stood there, peering out with his one serviceable eye under a heavy, bushy brow, and chewing curses to himself, he looked a man, if one ever breathed, unbeaten and unbeatable.

The captain's voice gusted out raw and brutelike, along the shambles of the deck.

"Hell of a thing, this is! And all along of a yellow wench. Devil roast all women! An' devil take the rotten, cowardly crew! If I'd had that crew I went black-birding with up the Gold Coast, not one o' those hounds would have boarded us. But they didn't get the she-dog back, did they? It's bad, bad, but might be worse, so help me!"

Again he laughed, with white teeth gleaming in his reddened beard, and lurched out on deck. He peered about him. A brown body lay before him, face upward, with grinning teeth. Briggs recognized the turtle-egg seller, who had thrown the kris. With a foul oath he kicked the body.

"*You* got paid off, anyhow," he growled. "Now you and Scurlock can fight it out together, in hell!"

He turned to the doctor, and limped along the deck.

"Doctor Filhiol!"

"Yes, sir?" answered the doctor, still busy with the man at the wheel.

"Make a short job o' that, and get to work on those two by the deck-house. We've got to muster all hands as quick as the Lord'll let us—got to get sail on her, an' away. These damned Malays will be worryin' at our heels again, if we don't."

"Yes, sir," said Filhiol, curtly. He made the bandage fast, took his kit, and started forward. Briggs laid a detaining hand on his arm—a hand that left a broad red stain on the rolled-up sleeve.

"Doctor," said he, thickly, "we've got to stand together, now. There's a scant half-dozen men, here, able to pull a rope; and with them we've got to make Singapore. Do your best, doctor—do your best!"

"I will, sir. But that includes cutting off your rum!"

The captain roared into boisterous laughter and slapped Filhiol on the back.

"You'll have to cut my throat first!" he ejaculated. "No, no; as long as I've got a gullet to swallow with, and the rum lasts, I'll lay to it. Patch 'em up, doctor, an' then—"

"You could do with a bit of patching, yourself."

The captain waved him away.

"Scratches!" he cried. "Let the sun dry 'em up!" He shoved the doctor forward, and followed him, kicking to right and left a ruck of weapons and débris. Together the men advanced, stumbling over bodies.

"Patch those fellows up the best you can," directed Briggs, gesturing at the pair by the deck-house. "One of 'em, anyhow, may be some good. We've got to save every man possible, now. Not that I love 'em, God knows," he added, swaying slightly as he stood there, with his blood-stained hand upon the rail. "The yellow-bellied pups! We've got to save 'em. Though if this was Singapore, I'd let 'em rot. At Singapore, Lascars are plenty, and beachcombers you can get for a song a dozen. Get to work now, sir, get to work!"

Life resumed something of order aboard the *Silver Fleece*, as she wore slowly down Motomolo Strait. The few Malays of the crew, who had survived the fight and had failed to make their escape with the retreating forces, were for the present kept locked in the deck-house. Briggs was taking no chances with another of the yellow dogs running *amok*.

The number of hands who mustered for service, including Briggs, Wansley and the doctor, was only nine. This remnant of a crew, as rapidly as weak and wounded flesh could compass it, spread canvas and cleaned ship. A grisly task that was, of sliding the remaining bodies over the rail and of sluicing down the reddened decks with buckets of warm seawater. More and more canvas filled—canvas cut and burned, yet still holding wind enough to drive the clipper. The *Silver Fleece* heeled gracefully and gathered way.

Slowly the scene of battle drew astern, marked by the thin smoke still rising from the wreckage of the proa. Slowly the haze-shrouded line of shore grew dim. A crippled ship, bearing the dregs of a mutilated crew, she left the vague, blue headland of Columpo Point to starboard, and so—sorely broken but still alive—passed beyond all danger of pursuit.

And as land faded, Captain Alpheus Briggs, drunk, blood-stained, swollen with malice and evil triumph, stood by the shattered taffrail, peering back at the vanishing scene of one more battle in a life that had been little save violence and sin. Freighted with fresh and heavy crimes he exulted, laughing in his blood-thick beard. The tropic sun beat down upon his face, bringing each wicked line to strong relief.

"Score one more for me," he sneered, his hairy fists clenched hard. "Hell's got you now, witch-woman, an' Scurlock an' all the rest that went against me. But I'm still on deck! They don't stick on *me*, curses don't. And I'll outlaugh that Eyeless Face—outlaugh it, by God, and come again. And so to hell with that, too!"

He folded steel-muscled arms across his bleeding, sweating chest, heaved a deep breath and gloried in his lawless strength.

"To hell with that!" he spat, once more. "I win—I always win! To hell with everything that crosses me!"

CHAPTER XII

AT LONG WHARF

Four months from that red morning, the *Silver Fleece* drew in past Nix's Mate and the low-buttressed islands in Boston Harbor, and with a tug to ease her to her berth, made fast at Long Wharf.

All signs of the battle had long since been obliterated, overlaid by other hardships, violences, evil deeds. Her bottom fouled by tropic weed and barnacles that had accumulated in West Indian waters, her canvas brown and patched, she came to rest. Of all the white men who had sailed with her, nearly two years before, now remained only Captain Briggs, Mr. Wansley, and the doctor. The others who had escaped the fight had all died or deserted on the home-bound journey. One had been caught by bubonic at Bombay, and two by beri-beri at Mowanga, on the Ivory Coast; the others had taken French leave as occasion had permitted.

Short-handed, with a rag-tag crew, the *Fleece* made her berth. She seemed innocent enough. The sickening stench of the slave cargo that had burdened her from Mowanga to Cuba had been fumigated out of her, and now she appeared only a legitimate trader. That she bore, deftly hidden in secret places, a hundred boxes of raw opium, who could have suspected?

As the hawsers were flung and the clipper creaked against the wharf, there came to an end surely one of the worst voyages that ever an American clipper-ship made. And this is saying a great deal. Those were hard days— days when Massachusetts ships carried full cargoes of Medford rum and Bibles to the West Coast, and came back as slavers, with black ivory groaning and dying under hatches—days when the sharks trailed all across the Atlantic, for the bodies of black men and women—hard days and evil ways, indeed.

Very spruce and fine was Captain Briggs; very much content with life and with the strength that in him lay, that excellent May morning, as with firm stride and clear eye he walked up State Street, in Boston Town. The wounds which would have killed a weaker man had long since healed on him. Up from the water-front he walked, resplendent in his best blue suit, and with a gold-braided cap on his crisp hair. His black beard was carefully trimmed and combed; his bronzed, full-fleshed face glowed with health and satisfaction; and the smoke of his cigar drifted behind him on the morning air. As he went he hummed an ancient chantey:

"Oh, Sharlo Brown, I love your datter,
  Awa-a-ay, my rollin' river!

Oh, Sharlo Brown, I love your datter,
Ah! Ah! We're bound with awa-a-ay,
'Cross the wide Missouri!"

Past the ship-chandlers' stores, where all manner of sea things lay in the windows, he made his way, and past the marine brokers' offices; past the custom-house and up along the Old State House; and so he came into Court Street and Court Square, hard by which, in a narrow, cobbled lane, the Bell-in-Hand Tavern was awaiting him.

All the way along, shipmasters and seafaring folk nodded respectfully to Alpheus Briggs, or touched their hats to him. But few men smiled. His reputation of hard blows and harder dealings made men salute him. But no man seized him by the hand, or haled him into any public house to toast his safe return.

Under the dark doorway of the Bell-in-Hand—under the crude, wooden fist that from colonial times, as even to-day, has held the gilded, wooden bell —Briggs paused a moment, then entered the inn. His huge bulk seemed almost to fill the dim, smoky, low-posted old place, its walls behung with colored woodcuts of ships and with fine old sporting prints. The captain raised a hand of greeting to Enoch Winch, the publican, passed the time of day with him, and called for a pewter of Four-X, to be served in the back room.

There he sat down in the half-gloom that seeped through the little windows of heavily leaded bull's-eye glass. He put his cap off, drew deeply at his cigar, and sighed with vast content.

"Back home again," he murmured. "A hell of a time I've had, and that's no lie. But I'm back home at last!"

His satisfaction was doubled by the arrival of the pewter of ale. Briggs drank deeply of the cold brew, then dried his beard with a handkerchief of purple silk. Not now did he smear his mouth with his hand. This was a wholly other and more elegant Alpheus Briggs. Having changed his latitude and raiment, he had likewise changed his manners.

He drained the pewter till light showed through the glass bottom—the bottom reminiscent of old days when to accept a shilling from a recruiting officer, even unaware, meant being pressed into the service; for a shilling in an empty mug was held as proof of enlistment, unless instantly detected and denied. Briggs smiled at memory of the trick.

"Clumsy stratagem," he pondered, "We're a bit slicker, to-day. In the old days it took time to make a fortune. Now, a little boldness turns the trick, just as I've turned it, this time!"

He rapped on the table for another pewter of Four-X. Stronger liquors would better have suited his taste, but he had certain business still to be carried out, and when ashore the captain never let drink take precedence of business.

The second pewter put Captain Briggs in a reminiscent mood, wherein memories of the stirring events of the voyage just ended mingled with the comforting knowledge that he had much money in pocket and that still more was bound to come, before that day's end. As in a kind of mental mirage, scenes arose before him—scenes of hardship and crime, now in security by no means displeasing to recall.

The affair with the Malay war fleet had already been half-obliterated by more recent violences. Briggs pondered on the sudden mutiny that had broken out, ten days from Bombay, led by a Liverpool ruffian named Quigley, who had tried to brain him with a piece of iron in a sock. Briggs had simply flung him into the sea; then he had faced the others with naked fists, and they had slunk away forward.

He and Wansley had later lashed them to the gangway and had given them the cat to exhaustion. Briggs felt that he had come out of this affair with honors. He took another draught of ale.

Beating up the West Coast, he recalled how he had punished a young Irishman, McCune, whom he had shipped at Cape Town. McCune, from the supposed security of the foretop-gallant yard, had cursed him for a black-hearted bucko. Without parley, Briggs had run up the ratlines, and had flung McCune to the deck. The man had lived only a few minutes. Briggs nodded with satisfaction. He clenched his right fist, hairy, corded, and turned it this way and that, glad of its power. Greatly did he admire the resistless argument that lay in all its bones and ligaments.

"There's no man can talk back to *me*!" he growled. "No, by the Judas priest!"

Now came less pleasing recollections. The slave cargo on the west-bound voyage had been unusually heavy. Ironed wrist and ankle, the blacks—men, women, children, purchased as a rather poor bargain lot from an Arab trader —had lain packed in the hold. They had been half starved when Briggs had loaded them, and the fever had already got among them. The percentage of loss had been a bit too heavy. Some death was legitimate, of course; but an excessive mortality meant loss.

The death rate had risen so high that Briggs had even considered bringing some of the black ivory on deck, and increasing the ration. But in the end he had decided to hold through, and trust luck to arrive in Cuba with enough slaves to pay a good margin. Results had justified his decision.

"I was right about that, too," thought he. "Seems like I'm always right—or else it's gilt-edged luck!"

Yet, in spite of all, that voyage had left some disagreeable memories. The reek and stifle of the hold, the groaning and crying of the blacks—that no amount of punishment could silence—had vastly annoyed the captain. The way in which his crew had stricken the shackles from the dead and from those manifestly marked for death and had heaved them overboard to the trailing sharks, had been only a trivial detail.

But the fact that Briggs's own cabin had been invaded by vermin and by noxious odors had greatly annoyed the captain. Not all Doctor Filhiol's burning of pungent substances in the cabin had been able to purify the air. Briggs had cursed the fact that this most profitable trafficking had involved such disagreeable concomitants, and had consoled himself with much strong drink.

Then, too, a five-day blow, three hundred miles west of the Cape Verdes, had killed off more than forty of his negroes and had made conditions doubly intolerable. Once more he formulated thoughts in words:

"Damn it! I might have done better to have scuttled her, off the African coast, and have drawn down my share of the insurance money. If I'd known what I was running into, that's just what I *would* have done, so help me! I made a devilish good thing of it, that way, in the old *White Cloud* two years ago. And never was so much as questioned!"

He pondered a moment, frowning blackly.

"Maybe I did wrong, after all, to bring the *Fleece* into port. But if I hadn't, I'd have had to sacrifice those hundred boxes of opium, that will bring me a clear two hundred apiece, from Hendricks. So after all, it's all right. I'm satisfied."

He drained the last of the Four-X, and carefully inspected his watch.

"Ten-fifteen," said he. "And I'm to meet Hendricks at ten-thirty at the Tremont House. I'll hoist anchor and away."

He paid his score with scrupulous exactness, for in such matters he greatly prided himself on his honesty, lighted a fresh cigar, and departed from the Bell-in-Hand.

Cigar in mouth, smoke trailing on the May morning, he made his way to School Street and up it. A fine figure of a mariner he strode along, erect, deep-chested, thewed and sinewed like a bull.

In under the columned portals of the old Tremont House—now long since only a memory—he entered, to his rendezvous with Hendricks, furtive buyer of the forbidden drug.

And as he vanishes beneath that granite doorway, for fifty years he passes from our sight.

CHAPTER XIII

AFTER FIFTY YEARS

If you will add into one total all that is sunniest and most sheltered, all that hangs heaviest with the perfume of old-fashioned New England gardens, all that most cozily combines in an old-time sailor's home, you will form a picture of Snug Haven, demesne of Captain Alpheus Briggs, long years retired.

Snug Haven, with gray-shingled walls, with massive chimney stacks projecting from its weather-beaten, gambreled roof, seemed to epitomize rest after labor, peace after strife.

From its broad piazza, with morning-glory-covered pillars, a splendid view opened of sea and shore and foam-ringed islets in the harbor of South Endicutt—a view commanding kelp-strewn foreshore, rock-buttressed headlands, sun-spangled cobalt of the bay; and then the white, far tower of Truxbury Light, and then the hazed and brooding mystery of open Atlantic.

Behind the cottage rose Croft Hill, sweet with ferns, with bayberries and wild roses crowding in among the lichen-crusted boulders and ribbed ledges, where gnarly, ancient apple-trees and silver birches clung. Atop the hill, a wall of mossy stones divided the living from the dead; for there the cemetery lay, its simple monuments and old, gray headstones of carven slate bearing some family names that have loomed big in history.

Along the prim box-hedge of Captain Briggs's front garden, the village street extended. Wandering irregularly with the broken shore line, it led past time-grayed dwellings, past the schoolhouse and the white, square-steepled church, to the lobstermen's huts, the storehouses and wharves, interspersed with "fish-flakes" that blent pungent marine odors with the fresh tang of the sea.

Old Mother Nature did her best, all along that street and in the captain's garden, to soften those sometimes insistent odors, with her own perfumes of asters and petunias, nasturtiums, dahlias, sweet fern, and fresh, revivifying caresses of poplar, elm and pine, of sumac, buttonwood and willow.

With certain westerly breezes—breezes that bore to Snug Haven the sad, slow chant of the whistling buoy on Graves Shoal and the tolling of the bell buoy on the Shallows—oakum and tar, pitch, salt and fish had the best of it in South Endicutt. But with a shift to landward, apple-tree, mignonette and phlox and other blooms marshalled victorious essences; and the little village by the lip of the sea grew sweet and warm as the breast of a young girl who dreams.

The afternoon on which Captain Alpheus Briggs once more comes to our sight—the 24th of June, 1918—was just one of those drowsy, perfumed afternoons, when the long roar of the breakers over Dry Shingle Reef seemed part of the secrets the breeze was whispering among the pine needles on Croft Hill, and when the droning of the captain's bees, among his spotted tiger-lilies, his sweet peas, cannas and hydrangeas, seemed conspiring with the sun-drenched warmth of the old-fashioned garden to lull man's spirit into rest and soothe life's fever with nepenthe.

Basking in the sunlight of his piazza, at ease in a broad-armed rocker by a wicker table, the old captain appeared mightily content with life. Beside him lay a wiry-haired Airedale, seemingly asleep yet with one eye ready to cock open at the captain's slightest move. A blue cap, gold-braided, hung atop one of the uprights of the rocking-chair; the captain's bushy hair, still thick, though now spun silver, contrasted with his deep-lined face, tanned brown. Glad expectancy showed in his deep-set eyes, clear blue as they had been full fifty years ago, eyes under bushy brows that, once black, now matched the silver of his hair.

White, too, his beard had grown. Once in a while he stroked it, nervously, with a strong, corded hand that seemed, as his whole, square-knit body seemed, almost as vigorous as in the long ago—the half-forgotten, wholly repented long ago of violence and evil ways. Not yet had senility laid its clutch upon Alpheus Briggs. Wrinkles had come, and a certain stooping of the powerful shoulders; but the old captain's blue coat with its brass buttons still covered a body of iron strength.

The telescope across his knees was no more trim than he. Carefully tended beard, well-brushed coat and polished boots all proclaimed Alpheus Briggs a proud old man. Though the soul of him had utterly changed, still Captain Briggs held true to type. In him no laxity inhered, no falling away from the strict tenets of shipshape neatness.

The captain appeared to be waiting for something. Once in a while he raised the telescope and directed it toward the far blue sheet of the outer harbor, where the headland of Pigeon Cliff thrust itself against the gray-green of the ship channel, swimming in a distant set of haze. Eagerly he explored the prospect, letting his glass rest on white lines of gulls that covered the tide-bars, on the whiter lines of foam over the reef, on the catboats and dories, the rusty coasting steamers and clumsy coal-barges near or far away. With care he sought among the tawny sails; and as each schooner tacked, its canvas now sunlit, now umber in shade, the captain's gaze seemed questioning: "Are you the craft I seek?"

The answer came always negative. With patience, Captain Briggs lowered his glass again and resumed his vigil.

"No use getting uneasy," said he, at last; and brought out pipe and tobacco from the pocket of his square-cut jacket. "It won't bring him a bit sooner. He wrote me he'd be here sometime to-day, and that means he surely will be. He's a Briggs. What he says he'll do he *will* do. No Briggs ever breaks a promise, and Hal is all clear Briggs, from truck to keelson!"

Waiting, pondering, the old man let his eyes wander over the Snug Haven of his last years; the place where he could keep contact with sunshine and seashine, with the salt breeze and the bite of old ocean, yet where comfort and peace profound could all be his.

A pleasant domain it was, and in all its arrangements eloquent of the old captain. There life had been very kind to him, and there his darkest moments of bereavement had been fought through, survived. Thither, more than five-and-forty years ago, he had brought the young wife whose love had turned his heart from evil ways and set his feet upon the better path from which, nearly half a century, they had not strayed.

In the upper front room his only son, Edward, had been born; and from the door, close at hand, he had followed the coffins that had taken away from him the three beings about whom, successively, the tendrils of his affection had clung.

First, the hand of death had closed upon his wife; but, profound as that loss had been, it had left to him his son. In this same house, that son had grown to manhood, and had himself taken a wife; and so for a few years there had been happiness again.

But not for long. The birth of Hal, the old man's grandson, had cost the life of Hal's mother, a daughter-in-law whom Captain Briggs had loved like his own flesh and blood; and, two years after, tragedy had once more entered Snug Haven. Edward Briggs, on his first voyage as master of a ship—a granite-schooner, between Rockport and Boston—had fallen victim of a breaking derrick-rope. The granite lintel that had crushed the body of the old captain's son had fallen also upon the captain's heart. Long after the grass had grown upon that third grave in the Briggs burial lot, up there on the hill overlooking the shining harbor, the old man had lived as in a dream.

Then, gradually, the fingers of little Hal, fumbling at the latchets of the old man's heart, had in some miraculous way of their own that only childish fingers possess, opened that crushed and broken doorway; and Hal had entered in, and once more life had smiled upon the captain.

After even the last leaves of autumn have fallen, sometimes wonderful days still for a little while warm the dying world and make men glad. Thus, with the captain. He had seemed to lose everything; and yet, after all, Indian summer still had waited for him. In the declining years, Hal had become his sunshine and his warmth, once more to expand his soul, once more to bid him love. And he had loved, completely, blindly, concentrating upon the boy, the last remaining hope of his family, an affection so intense that more than once the child, hurt by the fierce grip of the old man's arms, had cried aloud in pain and fright. Whereat the captain, swiftly penitent, had kissed and fondled him, sung brave sea chanteys to him, taught him wondrous miracles of splicing and weaving, or had fashioned boats and little guns, and so had brought young Hal to worship him as a child will when a man comes to his plane and is another, larger child with him.

Life would have ceased to hold any purpose or meaning for the captain, had it not been for Hal. The boy, wonderfully strong, had soon begun to absorb so much of the captain's affection that the wounds in his heart had ceased to bleed, and that his pain had given place to a kind of dumb acquiescence. And after the shock of the final loss had somewhat passed life had taken root again, in Snug Haven.

Hal had thriven mightily in the sea air. Body and mind, he had developed at a wonderful pace. He had soon grown so handsome that even his occasional childish fits of temper—quite extraordinary fits, of strange violence, though brief—had been forgiven by every one. He had needed but to smile to be absolved.

Life had been, for the boy, all "a wonder and a wild desire." The shadow of death had not been able to darken it. Before very long he had come to care little for any human relationship save with his grandfather. But the captain, proud of race, had often spoken to him of his father and his mother, or, leading Hal by the hand, had trudged up the well-worn path to the cemetery on the hill, to show the boy the well-kept graves.

So Hal had grown up. Shore and sea and sky had all combined to develop him. School and play, and all the wonders of cliff, beach, tide, and storm, of dories, nets, tackle, ships, and sea-things had filled both mind and body with unusual vigor.

The captain had told Hal endless tales of travel, had taught him an infinite number of sea-marvels. Before Hal had reached ten years, he had come to know every rope and spar of many rigs.

At twelve, he had built a dory; and, two years later with the captain's help, a catboat, in which he and the old man had sailed in all weathers. If there were any tricks of navigation that the boy did not learn, or anything about the mysterious doings of the sea, it was only because the captain himself fell short of complete knowledge.

In everything the captain had indulged him. Yet even though he had never inflicted punishment, and even though young Hal had grown up to have pretty much his own way, the captain had denied spoiling him.

"Only poor material will spoil," he had always said. "You can't spoil the genuine, thoroughbred stuff. No, nor break it, either. I know what I'm doing. Whose business is it, but my own?"

Sharing a thousand interests in common with Hal, the captain's love and hope had burned ever higher and more steadily. As the violent and grief-stricken past had faded gradually into a vague melancholy, the future had seemed beckoning with ever clearer cheer. The captain had come to have dreams of some day seeing Hal master of the biggest ship afloat. He had formed a hundred plans and dreamed a thousand dreams, all more or less enwoven with the sea. And though Hal, when he had finished school and had entered college, had begun to show strange aptitude for languages—especially the Oriental tongues—still the old man had never quite abandoned hope that some day the grandson might stand as captain on the bridge of a tall liner.

For many years another influence had had its part in molding Hal—the influence of Ezra Trefethen, whereof now a word or two. Ezra, good soul, had lived at Snug Haven ever since Hal's birth, less as a servant than as a member of the household. Once he had cooked for the captain, on a voyage out to Japan. His simple philosophy and loyalty, as well as his exceeding skill with saucepans, had greatly attached the captain to him—this being, you understand, in the period after the captain's marriage had made of him another and a better man.

When Hal's mother had died, the captain had given Ezra dominion over the "galley" at Snug Haven, a dominion which had gradually extended itself to the whole house and garden, and even to the upbringing of the boy.

Together, in a hit-or-miss way that had scandalized the good wives of South Endicutt, Briggs and Trefethen had reared little Hal. The captain had given no heed to hints that he needed a house-keeper or a second wife. Trefethen had been a powerful helper with the boy. Deft with the needle, he had sewed for Hal. He had taught him to keep his little room—his little "first mate's cabin," as he had always called it—very shipshape. And he had taught him sea lore, too; and at times when the captain had been abroad on the great waters, had taken complete charge of the fast-growing lad.

Thus the captain had been ever more and more warmly drawn towards Ezra. The simple old fellow had followed the body of the captain's son up there to the grave on the hill, and had wept sincerely in the captain's sorrow. Together, Briggs and Ezra had kept the cemetery lot in order. Evenings without number, after little Hal had been tucked into bed, the two ageing men had sat and smoked together.

Almost as partners in a wondrous enterprise, they two had watched Hal grow. Ezra had been just as proud as the captain himself, when the sturdy, black-haired, blue-eyed boy had entered high school and had won his place at football and on the running-track. When "Hal" had become "Master Hal," for him, on the boy's entering college, the old servitor had come to look upon him with something of awe, for now Hal's studies had lifted him beyond all possible understanding. Old Ezra had thrilled with pride as real and as proprietary as any Captain Briggs had felt.

Thus, the belovèd idol of the two indulgent old sea-dogs, Hal had grown up.

CHAPTER XIV

A VISITOR FROM THE LONG AGO

As the captain sat there expectantly on the piazza, telescope across his knees, dog by his side, a step sounded in the hallway of Snug Haven, and out issued Ezra, blinking in the sunshine, screwing up his leathery, shrewd, humorous face, and from under a thin palm squinting across the harbor.

"Ain't sighted him yit, cap'n?" demanded he, in a cracked voice. "It's past six bells o' the aft'noon watch. You'd oughta be sightin' him pretty soon, now, seems like."

"I think so, too," the captain answered. "He wrote they'd leave Boston this morning early. Seems as if they should have made Endicutt Harbor by now."

"Right, cap'n. But don't you worry none. They can't of fell foul o' nothin'. Master Hall, he's an A1 man. He'll make port afore night, cap'n, never you fear. He's *gotta*! Ain't I got a leg o' lamb on to roast, an' ain't I made his favorite plum-cake with butter-an'-sugar sauce? Aye, he'll tie up at Snug Haven afore sundown, never you fear!"

The captain only grunted; and old Trefethen, after careful but fruitless examination of the harbor, went back into the house again, very much like those figures on toy barometers that come out in good weather and retire in bad.

Left alone once more, the captain drew deeply at his pipe and glanced with satisfaction at his cozy domain. A pleasant place it was, indeed, and trimly eloquent of the hand of an old seafaring man. The precision wherewith the hedge was cut, the whitewashed spotlessness of the front gate—a gate on the "port" post of which was fastened a red ship's-lantern, with a green one on the "starboard"—and even the sanded walks, edged with conch-shells, all spelled "shipshape."

Trailing woodbine covered the fences to right and left, and along these fences grew thrifty berry bushes. Apple-trees, whereon green buttons of fruit had already set, shaded the lawn, interspersed with flower-beds edged with whitewashed rocks—flower-beds bright with hollyhocks, peonies and poppies.

Back of the house a vegetable-garden gave promise of great increase; and in the hen-yard White Leghorns and Buff Orpingtons pursued the vocations of all well-disposed poultry. A Holstein cow, knee-deep in daisies on the gentle hill-slope behind Snug Haven, formed part of the household; and last of all came the bees, denizens of six hives not far from the elm-shaded well.

But the captain's special pride centered in the gleaming white flagpole, planted midway of the front lawn—a pole from which flew the Stars and Stripes, together with a big blue house-flag bearing a huge "B" of spotless white. This flag and a little cannon of gleaming brass, from which on every holiday the captain fired a salute, formed his chief treasures; by which token you shall read the heart of the old man, and see that, for all his faring up and down the world, a certain curious simplicity had at the end developed itself in him.

Thus that June afternoon, sitting in state amid his possessions, the captain waited. Waited, dressed in his very best, for the homecoming of the boy on whom was concentrated all the affection of a nature now powerful to love, as in the old and evil days it had been violent to hate. His face, as he sat there, was virile, patriarchal, dignified with that calm nobility of days when old age is "frosty but kindly." With placid interest he watched a robin on the lawn, and listened to the chickadees' piping monotone in the huge maple by the gate. Those notes seemed to blend with the metallic music of hammer and anvil somewhere down the village street. *Tunk-tunk! Clink-clank-clink!* sang the hammer from the shop of Peter Trumett, as Peter forged new links for the anchor-chain of the *Lucy Bell*, now in port for repairs. Then a voice, greeting the captain from the rock-nubbled roadway, drew the old man's gaze.

"How do, cap'n?" called a man from the top of a slow-moving load of kelp. "I'm goin' up-along. Anythin' I kin do fer you?"

"Nothing, Jacob," answered Briggs. "Thank you, just the same. Oh, Jacob! Wait a minute!"

"Hoa, *s-h-h-h-h!*" commanded the kelp-gatherer. "What is it, cap'n?"

The old man arose, placed his telescope carefully in the rocking-chair, and slowly walked down toward the gate. The Airedale followed close. The dog's rusty-brown muzzle touched the captain's hand. Briggs fondled the animal and smiling said:

"I'm not going to leave you, Ruddy. None of us can go anywhere to-day. Hal's coming home. Know that? We mustn't be away when he comes!" The captain advanced once more. Half-way down the walk he paused, picked up a snail that had crawled out upon the distressful sand. He dropped the snail into the sheltering grass and went forward again. At the gate he stopped, leaned his crossed arms on the clean top-board, and for a moment peered at Jacob perched on the load of kelp that overflowed the time-worn, two-wheeled cart.

"What is it, cap'n?" Jacob queried. "Somethin' I kin do fer you?"

"No, nothing you can do for me, but something you can do for Uncle Everett and for yourself, if you will."

At sound of that name the kelp-gatherer stiffened with sudden resentment.

"Nothin' fer him, cap'n!" he ejaculated. "He's been accommodatin' as a hog on ice to me, an' the case is goin' through. Nothin' at all fer that damned —"

"Wait! Hold on, Jacob!" the old man pleaded, raising his hand. "You can't gain anything by violence and hate. I know you think he's injured you grievously. He thinks the same of you. In his heart I know he's sorry. You and he were friends for thirty years till this petty little quarrel came up. Jacob, is the whole boat worth cutting the cables of good understanding and letting yourselves drift on the reefs of hate? Is it, now?"

"You been talkin' with him 'bout me?" demanded Jacob irefully.

"Well, maybe I have said a few words to Uncle Everett," admitted the captain. "Uncle's willing to go half-way to meet you."

"He'll meet me nowheres 'cept in the court-room down to 'Sconset!" retorted Jacob with heat. "He done me a smart trick that time. I'll rimrack *him!*"

"We've all done smart tricks one time or another," soothed the old captain. The sun through the arching elms flecked his white hair with moving bits of light; it narrowed the keen, earnest eyes of blue. "That's human. It's better than human to be sorry and to make peace with your neighbor. Uncle Everett's not a bad man at heart, any more than you are. Half a dozen words from you would caulk up the leaking hull of your friendship. You're not going to go on hating uncle, are you, when you *could* shake hands with him and be friends?"

"Oh, ain't I, huh?" demanded Jacob. "Why ain't I?"

"Because you're a man and can think!" the captain smiled. "Harkness and Bill Dodge were bitter as gall six months ago, and Giles was ready to cut Burnett's heart out, but I found they were human, after all."

"Yes, but they ain't *me!*"

"Are you less a man than they were?"

"H-m! H-m!" grunted Jacob, floored. "I—I reckon not. Why?"

"I've got nothing more to say for now," the captain answered. "Good-by, Jacob!"

The kelp-gatherer pushed back his straw hat, scratched his head, spat, and then broke out:

"Mebbe it'd be cheaper, after all, to settle out o' court rather 'n' to law uncle. But shakin' hands, an' bein' neighbors with that—that—"

"Good day, Jacob!" the captain repeated. "One thing at a time. And if you come up-along to-morrow, lay alongside, and have another gam with me, will you?"

To this Jacob made no answer, but slapped his reins on the lean withers of his horse. Creakingly the load of seaweed moved away, with Jacob atop, rather dazed. The captain remained there at the gate, peering after him with a smile, kindly yet shrewd.

"Just like the others," he murmured. "Can't make port all on one tack. Got to watch the wind, and wear about and make it when you can. But if I know human nature, a month from to-day Jacob Plummer will be smoking his pipe down at Uncle Everett's sail-loft."

The sound of piping voices, beyond the blacksmith-shop, drew the old captain's attention thither. He assumed a certain expectancy. Into the pocket of his square-cut blue jacket he slid a hand. Along the street he peered—the narrow, rambling street sheltered by great elms through which, here and there, a glint of sunlit harbor shimmered blue.

He had not long to wait. Round the bend by the smithy two or three children appeared; and after these came others, with a bright-haired girl of twenty or thereabout. The children had school-bags or bundles of books tightly strapped. Keeping pace with the teacher a little girl on either side held her hands. You could not fail to see the teacher's smile, as wholesome, fresh and winning as that June day itself.

At sight of the captain the boys in the group set up a joyful shout and some broke into a run.

"Hey, lookit! There's cap'n!" rose exultant cries. "There's Cap'n Briggs!"

Then the little girls came running, too; and all the children captured him by storm. Excited, the Airedale set up a clamorous barking.

The riot ended only when the captain had been despoiled of the peppermints he had provided for such contingencies. Meanwhile the teacher, as trimly pretty a figure as you could meet in many a day's journeying, was standing by the gate, and with a little heightened flush of color was casting a look or two, as of expectancy, up at Snug Haven.

The old captain, smiling, shook his head.

"Not yet, Laura," he whispered. "He'll be here before night, though. You're going to let me keep him a few minutes, aren't you, before taking him away from me?"

She found no answer. Something about the captain's smile seemed to disconcert her. A warm flush crept from her throat to her thickly coiled, lustrous hair. Then she passed on, down the shaded street; and as the captain peered after her, still surrounded by the children, a little moisture blurred his eyes.

"God has been very good to me in spite of all!" he murmured. "Very, very good, and 'the best is yet to be'!"

He turned and was about to start back toward the house when the *cloppa-cloppa-clop* of hoofs along the street arrested his attention. Coming into view, past Laura and her group of scholars, an old-fashioned buggy, drawn by a horse of ripe years, was bearing down toward Snug Haven.

In the buggy sat an old, old man, wizen and bent. With an effort he reined in the aged horse. The captain heard his cracked tones on the still afternoon air:

"Pardon me, but can you tell me where Captain Briggs lives—Captain Alpheus Briggs?"

A babel of childish voices and the pointing of numerous fingers obliterated any information Laura tried to give. The old man, with thanks, clucked to his horse, and so the buggy came along once more to the front gate of Snug Haven. There it stopped.

Out of it bent a feeble, shrunken figure, with flaccid skin on deep-lined face, with blinking eyes behind big spectacles.

"Is that you, captain?" asked a shaking voice that pierced to the captain's heart with a stab of poignant recollection. "Oh, Captain—Captain Briggs—is that you?"

The captain, turning pale, steadied himself by gripping at the whitewashed gate. For a moment his staring eyes met the eyes of the old, withered man in the buggy. Then, in strange, husky tones he cried:

"God above! It—it can't be you, doctor? It can't be—Dr. Filhiol?"

———————————————————————

CHAPTER XV

TWO OLD MEN

"Yes, yes, it's Dr. Filhiol!" the little old man made answer. "I'm Filhiol. And you—Yes, I'd know you anywhere. Captain Alpheus Briggs, so help me!"

He took up a heavy walking-stick, and started to clamber down out of the buggy. Captain Briggs, flinging open the gate, reached him just in time to keep him from collapsing in the road, for the doctor's feeble strength was all exhausted with the long journey he had made to South Endicutt, with the drive from the station five miles away, and with the nervous shock of once more seeing a man on whom, in fifty years, his eyes had never rested.

"Steady, doctor, steady!" the captain admonished with a stout arm about him. "There, there now, steady does it!"

"You—you'll have to excuse me, captain, for seeming so unmanly weak," the doctor proffered shakily. "But I've come a long way to see you, and it's such a hot day—and all. My legs are cramped, too. I'm not what I used to be, captain. None of us are, you know, when we pass the eightieth milestone!"

"None of us are what we used to be; right for you, doctor," the captain answered with deeper meaning than on the surface of his words appeared. "You needn't apologize for being a bit racked in the hull. Every craft's seams open up a bit at times. I understand."

He tightened his arm about the shrunken body, and with compassion looked upon the man who once had trod his deck so strongly and so well. "Come along o' me, now. Up to Snug Haven, doctor. There's good rocking-chairs on the piazza and a good little drop of something to take the kinks out. The best of timber needs a little caulking now and then. Good Lord above! Dr. Filhiol again—after fifty years!"

"Yes, that's correct—after fifty years," the doctor answered. "Here, let me look at you a moment!" He peered at Briggs through his heavy-lensed spectacles. "It's you all right, captain. You've changed, of course. You were a bull of a man in those days, and your hair was black as black;—but still you're the same. I—well, I wish I could say that about myself!"

"Nonsense!" the captain boomed, drawing him toward the gate. "Wait till you've got a little tonic under your hatches, 'midships. Wait till you've spliced the main brace a couple of times!"

"The horse!" exclaimed Filhiol, bracing himself with his stout cane. He peered anxiously at the animal. "I hired him at the station, and if he should run away and break anything—"

"I'll have Ezra go aboard that craft and pilot it into port," the captain reassured him. "We won't let it go on the rocks. Ezra, he's my chief cook and bottle-washer. He can handle that cruiser of yours O. K." The captain's eyes twinkled as he looked at the dejected animal. "Come along o' me, doctor. Up to the quarterdeck with you, now!"

Half-supported by the captain, old Dr. Filhiol limped up the white-sanded path. As he went, as if in a kind of daze he kept murmuring:

"Captain Briggs again! Who'd have thought I could really find him? Half a century—a lifetime—Captain Alpheus Briggs!"

"Ezra! Oh, Ezra!" the captain hailed. Carefully he helped the aged doctor up the steps. Very feebly the doctor crept up; his cane clumped hollowly on the boards. Ezra appeared.

"Aye, aye, sir?" he queried, a look of wonder on his long, thin face. "What's orders, sir?"

"An old-time friend of mine has come to visit me, Ezra. It's Dr. Filhiol, that used to sail with me, way back in the '60's. I've got some of his fancy-work stitches in my leg this minute. A great man he was with the cutting and stitching; none better. I want you men to shake hands."

Ezra advanced, admiration shining from his honest features. Any man who had been a friend of his captain, especially a man who had embroidered his captain's leg, was already taken to the bosom of his affections.

"Doctor," said the captain, "this is Ezra Trefethen. When you get some of the grub from his galley aboard you, you'll be ready to ship again for Timbuctoo."

"I'm very glad to know you, Ezra," the doctor said, putting out his left hand—the right, gnarled and veinous, still gripped his cane. "Yes, yes, we were old-time shipmates, Captain Briggs and I." His voice broke pipingly, "turning again toward childish treble," so that pity and sorrow pierced the heart of Alpheus Briggs. "It's been a sad, long time since we've met. And now, can I get you to look out for my horse? If he should run away and hurt anybody, I'm sure that would be very bad."

"Righto!" Ezra answered, his face assuming an air of high seriousness as he observed the aged animal half asleep by the gate, head hanging, spavined knees bent. "I'll steer him to safe moorin's fer you, sir. We got jest the handiest dock in the world fer him, up the back lane. He won't git away from *me*, sir, never you fear."

"Thank you, Ezra," the doctor answered, much relieved. The captain eased him into a rocker, by the table. "There, that's better. You see, captain, I'm a bit done up. It always tires me to ride on a train; and then, too, the drive from the station was exhausting. I'm not used to driving, you know, and—"

"I know, I know," Briggs interrupted. "Just sit you there, doctor, and keep right still. I'll be back in half a twinkling."

And, satisfied that the doctor was all safe and sound, he stumped into the house; while Ezra whistled to the dog and strode away to go aboard the buggy as navigating officer of that sorry equipage.

Even before Ezra had safely berthed the horse in the stable up the lane, bordered with sweetbrier and sumacs, Captain Briggs returned with a tray, whereon was a bottle of his very best Jamaica, now kept exclusively for sickness or a cold, or, it might be, for some rare and special guest. The Jamaica was flanked with a little jug of water, with glasses, lemons, sugar. At sight of it the doctor left off brushing his coat, all powdered with the gray rock-dust of the Massachusetts north shore, and smiled with sunken lips.

"I couldn't have prescribed better, myself," said he.

"Correct, sir," agreed the captain. He set the tray on the piazza table. "I don't hardly ever touch grog any more. But it's got its uses, now and then. You need a stiff drink, doctor, and I'm going to join you, for old times' sake. Surely there's no sin in that, after half a century that we haven't laid eyes on one another!"

Speaking, he was at work on the manufacture of a brace of drinks.

"It's my rule not to touch it," he added. "But I've got to make an exception to-day. Sugar, sir? Lemon? All O. K., then. Well, doctor, here goes. Here's to—to—"

"To fifty years of life!" the doctor exclaimed. He stood up, raising the glass that Briggs had given him. His eye cleared; for a moment his aged hand held firm.

"To fifty years!" the captain echoed. And so the glasses clinked, and so they drank that toast, bottoms-up, those two old men so different in the long ago, so very different now.

When Filhiol had resumed his seat, the captain drew a chair up close to him, both facing the sea. Through the doctor's spent tissues a little warmth began to diffuse itself. But still he found nothing to say; nor, for a minute or two, did the captain. A little silence, strangely awkward, drew itself between them, now that the first stimulus of the meeting had spent itself. Where, indeed, should they begin to knit up so vast a chasm?

Each man gazed on the other, trying to find some word that might be fitting, but each muted by the dead weight of half a century. Filhiol, the more resourceful of wit, was first to speak.

"Yes, captain, we've both changed, though you've held your own better than I have. I've had a great deal of sickness. And I'm an older man than you, besides. I'll be eighty-four, sir, if I live till the 16th of next October. A man's done for at that age. And you've had every advantage over me in strength and constitution. I was only an average man, at best. You were a Hercules, and even to-day you look as if you might be a pretty formidable antagonist. In a way, I've done better than most, captain. Yes, I've done well in my way," he repeated. "Still, I'm not the man you are to-day. That's plain to be seen."

"We aren't going to talk about that, doctor," the captain interposed, his voice soothing, as he laid a strong hand on the withered one of Filhiol, holding the arm of the rocker. "Let all that pass. I'm laying at anchor in a sheltered harbor here. What breeze bore you news of me? Tell me that, and tell me what you've been doing all this time. What kind of a voyage have you made of life? And where are you berthed, and what cargo of this world's goods have you got in your lockers?"

"Tell me about yourself, first, captain. You have a jewel of a place here. What else? Wife, family, all that?"

"I'll tell you, after you've answered my questions," the captain insisted. "You're aboard my craft, here, sitting on my decks, and so you've got to talk first. Come, come, doctor—let's have your log!"

Thus urged, Filhiol began to speak. With some digressions, yet in the main clearly enough and even at times with a certain dry humor that distantly recalled his mental acuity of the long ago, he outlined his life-story.

Briefly he told of his retirement from the sea, following a wreck off the coast of Chile, in 1876—a wreck in which he had taken damage from which he had never fully recovered—and narrated his establishing himself in practice in New York. Later he had had to give up the struggle there, and had gone up into a New Hampshire village, where life, though poor, had been comparatively easy.

Five years ago he had retired, with a few hundred dollars of pitiful savings, and had bought his way into the Physicians' and Surgeons' Home, at Salem, Massachusetts. He had never married; had never known the love of a wife, nor the kiss of children. His whole life, the captain could see, had been given unhesitatingly to the service of his fellow-men. And now mankind, when old age had paralyzed his skill, was passing him by, as if he had been no more than a broken-up wreck on the shores of the sea of human existence.

Briggs watched the old man with pity that this once trim and active man should have faded to so bloodless a shadow of his former self. Close-shaven the doctor still was, and not without a certain neatness in his dress, despite its poverty; but his bent shoulders, his baggy skin, the blinking of his eyes all told the tragedy of life that fades.

With a pathetic moistening of the eyes, the doctor spoke of this inevitable decay; and with a heartfelt wish that death might have laid its summons on him while still in active service, turned to a few words of explanation as to how he had come to have news again of Captain Briggs.

Chance had brought him word of the captain. A new attendant at the home had mentioned the name Briggs; and memories had stirred, and questions had very soon brought out the fact that it was really Captain Alpheus Briggs, who now was living at South Endicutt. The attendant had told him something more —and here the doctor hesitated, feeling for words.

"Yes, yes, I understand," said Briggs. "You needn't be afraid to speak it right out. It's true, doctor. I *have* changed. God knows I've suffered enough, these long years, trying to forget what kind of a man I started out to be; trying to forget, and not always able to. If repentance and trying to sail a straight course now can wipe out that score, maybe it's partly gone. I hope so, anyhow; I've done my best—no man can do more than that, now, can he?"

"I don't see how he can," answered the doctor slowly.

"He can't," said the captain with conviction. "Of course I can't give back the lives I took, but so far as I've been able, I've made restitution of all the money I came by wrongfully. What I couldn't give back directly I've handed over to charity."

"My undoing," he went on, then paused, irresolute. "My great misfortune —was—"

"Well, what?" asked Filhiol. And through his glasses, which seemed to make his eyes so strangely big and questioning, he peered at Captain Briggs.

CHAPTER XVI

THE CAPTAIN SPEAKS

The captain clenched his right fist, and turned it to and fro, studying it with rueful attention.

"My undoing was the fact that nature gave me brute strength," said he. "Those were hard, bad days, and I had a hard, bad fist; and together with the hot blood in me, and the Old Nick, things went pretty far. Lots of the things I did were needless, cruel, and beyond all condemnation. If I could only get a little of the guilt and sorrow off my mind, that would be something."

"You're morbid, captain," answered Filhiol. "You've made all the amends that anybody can. Let's forget the wickedness, now, and try to remember the better part. You've changed, every way. What changed you?"

"Just let me have another look through the glass, and I'll tell you what I can."

Briggs raised his telescope and with it swept the harbor.

"H-m!" said he. "Nothing yet."

"Expecting some one, captain?"

"My grandson, Hal."

"Grandson! That's fine! The only one?"

"The only one." Briggs lowered his glass with disappointment. "He's the sole surviving member of the family, beside myself. All the rest are up there, doctor, in that little cemetery on the hilltop."

Filhiol's eyes followed the captain's pointing hand, as it indicated the burial-ground lying under the vagrant cloud-shadows of the fading afternoon, peaceful and "sweet with blade and leaf and blossom." In a pine against the richly luminous sky a bluejay was scolding. As a contrabass to the rhythm of the blacksmith's hammer, the booming murmur of the sea trembled across the summer air. The captain went on:

"I've had great losses, doctor. Bitter and hard to bear. After I fell in love and changed my way of life, and married and settled here, I thought maybe fate would be kind to me, but it wasn't. One by one my people were taken away from me—my wife, and then my son's wife, and last of all, my son. Three, I've lost, and got one left. Yet it isn't exactly as if I'd really lost them. I'm not one that can bury love, and forget it. My folks aren't gone. They're still with me, in a way.

"I don't see how people can let their kin be buried in strange places and forgotten. I want to keep mine always near me, where I can look out for them, and where I know they won't feel lonesome. I want them to be right near home, doctor, where it's all so friendly and familiar. Maybe that's an old man's foolish notion, but that's the way I feel, and that's the way I've had it."

"I—think I understand," the doctor answered. "Go on."

"They aren't really gone," continued Briggs. "They're still up there, very, very near to me. There's nothing mournful in the lot; nothing sad or melancholy. No, Ezra and I have made it cheerful, with roses and petunias and zinnias and all kinds of pretty flowers and bushes and vines. You can see some of those vines now on the monument." He pointed once more. "That one, off to starboard of the big elm. It's a beautiful place, really. The breeze is always cool up there, doctor, and the sun stays there longest of any spot round here. It strikes that hill first thing in the morning, and stays till last thing at night. We've got a bench there, a real comfortable one I made myself; not one of those hard, iron things they usually put in cemeteries. I've given Hal lots of his lessons, reading and navigation, up there. I go up every day a spell, and take the dog with me, and Ezra goes, too; and we carry up flowers and put 'em in jars, and holystone the monument and the headstones, and make it all shipshape. It's all as bright as a button, and so it's going to be, as long as I'm on deck."

"I think you've got the right idea, captain," murmured Filhiol. "Death, after all, is quite as natural a process, quite as much to be desired at the proper time, as life. I used to fear it, when I was young; but now I'm old, I'm not at all afraid. Are you?"

"Never! If I can only live to see Hal launched and off on his life journey, with colors flying and everything trig aloft and alow, I'll be right glad to go. That's what I've often told my wife and the others, sitting up there in the sunshine, smoking my pipe. You know, that's where I go to smoke and think, doctor. Ezra goes too, and sometimes we take the old checkerboard and have a game or so. We take the telescopes and sextant up, too, and make observations there. It kind of scandalizes some of the stiff-necked old Puritans, but Lord love you! I don't see any harm in it, do you? It all seems nice and sociable; it makes the death of my people seem only a kind of temporary going away, as if they'd gone on a visit, like, and as if Hal and Ezra and I were just waiting for 'em to come back.

"I tell you, doctor, it's as homy and comfortable as anything you ever saw. I'm truly very happy, up there. Yes, in spite of everything, I reckon I'm a happy man. I've got no end of things to be thankful for. I've prospered. Best of all, *the* main thing without which, of course, everything else wouldn't be worth a tinker's dam, I've got my grandson, Hal!"

"I see. Tell me about him, captain."

"I will. He's been two years in college already, and he's more than made good. He's twenty-one, and got shoulders on him like Goliath. You ought to see him at work in the gym he's fitted up in the barn! Oh, doctor, he's a wonder! His rating is A1, all through."

"I don't doubt it. And you say he's coming home to-day?"

"To-day—which makes this day a great, wonderful day for his old grandfather, and that's the living truth. Yes, he's coming home for as long as he'll stay with me, though he's got some idea of going out with the fishing-fleet, for what he calls local color. He's quite a fellow to make up stories; says he wants to go to sea a while, so he can do it right. Though, Lord knows, he's full enough of sea-lore and sea-skill. That's his grandfather's blood cropping out again, I suppose, that love for blue water. That's what you call heredity, isn't it, doctor?"

"H-m! yes, I suppose so," answered Filhiol, frowning a little. "Though heredity's peculiar. We don't always know just what it is, or how it acts. Still, if a well-marked trait comes out in the offspring, we call it heredity. So he's got your love of the sea, has he?"

"He surely has. There's salt in *his* blood, all right enough!"

"H-m! You don't notice any—any other traits in him that—remind you of your earlier days?"

"If you mean strength and activity, and the love of hard work, yes. Now see, for example. Any other boy would have come home by train, and lots of 'em would have traveled in the smoker, with a pack of cigarettes and a magazine. Does Hal come home that way? He does not! He writes me he's going to work his way up on a schooner, out of Boston, for experience. That's why I'm keeping my glass on the harbor. He told me the name of the schooner. It's the *Sylvia Fletcher*. The minute she sticks her jib round Truxbury Light, I'll catch her."

"*Sylvia Fletcher?*" asked the doctor. "That's an odd coincidence, isn't it?"

"What is?"

"Why, just look at those initials, captain. *Sylvia Fletcher*—S.F."

"Well, what about 'em?"

"*Silver Fleece.* That was S.F., too."

The captain turned puzzled eyes on his guest. He passed a hand over his white hair, and pondered a second or two. Then said he:

"That *is* odd, doctor, but what about it? There must be hundreds of vessels afloat, with those initials."

"By all means. Of course it can't mean anything. As you say, S.F. must be common enough initials among ships. So then, Hal's amphibious already, is he? What's he going to be? A captain like yourself?"

"I'd like him to be. I don't hardly think so, though," Briggs answered, a little distraught. Something had singularly disturbed him. Now and then he cast an uneasy glance at the withered little man in the chair beside him.

"It's going to be his own choice, his profession is," he went on. "He's got to settle that for himself. But I know this much—anything he undertakes, he'll make a success of. He'll carry it out to the last inch. He's a wonder, Hal is. Ah, a fellow to warm the heart! He's none of your mollycoddles, in spite of all the high marks and prizes he's taken. No, no, nothing at all of the mollycoddle."

The captain's face lighted up with pride and joy and a profound eagerness.

"There isn't anything that boy can't do, doctor," he continued. "Athletics and all that; and he's gone in for some of the hardest studies, too, and beaten men that don't do anything but get round-shouldered over books. He's taken work outside the regular course—strange Eastern languages, doctor. I hear there never *was* a boy like Hal. You don't wonder I've been sitting here all afternoon with my old spy-glass, do you?"

"Indeed I don't," Filhiol answered, a note of envy in his feeble voice. "You've had your troubles, just as we all have, but you've got something still to live for, and that's more than *I* can say. You've got everything, everything! It never worked out on you, after all, the curse—the black curse that was put on you fifty years ago. It was all nonsense, of course, and I knew it wouldn't. All that stuff is pure superstition and humbug—"

"Of course! Why, you don't believe such rubbish! I've lived that all down half a lifetime ago. Two or three times, when death took away those I loved, I thought maybe the curse of old Dengan Jouga was really striking me, but it wasn't. For that curse said *everything* I loved would be taken away, and there was always something left to live for; and even when I'd been as hard hit as a man ever was, almost, after a while I could get my bearings again and make sail and keep along on my course. Because, you see, I always had Hal to love and pin my hopes to. I've got him now. He's all I've got—but, God! how wonderfully much he is!"

"Yes, yes, you're quite right," the doctor answered. "He must be a splendid chap, all round. What does he look like?"

"I'm going to answer you in a peculiar way," said Briggs. "That boy, sir, that grandson of mine, he's the living spit and image of what I was, fifty-five or sixty years ago!"

"Eh, what? What's that you say?"

"It's wonderful, I tell you, to see the resemblance. His father—my son—didn't show it at all. A fine, handsome man he was, doctor, and a good man, too. Everybody liked him; he never did a bad thing in his life. He sailed a straight course, and went under his own canvas, all the way; and I loved him for an honest, upright man. But he wasn't brilliant. He never set the world on fire. He was just a plain, good, average man.

"But, Hal! Hal—ah, now there *is* something for you! He's got all the physique I ever had, at my best, and he's got a hundred per cent. more brains than ever I had. It's as if I could see myself, my youth and strength, rise up out of the grave of the past, all shining and splendid, doctor, and live again and make my soul sing with the morning stars, for gladness, like it says in the Bible or somewhere, sir!"

The old captain, quite breathless with his unaccustomed eloquence, pulling out a huge handkerchief, wiped his forehead where the sweat had started. He winked eyes wet with sudden moisture. Filhiol peered at him with a strange, brooding expression.

"You say he's just like you, captain?" asked he. "He's just the way you used to be, in the old days?"

"Why—no, not in all ways. God forbid! But in size and strength he's the equal of me at my best, or even goes ahead of that. And as I've told you before, he's got no end more brains than ever I had."

"How's the boy's temper?"

"Temper?"

"Ever have any violent spells?" The doctor seemed as if diagnosing a case. Briggs looked at him, none too well pleased.

"Why—no. Not as I know of," he answered, though without any emphatic denial. "Of course all boys sometimes slip their anchors, and run foul of whatever's in the way. That's natural for young blood. I wouldn't give a brass farthing for a boy that had no guts, would you?"

"No, no. Of course not. It's natural for—"

"*Ship ahoy!*" the captain joyfully hailed. His keen old eye had just caught sight of something, far in the offing, which had brought the glass to his eye in a second. "There she is, doctor! There's the *Sylvia Fletcher*, sure as guns!"

"He's coming, then?"

"Almost here! See, right to south'ard o' the light? That's the *Sylvia*, and my boy's aboard her. She'll be at Hadlock's Wharf in half an hour. He's almost home. Hal's almost home again!"

The captain stood up and faced the doctor, radiant. Joy, pride, anticipation beamed from his weather-beaten old face; his eyes sparkled, blue, with pure happiness. He said:

"Well, I'm going down to meet him. Do you want to go, too, doctor?"

"How far is it?"

"Mile, or a little better. I'll make it, easy, afore the *Sylvia* gets in. I'll be on the wharf, all right, to welcome Hal."

"I—I think I'll stay here, captain," the other answered. "I'm lame, you know. I couldn't walk that far."

"How about the horse? Ezra'll hitch up for you."

"No, no. It tires me to ride. I'm not used to so much excitement and activity. If it's all the same to you, I'll just sit here and wait. Give me a book, or something, and I'll wait for you both."

"All right, doctor, suit yourself," the captain assented. The relief in his voice was not to be concealed. Despite his most friendly hospitality, something in the doctor's attitude and speech had laid a chill upon his heart. The prospect of getting away from the old man and of meeting Hal quite alone, allured him. "I'll give you books enough for a week, or anything you like. And here in this drawer," as he opened one in the table, "you'll find a box of the best Havanas."

"No, no, I've given up smoking, long ago," the doctor smiled, thinly. "My heart wouldn't stand it. But thank you, just the same."

The figure of Ezra loomed in the doorway, and, followed by the dog, came out upon the porch.

"Sighted him, cap'n?" asked the old man joyfully. "I heered you hailin'. That's him, sure?"

"There's the *Sylvia Fletcher*," Briggs made answer. "You'll see Hal afore sundown."

"Gosh, ain't that great, though?" grinned Ezra, his leathery face breaking into a thousand wrinkles. "If I'd of went an' made that there cake, an' fixed that lamb, an' he hadn't of made port—"

"Well, it's all right, Ezra. Now I'm off. Come, Ruddy," he summoned the Airedale. "Master's coming!"

As the dog got up, the doctor painfully rose from his chair. Cane in hand, he limped along the porch.

"It's just a trifle chilly out here, captain," said he, shivering slightly. "May I go inside?"

"Don't ask, doctor. Snug Haven's yours, all yours, as long as you want it. Make yourself at home! Books, papers, everything in the library—my cabin, I call it. And if you want, Ezra'll start a fire for you in the grate, and get you tea or coffee—"

"No, no, thank you. My nerves won't stand them. But a little warm milk and a fire will do me a world of good."

"Ezra'll mix you an egg-nog that will make you feel like a fighting-cock. Now I must be going. Hal mustn't come ashore and not find me waiting. Come, Ruddy! Good-by, doctor. Good-by, Ezra; so long!"

"Tell Master Hal about the plum-cake an' the lamb!" called the faithful one, as Captain Briggs, a brave and sturdy figure in his brass-buttoned coat of blue and his gold-laced cap tramped down the sandy walk. "Don't fergit to tell him I got it special!"

At the gate, Briggs waved a cheery hand. The doctor, peering after him with strange, sad eyes, shook a boding head. He stood leaning on his stick, till Briggs had skirted the box-hedge and disappeared around the turn by the smithy. Then, shivering again—despite the brooding warmth of the June afternoon—he turned and followed Ezra into the house.

"After fifty years," he murmured, as he went. "I wonder if it could be— after fifty years?"

90

CHAPTER XVII

VISIONS OF THE PAST

Comfortably installed in a huge easy-chair beside the freshly built fire in the "cabin" of Snug Haven and with one of Ezra Trefethen's most artful egg-nogs within easy reach, the aged doctor leaned back, and sighed deeply.

"Maybe the captain's right," said he. "Maybe the boy's all right. It's possible; but I don't know, I don't know."

Blinking, his eyes wandered about the room, which opened off from an old-fashioned hallway lighted by glass panels at the sides of the front door, and by a leaded fanlight over the lintel; a hallway with a curved stairway that would have delighted the heart of any antiquarian. The cabin itself showed by its construction and furnishing that the captain had spent a great deal of thought and time and money. At first glance, save that the fireplace was an incongruous note, one would have thought one's self aboard ship, so closely had the nautical idea been carried out.

To begin with, the windows at the side, which opened out upon the orchard, were circular and rimmed with shining brass, and had thick panes inward-swinging like ships' portholes. A polished fir column, set a trifle on a slant, rose from floor to ceiling, which was supported on white beams, the form and curve of which exactly imitated marine architecture. This column measured no less than a foot and a half in diameter, and gave precisely the impression of a ship's mast. On it hung a chronometer, boxed in a case of polished mahogany, itself the work of the captain's own hand.

All the lamps were hung in gimbals, as if the good captain expected Snug Haven at any moment to set sail and go pitching away over storm-tossed seas. The green-covered table bore a miscellany of nautical almanacs; it accommodated, also, a variety of charts, maps and meteorological reports. The captain's own chair at that table was a true swinging-chair, screwed to the floor; and this floor, you understand, was uncarpeted, so that the holystoned planking shone in immaculate cleanliness as the declining sun through the portholes painted long, reddish stripes across it. Brass instruments lay on the table, and from them the sun flecked little high-lights against the clean, white paint of the cabin.

At the left of the table stood a binnacle, with compass and all; at the right, a four-foot globe, its surface scored with numerous names, dates and memoranda, carefully written in red ink. The captain's log-book, open on the table, also showed writing in red. No ordinary diary sufficed for Alpheus Briggs; no, he would have a regulation ship's log to keep the record of his daily life, or he would have no record at all.

In a rack at one side rested two bright telescopes, with an empty place for the glass now out on the piazza. Beneath this rack a sextant hung; and at one side the daily government weather-report was affixed to a white-painted board.

A sofa-locker, quite like a ship's berth, still showed the impress of the captain's body, where he had taken his after-dinner nap. One almost thought to hear the chanting of sea-winds in cordage, aloft, and the creak and give of seasoned timbers. A curious, a wonderful room, indeed! And as Dr. Filhiol studied it, his face expressed a kind of yearning eagerness; for to his fading life this connotation of the other, braver days brought back memories of things that once had been, that now could never be again.

Yet, analyzing everything, he put away these thoughts. Many sad years had broken the spirit in him and turned his thoughts to the worse aspects of everything. He shook his head again dubiously, and his thin lips formed the words:

"This is very, very strange. This is some form of mental aberration, surely. No man wholly sane would build and furnish any such grotesque place. It's worse, worse than I thought."

Contemplatively he sipped the egg-nog and continued his observations, while from the kitchen—no, the galley—sounded a clink of coppers, mingled with the piping song of old Ezra, interminably discoursing on the life and adventures of the unfortunate Reuben Ranzo, whose chantey is beknown to all seafaring men. The doctor's eyes, wandering to the wall nearest him, now perceived a glass-fronted cabinet, filled with a most extraordinary *omnium gatherum* of curios.

Corals, sponges, coir, nuts, pebbles and dried fruits, strange puffy and spiny fishes, specimens in alcohol, a thousand and one oddments jostled each other on the shelves.

Nor was this all to excite the doctor's wonder. For hard by the cabinet he now perceived the door of a safe, set into the wall, its combination flush with the white boards.

"The captain can't be so foolish as to keep his money in his house," thought Filhiol. "Not when there are banks that offer absolute security. But then, with a man like Captain Briggs, anything seems possible."

He drank a little more of Ezra's excellent concoction, and turned his attention to the one remaining side of the cabin, almost filled by the huge-throated fireplace and by the cobbled chimney.

"More junk!" said Dr. Filhiol unsympathetically.

Against the cobble-stones, suspended from hooks screwed into the cement, hung a regular arsenal of weapons: yataghans, scimitars, sabers and muskets—two of them rare Arabian specimens with long barrels and silver-chased stocks. Pistols there were, some of antique patterns bespeaking capture or purchase from half-civilized peoples. Daggers and stilettos had been worked into a kind of rough pattern. A bow and arrows, a "Penang lawyer," and a couple of boomerangs were interspersed between some knobkerries from Australia, and a few shovel-headed spears and African pigmies' blow-guns. All the weapons showed signs of wear or rust. In every probability, all had taken human life.

Odd, was it not, that the captain, now so mild a man of peace, should have maintained so grim a reliquary? But, perhaps (the doctor thought), Briggs had preserved it as a kind of strange, contrasting reminder of his other days, just as more than one reformed drunkard has been known to keep the favorite little brown jug that formerly was his undoing.

Filhiol, however, very deeply disapproved of this collection. Old age and infirmity had by no means rendered his disposition more suave. He muttered words of condemnation, drank off a little more of the egg-nog, and once again fell to studying the collection. And suddenly his attention concentrated, fixing itself with particular intentness on a certain blade that until then had escaped his scrutiny.

This blade, a Malay kris with a beautifully carved lotus-bud on the handle, seemed to occupy a sort of central post of honor, toward which the other knives converged. The doctor adjusted his spectacles and studied it for a long minute, as if trying to bring back some recollections not quite clear. Then he arose lamely, and squinted up at the blade.

"That's a kris," said he slowly. "A Malay kris. Good Lord, it couldn't be —*the* kris, could it?"

He remained a little while, observing the weapon. The sunlight, ever growing redder as the sun sank over Croft Hill and the ancient cemetery, flicked lights from the brass instruments on the table, and for a moment seemed to crimson the vicious, wavy blade of steel. The doctor raised a lean hand to touch the kris, then drew back.

"Better not," said he. "That's the one, all right enough. There's the groove, the poison groove. There couldn't be two exactly alike. I remember that groove especially. And curaré lasts for years; it's just as fatal now, as when it was first put on. That kris is mighty good to let alone!"

A dark, rusty stain on the blade set him shuddering. Blood, was it—blood, from the long ago? Who could say? The kris evoked powerful memories. The battle of Motomolo Strait rose up before him. The smoke from the fire in the grate seemed, all at once, that of the burning proa, drifting over the opalescent waters of that distant sea. The illusion was extraordinary. Dr. Filhiol closed his eyes, held tightly to the edge of the mantel, and with dilated nostrils sniffed the smoke. He remained there, transfixed with poignant emotions, trembling, afraid.

It seemed to him as if the shadowy hand of some malignant *jinnee* had reached out of the bleeding past, and had laid hold on him—a hand that seized and shook his heart with an envenomed, bony clutch.

"God!" he murmured. "What a time that was—what a ghastly, terrible time!"

He tried to shake off this obsessing vision, opened his eyes, and sank down into the easy-chair. Unnerved, shaking, he struck the glass still holding some of the egg-nog, and knocked it to the floor.

The crash of the breaking glass startled him as if it had been the crack of a rifle. Quivering, he stared down at the liquor, spreading over the holystoned floor. Upon it the red sunlight gleamed; and in a flash he beheld once more the deck of the old *Silver Fleece*, smeared and spotted with blood.

Back he shrank, with extended hands, superstitious fear at his heart. Something nameless, cold and terrible fingered at the latchets of his soul. It was all irrational enough, foolish enough; but still it caught him in its grip, that perfectly unreasoning, heart-clutching fear.

Weakly he pressed a shaking hand over his eyes. With bloodless lips he quavered:

"After fifty years, my God! After fifty years!"

CHAPTER XVIII

THE LOOMING SHADOW

Old Captain Briggs, meanwhile, absorbed in the most cheerful speculations, was putting his best foot forward on the road to Hadlock's Wharf. A vigorous foot it was, indeed, and right speedily it carried him. With pipe in full eruption, leaving a trail of blue smoke on the late afternoon air, and with boots creaking on the hard, white road, the captain strode along; while the Airedale trotted ahead as if he, too, understood that Master Hal was coming home.

He made his way out of the village and so struck into the road to Endicutt itself. "The mingled scents of field and ocean" perfumed the air, borne on a breeze that blent the odors of sea and weedy foreshore and salt marsh with those of garden and orchard, into a kind of airy nectar that seemed to infuse fresh life into the captain's blood. His blue eyes sparkled almost as brightly as the harbor itself, where gaily painted lobster-pot buoys heaved on the swells, where dories labored and where gulls spiraled.

Briggs seemed to love the sea, that afternoon, almost as he had never loved it—the wonderful mystery of tireless, revivifying, all-engendering sea. Joy filled him that Hal, in whose life lived all the hopes of his race, should have inherited this love of the all-mother, Ocean.

Deeply the captain breathed, as he strode onward, and felt that life was being very good to him. For the most part, rough hillocks and tangled clumps of pine, hemlock and gleaming birch hid the bay from him; but now and again these gave way to sandy stretches, leaving the harbor broad-spread and sparkling to his gaze. And as the old man passed each such place, his eyes sought the incoming canvas of the *Sylvia Fletcher*, that seemed to him shining more white, uprearing itself with more stately power, than that of any other craft.

Now and then he hailed the boy as if Hal could hear him across all that watery distance. His hearty old voice lost itself in the ebbing, flowing murmur of the surf that creamed up along the pebbles, and dragged them down with a long, rattling slither. Everything seemed glad, to Captain Briggs—dories hauled up on the sand; blocks, ropes and drying sails; lobster-pots and fish-cars; buoys, rusty anchors half-buried—everything seemed to wear a festive air. For was not Hal, now homeward bound, now almost here?

So overflowing were the old man's spirits that with good cheer even beyond his usual hearty greeting he gave the glad news to all along the road, to those he met, to those who stopped their labors or looked up from their rest in yards and houses, to give him a good-evening.

"It *is* a good evening for me, neighbor," he would say, with a fine smile, his beard snowy in the sun now low across the western hills. "A fine, wonderful evening! Hal's coming home to-night; he's on the *Sylvia Fletcher*, just making in past the Rips, there—see, you can sight her, yourself."

And then he would pass on, glad, triumphant. And as he went, hammers would cease their caulking, brushes their painting; and the fishers mending their russet nets spread over hedge or fence would wish him joy.

Here, there, a child would take his hand and walk with him a little way, till the captain's stout pace tired the short legs, or till some good mother from a cottage door would call the little one back for supper. Just so, fifty years ago, yellow-skinned Malay mothers had called their children within doors, at Batu Kawan, lest Mambang Kuning, the demon who dwelt in the sunset, should do them harm. And just so the sunset itself, that wicked night at the Malay *kampong*, had glowered redly.

A mist was now rising from the harbor and the marshland, like an exhalation of pale ghosts, floating vaguely, quite as the smoke had floated above Batu Kawan. The slowly fading opalescence of the sky, reddening over the hills, bore great resemblance to those hues that in the long ago had painted the sky above the jagged mountain-chain in that far land. But of all this the captain was taking no thought.

No, nothing could enter his mind save the glad present and the impending moment when he should see his Hal again, should feel the boy's hand in his, put an arm about his shoulder and, quite unashamed, give him a kiss patriarchal in its fine simplicity and love.

"It *is* a good evening!" he repeated. "A wonderful evening, friends. Why, Hal's been gone nearly six months. Gone since last Christmas. And now he's coming back to me, again!"

So he passed on. One thing he did not note: this—that though all the folk gave him Godspeed, no one inquired about Hal. That after he had passed, more than one shook a dubious head or murmured words of commiseration. Some few of the fisherfolk, leaning over their fences to watch after him, talked a little together in low tones as if they feared the breeze might bear their words to the old man.

Of all this the captain remained entirely unaware. On he kept, into the straggling outskirts of Endicutt. Now he could see the harbor only at rare intervals; but in the occasional glimpses he caught of it, he saw the *Sylvia Fletcher's* tops'ls crumpling down and perceived that she was headed in directly for the wharf. He hurried on, at a better pace. Above all things Hal must not come, and find no grandfather waiting for him. That, to the captain's mind, would have been unthinkable treason.

The captain strode along the cobblestoned main street, past the ship-chandlers' stores, the sail-lofts and quaint old shops, and so presently turned to the right, into Hadlock's Wharf. Here the going was bad, because of crates and barrels of iced fish and lobsters, and trucks, and a miscellany of obstructions. For a moment the captain was entirely blocked by a dray across the wharf, backing into a fish-shed. The driver greeted him with a smile.

"Hello, cap!" cried he. "Gee, but you're lookin' fine. What's up?"

"It's a great day for me," Briggs answered. "A rare fine day. Hal, my boy, is coming home. He's on the *Sylvia Fletcher*, just coming in from Boston. Can't you let me past, some way?"

"Why, sure! Back *up!*" the driver commanded, savagely jerking at the bit. "You can make it, now, I reckon."

Then, as Briggs squeezed by, he stood looking after the old, blue-clad figure. He turned a lump in his cheek, and spat.

"Gosh, ain't it a shame?" he murmured. "Ain't it a rotten, gorrammed shame?"

By the time Captain Briggs, followed by the faithful Ruddy, reached the stringpiece of the wharf, the schooner was already close. The captain, breathing a little fast, leaned against a tin-topped mooring-pile, and with eager eyes scrutinized the on-coming vessel. All along the wharf, the usual contingent of sailors, longshoremen, fishers and boys had already gathered. To none the captain addressed a word. All his heart and soul were now fast riveted to the schooner, from whose deck plainly drifted words of command, and down from whose sticks the canvas was fast collapsing.

With skilful handling and hardly a rag aloft, she eased alongside. Ropes came sprangling to the wharf. These, dragged in by volunteer hands, brought hawsers. And with a straining of hemp, the *Sylvia* hauled to a dead stop, groaning and chafing against the splintered timbers.

Jests, greetings, laughter volleyed between craft and wharf. The captain, alone, kept silent. His eager eyes were searching the deck; searching, and finding not.

"Hello, cap'n! Hey, there, Cap'n Briggs!" voices shouted. The mate waved a hand at him, and so did two or three others; but there seemed restraint in their greetings. Usually the presence of the captain loosened tongues and set the sailormen glad. But now—

With a certain tightening round the heart, the captain remained there, not knowing what to do. He had expected to see Hal on deck, waving a cap at him, shouting to him. But Hal remained invisible. What could have happened? The captain's eyes scrutinized the deck, in vain. Neither fore nor aft was Hal.

Briggs stepped on the low rail of the schooner and went aboard. He walked aft, to the man at the wheel. Ruddy followed close at heel.

"Hello, cap'n," greeted the steersman. "Nice day, ain't it?" His voice betrayed embarrassment.

"Is my boy, Hal, aboard o' you?" demanded Briggs.

"Yup."

"Well, where is he?"

"Below."

"Getting his dunnage?"

"Guess so." The steersman sucked at his cob pipe, very ill at ease. Briggs stared at him a moment, then turned toward the companion.

A man's head and shoulders appeared up the companionway. Out on deck clambered the man—a young man, black-haired and blue-eyed, with mighty shoulders and a splendidly corded neck visible in the low roll of his opened shirt. His sleeves, rolled up, showed arms and fists of Hercules.

"*Hal!*" cried the captain, a world of gladness in his voice. Silence fell, all about; every one stopped talking, ceased from all activities; all eyes centered on Hal and the captain.

"Hal! My boy!" exclaimed Briggs once more, but in an altered tone. He took a step or two forward. His hand, that had gone out to Hal, dropped at his side again.

He peered at his grandson with troubled, wondering eyes. Under the weathered tan of his face, quick pallor became visible.

"Why, Hal," he stammered. "What—what's happened? What's the meaning of—of all this?"

Hal stared at him with an expression the old man had never seen upon his face. The boy's eyes were reddened, bloodshot, savage with unreasoning passion. The right eye showed a bruise that had already begun to discolor. The jaw had gone forward, become prognathous like an ape's, menacing, with a glint of strong, white teeth. The crisp black hair, rumpled and awry, the black growth of beard—two days old, strong on that square-jawed face—and something in the full-throated poise of the head, brought back to the old captain, in a flash, vivid and horrible memories.

Up from that hatchway he saw himself arising, once again, tangibly and in the living flesh. In the swing of Hal's huge fists, the squaring of his shoulders, his brute expression of blood-lust and battle-lust, old Captain Briggs beheld, line for line, his other and barbaric self of fifty years ago.

"Good God, Hal! What's *this* mean?" he gulped, while along the wharf and on deck a staring silence held. But his question was lost in a hoarse shout from the cabin:

"Here, you young devil! Come below, an' apologize fer that!"

Hal swung about, gripped both sides of the companion, and leaned down. The veins in his powerful neck, taut-swollen, seemed to start through the bronzed skin.

"Apologize?" he roared down the companion. "To a lantern-jawed P. I. like you? Like hell I will!"

Then he stood back, lifted his head and laughed with deep-lunged scorn.

From below sounded a wordless roar. Up the ladder scrambled, simian in agility, a tall and wiry man of middle age. Briggs saw in a daze that this man was white with passion; he had that peculiar, pinched look about the nostrils which denotes the killing rage. Captain Fergus McLaughlin, of Prince Edward's Island, had come on deck.

"You——!" McLaughlin hurled at him, while the old man stood quivering, paralyzed. "If you was a member o' my crew, damn y'r lip—"

"Yes, but I'm not, you see," sneered Hal, fists on hips. "I'm a passenger aboard your rotten old tub, which is almost as bad as your grammar and your reputation." Contemptuously he eyed the Prince Edward's Islander, from rough woolen cap to sea-boots, and back again, every look a blistering insult. His huge chest, rising, falling, betrayed the cumulating fires within. The hush among the onlookers grew ominous. "There's not money enough in circulation to hire me to sign articles with a low-browed, sockless, bean-eating—"

McLaughlin's leap cut short the sentence. With a raw howl, the P. I. flung himself at Hal. Deft and strong with his stony-hard fists was McLaughlin, and the fighting heart in him was a lion's. A hundred men had he felled to his decks, ere now, and not one had ever risen quite whole, or unassisted. In the extremity of his rage he laughed as he sprang.

Lithely, easily, with the joy and love of battle in his reddened eyes, Hal ducked. Up flashed his right fist, a sledge of muscle, bone, sinew. The left swung free.

The impact of Hal's smash thudded sickeningly, with a suggestion of crushed flesh and shattered bone.

Sprawling headlong, hands clutching air, McLaughlin fell. And, as he plunged with a crash to the planking, Hal's laugh snarled through the tense air. From him he flung old Briggs, now in vain striving to clutch and hold his arm.

"Got enough apology, you slab-sided herring-choker?" he roared, exultant. "Enough, or want some more? Apologize? You bet—with these! Come on, you or any of your crew, or all together, you greasy fishbacks! *I'll* apologize you!"

Snarling into a laugh he stood there, teeth set, neck swollen and eyes engorged with blood, his terrible fists eager with the lust of war.

CHAPTER XIX

HAL SHOWS HIS TEETH

Fergus McLaughlin, though down, had not yet taken the count. True, Hal had felled him to his own deck, half-stunned; but the wiry Scot, toughened by many seas, had never yet learned to spell "defeat." For him, the battle was just beginning. He managed to rise on hands and knees. Mouthing curses, he swayed there. Hal lurched forward to finish him with never a chance of getting up; but now old Captain Briggs had Hal by the arm again.

"Hal, Hal!" he entreated. "For God's sake—"

Once more Hal threw the old man off. The second's delay rescued McLaughlin from annihilation. Dazed, bleeding at mouth and nose, he staggered to his feet and with good science plunged into a clinch.

This unexpected move upset Hal's tactics of smashing violence. The Scot's long, wiry arms wrapped round him, hampering his fist-work. Hal could do no more than drive in harmless blows at the other's back. They swayed, tripped over a hawser, almost went down. From the crew and from the wharf ragged shouts arose, of fear, anger, purely malicious delight, for here was battle-royal of the finest. The sound of feet, running down the wharf, told of other contingents hastily arriving.

"By gum!" approved the helmsman, forgetting to chew. He had more than once felt the full weight of McLaughlin's fist. "By gum, now, but Mac's in f'r a good takin'-down. If that lad don't fist him proper, I miss my 'tarnal guess. Sick 'im, boy!"

Blaspheming, Hal tore McLaughlin loose, flung him back, lowered his head and charged. But now the Scot had recovered a little of his wit. On deck he spat blood and a broken snag of tooth. His eye gleamed murderously. The excess of Hal's rage betrayed the boy. His guard opened. In drove a stinging lefthander. McLaughlin handed him the other fist, packed full of dynamite. The boy reeled, gulping.

"Come on, ye college bratlin'!" challenged the fighting Scot, and smeared the blood from his mouth. "This here ain't your ship—not yet!"

"My ship's any ship I happen to be on!" snarled Hal, circling for advantage. Mac had already taught him to be cautious. Old Captain Brigg's imploring cries fell from him, unheeded. "If this *was* my ship, I'd wring your neck, so help me God! But as it is, I'll only mash you to a jelly!"

"Pretty bairn!" gibed McLaughlin, hunched into battle-pose, bony fists up. "Grandad's pretty pet! Arrrh! Ye *would*, eh?" as Hal bored in at him.

He met the rush with cool skill. True, Hal's right went to one eye, closing it; but Hal felt the bite of knuckles catapulted from his neck.

Hal delayed no more. Bull-like, he charged. By sheer weight and fury of blows he drove Mac forward of the schooner, beside the deck-house. Amid turmoil, the battle raged. The jostling crowd, shoved and pushed, on deck and on the wharf, to see this epic war. Bets were placed, even money.

McLaughlin, panting, half-blind, his teeth set in a grin of rage, put every ounce he had left into each blow. But Hal outclassed him.

A minute, two minutes they fought, straining, sweating, lashing. Then something swift and terrible connected with Mac's jaw-point in a jolt that loosened his universe. Mac's head snapped back. His arms flung up. He dropped, pole-axed, into the scuppers.

For the first time in five-and-twenty years of fighting, clean and dirty, Fergus McLaughlin had taken a knockout.

A mighty shout of exultation, fear and rage loosened echoes from the old fish-sheds. Three or four of the crew came jostling into the circle, minded to avenge their captain. Sneering, his chest heaving, but ready with both fists, Hal faced them.

"Come on, all o' you!" he flung, drunk with rage, his face bestial. A slaver of bloody froth trickled from the corner of his mouth. "Come on!"

They hesitated. Gorilla-like, he advanced. Back through the crowd the overbold ones drew. No heart remained in them to tackle this infuriated fighting-machine.

Hal set both fists on his hips, flung up his head and panted:

"Apologize, will I? I, a passenger on this lousy tub, I'll apologize to a bunch of down-east rough-necks, eh? If there's anybody else wants any apology, I'm here!"

None caught up the gage of battle. Bursting with fury that had to vent itself, Hal swung toward McLaughlin. The Scot had landed on a coil of hawser in the scuppers, that had somewhat broken his fall. Hal reached down, hauled him up and flung him backward over the rail. Thrice he struck with a fist reddened by McLaughlin's blood. He wrenched at the unconscious man's arm, snarling like an animal, his face distorted, eyes glazed and staring. A crunching told of at least one broken bone.

Shouts of horror fell unheeded from his ears. He glared around.

"My Gawd, he's a-killin' on him!" quavered a voice. "We can't stan' by an' see him do murder!"

Old Briggs, nerved to sudden action, ran forward.

"Hal! For God's sake, Hal!"

"You stand back, grandad! He's my meat!"

Hal raised McLaughlin high above his head, with a sweep of wonderful power. He dashed the Scot to the bare planks with a horrible, dull crash, hauled back one foot and kicked the senseless man full in the mangled, blood-smeared face.

A communal gasp of terror rose up then. Men shrank and quivered, stricken with almost superstitious fear. All had seen fights aplenty; most of them had taken a hand in brawls—but here was a new kind of malice. And silence fell, tense, heart-searching.

Hal faced the outraged throng, and laughed with deep lungs.

"There's your champion, what's left of him!" cried he. "*He* won't bullyrag anybody for one while, believe me. Take him—I'm through with him!"

Of a sudden the rage seemed to die in Hal, spent in that last, orgiastic convulsion of passion. He turned away, flung men right and left, and leaped down the companion. Swiftly he emerged with a suit-case. To his trembling, half-fainting grandfather he strode, unmindful of the murmur of curses and threats against him.

"Come on, grandpop!" he said in a more normal tone. His voice did not tremble, as will the voice of almost every man after a storm of rage. His color was fresh and high, his eyes clear; his whole ego seemed to have been vivified and freshened, like a sky after tempest. "Come along, now. I've had enough of this rotten old hulk. I've given it what it needed, a good clean-up. Come on!"

He seized Captain Briggs by the elbow—for the old man could hardly stand, and now was leaning against the hatchway housing—and half guided, half dragged him over the rail to the wharf.

"Shame on you, Hal Briggs!" exclaimed an old lobsterman. "This here's a bad day's work you've done. When he was down, you booted him. We wun't fergit it, none of us wun't."

"No, and *he* won't forget it, either, the bragging bucko!" sneered Hal. "Uncle Silas, you keep out of this!"

"Ef that's what they l'arn ye down to college," sounded another voice, "you'd a durn sight better stay to hum. We fight some, on the North Shore, but we fight fair."

Hal faced around, with blazing eyes.

"Who said that?" he gritted. "Where's the son of a pup that said it?"

No answer. Cowed, everybody held silence. No sound was heard save the shuffling feet of the men aboard, as some of the crew lifted McLaughlin's limp form and carried it toward the companion, just as Crevay had been carried on the *Silver Fleece*, half a century before.

"Come on, gramp!" exclaimed Hal. "For two cents I'd clean up the whole white-livered bunch. Let's go home, now, before there's trouble."

"I—I'm afraid I can't walk, Hal," quavered the old man. "This has knocked me galley-west. My rudder's unshipped and my canvas in rags. I can't navigate at all." He was trembling as with a chill. Against his grandson he leaned, ashen-faced, helpless. "I can't make Snug Haven, now."

"That's all right, grampy," Hal assured him. "We'll dig up a jitney if you can get as far as the street. Come on, let's move!"

With unsteady steps, clinging to Hal's arm and followed by the dog, old Captain Briggs made his way up Hadlock's Wharf. Only a few minutes had elapsed since he had strode so proudly down that wharf, but what a vast difference had been wrought in the captain's soul! All the glad elation of his heart had now faded more swiftly than a tropic sunset turns to dark. The old man seemed to have shrunken, collapsed. Fifteen little minutes seemed to have bowed down his shoulders with at least fifteen years.

"Oh, Hal, Hal!" he groaned, as they slowly made their way towards the street. "Oh, my boy, how could you ha' done that?"

"How could I? After what he said, how *couldn't* I?"

"What a disgrace! What a burning, terrible disgrace! You—just back from college—"

"There, there, grandpop, it'll be all right. Everybody'll be glad, when they cool off, that I handed it to that bully."

"This will make a terrible scandal. The *Observer* will print it, and—"

"Nonsense! You don't think they'd waste paper on a little mix-up aboard a coasting-schooner, do you?"

"This is more than a little mix-up, Hal. You've stove that man's hull up, serious. There's more storm brewing."

"What d'you mean, more storm?"

"Oh, he'll take this to court. He'll sue for damages."

"He'd better not!" snapped Hal, grimly. "I've got more for him, where what I handed him came from, if he tries it!"

"Hal, you're—breaking my old heart."

"D'you think, grandpa, I was going to stand there and swallow his insults? Do you think I, a Briggs, was going to let that slab-sided P.I. hand me that rough stuff? Would *you* have stood for it?"

"I? What do you mean? How could I fight, at my age?"

"I mean, when you were young. Didn't *you* ever mix it, then? Didn't you have guts enough to put up your fists when you had to? If you didn't, you're no grandfather of mine!"

"Hal," answered the old man, still holding to his grandson as they neared the street, "what course I sailed in my youth is nothing for you to steer by now. Those were rough days, and these are supposed to be civilized. That was terrible, terrible, what you did to McLaughlin. The way you flung him across the rail, there, and then to the deck, and—kicked him, when he was down—kicked him in the face—"

"It's all right, I tell you!" Hal asserted, vigorously. He laughed, with glad remembrance. "When I fight a gentleman, I fight like a gentleman. When I fight a ruffian, I use the same tactics. That's all such cattle understand. My motto is to hit first, every time. That's the one best bet. The second is, hit hard. If you're in a scrap, you're in it to win, aren't you? Hand out everything you've got—give 'em the whole bag of tricks, all at one wallop. That's what *I* go by, and it's a damn good rule. You, there! Hey, there, jitney!"

The discussion broke off, short, as Hal sighted a little car, cruising slowly and with rattling joints over the rough-paved cobbles.

CHAPTER XX

THE CAPTAIN COMMANDS

The jitney stopped.

"Oh, hello, Sam! That you?" asked Hal, recognizing the driver.

"Horn spoon! Ef it ain't Hal!" exclaimed the jitney-man. "Back ag'in, eh? What the devil *you* been up to? Shirt tore, an' one eye looks like you'd been —"

"Oh, nothing," Hal answered, while certain taggers-on stopped at a respectful distance. "I've just been arguing with McLaughlin, aboard the *Sylvia Fletcher*. It's nothing at all." He helped his grandfather into the car and then, gripping the Airedale so that it yelped with pain, he pitched it in. "How much do you want to take us down to Snug Haven?"

"Well—that'll be a dollar 'n' a half, seein' it's you."

"You'll get one nice, round little buck, Sam."

"Git out! You, an' the cap'n, an' the dog, an' a tussik! Why—"

Hal climbed into the car. He leaned forward, his face close to Sam's. The seethe of rage seemed to have departed. Now Hal was all joviality. Swiftly the change had come upon him.

"Sam!" he admonished. "You know perfectly well seventy-five cents would be robbery, but I'll give you a dollar. Put her into high."

The driver sniffed Hal's breath, and nodded acceptance.

"All right, seein' as it's you," he answered. He added, in a whisper: "Ain't got nothin' on y'r hip, have ye?"

"Nothing but a bruise," said Hal. "*Clk-clk!*"

The jitney struck its bone-shaking gait along the curving street of Endicutt. No one spoke. The old captain, spent in forces and possessed by bitter, strange hauntings, had sunk far down in the seat. His beard made a white cascade over the smart blue of his coat. His eyes, half-closed, seemed to be visioning the far-off days he had labored so long to forget. His face was gray with suffering, beneath its tan. His lips had set themselves in a grim, tight line.

As for Hal, he filled and lighted his pipe, then with a kind of bored tolerance eyed the quaint old houses, the gardens and trim hedges.

"Some burg!" he murmured. "Some live little burg to put in a whole summer! Well, anyhow, I started something. They ought to hand me a medal, for putting a little pep into this prehistoric graveyard."

Then he relapsed into contemplative smoking.

Presently the town gave place to the open road along the shore, now bathed in a thousand lovely hues as sunset died. The slowly fading beauty of the seascape soothed what little fever still remained in Hal's blood. With an appreciative eye he observed the harbor. The town itself might seem dreary, but in his soul the instinctive love of the sea awoke to the charms of that master-panorama which in all its infinite existence has never twice shown just the same blending of hues, of motion, of refluent ebb and fall.

Along the dimming islands, swells were breaking into great bouquets of foam. The murmurous, watery cry of the surf lulled Hal; its booming cadences against the rocky girdles of the coast seemed whispering alluring, mysterious things to him. In the offing a few faint specks of sail, melting in the purple haze, beckoned: "Come away, come away!"

To Captain Briggs quite other thoughts were coming. Not now could the lure of his well-loved ocean appeal to him, for all the wonders of the umber and dull orange west. Where but an hour ago beauty had spread its miracles across the world, for him, now all had turned to drab. A few faint twinkles of light were beginning to show in fishers' cottages; and these, too, saddened the old captain, for they minded him of Snug Haven's waiting lights—Snug Haven, where he had hoped so wonderfully much, but where now only mournful disillusion and bodings of evil remained.

The ceaseless threnody of the sea seemed to the old man a requiem over dead hopes. The salt tides seemed to mock and gibe at him, and out of the pale haze drifting seaward from the slow-heaving waters, ghosts seemed beckoning.

All at once Hal spoke, his college slang rudely jarring the old captain's melancholy.

"That was some jolt I handed Mac, wasn't it?" he laughed. "He'll be more careful who he picks on next time. That's about what he needed, a good walloping."

"Eh? What?" murmured the old man, roused from sad musings.

"Such people have to get it handed to them once in a while," the grandson continued. "There's only one kind of argument they understand—and that's this!"

107

He raised his right fist, inspected it, turning it this way and that, admiring its massive power, its adamantine bone and sinew.

"Oh, for Heaven's sake, Hal, don't do that!" exclaimed the captain. With strange eyes he peered at the young man.

Hal laughed uproariously.

"Some fist, what?" he boasted. "Some pacifier!"

As he turned toward the old man, his breath smote the captain's senses.

"Lord, Hal! You haven't been drinking, have you?" quavered Briggs.

"Drinking? Well—no. Maybe I've had one or two, but that's all."

"One or two what, Hal?"

"Slugs of rum."

"Rum! Good God!"

"What's the matter, now? What's the harm in a drop of good stimulant? I asked him for a drink, and he couldn't see it, the tightwad! I took it, anyhow. That's what started all the rough-house."

"Great heavens, Hal! D'you mean to tell me you're drinking, now?"

"There, there, gramp, don't get all stewed up. All the fellows take a drop now and then. You don't want me to be a molly-coddle, do you? To feel I can't take a nip, once in a while, and hold it like a gentleman? That's all foolishness, grampy. Be sensible!"

The old man began to shiver, though the off-shore breeze blew warm. Hal made a grimace of vexation. His grandfather answered nothing, and once more silence fell. It lasted till the first scattering houses of South Endicutt came into view in the fading light.

The driver, throwing a switch, sent his headlights piercing the soft June dusk. The cones of radiance painted the roadside grass a vivid green, and made the whitewashed fences leap to view. Hedges, gardens, gable-ends, all spoke of home and rest, peace and the beatitude of snug security. Somewhere the sound of children's shouts and laughter echoed appealingly. The tinkle of a cow-bell added its music; and faint in the western sky, the evening star looked down.

And still Captain Briggs held silent.

A little red gleam winked in view—the port light of Snug Haven.

"There's the old place, isn't it?" commented Hal, in a softer tone. He seemed moved to gentler thoughts; but only for a moment. His eye, catching a far, white figure away down by the smithy, brightened with other anticipations than of getting home again.

"Hello!" he exclaimed. "That's Laura, isn't it? Look, gramp—isn't that Laura Maynard?"

Peering, Captain Briggs recognized the girl. He understood her innocent little subterfuge of being out for a casual stroll just at this time. His heart, already lacerated, contracted with fresh pain.

"No, no, Hal," he exclaimed. "That can't be Laura. Come now, don't be thinking about Laura, to-night. You're tired, and ought to rest."

"Tired? Say, that's a good one! When was I ever tired?"

"Well, *I'm* tired, anyhow," the captain insisted, "and I want to cast anchor at the Haven. We've got company, too. It wouldn't look polite, if you went gallivanting—"

"Company? What company?" demanded Hal, as the car drew up toward the gate.

"A very special friend of mine. A man I haven't seen in fifty years. An old doctor that once sailed with me. He's waiting to see you, now."

"Another old pill, eh?" growled the boy, sullenly, his eyes still fixed on the girl at the bend of the road. "There'll be time enough for Methuselah, later. Just now, it's me for the skirt!"

The car halted. The captain stiffly descended. He felt singularly spent and old. Hal threw out the suit-case, and lithely leaped to earth.

"Dig up a bone for Sam, here," directed Hal. "Now, I'll be on my way to overhaul the little dame."

"Hal! That's *not* Laura, I tell you!"

"You can't kid me, grampy! That's the schoolma'm, all right. I'd know her a mile off. She's some chicken, take it from me!"

"Hal, I protest against such language!"

"Oh, too rough, eh?" sneered the boy. "Now in your day, I suppose you used more refined English, didn't you? Maybe you called them—"

"Hal! That will do!"

"So will Laura, for me. She's mine, that girl is. She's plump as a young porpoise, and I'm going after her!"

The captain stood aghast, at sound of words that echoed from the very antipodes of the world and of his own life. Then, with a sudden rush of anger, his face reddening formidably, he exclaimed:

"Not another word! You've been drinking, and you're dirty and torn—no fit man, to-night, to haul up 'longside that craft!"

"I tell you, I'm going down there to say good evening to Laura, anyhow," Hal insisted, sullenly. "I'm going!"

"You are *not*, sir!" retorted Briggs, while Sam, in the car, grinned with enjoyment. "You're *not* going to hail Laura Maynard to-night! Do you want to lose her friendship and respect?"

"Bull! Women like a little rough stuff, now and then. This 'Little Rollo' business is played out. Go along in, if you want to, but I'm going to see Laura."

"Hal," said the old man, a new tone in his voice. "This is carrying too much canvas. You'll lose some of it in a minute, if you don't reef. I'm captain here, and you're going to take my orders, if it comes to that. The very strength you boast of and misuse so brutally is derived from money I worked a lifetime for, at sea, and suffered and sinned and bled and almost died for!" The old captain's tone rang out again as in the old, tempestuous days when he was master of many hard and violent men. "Now, sir, you're going to obey me, or overside you go, this minute—and once you go, you'll never set foot on my planks again! Pick up your dunnage, sir, and into the Haven with you!"

"Good *night!*" ejaculated Hal, staring. Never had the old man thus spoken to him. Stung to anger, though Hal was, he dared not disobey. Muttering, he picked up the suit-case. The dog, glad to be at home once more, leaped against him. With an oath, Hal swung the suit-case; the Airedale, yelping with pain, fawned and slunk away.

"Into the Haven with you!" commanded Briggs, outraged to his very heart. "*Go!*"

Hal obeyed, with huge shoulders hulking and drooping in their plenitude of evil power, just like the captain's, so very long ago. Alpheus Briggs peered down the street at the dim white figure of the disappointed girl; then, eyes agleam and back very straight, he followed Hal toward Snug Haven—the Haven which in such beatitude of spirit he had left but an hour ago—the Haven to which, filled with so many evil bodings, he now was coming back again.

"Oh, God," he murmured, "if this thing must come upon me, Thy will be done! But if it can be turned aside, spare me! Spare me, for this is all my life and all my hope! Spare me!"

CHAPTER XXI

SPECTERS OF THE PAST

Hal's boots, clumping heavily on the porch, aroused the captain from his brief revery of prayer. Almost at once the new stab of pain at realization that Dr. Filhiol must see Hal in this disheveled, half-drunken condition brought the old man sharply back to earth again. Bitter humiliation, brutal disillusionment, sickening anti-climax! The captain stifled a groan. Fate seemed dealing him a blow unreasonably hard.

A chair scraped on the porch. Briggs saw the bent and shriveled form of Dr. Filhiol arising. The doctor, rendered nervous by the arsenal and by the cabinet of curios, which all too clearly recalled the past, had once more gone out upon the piazza, to await the captain's return. Warmed by the egg-nog within, and outwardly by a shawl that Ezra had given him, now he stood there, leaning on his cane. A smile of anticipation curved his shaven, bloodless lips. His eyes blinked eagerly behind his thick-lensed glasses.

"Home again, eh?" he piped. "Good! So then this is the little grandson back from college? Little! Ha-ha! Why, captain, he'd make two like us!"

"This is Hal," answered the captain briefly. "Yes, this is my grandson."

The doctor, surprised at Briggs's curt reply, put out his hand. Hal took it as his grandfather spoke the doctor's name.

"Glad to know you, doctor!" said he in a sullen voice, and let the hand drop. "Excuse me, please! I'll go in and wash up."

He turned toward the door. With perturbation Filhiol peered after him. Then he glanced at the captain. Awkwardly silence fell, broken by a cry of joy from the front door.

"Oh, Master Hal!" ejaculated Ezra. "Ef it ain't Master Hal!"

The servitor's long face beamed with jubilation as he seized the suit-case with one hand and with the other clapped Hal on the shoulder. "Jumpin' jellyfish, but you're lookin' fine an' stout! Back from y'r books, ain't ye? Ah, books is grand things, Master Hal, 'specially check-books, pocketbooks, an' bank-books. Did the cap'n tell ye? He did, didn't he?"

"Hello, Ez!" answered Hal, still very glum. "Tell me what?"

"'Bout the plum-cake an' lamb?" asked Ezra anxiously as Hal slid past him into the house. "I remembered what you like, Master Hal. I been workin' doggone hard to git everythin' jest A1 fer you!"

His voice grew inaudible as he followed Hal into Snug Haven. The captain and the doctor gazed at each other a long, eloquent moment in the vague light. Neither spoke. Filhiol turned and sat down, puzzled, oppressed.

Briggs wearily sank into another chair. Hal's feet stumbling up the front stairs echoed with torment through his soul. Was that the stumbling of haste, or had the boy drunk more than he had seemed to? The captain dropped his cap to the porch-floor. Not now did he take pains to hang it on top of the rocking-chair. He wiped his forehead with his silk handkerchief, and groaned.

The doctor kept silence. He understood that any word of his would prove inopportune. But with pity he studied the face of Captain Briggs, its lines accentuated by the light from the window of the cabin.

Presently the captain sighed deep and began:

"I'm glad you're here on my quarterdeck with me to-night, doctor. Things are all going wrong, sir. Barometer's way down, compass is bedeviled, seams opening fore and aft. It's bad, doctor—very, very bad!"

"I see there's something wrong, of course," said Filhiol with sympathy.

"Everything's wrong, sir. That grandson of mine—you—noticed just what was the matter with him?"

"H-m! It's rather dark here, you know," hedged Filhiol.

"Not so dark but what you understood," said Briggs grimly. "When there's a storm brewing no good navigator thinks he can dodge it by locking himself in his cabin. And there *is* a storm brewing this time, a hurricane, sir, or I've missed all signals."

"Just what do you mean, captain?"

"Violence, drink, women—wickedness and sin! You smelled his breath, didn't you? You took an observation of his face?"

"Well, yes. He's been drinking a little, of course; but these boys in college —"

"He very nigh killed the skipper of the *Sylvia Fletcher*, and there'll be the devil to pay about it. It was just luck there wasn't murder done before my very eyes. He's been drinking enough so as to wake a black devil in his heart! Enough so he's like a roaring bull after the first pretty girl in the offing."

"There, there, captain!" The doctor tried to soothe him, his thin voice making strange contrast with the captain's booming bass. "You're probably exaggerating. A little exuberance may be pardoned in youth," his expression belied his words. "Remember, captain, when *you* were—"

"That's just what's driving me on the rocks with grief and despair!" the old man burst out, gripping the arms of the rocker. "God above! It's just the realization of my own youth, flung back at me now, that's like to kill me! That boy, so help me—why, he's thrown clean back fifty years all at one crack!"

"No, no, not that!"

"He has, I tell you! He's jumped back half a century. *He* don't belong in this age of airplanes and wireless. *He* belongs back with the clipper-ships and —"

"Nonsense, captain, and you know it!"

"It's far from nonsense! There's a bad strain somewhere in my blood. I've been afraid a long time it was going to crop out in Hal. There's always been a tradition in my family of evil doings now and then. I don't know anything certain about it, though, except that my grandfather, Amalfi Briggs, died of bursting a blood-vessel in his brain in a fit of rage. That was all that saved him from being a murderer—he died before he could kill the other man!"

Silence came, save for the piping whistle of an urchin far up the road. The ever-rising, falling suspiration of the sea breathed its long caress across the land, on which a vague, pale sheen of starlight was descending.

Suddenly, from abovestairs, sounded a dull, slamming sound as of a bureau-drawer violently shut. Another slam followed; and now came a grumbling of muffled profanity.

"All that saved my grandfather from being a murderer," said Briggs dourly, "was the fact that he dropped dead himself before he could cut down the other man with the ship-carpenter's adze he had in his hand."

"Indeed? Your grandfather must have been rather a hard specimen."

"Only when he was in anger. At other times you never saw a more jovial soul! But rage made a beast of him!"

"How was your father?"

"Not that way in the least. He was as consistently Christian a man as ever breathed. My son—Hal's father—was a good man, too. Not a sign of that sort of brutality ever showed in him."

"I think you're worrying unnecessarily," judged the doctor. "Your grandson may be wild and rough at times, but he's tainted with no hereditary stain."

"I don't know about that, doctor," said the captain earnestly. "For a year

114

or two past he's been showing more temper than a young man should. He's not been answering the helm very well. Two or three of the village people here have already complained to me. I've never been really afraid till to-night. But now, doctor, I *am* afraid—terribly, deadly afraid!"

The old man's voice shook. Filhiol tried to smile.

"Let the dead past bury its dead!" said he. "Don't open the old graves to let the ghosts of other days walk out again into the clear sunset of your life."

"God knows I don't want to!" the old man exclaimed in a low, trembling voice. "But suppose those graves open themselves? Suppose they won't stay shut, no, not though all the good deeds from here to heaven were piled atop of them, to keep them down? Suppose those ghosts rise up and stare me in the eyes and won't be banished—what then?"

"Stuff and nonsense!" gibed Filhiol, though his voice was far from steady. "You're not yourself, captain. You're unnerved. There's nothing the matter with that boy except high spirits and overflowing animal passions."

"No, no! I understand only too well. God is being very hard to me! I sinned grievous, in the long ago! But I've done my very best to pay the reckoning. Seems like I haven't succeeded. Seems like God don't forget! He's paying me now, with interest!"

"Captain, you exaggerate!" the doctor tried to assure him, but Briggs shook his head.

"Heredity skips that way sometimes, don't it?" asked he.

"Well—sometimes. But that doesn't prove anything."

"No, it don't prove anything, but what Hal did to-night *does*! Would a thing like that come on sudden that way? Would it? A kind of hydrophobia of rage that won't listen to any reason but wants to break and tear and kill? I mean, if that kind of thing was in the blood, could it lay hid a long time and then all of a sudden burst out like that?"

"Well—yes. It might."

"I seem to remember it was the same with me the first time I ever had one of those mad fits," said the captain. "It come on quick. It wasn't like ordinary getting mad. It was a red torrent, delirious and awful—something that caught me up and carried me along on its wave—something I couldn't fight against. When I saw Hal with his teeth grinning, eyes glassy, fists red with McLaughlin's blood, oh, it struck clean through my heart!

"It wasn't any fear of either of them getting killed that harpooned me, no, nor complications and damages to pay. No, no, though such will be bad enough. What struck me all of a heap was to see myself, my very own self that used to be. If I, Captain Alpheus Briggs, had been swept back to 1868 and set down on the deck of the *Silver Fleece*, Hal would have been my exact double. I've seen myself just as I was then, doctor, and it's shaken me in every timber. There I stood, I, myself, in Hal's person, after five decades of weary time. I could see the outlines of the same black beard on the same kind of jaw—same thick neck and bloody fists; and, oh, doctor, the eyes of Hal. His eyes!"

"His eyes?"

"Yes. In them I saw my old, wicked, hell-elected self—saw it glaring out, to break and ravish and murder!"

"Captain Briggs!"

"It's true, I'm telling you. I've seen a ghost this evening. A ghost—"

He peered around fearfully in the dusk. His voice lowered to a whisper:

"A ghost!"

Filhiol could not speak. Something cold, prehensile, terrible seemed fingering at his heart! Ruddy, the Airedale, raised his head, seemed to be listening, to be seeing something they could not detect. In the dog's throat a low growl muttered.

"What's *that*?" said the captain, every muscle taut.

"Nothing, nothing," the doctor answered. "The dog probably hears some one down there by the hedge. This is all nonsense, captain. You're working yourself into a highly nervous state and imagining all kinds of things. Now —"

"I tell you, I saw the ghost of my other self," insisted Briggs. "There's worse kinds of ghosts than those that hang around graveyards. I've always wanted to see that kind and never have. Night after night I've been up there to the little cemetery on Croft Hill, and sat on the bench in our lot, just as friendly and receptive as could be, ready to see whatever ghost might come to me, but none ever came. I'm not afraid of the ghosts of the dead! It's ghosts of the living that strike a dread to me—ghosts of the past that ought to die and can't—ghosts of my own sins that God won't let lie in the grave of forgiveness—"

"*S-h-h-h!*" exclaimed the doctor. He laid a hand on the captain's, which was clutching the arm of the rocker with a grip of steel. "Don't give way to such folly! Perhaps Hal did drink a little, and perhaps he did thrash a man who had insulted him. But that's as far as it goes. All this talk about ghosts

116

and some hereditary, devilish force cropping out again, is pure rubbish!"

"I wish to God above it *was*!" the old man groaned. "But I know it's not. It's there, doctor, I tell you! It's still alive and in the world, more terrible and more malignant than ever, a living, breathing thing, evil and venomous, backed up with twice the intelligence and learning I ever had, with a fine, keen brain to direct it and with muscles of steel to do its bidding! Oh, God, I know, I *know*!"

"Captain Briggs, sir," the doctor began. "This is most extraordinary language from a man of your common sense. I really do not understand—"

"Hush!" interrupted the captain, raising his right hand. On the stairway feet echoed. "Hush! He's coming down!"

Silent, tense, they waited. The heavy footfalls reached the bottom of the stair and paused there a moment. Briggs and the doctor heard Hal grumbling something inarticulate to himself. Then he walked into the cabin.

CHAPTER XXII

DR. FILHIOL STANDS BY

Through the window both men could see him. The cabin-lamp over the captain's table shed soft rays upon the boy as he stood there unconscious of being observed.

He remained motionless a moment, gazing about him, taking account of any little changes that had been wrought in the past months. At sight of him the old captain, despite all his bodings of evil, could not but thrill with pride of this clean-limbed, powerful-shouldered grandson, scion of the old stock, last survivor of his race, and hope of all its future.

Hal took a step to the table. The lithe ease and power of his stride impressed the doctor's critical eye.

"He's all right enough, captain," growled Filhiol. "He's as normal as can be. He's just overflowing with animal spirits, strength, and energy. Lord! What wouldn't you or I give to be like that—again?"

"I wouldn't stand in those boots of his for all the money in Lloyd's!" returned the captain in a hoarse whisper. "For look you, doctor, I have lived my life and got wisdom. My fires have burned low, leaving the ashes of peace —or so I hope. But that lad there, ah! there's fires and volcanoes enough ahead for him! Maybe those same fires will kindle up my ashes, too, and sear my heart and soul! I thought I was entitled to heave anchor and lay in harbor a spell till I get my papers for the unknown port we don't any of us come back from, but maybe I'm mistaken. Maybe that's not to be, doctor, after all."

"What rubbish!" retorted Filhiol. "Look at him now, will you? Isn't he peaceful, and normal enough for anybody? See there, now, he's going to take a book and read it like any well-behaved young man."

Hal had, indeed, taken a book from the captain's table and had sat down with it before the fireplace. He did not, however, open the book. Instead, he leaned back and gazed intently up at the arsenal. He frowned, nodded, and then broke into a peculiar smile. His right fist clenched and rose, as if in imagination he were gripping one of those weapons, with Fergus McLaughlin as his immediate target.

Silence fell once more, through which faintly penetrated the far-off, nasal minor of old Ezra, now engaged upon an endless chantey recounting the adventures of one "Boney"—*alias* Bonaparte. Peace seemed to have descended upon Snug Haven, but only for a minute.

For all at once, with an oath of impatience, Hal flung the book to the floor. He stood up, thrust both hands deep into his pockets, and fell to pacing the floor in a poisonous temper.

Of a sudden he stopped, wheeled toward the captain's little private locker and strode to it. The locker door was secured with a brass padlock of unusual strength. Hal twisted it off between thumb and finger as easily as if it had been made of putty. He flung open the door, and took down a bottle.

He seized a tumbler and slopped it levelful of whisky, which he gulped without a wink. Then he smeared his mouth with the back of his hand and stood there evil-eyed and growling.

"*Puh!* That's rotten stuff!" he ejaculated. "Grandpop certainly does keep a punk line here!" Back upon the shelf he slammed the bottle and the glass. "Wonder where that smooth Jamaica's gone he used to have?"

"God above! Did you see that, doctor?" breathed the old captain, gripping at the doctor's hand. "He downed that like so much water. Isn't that the exact way I used to swill liquor? By the Judas priest, I'll soon stop *that!*"

Filhiol restrained him.

"Wait!" he cautioned as the two old men peered in, unseen, through the window. "Even that doesn't prove the original sin you seem determined to lay at the boy's door. He's unnerved after his fight. Let's see what he'll do next. If we're going to judge him, we've got to watch a while."

Old Briggs sank back into his chair, and with eyes of misery followed the boy, hope of all his dreams. Hal's next move was not long delayed.

"Ezra!" they heard him harshly call. "You, Ezra! Come *here!*"

The chantey came to a sudden end. A moment, and Ezra appeared in the doorway leading from the cabin to the "dining-saloon."

"Well, Master Hal, what is it?" smiled the cook, beaming with affection. In one hand he held a "copper," just such as aboard the *Silver Fleece* had heated water for the scalding of the Malays. "What d'you want, Master Hal?"

"Look here, Ezra," said the boy arrogantly, "I've been trying to find the rum grandpop always keeps in there. Couldn't locate it, so I've been giving this whisky a trial, and—"

"When whisky an' young men lay 'longside one another, the whisky don't want a trial. It wants lynchin'!"

"I'm not asking *your* opinion!" sneered Hal.

"Yes, but I'm givin' it, Master Hal," persisted Ezra. "When the devil goes fishin' fer boys, he sticks a petticoat an' a bottle o' rum on the hook."

"Get me the Jamaica, you!" demanded Hal with growing anger. "I've got no time for your line of bull!"

"Lots that ain't got no time for nothin' in this world will have time to burn in the next! You'll get no rum from me, Master Hal. An' what's more, if I'd ha' thought you was goin' to slip your cable an' run ashore in any such dognation fool way on a wave o' booze, I'd of hid the whisky where *you* wouldn't of run it down!"

"You'd have hidden it!" echoed Hal, his face darkening, the veins on neck and forehead beginning to swell. "You've got the infernal nerve to stand there —you, a servant—and tell me you'd hide anything away from me in my own house?"

"This here craft is registered under your grandpa's name an' is sailin' under his house-flag," the old cook reminded him. His face was still bland as ever, but in his eyes lurked a queer little gleam. "It ain't the same thing at all —not yet."

"Damn your infernal lip!" shouted Hal, advancing. Captain Briggs, quivering, half-rose from his chair. "You've got the damned impudence to stand there and dictate to *me*?"

"Master Hal," retorted Ezra with admirable self-restraint, "you're sailin' a bit too wide wide o' your course now. There's breakers ahead, sir. Look out!"

"I believe you've been at the Jamaica yourself, you thieving son of Satan!" snarled Hal. "I'll not stand here parleying with a servant. Get me that Jamaica, or I'll break your damned, obstinate neck!"

"Now, Master Hal, I warn you—"

"To hell with you!"

"With me, Master Hal? With old Ezra?"

"With everything that stands in my way!"

Despite Hal's furious rage the steadfast old sailor-man still resolutely faced him. Captain Briggs, now again hearing almost the identical words he himself had poured out in the cabin of the *Silver Fleece*, sank back into his chair with a strange, throaty gasp.

"Doctor!" he gulped. "Do you hear that?"

"Wait!" the doctor cautioned, leaning forward. "This is very strange. It is, by Jove, sir! Some amazing coincidence, or—"

"Next thing you know he'll knock Ezra down!" whispered the captain, staring. He seemed paralyzed, as though tranced by the scene. "That's what I did to the cabin-boy, when my rum was wrong. Remember? It's all coming round again, doctor. It's a nightmare in a circle—a fifty-year circle! Remember Kuala Pahang? She—she died! I wonder what woman's got to die this time?"

"That's all pure poppycock!" the doctor ejaculated. He was trembling violently. With a great effort, leaning heavily on his stick, he arose. Captain Briggs, too, shook off the spell that seemed to grip him and stood up.

"Hal!" he tried to articulate; but his voice failed him. Turning, he lurched toward the front door.

From within sounded a cry, a trampling noise. Something clattered to the floor.

"Hal! My God, Hal!" the captain shouted hoarsely.

As he reached the door Ezra came staggering out into the hall, a hand pressed to his face.

"Ezra! What is it? For Heaven's sake, Ezra, what's Hal done to you?"

The old man could make no answer. Limply he sagged against the newel-post, a sorry picture of grief and pain. The captain put an arm about his shoulders, and with burning indignation cried:

"What did he do? Hit you?"

Ezra shook his head in stout negation. Even through all the shock and suffering of the blow, his loyalty remained sublimely constant.

"Hit me? Why, no, sir," he tried to smile, though his lips were white. "*He* wouldn't strike old Ezra. There's no mutiny aboard this little craft of ours. Two gentlemen may disagree, an' all that, but as fer Master Hal strikin' me, no, *sir!*"

"But I heard him say—"

"Oh, that's nothin', cap'n," the old cook insisted, still, however, keeping his cheek-bone covered with his hand. "Boys will be boys. They're a bit loose with their jaw-tackle, maybe. But there, there, don't you git all har'red up, captain. Men an' pins is jest alike, that way—no good ef they lose their heads. Ca'm down, cap'n!"

"What's that on your face. Blood?"

"Blood, sir? How would blood git on my doggone face, anyhow? That's— h-m—"

"Don't you lie to me, Ezra! I'm not blind. He cut you with something! What was it?"

"Honest to God, cap'n, he never! I admit we had a bit of an argyment, an' I slipped an' kind of fell ag'in' the—the binnacle, cap'n. I'll swear that on the ship's Bible!"

"Don't you stand there and perjure your immortal soul just to shield that boy!" Briggs sternly reproved, loving the old man all the more for the brave lie. "But I know you will, anyhow. What authority have I got aboard my own ship, when I can't even get the truth? Ezra, you wouldn't admit it, if Hal took that kris in there and cut your head off!"

"How could I then, sir?"

"That'll do, Ezra! Where is he now?"

"I don't know, sir."

"I'll damn soon find out!" the captain cried, stung to the first profanity of years. He tramped into the cabin, terrible.

"Come here, sir!" he cried in a tone never before heard in Snug Haven.

No answer. Hal was not there. Neither was the bottle of whisky. A chair had been tipped over, and on the floor lay the captain's wonderful chronometer, with shattered glass.

This destruction, joined to Ezra's innocent blood, seemed to freeze the captain's marrow. He stood there a moment, staring. Then, wide-eyed, he peered around.

"Mutiny and bloodshed," he whispered. "God deliver us from what's to be! Hal Briggs, sir!" he called crisply. "Come here!" The captain, terrible in wrath, strode through the open door.

A creaking of the back stairs constituted the only answer. The captain hurried up those stairs. As he reached the top he heard the door of Hal's room shut, and the key turn.

"You, sir!" he cried, knocking violently at the panels. A voice issued:

"It's no use, gramp. I'm not coming out, and you're not coming in. It's been nothing but hell ever since I struck this damn place. If it doesn't stop I'm going to get mad and do some damage round here. All I want now is to be let alone. Go 'way, and don't bother me!"

"Hal! Open that door, sir!"

Never a word came back. The captain knocked and threatened, but got no reply.

At last, realizing that he was only lowering his dignity by such vain efforts, he departed. His eyes glowered strangely as he made his way downstairs.

Ezra had disappeared. But the old doctor was standing in the hallway, under the gleam of a ship's lantern there. He looked very wan and anxious.

"Captain," said he, with timid hesitation. "I feel that my presence may add to your embarrassment. Therefore, I think I had best return to Salem this evening. If you will ask Ezra to harness up my horse, I'll be much obliged."

"I'll do nothing of the kind, doctor! You're my friend and my guest, and you're not going to be driven out by any such exhibition of brutal bad manners! I ask you, sir, to stay. I haven't seen you for fifty years, sir; and you do no more than lay 'longside, and then want to hoist canvas again and beat away? Never, sir! Here you stay, to-night, aboard me. There's a cabin and as nice a berth as any seafaring man could ask. Go and leave me now, would you? Not much, sir!"

"If you really want me to stay, captain—"

Briggs took Filhiol by the hand and looked steadily into his anxious, withered face.

"Listen," said he, in a deep, quiet tone. "I'm in trouble, doctor. Deep, black, bitter trouble. Nobody in this world but you can help me steer a straight course now, if there's any way *to* steer one, which God grant! Stand by me now, doctor. You did once before on the old *Silver Fleece*. I've got your stitches in me yet. Now, after fifty years, I need you again, though it's worse this time than any knife-cut ever was. Stand by me, doctor, for a little while. That's all I ask. *Stand by!*"

CHAPTER XXIII

SUNSHINE

The miracle of a new day's sunshine—golden over green earth, foam-collared shore and shining sea—brought another miracle almost as great as that which had transformed somber night to radiant morning. This miracle was the complete reversal of the situation at Snug Harbor, and the return of peace and happiness. But all this cannot be told in two breaths. We must not run too far ahead of our story.

So, to go on in orderly fashion we must know that Ezra's carefully prepared supper turned out to be a melancholy failure. The somber dejection of the three old men at table, and then the miserable evening of the captain and the doctor on the piazza, talking of old days with infinite regret, of the present with grief and humiliation, of the future with black bodings, made a sorry time of it all.

Night brought but little sleep to Captain Briggs. The doctor slept well enough, and Ezra seconded him. But the good fortune of oblivion was not for the old captain. Through what seemed a black eternity he lay in the bunk in his cabin, brooding, agonizing, listening to the murmur of the sea, the slow tolling of hours from the tall clock in the hallway. The cessation of the ticking of his chronometer left a strange vacancy in his soul. Deeply he mourned it.

After an infinite time, half-sleep won upon him, troubled by ugly dreams. Alpheus Briggs seemed to behold again the stifling alleyways of the Malay town, the carabaos and chattering gharrimen, the peddlers and whining musicians, the smoky torch-flares and dark, slow-moving river. He seemed to smell, once more, the odors of spice and curry, the smoke of torches and wood fires, the dank and reeking mud of the marshy, fever-bitten shore.

And then the vision changed. He was at sea again; witnessing the death of Scurlock, the boy and Kuala Pahang, in the blood-tinged waters. Came the battle with the Malays, in the grotesque exaggerations of a dream; and then the torments of the hell-ship, cargoing slaves. The old captain seemed stifled by the reek and welter of that freight; he seemed to hear their groans and cries —and all at once he heard again, as in a voice from infinite distances, the curse of Shiva, flung at him by Dengan Jouga, witch-woman of the Malay tribesmen:

"The evil spirit will pursue you, even beyond the wind, even beyond the Silken Sea! Vishnu will repay you! Dead men shall come from their graves, like wolves, to follow you. Birds of the ocean foam will poison you. Life will become to you a thing more terrible than the venom of the katchubong flower, and evil seed will grow within your heart.

"Evil seed will grow and flourish there, dragging you down to death, down to the longing for death, and yet you cannot die! And the blind face in the sky will watch you, *sahib*—watch you, and laugh, because you cannot die! That is the curse of Vishnu on your soul!"

In the captain's dream, the groaning and crying of the wounded and perishing men aboard the *Silver Fleece* seemed to blend with that of the dying slaves. And gradually all this echoing agony transmuted itself into a sinister and terrible mirth, a horrifying, ghastly laughter, far and strange, ceaseless, monotonous, maddening.

Somewhere in a boundless sky of black, the captain seemed to behold a vast spiral, whirling, ever-whirling in and in; and at its center, vague, formless yet filled with menace, he dimly saw an eyeless face, indeed, that still for all its blindness seemed to be watching him. And as it watched, it laughed, blood-freezingly.

Captain Briggs roused to his senses. He found himself sitting up in bed, by the open window, through which drifted the solemn roar and hissing backwash of a rising surf. A pallid moon-crescent, tangled in spun gossamer-fabric of drifting cloud, cast tenuous, fairy shadows across the garden. Staring, the captain rubbed his eye.

"Judas priest!" he muttered. "What—where—Ah! Dreaming, eh? Only dreaming? Thank God for that!"

Then, with a pang of transfixing pain, back surged memories of what had happened last night. He slid out of bed, struck a match and looked at his watch. The hour was just a bit after two.

Noiselessly Briggs crept from his room, climbed the stairs and came to Hal's door. The menace of Kuala Pahang still weighed terribly upon him. Something of the vague superstitions of the sea seemed to have infused themselves into the captain's blood. Shuddering, he remembered the curse that now for years had lain forgotten in the dusty archives of his youth; remembered even more than he had dreamed; remembered the words of the *nenek kabayan*, the witch-woman—that strange, yellow, ghostlike creature which had come upon him silently over his rum and gabbling in the cabin of the hell-ship:

"Something you love—love more than your own life—will surely die. You will die then, but still you will not die. You will pray for death, but death will mock and will not come!"

The old captain shivered as he stood before the door of Hal's room. Suppose the ancient curse really had power? Suppose it should strike Hal, and Hal should die! What then?

For a moment he heard nothing within the room, and his old heart nearly stopped, altogether. But almost at once he perceived Hal's breathing, quiet and natural.

"Oh, thank God!" the captain murmured, his soul suddenly expanding with blest relief. He remained there a while, keeping silent vigil at the door of his well-loved boy. Then, satisfied that all was well, he retraced his steps, got back into bed, and so presently fell into peaceful slumber.

A knocking at his door, together with the voice of Ezra, awoke him.

"Cap'n Briggs, sir! It's six bells o' the mornin' watch. Time to turn out!"

The captain blinked and rubbed his eyes.

"Come in, Ezra," bade he, mustering his wits. "H-m!" he grunted at sight of Ezra's cheek-bone with an ugly cut across it. "The doctor up yet?"

"Yes, sir. He's been cruisin' out 'round the lawn an' garden an hour. He's real interestin', ain't he? But he's too kind o' mournful-like to set right on *my* stomach. Only happy when he's miserable. Men's different, that way, sir. Some heaves a sigh, where others would heave a brick."

"That'll do, Ezra. What's there to record on the log, so far?" asked Briggs, anxiously.

"First thing this A. M. I'm boarded by old Joe Pringle, the peddler from Kittery. Joe, he wanted to sell us anythin' he could—a jew's-harp, history o' the world, Salvation Salve, a phonograft, an Eyetalian queen-bee, a—"

"Hold hard! I don't care anything about Joe. What's the news this morning about—about—"

"News, sir? Well, the white Leghorn's bringin' off a nestful. Five's hatched already. Nature's funny, ain't it? We git chickens from eggs, an' eggs from chickens, an'—"

"*Will* you stop your fool talk?" demanded the captain. He peered at Ezra with disapproval. To his lips he could not bring a direct question about the boy; and Ezra was equally unwilling to introduce the subject, fearing lest some word of blame might be spoken against his idol. "Tell me some news, I say!" the captain ordered.

"News, cap'n? Well, Dr. Filhiol, there, fed his nag enough of our chicken-feed to last us a week. The doc, he calls the critter, Ned. But I think Sea Lawyer would be 'bout right."

"Sea Lawyer? How's that?"

"Well, sir, it *can* draw a conveyance, but it's doggone poor at it."

"Stop your foolishness, Ezra, and tell me what I want to know. How's Hal this morning? Where is he, and what's he doing?"

"Master Hal? Why, he's all right, sir."

"He is, eh?" The captain's hands were clenched with nervousness.

Ezra nodded assent.

"Don't ye worry none about Master Hal," said he gravely. "Worry's wuss'n a dozen leaks an' no pump. Ef ye *must* worry, worry somebody else."

"What's the boy doing? Drinking again?"

"Not a drink, cap'n. Now my idea about liquor is—"

"Judas priest!" interrupted Briggs. "You'll drive me crazy! If the world was coming to an end you'd argue with Gabriel. You say Hal's not touched it this morning?"

"Nary drop, sir."

"Oh, that's good news!"

"Good news is like a hard-b'iled egg, cap'n. You don't have to break it easy. Hal's fine an' fit this mornin', sir. I thought maybe he might hunt a little tot o' rum, this mornin', but no; no, sir, he's sober as a deacon. The way he apologized was as han'some."

"Apologized? Who to?"

"Me an' the doctor. He come out to the barn, an' begged our pardons in some o' the doggondest purtiest language I ever clapped an ear to. He's slick. Everythin's all right between Master Hal an' I an' the doctor. After he apologized he went fer a swim, down to Geyser Rock."

"Did, eh? He's wonderful in the water! Not another man in *this* town dares take that dive. I—I'm mighty glad he had the decency to apologize. Hal's steering the right course now. He's proved himself a man anyhow. Last night I'd almost lost faith in him and in all humanity."

"It ain't so important fer a man to have faith in humanity as fer humanity to have faith in him," affirmed the old cook. "Now, cap'n, you git up, please. You'll want to see Master Hal afore breakfast. Listen to me, cap'n, don't never drive that boy out, same's I was drove. Master Hal's sound an' good at heart. But he's had his own head too long now fer you to try rough tactics."

"Rough! When was I ever rough with Hal?"

"Mebbe if you had of been a few times when he was small it'd of been better. But it's too late now. Let him keep all canvas aloft; but hold a hard helm on him. Hold it hard!"

The sound of singing somewhere across the road toward the shore drew the captain's attention out the window. Striding home from his morning plunge, Hal was returning to Snug Harbor, "coming up with a song from the sea."

The captain put on his bathrobe, then went to the window and sat down there. He leaned his arms on the sill, and peered out at Hal. Ezra discreetly withdrew.

No sign seemed visible on Hal of last night's rage and war. Sleep, and the exhilaration of battling with the savage surf along the face of Geyser Rock, had swept away all traces of his brutality. Molded into his wet bathing-suit that revealed every line of that splendidly virile body, he drew near.

All at once he caught sight of Captain Briggs. He stopped his song, by the lantern-flanked gateway, and waved a hand of greeting.

"Top o' the morning to you, grandfather!" cried he. There he stood overflooded with life, strength, spirits. His body gleamed with glistening brine; his face, lighted by a smile of boyish frankness, shone in the morning sun. His thick, black hair that he had combed straight back with his fingers, dripped seawater on his bronzed, muscular shoulders.

"God, what a man!" the captain thought. "Hard as nails, and ridged with muscle. He's only twenty-one, but he's better than ever I was, at my best!"

And once again, he felt his old heart expand with pride and hope—hope that reached out to lay eager hold upon the future and its dreams.

"I want to see you, sir, before breakfast," said the captain.

Hal nodded comprehension. From the hedge he broke a little twig, and held it up.

"Here's the switch, gramp," said he whimsically. "You'd better use it now, while I've got bare legs."

The old man had to smile. With eyes of profound affection he gazed at Hal. Sunlight on his head and on Hal's struck out wonderful contrasts of snow and jet. The luminous, celestial glow of a June morning on the New England coast—a morning gemmed with billions of dewdrops flashing on leaf and lawn, a morning overbrooded by azure deeps of sky unclouded—folded the world in beauty.

A sense of completion, of loveliness fulfilled compassed everything. Autumn looks back, regretfully. Winter shivers between memories and hopes. Spring hopes more strongly still—but June, complete and resting, says:

"Behold!"

Such was that morning; and the captain, looking at his boy, felt its magic soothing the troubled heart within him. On the lawn, two or three robins were busy. Another, teetering high on the plumy crest of a shadowing elm, was emptying its heart of melody.

A minute, old man and young looked steadily at each other. Then Hal came up the white-sanded walk, between the two rows of polished conches. He stopped at the old man's window.

"Grandfather," said he in a low tone. "Will you listen to me, please?"

"What have you got to say, sir?" demanded Briggs, and stiffened his resolution. "Well, sir?"

"Listen, grandfather," answered Hal, in a very manly way, that harmonized with his blue-eyed look, and with his whole air of ingenuous and boyish contrition. He crossed his bare arms, looked down a moment at the sand, dug at it a little with a toe, and then once more raised his head. "Listen, please. I've got just one thing to ask. Please don't lecture me, and don't be harsh. I stand here absolutely penitent, grandfather, begging to be forgiven. I've already apologized to Dr. Filhiol and Ezra—"

"So I understand," put in Briggs, still striving hard to make his voice sound uncompromising. "Well?"

"Well, grandfather—as for apologizing to you, that's kind of a hard proposition. It isn't that I don't want to, but the relations between us have been so close that it's pretty hard to make up a regular apology. You and I aren't on a basis where I really *could* apologize, as I could to anybody else. But I certainly did act the part of a ruffian on the *Sylvia Fletcher*, and I was certainly a rotter here last night. There's only one other thing—"

"And what's that, sir?" demanded Briggs. The captain still maintained judicial aloofness, despite all cravings of the heart. "What's that?"

"I—you may not believe it, gramp, but it's true. I really don't remember hardly anything about what happened aboard the schooner or here. I suppose I can't stand even a couple of drinks. It all seems hazy to me now, like a kind of nightmare. It's all indistinct, as if it weren't me at all, but somebody else. I feel just as if I'd been watching another man do the things that I really know I myself *did* do. The feeling is that somebody else took my body and used it, and made it do things that I myself didn't want it to do. But I was powerless to stop it. Grampy, it's true, true, *true!*"

He paused, looking at his grandfather with eyes of tragic seriousness. Old

Briggs shivered slightly, and drew the bathrobe more tightly around his shoulders.

"Go on, Hal."

"Well, there isn't much more to say. I know there'll be consequences, and I'm willing to face them. I'll cut out the booze altogether. It was foolish of me to get into it at all, but you know how it is at college. They all kidded me, for not drinking a little, and so—well. It's my own fault, right enough. Anyhow, I'm done. You'll forget it and forgive it, won't you, grandpa?"

"*Will* I, my boy?" the old man answered. He blinked to keep back the tears. "You know the answer, already!"

"You really mean that, gramp?" exclaimed Hal, with boyish enthusiasm. "If I face the music, whatever it is, and keep away from any encores, will you let me by, this time?"

The captain could answer only by stretching out his hand and gripping Hal's. The boy took his old, wrinkled hand in a grip heartfelt and powerful. Thus for a moment the two men, old and young, felt the strong pressure of palms that cemented contrition and forgiveness. The captain was first to speak.

"Everything's all right now, Hal," said he, "so far's I'm concerned. Whatever's wrong, outside Snug Haven, can be made right. I know you've had your lesson, boy."

"I should say so! I don't need a second."

"No, no. You'll remember this one, right enough. Well, now, least said soonest mended. It was pretty shoal water there, one while. But we're floating again, and we're not going to run on to any more sandbars, are we? Ah, there's Ezra blowing his bo'sun's whistle for breakfast. Let's see which of us gets to mess-table first!"

CHAPTER XXIV

DARKENING SHADOWS

Breakfast—served on a regulation ship's table, with swivel-chairs screwed to the floor and with a rack above for tumblers and plates—made up by its overflowing happiness for all the heartache of the night before. Hal radiated life and high spirits. The captain's forebodings of evil had vanished in his newly-revivified hopes. Dr. Filhiol became downright cheerful, and so far forgot his nerves as to drink a cup of weak coffee. As for Ezra, he seemed in his best form.

"Judgin' by your togs, Master Hal," said he, as Hal—breakfast done—lighted his pipe and blew smoke up into the sunlit air, "I cal'late Laura Maynard's got jest the same chances of not takin' a walk with you, this mornin', that Ruddy, here, has got of learnin' them heathen Chinee books o' yourn. It says in the Bible to love y'r neighbor as y'rself, so you got Scripture backin' fer Laura."

"Plus the evidence of my own senses, Ezra," laughed the boy, as he drew at his pipe. His fresh-shaven, tanned face with those now placid blue eyes seemed to have no possible relation with the mask of vicious hate and rage of the night before.

As he sat there, observing Ezra with a smile, he appeared no other than an extraordinary well-grown, powerfully developed young man.

"Must have been the rum that did it," the captain tried to convince himself. "Works that way with some people. They lose all anchors, canvas, sticks and everything—go on the rocks when they've only shipped a drink or two. There'll be no more rum for Hal. He's passed his word he's through. That means he *is* through, because whatever else he may or may not be, he's a Briggs. So then, that's settled!"

"Now that you've put me in mind of Laura, I think I *will* take a walk down-street," said Hal. "I might just possibly happen to meet her. Glad you reminded me, Ezra."

"I guess you don't need much remindin'," replied the old cook solemnly. "But sail a steady course an' don't carry too much canvas. You're too young a cap'n to be lookin' for a mate, on the sea o' life. Go slow. You can't never tell what a woman or a jury'll do, an' most women jump at a chanst quicker 'n what they do at a mouse. Go easy!"

"For an old pair of scissors with only one blade, you seem to understand the cut of the feminine gender pretty well," smiled the boy.

"Understand females?" replied Ezra, drawing out a corn-cob and a pouch of shag. "Not me! Some men think they do, but then, some men is dum fools. They're dangerous, women is. No charted coast, no lights but love-light, an' that most always turns out to be a will-o'-the-wisp, that piles ye up on the rocks. When a man gits stuck on a gal, seems like he's like a fly stuck on fly-paper—sure to git his leg pulled."

Hal laughed again, and departed with that kind of casual celerity which any wise old head can easily interpret. Ezra, striking into a ditty with a monotonous chorus of "Blow the man down," began gathering up the breakfast-dishes. The captain and his guest made their way to the quarterdeck and settled themselves in rockers.

Briggs had hardly more than lighted his pipe, when his attention was caught by a white-canvas-covered wagon, bearing on its side the letters: "R. F. D."

"Hello," said he, a shade of anxiety crossing his face. "Hello, there's the mail."

He tried to speak with unconcern, but into his voice crept foreboding that matched his look. As he strode down the walk, Filhiol squinted after him.

"It's a sin and shame, the way he's worried now," the doctor murmured. "That boy's got the devil in him. He'll kill the captain, yet. A swim, a shave and a suit of white flannels don't change a man's heart. What's bred in the bone—"

Captain Briggs came to a stand at the gate. His nervousness betrayed itself by the thick cloud of tobacco-smoke that rose from his lips. Leisurely the mail-wagon zigzagged from side to side of the street as the postman slid papers and letters into the boxes and hoisted the red flags, always taking good care that no card escaped him, unread.

"Mornin', cap'n," said the postman. "Here's your weather report, an' here's your 'Shippin' News.' An' here's a letter from Boston, from the college. You don't s'pose Hal's in any kind o' rookus down there, huh? An' here's a letter from Squire Bean, down to the Center. Don't cal'late there's any law-doin's, do you?"

"What do you mean?" demanded the captain, trying to keep a brave front. "What could there be?"

"Oh, *you* know, 'bout how Hal rimracked McLaughlin. I heered tell, down-along, he's goin' to sue for swingein' damages. Hal durn nigh killed the critter."

"Who told you?" demanded the captain.

"Oh, they're all talkin'. An' I see Mac, myself, goin' inta the squire's house on a crutch an' with one arm in a sling, early this mornin'. This here letter must of been wrote right away after that. Course I hope it ain't nuthin', but looks to me like 'tis. Well—"

He eyed the captain expectantly, hoping the old man might open the letter and give the news which he could bear to all and sundry. But, no; the captain merely nodded, thrust the letters into the capacious breast-pocket of his square-rigged coat and with a non-committal "Thank you," made his way back to the piazza.

His shoulders drooped not, neither did his step betray any weakness. The disgruntled postman muttered something surly, clucked to his horse, and in disappointment pursued his business—the leisurely handling of Uncle Sam's mail and everybody's private affairs.

The same robin—or perhaps, after all, it was a different one—was singing in the elm, as Alpheus Briggs returned to the house. Down the shaded street the metallic rhythm of the anvil was breaking through the contrabass of the surf. But now this melody fell on deaf ears, for Captain Briggs. Heavily he came up the steps, and with weariness sank down in the big rocker. Sadly he shook his head.

"It's come, I'm afraid," said he dejectedly. "I was hoping it wouldn't. Hoping McLaughlin would let it go. But that was hoping too much. He's no man to swallow a beating. See here now, will you?"

The captain pulled out his letter from Squire Bean, and extended it to Filhiol.

"Local attorney?" asked the doctor, with a look of anxiety.

"Yes," answered the captain. "This letter means only one thing. Barometer's falling again. We'll have to take in more canvas, sir."

He tore the envelope with fingers now trembling. The letter revealed a crabbed hand-writing, thus:

Endicutt, Massachusetts,

June 19, 1918.

CAPTAIN ALPHEUS BRIGGS,

South Endicutt.

DEAR SIR: Captain Fergus McLaughlin has placed in my hands the matter of the assault and battery committed upon him by your grandson, Hal Briggs. Captain McLaughlin is in bad shape, is minus a front tooth, has his right arm broke, and cannot walk without a crutch. You are legally liable for these injuries, and would be immediately summoned into court except Capt. McLaughlin has regard for your age and position in the community. There is, however, no doubt, legal damages coming to the Capt. If you call, we can discuss amt. of same, otherwise let the law take its course.

Resp'ly,

JOHAB BEAN, J. P.,

Ex-Candidate for Judge of Dis't Court.

Captain Briggs read this carefully, then, tugging at his beard, passed it over to Dr. Filhiol.

"It's all as I was afraid it would be," said the captain. "McLaughlin's not going to take the medicine he's really deserved for long years of buckoing poor devils. No, doctor. First time he meets a *man* that can stand up to him and pay him back with interest, he steers a course for the law. That's your bully and your coward! Thank God, for all my doings, I never fought my fights before a judge or jury! It was the best man win, fist to fist, or knife to knife if it came to that—but the law, sir, never!"

"Well, that doesn't matter now," said Filhiol. "I'm afraid you're in for whacking damages. Hal's lucky that he wasn't a signed-on member of the crew. There'd have been mutiny for you to get him out of, and iron bars. Lucky again, he didn't hit just a trifle harder. If he had, it might have been murder, and in this State they send men to the chair for that. Yes, captain, you're lucky it's no worse. If you have only a hundred or two dollars to pay for doctor's bills and damages, you'll be most fortunate."

"A hundred or two dollars!" ejaculated the captain. "Judas priest! You don't think there'll be any such bill as that for repairs and demurrage on McLaughlin's hulk, do you?"

"I think that would be a very moderate sum," answered Filhiol. "I'm willing to stand back of you, captain, all the way. I'll go into court and examine McLaughlin, myself, as an expert witness. It's more than possible Squire Bean is exaggerating, to shake you down."

"You'll stand back of me, doctor?" exclaimed the captain, his face lighting up. "You'll go into court, and steer me straight?"

"By all means, sir!"

Briggs nearly crushed the doctor's hand in a powerful grip.

"Well spoken, sir!" said he. "It's like you, doctor. Well, all I can do is to thank you, and accept your offer. That puts a better slant to our sails, right away. Good, sir—very, very good!"

His expression was quite different as he tore open the letter from the college. Perhaps, after all, this was only some routine communication. But as he read the neat, typewritten lines, a look of astonishment developed; and this in turn gave way to a most pitiful dismay.

The captain's hands were shaking, now, so that he could hardly hold the letter. His face had gone quite bloodless. All the voice he could muster was a kind of whispering gasp, as he stretched out the sheet of paper to the wondering Filhiol:

"Read—read that, doctor! The curse—the curse! Oh, God is being very hard on me, in my old age! Read *that!*"

CHAPTER XXV

TROUBLED SOULS

Dr. Filhiol trembled as he took the letter and read:

Cambridge, Massachusetts,

June 18, 1918.

DEAR SIR:

I regret that I must write you again in regard to your grandson, Haldane Briggs, but necessity leaves no choice. This communication does not deal with an unimportant breach of discipline, such as we overlooked last year, but involves matters impossible to condone.

During the final week of the college year Mr. Briggs's conduct cannot be too harshly stigmatized. Complaint has been entered against him for gambling and for having appeared on the college grounds intoxicated. On the evening of Thursday last Mr. Briggs attempted to bring liquor into a college dormitory, and when the proctor made a protest, Mr. Briggs assaulted him.

In addition, we find your grandson has not applied the money sent by you to the settlement of his term bill, but has diverted it for his own uses. The bill is herewith enclosed, and I trust that you will give it your immediate attention.

Mr. Briggs, because of his undesirable habits, has not recently been properly attending to his courses, with the exception of his Oriental language work, in which he has continued to take a real interest. His examination marks in other studies have been so high as to lead to an inquiry, and we find that Mr. Briggs has been hiring some person unknown to take his place in three examinations and to pass them for him—a form of cheating which the large size of some of our courses unfortunately renders possible.

Any one of Mr. Briggs's infractions of the rules would result in his dismissal. Taken as a total, they render that dismissal peremptory and final. I regret to inform you that your grandson's connection with the university is definitely terminated.

Regretting that my duty compels me to communicate news of such an unpleasant nature, I am,

Very sincerely yours,

HAWLEY D. TRAVERS, A.B., A.M., LL.B.

To CAPTAIN ALPHEUS BRIGGS,

South Endicutt, Massachusetts.

Down sank the head of Captain Briggs. The old man's beard flowed over the smart bravery of his blue coat, and down his weather-hardened cheeks trickled slow tears of old age, scanty but freighted with a bitterness the tears of youth can never feel.

For a moment the captain sat annihilated under life's most grievous blow —futility and failure after years of patient labor, years of saving and of self-denial, of hopes, of dreams. One touch of the harsh finger of Fate and all the gleaming iridescence of the bubble had vanished. From somewhere dark and far a voice seemed echoing in his ears:

"Even though you flee to the ends of the earth, my curse will reach you. You shall pray to die, but still you cannot die! What is written in the Book must be fulfilled!"

Suddenly the captain got up and made his way into the house. Like a wounded animal seeking its lair he retreated into his cabin.

The doctor peered after him, letter in hand. From the galley Ezra's voice drifted in nasal song, with words strangely trivial for so tragic a situation:

"Blow, boys, blow, for Californ-io!
There's plenty of gold, so I've been told,
On the banks of Sacramento!"

"H-m!" grunted the doctor. "Poor old captain! God, but this will finish him! That Hal—damn that Hal! If something would only happen to him now, so I could have him for a patient! I'm a law-abiding man, but still—"

In the cabin Briggs sank down in the big rocking-chair before the fireplace. He was trembling. Something cold seemed clutching at his heart like tentacles. He looked about, as if he half-thought something were watching him from the far corner. Then his eye fell on the Malay kris suspended against the chimney. He peered at the lotus-bud handle, the wavy blade of steel, the dark groove where still lay the poison, the *curaré*.

"Merciful God!" whispered Captain Briggs, and covered his eyes with a shaking hand. He suddenly stretched out hands that shook. "Oh, haven't I suffered enough and repented enough? Haven't I labored enough and paid enough?" He pressed a hand to his forehead, moist and cold. "He's all I've got, Lord—the boy is all I've got! Take me, *me*—but don't let vengeance come through *him*! The sin was mine! Let me pay! Don't drag him down to hell! Take me—but let him live and be a man!"

No answer save that Briggs seemed to hear the words of the old witch-woman ringing with all the force of long-repressed memories:

"Your blood, your blood I will have! Even though you flee from me forever, your blood will I have!"

"Yes, yes! My blood, not his!" cried the old captain, standing up. Haggard, he peered at the kris, horrible reminder of a past he would have given life itself to obliterate so that it might not go on forever poisoning his race. There the kris hung like a sword of Damocles forever ready to fall upon his heart and pierce it. And all at once a burning rage and hate against the kris flared up in him. That thing accursed should be destroyed. No longer should it hang there on his fireplace to goad him into madness.

Up toward the kris he extended his hand. For a moment he dared not lay hold on it; but all at once he forced himself to lift it from its hooks. At touch of it again, after so long a time, he began to tremble. But he constrained himself to study it, striving to fathom what power lay in it. Peering with curiosity and revulsion he noted the lotus-bud, symbol of sleep; the keen edge spotted with dark stains of blood and rust; the groove with its dried poison, one scratch thereof a solvent for all earthly problems whatsoever.

And suddenly a new thought came to him. His hand tightened on the grip. His head came up, his eye cleared, and with a look half of amazement, half triumph, he cried:

"I've got the answer here! The answer, so help me God! Before that boy of mine goes down into the gutter—before he defiles his family and all the memories of his race, here's the answer. Lord knows I hope he will come about on a new tack yet and be something he ought to be; but if he don't, he'll never live to drag our family name down through the sewer!"

Savage pride thrilled the old man. All his hope yearned toward the saving of the boy; but, should that be impossible, he knew Hal would not sink to the dregs of life.

The kris now seemed beneficent to Captain Briggs. Closely he studied the blade, and even drew his thumb along the edge, testing its keenness. Just how, he wondered, did the poison work? Was it painless? Quick it was; that much he knew. Quick and sure. Not in anger, but with a calm resolve he stood there, thinking. And like the after-swells of a tempest, other echoes now bore in upon him—echoes of words spoken half a hundred years ago by Mahmud Baba:

"Even though I wash coal with rosewater a whole year long, shall I ever make it white? Even though the rain fall a whole year, will it make the sea less salt? One drop of indigo—and lo! the jar of milk is ruined! Seed sown upon a lake will never grow!"

Again the captain weighed the kris in hand.

"Maybe the singer was right, after all," thought he. "I've done my best. I've given all I had to give. He'll have his chance, the boy shall, but if, after that—"

CHAPTER XXVI

PLANS FOR RESCUE

"For Heaven's sake, captain, what are you up to there?"

The voice of Filhiol startled Briggs. In the door of the cabin he saw the old man standing with a look of puzzled anxiety. Through the window Filhiol had seen him take down the kris; and, worried, he had painfully arisen and had hobbled into the house. "Better put that knife up, captain. It's not a healthy article to be fooling with."

"Not, eh?" asked the captain. "Pretty bad poison, is it?"

"Extremely fatal."

"Even dried, this way?"

"Certainly! Put it up, captain, I beg you!" The doctor, more and more alarmed, came into the cabin. "Put it up!"

"What does it do to you, this *curaré* stuff?" insisted the captain.

"Various things. And then—"

"Then you die? You surely die?"

"You do, unless one very special antidote is applied."

"Nobody in this country has that, though!"

"Nobody but myself, so far as I know."

"You've got it?" demanded the captain, amazed. "Where the devil would *you* get it?"

"Out East, where you got that devilish kris! You haven't forgotten that Parsee in Bombay, who gave me the secret cure, after I'd saved him from cholera? But that's neither here nor there, captain! That kris is no thing to be experimenting with. Put it up now, I tell you! We aren't going to have any foolishness, captain. Not at our age, mind you! Put it up, now."

Unwillingly the captain obeyed. He hung the weapon up once more, while Filhiol eyed him with suspicious displeasure.

"It would be more to the point to see how we're going to get the boy out of his trouble again," the doctor reproved. "If you can't meet this problem without doing something very foolish, captain, you're not the man I think you!"

Briggs made no answer, but hailed:

"Ezra! Oh, Ezra!"

The old man's chantey—it now had to do with one "Old Stormy," alleged to be "dead and gone"—promptly ceased. Footfalls sounded, and Ezra appeared. The cut on his cheek showed livid in the tough, leathery skin.

"Cap'n Briggs, sir?" asked he.

"The doctor and I are going to take a little morning cruise down to Endicutt in the tender—the buggy, I mean."

"An' you want me to h'ist sail on Bucephalus, sir? All right! That ain't much to want, cap'n. Man wants but little here below, an that's jin'ly all he gits, as the feller says. Right! The Sea Lawyer'll be anchored out front, fer you, in less time than it takes to box the compass!"

Ezra saluted and disappeared.

"I don't know what I'd do without Ezra," said the captain. "There's a love and loyalty in that old heart of his that a million dollars wouldn't buy. Ezra's been through some mighty heavy blows with me. If either of us was in danger, he'd give his life freely, to save us. No doubt of that!"

"None whatever," assented the doctor, as they once more made their way out to the porch. He blinked at the shimmering vagrancy of light that sparkled from the harbor through the fringe of birches and tall pines along the shore. "Going down to see Squire Bean? Is that it?"

"Yes. The quicker we settle that claim the better. You'll go with me, eh?"

"If I'm needed—yes."

"Well, you *are* needed!"

"All right. But, after that, I ought to be getting back to Salem."

"You'll get back to nowhere!" ejaculated Briggs. "They can spare you at the home a few days. You're needed here on the bridge while this typhoon is blowing. Here you are and here you stay till the barometer begins to rise!"

"All right, captain, as you wish," he conceded, his will overborne by the captain's stronger one. "But what's the program?"

"The program is to pay off everything and straighten that boy out and make him walk the chalk-line. Between the four of us—you and I and Laura and Ezra—if we can't do it, we're not much good, are we?"

"Laura? Who is this Laura, anyhow? What kind of a girl is she?"

140

"The very best," answered Briggs proudly. "Hal wouldn't go with any other kind. She's the daughter of Nathaniel Maynard, owner of a dozen schooners. A prettier girl you never laid eyes to, sir!"

"Educated woman?"

"Two years through college. Then her mother had a stroke, and Laura's home again. She's taken the village school, just to fill up her time. A good girl, if there ever was one. Good as gold, every way. I needn't say more. I love her like a daughter. I suppose if I could have my dearest wish—"

"You'd have Hal marry her?"

"Just that; and I'd see the life of my family carried on stronger, better and more vigorous. I'd see a child or two picking the flowers here, and feel little hands tugging at my old gray beard and—but, Judas priest! I'm getting sentimental now. No more of that, sir!"

"I think I understand," the doctor said in another tone. "We've got more than just Hal to save. We've got a woman's happiness to think of. She cares for him, you think?"

Briggs nodded silently.

"It's quite to be expected," commented the doctor. "He certainly can be charming when he tries. There's only one fly in the honey-pot. Just one—his unbridled temper and his seemingly utter irresponsibility.

"You know yourself, captain, his actions this morning have been quite amazing. He starts out to see this girl of his, right away, without giving his bad conduct a second thought. The average boy, expelled from college, would have come home in sackcloth and ashes and would have told you all about it. Hal never even mentioned it. That's almost incredible."

"Hal's not an average kind of boy, any more than *I* was!" put in the captain proudly.

"No, he doesn't seem to be," retorted the physician, peppery with infirmity and shaken nerves. "However, I'm your guest and I won't indulge in any personalities. Whatever comes I'm with you!"

The captain took his withered hand in a grip that hurt, and for a moment there was silence. This silence was broken by the voice of Ezra, driving down the lane:

"All ready, cap'n! All canvas up, aloft an' alow, an' this here craft ready to make two knots an hour ef she don't founder afore you leave port! Fact is, I think Sea Lawyer's foundered already!"

Together captain and doctor descended the path to the front gate. In a few minutes Ezra, bony hands on hips, watched the two men slowly drive from sight round the turn by the smithy. Grimly the old fellow shook his head and gripped his pipe in some remnants of teeth.

"I don't like Pills," grumbled he. "He's a tightwad; never even slipped me a cigar. He's one o' them fellers that stop the clock, nights, to save the works. S'pose I'd oughta respect old age, but old age ain't always to be looked up to, as, fer instance, in the case of eggs. He's been ratin' Master Hal down, I reckon. An' that wun't *do!*"

Resentfully Ezra came back to the house and entered the hall. Into the front room Ezra walked, approached the fireplace and for a moment stood there, carefully observing the weapons. Then he reached up and straightened the position of the "Penang lawyer" club, on its supporting hooks.

"I got to git that jest right," said he. "Jest exactly right. Ef the cap'n should see 'twas a mite out o' place he might suspicion that was what Master Hal hit me with. So? Is that right, that way?"

With keen judgment he squinted at the club and gave it a final touch. The kris, also, he adjusted.

"I didn't know Hal touched the toad-stabber, too," he remarked. "But I guess he must of. It's been moved some, that's sure.

"I guess things'll do now," judged he, satisfied. "There's many a slip 'twixt the cup an' the lip, but there's a damn sight more after the cup has been *at* the lip. That's all that made Master Hal slip. He didn't know, rightly, what he was up to. Forgive the boy? God bless him, you bet! A million times over!

"But that doctor, now, what's been ratin' Master Hal down—no, no, he'll never be no friend o' *mine!* Well, this ain't gittin' dinner ready fer Master Hal. A boy what can dive off Geyser Rock, an' lick McLaughlin, an' read heathen Chinee, an' capture the purtiest gal in *this* town, is goin' to be rationed proper, or I'm no cook aboard the snuggest craft that ever sailed a lawn, with lilacs on the port bow an' geraniums to starb'd!"

Ezra gave a final, self-assuring glance at the Malay club that had so nearly ended his life, and turned back to his galley with a song upon his lips:

"A Yankee ship's gone down the river,
Her masts an' yard they shine like silver.

Blow, ye winds, I long to hear ye!
Blow, boys, blow!

Blow to-day an' blow to-morrer,
Blow, boys, bully boys, blow!

How d'ye know she's a Yankee clipper?

By the Stars and Stripes that fly above her!

Blow, boys, blow!

An' who d'ye think is captain of her?
One-Eyed Kelly, the Bowery runner!

Blow, boys, bully boys, blow!

An' what d'ye think they had fer dinner?
Belayin'-pin soup an' monkey's liver!

Blow, ye winds, I long to hear ye!
Blow, boys, blow!

Blow to-day an' blow to-morrer,
Blow, boys, bully boys, blow!"

CHAPTER XXVII

GEYSER ROCK

Hal Briggs had little thought of trouble as he strode away in search of Laura. Very hot was his blood as he swung down the shaded street toward the house of Nathaniel Maynard, father of the girl. Some of the good folk frowned and were silent as he greeted them, but others had to smile and raise a hand of recognition. Still at some distance from Laura's house, the boy caught sight of a creamy-toned voile dress among the hollyhocks in the side yard. He whistled, waved his hand, hurried his pace. And something leaped within him, so that his heart beat up a little thickly, as the girl waved an answering hand.

Another look came to his eyes. Another light began to burn in their blue depths.

"Geyser Rock!" he whispered. "By God, the very place!"

Geyser Rock boldly fronts the unbroken sweep of the sea at Thunder Head. Up it leaps, sheer two hundred feet, from great deeps. Fifty feet from the barnacle-crusted line of high-tide a ledgelike path leads to the face of the cliff. From this ledge Hal often took the plunge that had won him local fame —a plunge into frothing surf that even in the calmest of midsummer days was never still.

Few visitors ever struggle up through sumacs, brakes and undergrowth, to gain the vantage-point of the pinnacle. Rolling boulders, slippery ledge and dizzying overlook upon the shining sea deter all but the hardy. The very solitude of the place had greatly endeared it to Hal. To him it was often a solace and a comfort after his strange fits of rage and viciousness.

All alone, up in that isolated height, he had passed long hours reading, smoking, musing in the tiny patch of grass there under the canopy of the white-birches' filigree of green, or under the huge pine that carpeted the north slope of the crest with odorous, russet spills. Some of his happiest hours had been spent on the summit, through the tree-tops watching sky-shepherds tend their flocks across the pastures infinitely far and blue above him.

Strangely secluded was the top of Geyser Rock. Though it lay hardly a pistol-shot from the main coast-road, it seemed almost as isolated as if it had been down among the Celebes.

For that reason Hal loved it best of all, with its grasses, flowers, ferns and tangled thickets, its rock-ridges filigreed with silvery lichens or sparkling with white quartz-crystals. From this aerie Hal could glimpse a bit of the village; the prim church spire; the tiny, far gravestones sleeping on Croft Hill. The solitude of this, his own domain by right of conquest, had grown ever more dear and needful to him as he had advanced toward manhood.

Such was the place toward which Laura and he were now walking along the road, with tilled fields and rock-bossed rolling hills to right of them; and, to their left, the restless flashings of the sea.

Laura had never been more charming. Her happiness in his return had flushed her cheeks with color and had brightened her eyes—thoughtful, deep, loyal eyes—till they looked clear and fresh as summer skies after rain.

Everything wholesome and glad seemed joined in Laura; her health and spirits were like the morning breeze itself that came to court the land, from the golden sparklings that stretched away to the shadowed, purple rim of the ocean. The June within her heart mirrored itself through her face, reflecting the June that overbrooded earth and sea and sky.

Hal sensed all this and more, as with critical keenness he looked down at her, walking beside him. He noted the wind-blown hair that shaded her eyes; he saw the health and vigor of that lithe, firm-breasted young body of hers. His look, brooding, glowed evilly. Fifty years ago thus had his grandsire's eyes kindled at sight of Kuala Pahang in her tight little Malay jacket. And as if words from the past had audibly echoed from some vibrant chord in the old-time captain's symphony of desire, once more the thought formed in his brain:

"She's mine, the girl is! She's plump as a young porpoise, and, by God, I'm going to have her!"

The words he uttered, though, were far afield from these. He was saying:

"So now, Laura, you see I wasn't really to blame, after all. 'A lie runs round the world, while truth is getting on its sandals.' That proverb's as true here as in Siam, where it originated. People are saying I was drunk and brutal, and all that, when the fact is—"

"I know, Hal," she answered, her eyes troubled. "I know how this country gossip exaggerates. But, even so, did you do right in beating Captain McLaughlin as you did?"

"It was the only thing I *could* do, Laura!" he protested. "The bully tried to humiliate me. I—I just licked him, that's all. You wouldn't want me to be a milksop, would you?"

"No, not that, Hal. But a fair fight is one thing and brutality is another. And then, too, they say you'd been drinking."

He laughed and slid his hand about her arm.

"I give you my word of honor, Laura, all I'd had was just a little nip to take the sea-chill out of my bones. Come, now, look at me, and tell me if I look like a thug and a drunkard!"

He stopped in the deserted road, swung the girl round toward him, and laid his hands on her shoulders. Through the sheer thinness of her dress he felt the warmth of her. The low-cut V of her waist tempted him, dizzyingly, to plant a kiss there; but he held steady, and met her questioning eyes with a look that seemed all candor.

For a long moment Laura kept silence, searching his face. Far off, mournfully the bell-buoy sent in its blur of musical tolling across the moving sea-floor.

"Well, Laura, do I look a ruffian?" asked Hal again, smiling.

Laura's eyes fell.

"I'm going to believe you, Hal, whatever people say," she whispered. "I'm sorry it happened at all, but I suppose that's the way of a man. You won't do anything like that again, though, will you?"

"No—dear! Never!"

He drew her toward him, but she shook her head and pressed him back. Wise with understanding, from sources of deep instinct, he let her go. But now the fires in his eyes were burning more hotly. And as they once more started down along the road he cast on her a glance of quick and all-inclusive desire.

Silence a minute or two. Then Hal asked:

"Laura, have you ever been up Geyser Rock?"

"No. Why?" Her look was wondering.

"Let's go!"

"That's pretty rough climbing for a girl, isn't it?"

"Not for a girl like you, Laura. You can make it, all right. And the view— oh, wonderful!" His enthusiasm quickened now that he saw her coming to his hand. "On a clear day you can see Cape Ann, to northward, and Cross Rip Light, to the south. See that big Norway pine right there? That's where the path leads in. Come on, Laura!"

"I—I don't know—"

"Afraid?"

"Not where *you* are, Hal, to protect me!"

He took her hand and drew her into the thick-wooded path, in under the cool green shadows, gold-sprinkled with the magic of the sun's morris-dance of little elfin light-fairies. New strength seemed to flood him. His heart, beginning to beat quickly, flushed his face with hot blood. Something as yet unawakened, something potent, atavistic, something that had its roots twined far into the past, surged through his veins.

"Come on, Laura!" he repeated. "Come on, I'll show you the way!"

Half an hour had passed before they stood upon the summit. They had perhaps lingered a bit more than needful, even with so many leaves and flowers to pick and study over; and, moreover, part of the way their progress had been really difficult. Hal had carried her in his arms up some of the more dangerous pitches—carried her quite as if she had been a child. The clinging of her arms to his shoulders, the warmth and yielding of her, the blowing of her hair across his face, the faint perfume of her alluring femininity had kindled fires that glowed from his eyes—eyes like the eyes of Alpheus Briggs in the old days when the Malay girl had been his captive. Yet still the atavisms in him had been stifled down. For Hal was sober now. And still the metes and bounds of civilization and of law had held the boy in leash.

Thus they had reached the summit. Far up past the diving-ledge they had made their way, and so had climbed to the little sheltered nook facing the sky.

"I think you're wonderful, Laura!" Hal said as he pressed aside the bushes for her to enter the grassy sward. His voice was different now; his whole manner had subtly altered. No longer words of college argot came to his lips. "I think you're really very wonderful! There's not another girl in this town who'd take a risk like this!"

"It's nothing, Hal," she answered, looking up at him in the sunshine with a smile. "I told you before I couldn't possibly be afraid where you were. How *could* I be afraid?"

"Lots of girls would be, all the same," said he. "You're just a wonder. Well, now, let's go over there to the edge. I won't let you fall. I want you to see the view. Just through that fringe of birches there you'll see it."

With quickened breath the girl peered down through the trees, at land and sea spread far below, while Hal's arm held her from disaster. Branches and twigs had pulled at her, in the ascent. Her voile dress showed a tear or two;

and all about her face the disordered hair strayed as the sea-breeze freshened over the top of Geyser. The boy kept silence that matched hers. A kind of vague, half-realized struggle seemed taking place in him—a conflict between the sense of chivalry, protecting this woman in his absolute power, and the old demon-clutch that reached from other days and other places.

Now, though his thoughts and hers lay far apart as the world's poles, each felt something of the same mysterious oppression. For the first time quite alone together, up there aloft in that snug, sun-warm nest embowered in greenery, a kind of mystic and half-sensed languor seemed to envelop them; a yearning that is older than old Egypt; a wonder and a dream.

Hal's arm tightened a very little 'round her body. She felt it tremble, and, wondering, understood that she, too, felt a little of that tremor in her own heart. She realized in a kind of half-sensed way that more dangers lay here than the danger of falling from the cliff. Yet in her soul she knew that she was glad to be there.

CHAPTER XXVIII

LAURA UNDERSTANDS

Thus she remained, holding to a silver birch, leaning out a little toward the chasm. Up from the depths echoed a gurgling roar as the white fury drenched and belabored the gray, sheer wall, then fell back, hissing.

For a moment Laura peered down, held by the boy's encircling arm. She looked abroad upon the sun-shining waters flecked with far, white boats and smudged with steamer-smoke. Then she breathed deep and lifted up her face toward the gold filigree of sun and leaf, and sighed:

"Oh, it's wonderful, Hal! I never even guessed it could be anything like this!"

"Wonderful isn't the name for it, Laura," he answered. He pointed far. "See the lighthouse? And Cape Ann in the haze? And the toy boats? Everything and everybody's a toy now except just you and me. We're the only real people. I wish it were really so, don't you?"

"Why, Hal? What would you do if it were?"

"Oh," he answered with that heart-warming smile of his, "I'd take you in a yacht, Laura, away off to some of those wonderful places the Oriental poems tell about. We'd sail away 'through the Silken Sea,' and 'Beyond the Wind,' wherever that is. Wouldn't you like to go there with me, dear?"

"Yes. But—"

"But what, Laura?" His lips were almost brushing the curve of her neck, where the wind-blown hair fell in loose ringlets. "But what?"

"I—I mustn't answer that, Hal. Not now!"

"Why not now?"

"While you're still in college, Hal? While there's so much work and struggle still ahead of you?"

The boy frowned, unseen by her, for her eyes were fixed on the vague horizons beyond which, no doubt, lay Silken Seas and far, unknown places of enchantment beyond all winds whatsoever. Not thus did he desire to be understood by Laura. The whim of June shrinks from being mistaken for a thing of lifelong import. Laura drew back from the chasm and faced him with a little smile.

"It's very wrong for people to make light of such things," she said. Her look lay steadily upon his face. "While the sun is shining it's so easy to say more than one means. And then, at the first cloud, the fancy dies like sunlight fading."

"But this isn't a mere fancy that I feel for you," Hal persisted, sensing that he had lost ground with her. "I've had plenty of foolish ideas about girls. But this is different. It's so very, very different every way!" His voice, that he well knew how to make convincing, really trembled a little with the thrill of this adventuring.

"I wish I could believe you, Hal!"

He drew her toward him again. This time she did not resist. He felt the yielding of her sinuous young body, its warmth and promise of intoxication.

"You *can* believe me, Laura! Only trust in me!"

"I—I don't know, Hal. I know what men are. They're all so much alike."

"Not all, dear! You ought to know me well enough to have confidence in me. Think of the long, long time we've known each other. Think of the years and years of friendship! Why, Laura, we've known each other ever since we were a couple of children playing on the beach, writing each other's names in the sand—"

"For the next high tide to wash away!"

"But we're not children now. There's something in my heart no tide can obliterate!"

"I hope that's true, Hal. But you're not through college yet. Wait till you are. You've got to graduate with flying colors, and make your dear old grandfather the proudest man in the world, and be the wonderful success I know you're going to be! And make me the happiest girl! You will, won't you?"

"I'll do anything in the world for you, Laura!" he exclaimed. His face, flushed with enkindling desire, showed no sign of shame or dejection. Laura knew nothing of his débâcle at the university. Of course she must soon know; but all that still lay in the future. And to Hal nothing mattered now but just the golden present with its nectar in the blossom and its sunshine on the leaf. He drew her a little closer.

"Tell me," he whispered. "Do you really care?"

"Don't ask me—yet!" she denied him, turning her face away. "Come, let's be going down!"

"Why, we've only just come!"

"I know, but—"

"You needn't be afraid of *me!*" he exclaimed. "You aren't, are you, dear?"

"No more than I am of myself," she answered frankly, while her throat and face warmed with blood that suddenly burned there. "We—really oughtn't to be alone like this, Hal."

He laughed and opened his arms to let her go. For a moment she stood looking up at him; then her eyes, too innocent to find the guile in his, smiled with pure-hearted affection.

"Forgive me, Hal!" said she. "I didn't mean that. But, you know, when you put your arms round me like that—"

"I won't do it again," he answered, instinct telling him the bird would take fright if the trap seemed too tightly closed. He dropped his arms, the palms of his hands spread outward. "You see, when you tell me to let you go, I mind you?"

"Yes, like the good, dear boy you are!" she exclaimed with sudden, impulsive affection. She reached up, took his face in both hands and studied his eyes. He thought she was about to kiss him, and his heart leaped. He quivered to seize her, to burn his kisses on her lips, there in the leafy, sun-glimmering shade; but already Laura's arms had fallen, and she had turned away, back toward the path that would lead them downward from this tiny enchanted garden to the common level of the world again.

"Come, Hal," said she, "we must be going now!"

He nodded, his eyes glowering coals of desire, and followed after. Was the bird, then, going to escape his hand? A sinister look darkened his face; just such a look as had made Captain Briggs a brute when he had shouldered his way into his cabin aboard the *Silver Fleece*, to master the captive girl.

"Laura, wait a minute, please!" begged Hal.

"Well, what is it?" she asked, half-turning, a beautiful, white, gracious figure in the greenery—a very wood-nymph of a figure, sylvan, fresh, enwoven with life's most mystic spell—the magic of youth.

"You haven't seen half my little Mysterious Island up here!"

"Mysterious Island?" asked she, pleased by the fanciful whim. "You call it that, do you?"

"Yes, I've always called it that ever since I read Jules Verne, when I was only a youngster. I've never told anybody, though. I haven't told that, or a hundred other imaginings." He had come close to her again, had taken her by the arm, was drawing her away from the path and toward the little flower-enameled greensward among the boulders crowned with birch and pine. "You're the only one that knows my secret, Laura. You'll never, never tell, now, will you?"

"Never!" she answered, uneasiness dispelled by his frank air. "Do you imagine things like that, too, Hal? I thought I was the only one around here who ever 'pretended.' Are you a dreamer, too?"

"Very much a dreamer. Sit down here, Laura, and let me tell you some of my dreams."

He sat down in the grass, and drew her down beside him. She yielded "half willing and half shy." For a moment he looked at her with eyes of desire. Then, still holding her hand, he said:

"It was all fairies and gnomes up here when I first came. Fairyland in those boyhood days. After a while the fairies went away and pirates began to come; pirates and Indians and a wild crew. I was sometimes a victim, sometimes a member of the brotherhood. There's treasure buried all 'round here. Those were the days when I was reading about Captain Kidd and Blackbeard. You understand?"

"Indeed I *do*! Go on!"

He laughed, as her mood yielded under the subtle mastery of his voice, his eyes.

"Oh, but it's a motley crew we've been up here, the pirates and I!" said he, leaning still closer. "'Treasure Island' peopled the place with adventurers —Long John Silver, and Pew and the Doctor, and all the rest. 'Robinson Crusoe' swept them all away, all but Man Friday; and then the savages had to come. If there's anything at all I haven't suffered in the way of shipwreck, starvation, cannibals and being rescued just in the nick of time up here, really I don't know what it is. And since I've grown up, though of course I can't 'pretend' any more, I've always loved this place to day-dream in, and wonder in, about the thing that every man hopes will come to him some day."

"And what's that, Hal?" she asked in a lower voice.

"Love!" he whispered. "Love—and you!"

"Hal, is that really true?"

"Look at me, Laura, and you'll know!"

She could not meet his gaze. Her eyes lowered. He drew his arm about her as she drooped a little toward him.

152

"Listen to me!" he commanded, masterfully lying. "There's never been anybody but you, Laura. There never will be. You've been in all my dreams, by night, my visions by day, up here in fairyland!"

His words were coming impetuously now. In his eyes the golden flame of desire was burning hot.

"You're everything to me! Everything! I've sensed it for a long time, but only in the last month or two I've really understood. It all came to me in a kind of revelation, Laura, one day when I was translating a poem from the Hindustani."

"A poem, Hal?" The girl's voice was tremulous. Her eyes had closed. Her head, resting on his shoulder, thrilled him with ardor; and in his nostrils the perfume of her womanhood conjured up shimmering dream-pictures of the Orient—strange lands that, though unseen, he mysteriously seemed to know. "Tell me the poem, dear!" Laura whispered. "A love-poem?"

"Such a love-poem! Listen, sweetheart! It's a thousand years old, and it comes from the dim past to tell you what I feel for you. It runs this way:

"Belovèd, were I to name the blossoms of the spring,
And all the fruits of autumn's bounteousness;
Were I to name all things that charm and thrill,
And earth, and Heaven, all in one word divine,

I would name thee!

"Had I the gold of Punjab's golden land,
Had I as many diamonds, shining bright
As leaves that tremble in a thousand woods,
Or sands along ten thousand shining seas;
Had I as many pearls of shifting hue
As blades of grass in fields of the whole world,
Or stars that shine on the broad breast of night,
I'd give them all, a thousand, thousand times,

To make thee mine!"

For a minute, while Hal watched her with calculation, Laura kept silence. Then she looked up at him, dreamy-eyed, and smiled.

"That's wonderful, Hal. I only wish you meant it!"

"You *know* I do! I want you, Laura—God, how much! You're all I need to make my fairyland up here a heaven!"

"What—what do you mean, Hal? Are you asking me to—to be your wife?"

His face contracted, involuntarily, but he veiled his true thought with a lie. What mattered just a lie to gain possession of her in this golden hour of sunshine?

"Yes, yes, of course!" he cried, drawing her to his lips in a betraying kiss
—a kiss, to her, culminant with wonder and mystic with a good woman's
aspiration for a life of love and service—a kiss, to him, only a trivial incident,
lawless, unbridled. At heart he cursed the girl's pure passion for him. Not this
was what he wanted; and dimly, even through the flame of his desire, he
could see a hundred complications, perils. But now the lie was spoken—and
away with to-morrow!

Again he kissed the girl, sensing, in spite of his desire, the different
quality of her returning kiss. Then she smiled up at him, and with her hand
smoothed back the thick, black hair from his forehead.

"It's all so wonderful, Hal!" she whispered fondly. "I can't believe it's
true. But it is true, isn't it? Even though we've got to wait till you get through
college. I'm willing to. I love you enough, Hal, to wait forever. And you will,
too, won't you?"

"Of—of course I will!"

"And it's really, really true? It's not just a fairy dream of wonderland, up
here, that will vanish when we go down to the world again?"

"No, no, it's all true, Laura," he was forced to answer, baffled and at a
loss. Not at all was this adventure developing as he had planned it. Why,
Laura was taking it seriously! Laura was acting like a child—a foolish,
preposterous child! The web that he had hoped to spread for her undoing had,
because of her own trusting confidence, been tangled all about himself.

Abashed and angry, he sought some way to break its bonds. Another
poem rose to memory, a poem that he hoped might make her understand. He
had read it the day before in a little book called "The Divine Image," and it
had instantly burned itself into his brain. Now said he:

"Listen, dear. I've got another verse for you. It's called: 'His Woman.'"

"And I'm really yours, forever?"

"Of course you are, dear! Listen, now:

"'In the pale, murmuring dawn she lay
Alone, with nothing more to lose.

Her eyes one warm, soft arm espied,

And lips too tired to voice her pride
Caressed and kissed a bruise.'"

The girl looked up at him a moment, circled with his arm, as she lay there
content. For a little she seemed not to understand. Then, slowly, a puzzled
look and then a look of hurt rose to her eyes.

154

"Hal, you—you mustn't—"

"Why mustn't I, dear?"

She tried to answer, but his lips upon her mouth stifled her speech.

Swift fear leaped through her as she fought away from him.

"Oh, Hal!" she cried. "What—what are you looking at me that way for? Your eyes, Hal—your eyes—"

In vain he tried to kiss her. Her face was turned away, her hands repulsing him.

"Kiss me, Laura! Kiss me!"

"No, no—not now! Oh, Hal, you have only yourself to resist. I have you to resist, and myself, too!"

The thought gave him a minute's pause. Did some instinct of chivalry, deep-buried, try for a second to struggle up through his evil heritage, or was it but surprise that loosed his grip upon her so that she escaped his hands, his arms?

"God forgive you, Hal, for having killed the most wonderful treasure I had—my faith in you!" she cried from where she stood now, looking down at him with tragic eyes of disillusion. "Oh, God forgive you!"

He would have spoken, but she turned and fled toward the tangled thicket through which the path led downward.

"Laura! Wait!" He sprang to his feet, peering after her with hateful eyes. No answer as she vanished through the greenery.

For all his rage and passion, Hal realized how absurd a figure he would make, pursuing her. Swift anger swept over him, broke all down, rushed in uncontrolled floods.

A moment he stood there, brutal, venomous. Then with a laugh, the echo of that which had sounded when Alpheus Briggs had flung the Malay girl to death, he clutched at his thick hair, tugging at it with excess of madness. He broke into wild curses that rose against the sky with barbarous blasphemy.

Foam slavered upon his lips. His face grew black; the veins stood out upon his neck and temples. A madman, he trampled through the bushes, stamping, striking, lusting to kill.

So for a time he raged in blind, stark passion; while Laura, shaken and afraid, bleeding at her heart of hearts, made her way all alone back to the safety of the seashore road.

155

At last, his rage burned out, Hal flung himself down in the grass. Face buried in hands, teeth set in bleeding lip, he lay there.

And over him the heavens, like an eyeless face, smiled down with calm, untroubled purpose.

CHAPTER XXIX

THE GARDEN OF GETHSEMANE

Sadly returning home, Laura stopped for a moment at her garden gate to make quite sure her father was not in the side yard. With all her girlish dreams broken and draggled, the heartbroken girl stood looking at the flowers that only an hour before had seemed so wondrous gay. And all at once she heard the sound of wheels upon the road. Turning, she saw old Captain Briggs and Dr. Filhiol slowly driving toward Snug Haven.

Half-minded to retreat inside the garden, still she stood there, for already Captain Briggs had raised a hand in greeting. Every feature of the old captain's face was limned with grief. His shoulders seemed to sag, bowed down with heavier weight than his almost eighty years could pile upon them.

So the girl remained at the gate, greatly sorrowing; and peered after the two old men. Though she could not guess the captain's trouble, her woman's instinct told her this trouble bore on Hal. And over her own grief settled still another cloud that darkened it still more.

Puzzled, disillusioned, she swung the gate and entered the prim paths bordered with low box-hedges. No one saw her. Quietly she entered the house and crept up-stairs to her own room. There, in that virginal place, she dropped down on her old-fashioned, four-posted bed of black walnut, and buried her face in the same pillows to which, girl-like, she had often confided so many innocent and tender dreams.

As the girl lay there, crying for the broken bauble, love, crushed in the brutal hand of Hal, old Captain Briggs and Dr. Filhiol—once more back on the quarterdeck of Snug Haven—settled themselves for dejected consultation.

"I never did expect 'twould be as much as that," the captain said, mechanically stuffing his pipe. "I reckoned maybe fifty dollars would pay demurrage and repairs on Mac. McLaughlin isn't worth more, rig and all. But, Judas priest, two hundred and a half! That's running into money. Money I can ill afford to pay, sir!"

"I know," the doctor answered. "It's cruel extortion. But what can you do, captain? McLaughlin holds the tiller now. He can steer any course he chooses. The fact that he started at five hundred, plus the apology that he demands from Hal on the deck of the *Sylvia* in front of the whole crew, and that we've pared him down to two hundred and fifty, plus the apology—that's a very great gain. It's bad, I know, but not so bad as having had the boy locked up, charged with felonious assault. It's not so bad as that, sir!'"

"No, no, of course not," Briggs agreed. "I suppose I've got to pay, though Lord knows, sir, the money's needed terribly for other things, now that the college bill has got to be settled all over again!"

"I know it's hard," sympathized the doctor, "but there's no help for it. Wipe the slate clean, and give Hal another start. That's all you *can* do."

The old captain remained smoking and brooding a while, with sunshine on his head. At last his eyes sought the far, deep line of blue that stretched against the horizon—the sea-line, lacking which the old man always sensed a vacancy, a loss.

"Close on to six bells," judged he, "by the way the sun's shining on the water. Wonder where the boy can be? I've got to have a proper gam with him."

"Why? Where ought he to be?" the doctor asked.

"He must have put back into port, after his little cruise with Laura, this morning. We sighted her, moored at her front gate, you remember?"

"H-m! You don't suppose there's trouble brewing there too, do you? I thought the girl looked upset, didn't you?"

"*I* didn't notice anything. What seemed to be the matter?"

"I thought she'd been crying a bit."

The captain clenched his fist.

"By the Judas priest!" he exclaimed fervently. "If I thought Hal had been abusing that girl, I'd make it hot for him! That's *one* thing I won't stand!" He peered down the road with narrowing eyes, then got up and went to the front door. "Hal, oh, Hal!" he cried.

No answer. The captain's voice echoed emptily in the old-fashioned hallway.

"Not here, anyhow," said he, returning to his rocker. "Well, we won't accuse him of anything else till we know. I only hope he hasn't written any more black pages on the log by mishandling Laura."

Wearily his eyes sought Croft Hill. Of a sudden unbidden tears blurred his sight.

"*There's* a peaceful harbor for old, battered craft, anyhow," he murmured, pointing. "I sometimes envy all the tired folk that's found sleep and rest up there in their snug berths, while we still stand watch in all weathers. If, after all I've worked and hoped for, there's nothing ahead but breakers, I'll envy them more than ever."

"Come now, captain!" Filhiol tried to cheer him. "Maybe it was only a little lovers' quarrel that sent Laura home. There's never all smooth sailing, with maid and man for a crew. Let's wait a while and see."

"Yes, wait and think it over," said the captain. "There's only one place for me, doctor, when things look squally, and that's with my folks on the hill. Guess I'll take a walk up there now and talk it over with them. Come with me, will you?"

Filhiol shook his head.

"Too much for me, that hill is," he answered. "If you don't mind, I'll sit right here and watch the sea."

"Suit yourself, doctor." And Captain Briggs arose. "When Ezra comes down the lane tell him not to bother with dinner. A little snack will do. Let's each of us think this thing out, and maybe we can chart the proper course between us."

He stood a moment in the sunshine, then, bare-headed, went down the steps and turned into the path that would lead him up Croft Hill. He stopped, gathering a handful of bright flowers—zinnias, hollyhocks, sweet peas—for his ever-remembered dead. Then he went on again.

"Poor old chap!" said Dr. Filhiol. "The curse is biting pretty deep. That's all poppycock, that Malay cursing; but the curses of heredity are stern reality. There's a specific for every poison in the world. Even the dread *curaré* has one. But for the poison of heredity, what remedy is there? Poor old captain!"

Alpheus Briggs, with bowed head, climbed up the winding way among the blackberry bushes, the sumacs and wild roses dainty-sweet; and so at last came to the wall pierced with the whitewashed gate that he himself kept always in repair.

Into the cemetery, his Garden of Gethsemane, he penetrated, by paths flanked with simple and pious stones, many of hard slate carved with death's-heads, urns, cherubs and weeping-willows, according to the custom of the ancient, godly days. Thus to his family burial lot he came, and there laid his offering upon the graves he loved; and then sat down upon the bench there, for meditation in this hour of sorrow and perplexity.

And as sun and sky and sea, fresh breeze and drifting cloud, and the mild influences of his lifelong friend, tobacco, all worked their soothings on him, he presently plucked up a little heart once more. The nearness of his dead bade him have hope and courage. He felt, in that quiet and solemn place, the tightening of his family bonds; he felt that duty called him to lift even these new and heavy burdens, to bear them valiantly and like a man.

With the graves about him and the sea before, and over all the heavens, calm returned. And sorrow—which, like anger, cannot long be keen—faded into another thought: the thought of how he should make of Hal the man that he would have him be.

How restful was this sunlit hilltop, where he knew that soon he, too, must sleep! The faint, far cries of gulls drifted in to him with the bell-buoy's slow tolling; and up from the village rose the music of the smitten anvil. That music minded him of a Hindustani poem Hal once had read to him—a poem about the blacksmith, Destiny, beating out showers of sparks upon the cosmic anvil in the night of eternity, each spark a human soul; and each, swiftly extinguished, worth just as much to Destiny as earthly anvil sparks are to the human toiler at the forge—as much and no more.

The poem had thus ended:

"All is Maya, all is illusion! Why struggle, then?
To walk is better than to run; to stand is better than to walk.
To sit is better than to stand; to lie is better than to sit.
To sleep is better than to wake; to dream is better than to live.
Better still is a sleep that is dreamless,

    And death is best of all!"

"I wonder if that's true?" the captain mused. "I wonder if life *is* all illusion and death alone is real?"

Thus meditating, he felt very near the wife and son who lay there beneath the flowers he had just laid on the close-cut sod. The cloud-shadows, drifting over the hilltop, seemed symbols of the transitory passage of man's life, unstable, ever drifting on, and leaving on the universe no greater imprint than shadows on the grass. He yearned toward those who had gone to rest before him; and though not a praying man, a supplication voiced itself in him:

"Oh, God, let me finish out my work, and let me rest! Let me put the boy on the right course through life, and let me know he'll follow it—then, let me steer for the calm harbor where Thou, my Pilot, wilt give me quiet from the storm!"

Thus the old captain sat there for a long time, pondering many and sad things; and all at once he saw the figure of a man in white coming along the road. The captain knew him afar.

"There's Hal now," said he. "I wonder where he's been and what this all means?"

A new anxiety trembled through his wounded heart, that longed for nothing now but love and trust. Up rose the old captain, and with slow steps walked to the eastern wall of the cemetery. There he waited patiently.

Presently Hal came into sight, round the shoulder of Croft Hill.

"Ahoy, there! Hal! Come here—I want to see you!"

The old man's cry dropped with disagreeable surprise into Hal's sinister reflections. Hal looked up, and swore to himself. He sensed the meaning of that summons.

"There's another damned scene coming," thought Hal. "Why the hell can't he let me alone now? Why can't everybody let me alone?"

Nothing could now have been more inopportune than an interview with his grandfather. Hal—his rage burned out to ashes—had come down from Geyser Rock, and had turned homeward in evil humor. And as he had gone he had already begun to lay out tentative plans for what he meant to do.

"It's all bull, what Laura handed me!" he had been thinking when the captain's summons had intruded. "Am I going to let her throw me that way? I guess *not*! I'll land her yet; but not here, not here! I can't stick here. The way I'm in wrong with the college, and now this new rough-house with Laura, will certainly put the crimp in me. What I've got to do is clear out. And I won't go alone, at that. If I only had a twenty-five footer! I could get her aboard of it some way. The main thing's a boat. The rest is easy. I could let them whistle, all of them. The open sea—that's the thing! That's a man's way to do things— not go sniveling 'round here in white flannels all summer, letting a girl hand it to me that way!

"God, if I could only raise five hundred bucks! I could get Jim Gordon's *Kittiwink* for that, and provision it, too. Make a break for Cuba, or Honduras; why, damn it, I could go round the world—go East—get away from all this preaching and rough-house—live like a man, by God!"

The captain's hail shattered Hal's dreams.

"Devil take the old man!" snarled Hal to himself as he scowled up at the figure on the hilltop. "What's he want *now*? And devil take all women! They're like dogs. Beat a dog and a woman, and you can't go wrong. I'll play this game to win yet, and make good! Hello, up there?" he shouted in reply to the captain. "What d'you want of me?"

"I want to talk with you, Hal," the old man's voice came echoing down. "Come here, sir!"

Another moment Hal hesitated. Then, realizing that he could not yet raise the banner of open rebellion, he turned and lagged toward the road that led up the south side of the hill.

As he climbed, he put into the background of his brain the plans he had been formulating, and for the more pressing need of the future began framing plausible lies.

He lighted a Turkish cigarette as he entered the graveyard, to give himself a certain nonchalance; and so, smoking this thing which the old captain particularly abominated, swinging his shoulders, he came along the graveled walk toward the family burying lot, where once more Captain Briggs had sat down upon the bench to wait for him.

CHAPTER XXX

HIS WORD OF HONOR

The old man said nothing at all, as Hal drew near, but only peered at him from under those white-thatched brows of his, with eyes of stern reproach. This still further quickened Hal's apprehension and blew to a kindling fire the glowing embers of venomous ill-humor.

For all his swagger, Hal could not bring himself to look the captain in the eye. Hands in pockets, cigarette in lips, he came close and stood there; and with defiant surliness on his tanned face managed to say:

"Well, gramp, what now? Getting ready to pan me properly, are you? If so, when ready, Gridley, you can fire!"

"Hal," answered the old man, "that's the last impertinence you're ever going to utter to me! So remember. Sit down and answer my questions."

"I can take it standing, all right!" said Hal, defiant still.

"I said, sit down, sir!"

Making no answer this time, the boy hulked his surly way toward the ancient, flat-topped tomb, the granite slab of which—supported on six stone pillars—bore the name "Amalfi Briggs."

"Not there, sir!" exclaimed the captain sternly. "Have you no respect for either dead or living? Here on this bench beside me! Sit down, I tell you!"

Hal slouched down beside his grandfather, his huge shoulders sagging. A strange resemblance grew visible between these two—young man and old; black-haired and white.

"Well, now what is it?" demanded Hal with an oblique glance.

"The first thing, sir, is that I'm going to be obeyed, without question and without any back talk. I never took it aboard my ships, and I'm not going to stand any impertinence. I'm an old man, but I'm still captain of Snug Harbor. As long as there's a breath of air in my lungs or a drop of blood in my veins, I'm going to give orders there; and those that don't like them will have to sail with some other skipper. Do you understand *that*?"

"Yes, sir," answered the boy, more subdued in tone. This new note of his grandfather's told him real business was up-wind.

"Very well, then. That's understood," continued Alpheus, grimly. "You are subordinate to me. That point ought never to have been raised at all, and with a right-minded grandson it never would have been. But since you've shown yourself rebellious, it's got to be. I'm master, and you're man. Don't ever forget that, sir. If you do, into the small boat you go, and away; and, once you've gone, there's no Jacob's-ladder down the side for you ever again!"

"All right, sir. What next?"

"Next, throw away that infernal cigarette, sir. There'll be no cigarettes smoked here in presence of our dead!"

"But, gramp, you've been smoking that rank old pipe here!"

The cigarette, dashed from Hal's mouth, would have burned a hole in the white flannel trousers had not Hal swiftly brushed its fire away. Hal's eyes glowered with swift anger, but he held his tongue. The captain began again:

"Where have you been, sir?"

"Been? Why—nowhere—just taking a walk with Laura. That's all."

"H-m! Why didn't you come back with her?"

"She—got mad at something, and—"

Hal's face grew ugly. With savage eyes he regarded the old man.

"Mad at what? What did you say to her?"

"Nothing, gramp, so help me! She got jealous about another girl in Boston, that's all."

"Very well, sir. I hope that *is* all. If you've been lying to me, or if you've hurt one hair of that girl's head, it'll be a bad day for you, sir! Now then, listen to me! You've got me into shoal waters, on a lee shore, with your evil ways. Yes, and you've got yourself there, too. I've been to see Squire Bean this morning, on account of your assault on Fergus McLaughlin."

"Assault, nothing! That was a fair fight, and I trimmed him."

"Legally, it's assault and battery. Do you know how much it's going to cost me to keep you out of court and clear the name of Briggs? Cash money, sir. Money that would have been yours later, but that I've got to take out of my safe now because of your evil doings?"

"Out of the safe?" asked Hal, his thoughts diverted into a new channel. He was going to add: "I thought you kept your money in the Endicutt National." But he nipped the words before they could escape him. The captain, too wrought up to notice the gleam in his grandson's eyes or the evil portent of the question, repeated:

"Do you know how much it's going to cost me, sir?"

"Search *me!*"

"Two hundred and fifty dollars, sir."

"You're kidding!"

"That will do, sir, for that kind of language in hearing of our family dead!"

"Excuse me, gramp—I forgot myself!" Hal apologized, feigning contrition. "You don't mean to tell me McLaughlin has the nerve to ask that much—and can collect it?"

"He asked five hundred, but Dr. Filhiol's help reduced the claim. I've agreed to pay. That's a hard blow to me, Hal, but there's far worse. I got a letter from the college this morning that carried away all canvas. It brought me heavy, bad news, Hal!"

"I thought so," said Hal moodily, his eyes fixed on the close-trimmed grass. "It was bound to come! I'm fired from college!"

"And yet you went gallivanting off with Laura, and never even reported it to me!"

"I knew you'd find it out soon enough. Yes, I'm on the shelf with the rest of the canned goods!"

"Dishonorably discharged from the service, sir! And for what cause?"

"How do *I* know what that sour old pill, Travers, has framed up on me?" demanded Hal angrily. "He's the kind of guy that would make murder out of killing a mosquito. If a fellow takes a single drink, or looks at a skirt—a girl, I mean—he's ready to chop his head off!"

"Is, eh?" demanded the old captain sternly. "So you deny having been drunk and disorderly, having committed an assault on a proctor, having stolen the money I sent you for your bill, and having cheated in examinations? Here in this place of solemn memories you deny all that?"

"I—I—" Hal began, but the tale of his misdemeanors was too circumstantial for even his brazen effrontery.

"You deny it, sir?"

"Oh, what's the use, gramp?" Hal angrily flung at him. "Everything's framed up against me! I'm sick of the whole thing, anyhow. College is a frost. I never fell for it at all. You tried to wish it on me, when everything I wanted in the world was to go to sea. It's all true. Let it go at that!"

"So then, sir, I still have a heavy bill at college to pay, besides the disgrace of your discharge?"

"Oh, I suppose so! I'm fired. Glad I *am*! Glad I'm done with the whole damned business!"

"Sir! Mind your tongue!"

"I'm glad, I tell you!" The boy's face seemed burning with interior fires, suddenly enkindled. "I quit everything. Give me a boat, gramp—anything that'll sail—a twenty-five footer, and let me go! I don't ask you for a dollar. All I ask is a boat. Give me that, and I swear to God I'll never trouble you again!"

"A boat, Hal? What do you mean, sir?" Startled, the captain peered at him.

"Oh, God!" Hal cried with sudden passion. "A boat—that's all I want now! I'm dying here! I was dying in college, choking to death by inches!" He stood up, raised his head, and flung his arms towards the sea. He cried from his black heart's depths:

"Let me go! Oh, let me go, let me go!"

"Go? Go where?"

"Lord, how do *I* know? All I want is to go somewhere, away from here. This place is cursed! I'm cursed here, and so are you, as long as I'm around!"

"Cursed, Hal?" whispered the captain, tensely. "What gives you that idea?"

"I know it! This village bounded on one side by nothing and on the other by a graveyard—I can't stand it, and I won't! Let me go somewhere, anywhere, out to sea, where it's calling me out over beyond *there*!" He gestured mightily at the lure of the horizon. "Let me go out past the Silken Sea, beyond the Back of the Wind!"

Panting a little he grew silent, with clenched fists, face flushed and veins swollen on neck and brow. The old man, staring, shivered at sound of the strange Malay words, now suddenly spoken again after half a century—words that echoed ghostlike in the empty chambers of the past. He peered at Hal, as at an apparition. His face, pale under its weather-beaten tan, drew into lines of anguish.

"Let me go!" the boy flung at him again. "You've got to let me go!"

"Sit down, sir!" the captain made shift to answer. "This is sheer lunacy. What, sir? You want to give up your career, your family, everything? You want to take a small boat and go sailing off into nowhere? Why, sir, Danvers

Asylum is the place for you. No more such talk, sir; not another word!"

"I don't care what you say, I'm going, anyhow," Hal defied him. "I'm not going to rot in this dump. It's no place for a live man, and you know it!"

"You've got no money to be buying boats, Hal! No, nor no skipper's papers, either. By the Judas priest, sir, but you're crazy! You'll be talking piracy next, or some such nonsense."

"I don't care what I talk," the boy retorted. "I'm sick of this! I'm through! I'm going to live, and be myself, and be—"

"You'll be a corpse or a jail-bird, if that's the course you're sailing!" the captain cut in. "This is a civilized world you're living in now."

"Civilized! My God, civilized! That's all I hear—civilized! When you were my age were *you* always civilized? Were *you* kept on dry land instead of going to sea? Were *you* buried in college, learning damned, dry rubbish?"

"Dry rubbish? Your Oriental studies dry rubbish?"

"I don't have to go to college for those! What you know of the East, did you learn it out of books? You did not! You learned it out of life! Learned it yourself, 'somewhere east of Suez.' Well, the temple-bells are calling me, too; and yet you pen me up in this crabbed little New England village, where they don't even know there *are* temple-bells! It's choking me to death, I tell you!" He caught at his throat, as if striving for air. "But you don't understand. You're old now, and you've 'put it all behind you, long ago and far away,' and now you ask me to be civilized!"

"You mean to tell me, sir," the captain asked, his voice trembling, "that you'd abandon me, after the way I've worked for you? You'd abandon the family and the home? You'd leave that good, pure girl, Laura, just for a whim like this? I appeal to you, my boy, in the name of the family—"

"It's no use, grandfather. You've got to let me go!" Unmoved he heard the old man plead:

"Have you no love for me, then? I'm in my declining years. Without you what would be left? I've lived for you, Hal, and in the hope of what you'd be some day. I've hoped you'd marry Laura—I've dreamed of grandchildren, of new light in the sunset that's guiding me to the western harbor. I've wanted nothing but to give the end of my life to you and for you, Hal—nothing but that!" In the captain's eyes gleamed a tear. Hal, noting it, felt secret scorn and mockery. "I'm willing to overlook everything that's past and give you a fresh start. God knows, I'd gladly lay down my life for you! Because, Hal—you know I love you, boy!"

Hal glanced appraisingly at the entreating old figure on the bench, at the white head, the tear-blurred eyes, the trembling outstretched hands. To what point, he wondered with sinister calculation, could he turn this blind affection to his own uses? He kept a moment's silence, then said in a tone that skilfully simulated humilitude:

"I suppose I *am* a fool to have such thoughts, after all. What is it you want me to do?"

"First, I want you to get off the lee shore. I'll pay your debts, Hal, and clear you. There are other colleges, and as for McLaughlin, the money and apology will satisfy him."

"Apology? What apology?"

"Oh, he demands an apology from you, you understand?"

"He does, eh? Like—h-m! Well, I suppose I can do that." Hal kept his lying tongue to the deception now essential to the success of his plans.

"Finely spoken, sir, and like a man!" exclaimed Captain Briggs, with sudden joy and hope. "I knew you'd come to it. You're sound at heart, boy— sound as old oak. You're a Briggs, after all!"

"When do I have to make this apology?" asked Hal, with a searching look. "Not right away?"

"No. I'm going to pay the money this afternoon. In a day or two you can go aboard the schooner—"

"The schooner? You mean I've got to see him *there*?"

"Well, yes. You see, he insists on the apology where the assault was done. You're to give it in front of all the crew. I know that'll be hard sailing, against stiff winds of pride, but you'll come through. You'll prove yourself a man, for your own sake as well as Laura's and mine, won't you?"

Hal's fists were clenched tight as he answered:

"Yes, of course. I'll go through." His eyes were the eyes of murder, but the old captain saw only his boy coming back to him again, dutiful and ready for a new start in life. "I'll do it, sir. Count on me!"

"Your hand, sir!"

The captain's hand met his grandson's in a grip that, on one side, was all confidence and love; on the other, abysmal treachery and wickedness. Hal said as the grasp loosened:

"I'm asking only one little favor of you."

"What's that, boy?"

"Till this thing is all settled, let's not talk about it any more. No more than is strictly necessary. Please don't discuss it with the doctor, or with Ezra!"

"Ezra knows nothing. The doctor may talk a little, but I'll discourage it. From now on, Hal, there'll be very little said."

"If you see Laura—"

"Not a word to her. And from now on, Hal, you're going to make amends for what you've done, and live it down, and prove yourself a man?"

"Why, sure!"

"You mean that, boy?"

"Of course I mean it! What shall I swear it on? The blue-throated Mahadeo of the Hindus, or Vishnu the Destroyer, or Ratna Mutnu Manikam, the Malay Great God of Death? All three, if you say so!"

The captain shivered again, as if the cold breath of ghosts from far, terrible graves had suddenly blown upon him.

"I wish you wouldn't talk that way, Hal," said he tremulously. "Just give me your word of honor. Will you?"

"Yes, sir!"

"As a gentleman?"

"As a 'gentleman—unafraid!'"

Captain Briggs got up from the bench among the tombs and put his tired old arm through the strong, vigorous one of Hal, with a patriarchal affection of great nobility.

"Come, boy!" said he, happy with new hopes. "Come, we must be getting under way for Snug Haven—for the little home you're going to be so worthy of and make so happy. The home where, some of these fine days, I know you'll bring Laura to comfort and rejoice me. Come, boy, now let's be going down the hill!"

Together he and Hal made their way toward the gate in the old stone wall, warm in the sunlight of June.

A smile was on the captain's time-worn face, a smile of joy and peace. Hal was smiling, too, but with mockery and craft and scorn.

"That's the time I handed it out right and stalled him proper!" he was thinking as they started down the winding path amid the sumacs and wild roses. "He's easy, gramp is—a cinch! Getting moldy in the attic. He'll fall for anything. Now, if Laura'd only been as easy! If she *had*—"

Heavily, but still smiling, the old man leaned upon Hal's arm, finding comfort in the strength of the lusty young scion of the family which, save for this one hope, must perish.

"God has been very good to me, after all!" the captain thought as they went down the hill. "I feared God was going to punish me; but, after all, He has been kind! 'My cup runneth over—He leadeth me beside the still waters,' at last, after so many stormy seas! Sunset of life is bringing peace—and somewhere my Pilot's waiting to tell me I have paid my debt and that I'm entering port with a clean log!"

And Hal? What was Hal thinking now?

"Cinch is no name for it! The old man's called off all rough-house for a day or two. One day's enough. Just twenty-four hours. That's all—that's all I need!"

CHAPTER XXXI

THE SAFE

Though a freshening east wind was now beginning to add a raw salt tang to the air, troubled by a louder suspiration of surf, and though the fluttering of the poplar-leaves, which now had begun to show their silvery undersides, predicted rain, all was bright sunshine in the old man's heart.

The drifting clouds in no wise lessened the light for Captain Briggs. Nodding flower and piping bird, grumbling bee and brisk, varnished cricket in the path all bore him messages of cheer. His blue eyes mirrored joy. For, after all that he had suffered and feared, lo! here was Hal come back to him again, repentant, dutiful and kind.

"God is being very good to me after all," the old captain kept thinking. "'His mercy endureth forever, and He is very, very good!'"

Dr. Filhiol, sitting at the window of his room, up-stairs, watched the captain and Hal with narrowed eyes that harbored suspicion. His lips drew tight, but he uttered no word. Hal, glancing up, met his look with instinctive defiance. Boldness and challenge leaped into his eyes. Filhiol understood his threat:

"Keep yourself out of this or take all consequences!"

And again the thought came to the doctor:

"What wouldn't I give to have you for a patient of mine? Just for one hour!"

The captain and Hal disappeared 'round the ell, in which Filhiol had his room; but even after he had lost them to sight, he sensed the fatuous self-deception of the old man and the cruel baseness of the young one. Hal's overstrained effort at good fellowship grated on the doctor's nerves with a note as false as his forced smile. He longed to warn the captain—and yet! How could he make Briggs credit his suspicions? Impossible, he realized.

"Poor captain!" he murmured. "Poor old captain!" And so he sat there, troubled and very sad.

He heard their feet on the porch, then heard Hal coming up-stairs, alone. Along the passageway went Hal, muttering something unintelligible. Presently he returned down-stairs again and went into the yard. Filhiol swung his blinds shut. Much as he hated to play the spy, instinct told he must.

Hal now had his pipe, and carried books and paper. With these he sat down on the rustic seat that encircled one of the captain's big elms—a seat before which a table had been built, for *al fresco* meals, or study. He opened one of the books and began writing busily, while smoke curled on the breeze now growing damp and raw. Even the doctor could not but admit Hal made an attractive figure in his white flannels.

"Pure camouflage, that study is," pondered the doctor. "That smile augurs no good." Down-stairs he heard Briggs moving about, and pity welled again. "This is bad, bad. There's something in the wind, *I* know. Tss-tss-tss! What a wicked, cruel shame!"

Down in the cabin, Captain Briggs's appearance quite belied the doctor's pity. Every line of his venerable face showed deep content. In his eyes lay beatitude.

"Thank God, the boy's true-blue, after all!" he murmured. "Just a little wild, perhaps, but he's a Briggs—he's sound metal at the core. Thank God for that!"

He opened the top drawer of his desk, took out a little slip of paper that helped refresh his memory, and approached the safe. Right, left, he turned the knob, as the combination on the paper bade him; then he swung open the doors, and pulled out a little drawer.

"Cap'n Briggs, sir!"

At sound of Ezra's voice in the doorway, he started almost guiltily.

"Well, what is it?"

"Anythin' you're wantin' down to Dudley's store, sir?"

"No, Ezra." The captain's answer seemed uneasy. Under the sharp boring of Ezra's steely eyes, he quailed. "No, there's nothing."

"All right, cap'n!" The old cook remained a moment, observing. Then with the familiarity of long years, he queried:

"Takin' money again, be you? Whistlin' whales, cap'n, that won't do!"

"Ezra! What d'you mean, sir!"

"You know, cap'n, we're gittin' mighty nigh the bottom o' the locker."

"You're sailing a bit wide, Ezra!"

"Mebbe, sir." The honest old fellow's voice expressed deep anxiety. "But you an' me is cap'n an' mate o' this here clipper, an' money's money."

The voices drifting out the open window brought Hal's head up, listening.

172

The doctor, peering through the blinds, saw him hesitate a moment, peer 'round, then cross the lawn to where, screened by the thick clump of lilac-bushes, he could peek into the room.

"Money's money, cap'n," repeated Ezra. "We hadn't oughta let it go too fast."

"There's lots of better things in this world than money, Ezra," said the captain, strangely ill at ease.

"Mebbe, sir, but it takes money to buy 'em," the cook retorted. "I ain't a two-dollar-worry man fer a one-dollar loss, but still I know a dollar's a good little friend."

"Happiness is better," affirmed the captain. "What I'm going to spend this money for now will bring me happiness. Better than all the money in the world, is being contented with your lot."

"Yes, sir, if it's a lot of money, or a corner lot in a live town. *I* think there's six things to make a man happy. One is a good cook an' the other five is cash. However, fur be it from me to argy with you. I got to clear fer Dudley's, or there wun't be no dinner."

Ezra withdrew.

"It's that damn McLaughlin, I betcha," he pondered. "I got an intuition the cap'n's got to pay him heavy. Intuition's a guess, when it comes out right; an' I'll bet a schooner to a saucepan I'm right this time. If I was half the man I used to be, it wouldn't be money McLaughlin'd be gittin', but *this!*" Menacingly, he doubled his fist.

Captain Briggs took from the safe a packet of bills and counted off four hundred dollars. This money he put into his wallet. Hal watched every move; while above, from behind the blinds, Dr. Filhiol observed him with profound attention.

"We *are* getting a bit low in the treasury," admitted the captain, inspecting the remainder of the cash. "Only a matter of seven hundred and fifty left, to stand us till January. A bit low, but we'll manage some way or other. Sail close to the wind, and make it. After all, what's a little money when the boy's whole life is at stake?"

He put the remaining bills back and closed the safe. To the desk he walked, dropped the combination into it and shut it, tight. Silently Hal slid back to his seat under the elm, and once more set himself to writing.

Filhiol peered down at him with animosity.

"A nice little treatment of strychnine or *curaré* might make a proper man of you, you brute," he muttered, "but, by the living Lord, I don't think anything else could!"

CHAPTER XXXII

THE READING OF THE CURSE

The kitchen door slammed. Ezra, turning the corner of the house, paused to gaze with admiration at Hal.

"Hello, Master Hal, sir," said he. "Always studyin', ain't you?" Voice and expression alike showed intense pride. Above, Filhiol bent an ear of keenest attention. "Ain't many young fellers in this town would be workin' over books, when there's petticoats in sight."

"You don't approve of the girls, eh?" asked Hal with a smile. A smile of the lips alone, not of the eyes.

"No, sir, I don't," answered Ezra with resentment—for once upon a time a woman had misused him, and the wound had never healed. "They ain't what I call good reliable craft, sir. Contrary at the wheel, an' their rig costs more 'n what their hull's wu'th. No, sir, I ain't overly fond of 'em."

"Your judgment's not valid," said Hal. He seemed peculiarly expansive, as if for some reason of his own he wanted to win Ezra to still greater affection. "What do *you* know about women, an old bach like you?"

"I know!" affirmed Ezra, coming over the lawn to the table. "Men are like nails—when they're drove crooked, they're usually drove so by a woman. Women can make a fool of almost any man, ef nature don't git a start on 'em."

Hal laughed. A certain malevolent content seemed radiating from him. Lazily he leaned back, and drew at his pipe. "Right or wrong, you've certainly got definite opinions. You know your own mind. You believe in a man knowing himself, don't you?"

"Ef some men knowed themselves they'd be ashamed o' the acquaintance," opined Ezra. "An' most women would. No, sir, I don't take no stock in 'em. There ain't nothin' certain about love but the uncertainty. Women ain't satisfied with the milk o' human kindness. They want all the cream. What they expect is a sealskin livin' on a mushrat salary. Love's a kind of paralysis—kind of a stroke, like. Sometimes it's only on one side an' there's hope. But ef it gits on both sides, it's hopeless."

"Love makes the world go 'round, Ezra!"

"Like Tophet! It only makes folks' heads spin, an' they *think* the world's goin' 'round, that's all. Nobody knows the value of a gold-mine or a woman, but millions o' men has went busted, tryin' to find out! Not fer me, this here lovin', sir," Ezra continued with eloquence. "I never yet see a matrimonial match struck but what somebody got burned. Marriage is the end o' trouble, as the feller says—but which end? I ask you!"

"You needn't ask *me*, Ezra; I'm no authority on women. There's a nice little proverb in this book, though, that you ought to know."

"What's that, Master Hal?"

"Here, I'll find it for you." Hal turned a few pages, paused, and read: "'*Bounga sedap dipakey, layou dibouang.*'"

"Sufferin' snails! What *is* that stuff, anyhow? Heathen Chinee?"

"That's Malay, Ezra," Hal condescended. The doctor, listening, felt a strange little shiver, as of some reminiscent fear from the vague long-ago. Those words, last heard at Batu Kawan, fifty years before, now of a sudden rose to him like specters of great evil. His attention strained itself as Hal went on:

"That's a favorite Malay proverb, and it means: 'While the flower is pleasing to man, he wears it. When it fades, he throws it away.'"

"Meanin' a woman, o' course? Uhuh! *I* see. Well, them heathens has it pretty doggone nigh correct, at that, ain't they? So that there is Malay, is it? All them twisty-wisty whirligigs? An' you can read it same as if it was a real language?"

"It *is* a real language, Ezra, and a very beautiful one. I love it. You don't know how much!" A tone of real sincerity crept into the false camaraderie of Hal's voice. Filhiol shook his head. Vague, incomprehensible influences seemed reaching out from the vapors of the Orient, fingering their way into the very heart of this trim New England garden, in this year of grace, 1918. The doctor suddenly felt cold. He crouched a little closer toward the blinds.

"Holy halibut, Master Hal!" exclaimed Ezra in an awed tone, peering at the book. "What a head you got on you, sir! Fuller o' brains than an old Bedford whaler is o' rats!"

"You flatter me, Ezra. Think so, do you?"

"I know so! Ef I'd had your peak I wouldn't of walloped pots in a galley all my natural. But I wan't pervided good. My mind's like a pint o' rum in a hogshead—kind of broad, but not very deep. It's sort of a phonograph mind— makes me talk a lot, but don't make me say nothin' original. So that's Malay, is it? Well, it's too numerous fer *me*. There's only one kind o' Malay I know about, an' that's my hens. They may lay, an' then again they may not. That's grammatical. But this here wiggly printin'—no, no, it don't look reasonable. My eye, what a head! Read some more, will you?"

"Certainly, if you like it," said Hal, strangely obliging. "Here's something I've been translating, in the line of cursing. They're great people to curse you, the Malays are, if you cross them. Their whole lives are full of vengeance—that's what makes them so interesting. Nothing weak, forgiving or mushy about *them*!" He picked up the paper he had been writing on, and cast his eyes over it, while Ezra looked down at him with fondly indulgent pride. "Here is part of the black curse of Vishnu."

"Who's he?"

"One of their gods. The most avenging one of the lot," explained Hal. The doctor, crouching behind the blinds, shivered.

"Gods, eh? What's this Vishnu feller like?" asked Ezra, with a touch of uneasiness. "Horns an' a tail?"

"No. He's got several forms, but the one they seem most afraid of is a kind of great, blind face up in the sky. A face that—even though it's blind—can watch a guilty man all his life, wherever he goes, and ruin him, crucify him, bring him to destruction, and laugh at him as he's dying."

"*Brrr!*" said Ezra. He seemed to feel something of the same cold that had struck to the doctor's heart—a greater cold than could be accounted for by the veiling of the sun behind the clouds now driving in from the sea, or by the kelp-rank mists gathering along the shore. "You make me feel all creepylike. You're wastin' your time on such stuff, Master Hal, same as a man is when he's squeezing a bad lemon or an old maid. None o' that cursin' stuff fer me!"

"Yes, yes, you've got to listen to it!" insisted Hal maliciously. Ezra's trepidation afforded him great enjoyment. "Here's the way it goes:

"'The curse of Vishnu, the great black curse, can never end unsatisfied when it has once been laid upon a human head. Beyond the land it carries, and beyond the sea, beyond the farthest sea unsailed. Beyond the day, the month, the year, it carries; and even though the accursèd one flee forever, in some far place and on some far day it will fall on him or his!'"

"Great grampus!" cried the old man, retreating a little with wide eyes. "That's *some* cussin', all right!"

The doctor sensed an insistent fear that would not be denied. What if old Captain Briggs should overhear this colloquy? What if Ezra should repeat to him these words that, now arising from the past, echoed with ominous purport? At realization of possible consequences, Filhiol's heart contracted painfully.

"Damn you, Hal!" thought he, peering out through the blinds. "Damn you and your Malay books. If any harm comes to the captain, through you, look out!"

"Some awful cussin'," Ezra repeated. "I wouldn't want to have no sech cuss as that rove onta *me*! You b'lieve that stuff, do ye?"

"Who am I to disprove it?"

"Ain't there no way to kedge off, ef you're grounded on a cuss like that?"

"Only one, Ezra, according to this book."

"What way's that?"

"Well," and Hal once more glanced at the paper, "well, this is what the book says:

"'The curse must be fulfilled, to the last breath, for by Shiva and the Trimurthi, what is written is written. But if he through whom the curse descendeth on another is stricken to horror and to death, then the Almighty Vishnu, merciful, closes that page. And he who through another's sin was cursed, is cleansed. Thus may the curse be fulfilled. But always one of two must die. *Tuan Allah poonia krajah!* It is the work of the Almighty One! One of two must die!'"

"Gosh!" ejaculated Ezra. "I reckon that'll be about enough fer me, Master Hal. Awful, ain't it?"

"Don't like Malay, after all?" laughed Hal.

"Can't say as I'm pinin' fer it. But you got some head on you, to read it off like that. I s'pose it's all right in its way, but I don't relish it overly, as the feller said when he spilled sugar on his oysters. Well," and he glanced at the lowering clouds and the indrifting sea-fog that with the characteristic suddenness of the north shore had already begun to throw its chilly blanket over the world, "well, this ain't gittin' to Dudley's store, is it? Lord, sir, what a head you got on you!"

With admiring ejaculations the old man started down the path once more. The doctor, filled with stern thoughts, remained watching Hal, who had now gone back to his writing.

"What a fatality!" pondered the doctor, unable to suppress a certain superstitious dread. Not all his scientific training could quite overcome the deep-rooted superstition that lies in the bottom of every human heart. "The black curse of Vishnu again, with this new feature: '*One of two must die!*' What the devil does all this mean now?"

A crawling sensation manifested itself along his spine. Silent shapes seemed standing behind him in the corners of the room darkened by the closing of the blinds. Trained thinker though he was, he could not shake off this feeling, but remained crouching at the window, a prey to inexplicable fear. The words Hal had spoken, echoing along dim corridors of the past, still seemed vibrating in his heart with unaccustomed pain.

"Nonsense!" he growled at last. "It's all nonsense—nothing but a sheer coincidence!" He tried to put the words away, but still they sounded in his ears: "*One of two must die! Always one of two must die!*"

Another thought, piercing him, brought him up standing with clenched fists.

"If the captain ever gets hold of that idea, what then? If he ever does —*what then?*"

Brooding he paced up and down the room, limping painfully, for without his cane he could hardly walk even a few steps. And almost at once his fear curdled into hate against the sleek, white-flanneled fellow, sitting there under the elm, calmly translating words that might mean agony and death to the old grandsire.

Filhiol's mind became confused. He knew not what to think, nor yet which way to turn. What events impended? He recalled the way Hal had peered stealthily into the cabin, and how he had then slid back to his seat under the elm. Was Hal plotting some new infamy? What could be done to warn the captain, to make that blindly loyal heart accept the truth and act upon it?

Tentacles of some terrible thing seemed enmeshing both Filhiol and the old captain—some catastrophe, looming black, impossible to thrust aside. But it was not of himself that Filhiol was thinking. Only the image of the captain, trusting, confident, arose before him.

Filhiol set his teeth in a grimace of hate against the figure at work out there under the big elm.

"I've probably done my share of evil in this world," thought he, "but I could wipe it all out with one supremely good action. If I could put an end to *you*—"

All unconscious, Hal continued at his work. As he wrote, he smiled a little. The smile was sinister and hard.

What thoughts did it reflect?

CHAPTER XXXIII

ROBBERY

Dinner brought the four men together: Filhiol glum and dour, Hal in his most charming mood, the captain expansive with new-found happiness, and old Ezra bubbling with aphorisms.

Silent and brooding, Filhiol turned the situation in his mind, asking himself a hundred times what he could do to avert catastrophe impending.

Decision, after dinner, crystallized into action. First of all the doctor interviewed Ezra in the galley, and from him extracted a binding promise to make no mention before Captain Briggs, of anything concerning Malay life, or books, or curses, or whatever.

"I can't explain now, Ezra," said he, "but it's most important. As a physician, I prohibit your speaking of these matters here. You understand?"

"Yes, sir. I dunno's I'm over an' above keen to obey you, sir, but ef it's fer the cap'n's good, that's enough fer me."

"It *is* for the captain's good, decidedly!" affirmed the doctor, and left old Ezra to think it over. One source of danger, he now felt confident, had been dammed up.

Ezra was still thinking it over when the captain told him to harness Sea Lawyer for a drive to Endicutt. In spite of the fine, drifting rain that had set in, Briggs was determined to go, for until McLaughlin's claim and the college bill had been settled, the money he had taken from the safe for that purpose was burning in his pocket. He insisted on going quite alone, despite protests from Filhiol and Ezra. Even though all the sunlight had died from the darkening sky, it seemed still shining in the old man's eyes as he drove off to pay the hard-saved money that now—so he believed—would put Hal on the upward road once more.

"Hal," said the doctor, when the old captain had slowly jogged out of sight, "I've got a few words to say to you, out on the porch. Give me five minutes, please?"

"Why, surest thing you know! Just let me get my pipe, and I'll be with you."

He seemed all engaging candor—just a big, powerful fellow, open of face and manner, good-humored and without guile. As he rejoined the doctor,

Filhiol wondered whether, after all, his analysis might not be wrong. But no, no. Something at the back of Hal's blue-eyed look, something arrogant with power, something untamed, atavistic, looked out through even the most direct glance. Filhiol knew that he was dealing with no ordinary force. And, carefully choosing his words, he said:

"Listen, young man. I'm going to ask a favor of you."

"My grandfather's guest has only to ask, and it's done," smiled Hal, as he settled himself in one of the rockers, and hoisted his white-shod feet to the porch-rail.

"You know, Hal," the doctor commenced, "your grandfather has been greatly distressed about your conduct."

"Well, and what then?" asked Hal, his eyes clouding.

"He has a strange idea that some of the misdeeds of his youth, long since atoned for, are being visited upon you, and that he's responsible for—h-m—certain irregularities of your conduct."

"Yes?"

"In short, he half believes a curse is resting on you, because of him. It would be most deplorable to let that belief receive corroboration from any source, as for example, from any of your Oriental studies."

Hal shot a keen glance at the old man. This was indeed getting under the hide, with a vengeance. The glance showed fear, too. Had Filhiol, then, been spying on him? Had he, by any chance, seen him peeking in at the window, through the lilac-bushes? Hal's evil temper began to stir, and with it a very lively apprehension.

"What are you driving at, anyhow?" demanded he, sullenly.

"I want you to keep your Oriental stuff completely in the background for a while. Not to talk with him about it, and especially to avoid all those fantastic curses."

"Oh, is that all?" asked Hal, relieved. "Well, that's easy."

The doctor sighed with relief.

"That makes me feel a bit better," said he. "We've got to do our best to protect the captain against himself. I know you'll coöperate with me to keep him out of any possible trouble."

"Surest thing you know, doctor!" exclaimed Hal. "I've been a fool and worse, I know, but that's all over. I've taken a fresh start that will help me travel far. You'll see."

He put out his hand.

"Let's shake on it," he smiled winningly.

A moment their eyes met. Then Filhiol said:

"I'm sorry if I've misjudged you. Let's just forget it. You don't know how much relieved I feel."

"I feel better, too," said Hal. "Things are going to take a decidedly new turn."

"It's fine to hear you say that!" exclaimed the doctor, almost convinced that at last he had struck a human stratum in the boy's heart. "I can take my after-dinner nap with a great deal easier mind now. Good-by."

He limped into the house, not perhaps fully confident of Hal, but at any rate more inclined to believe him amenable to reason. Hal, peering after him, whispered a terrific blasphemy under his breath.

"You damned buttinsky!" he growled, black with passion. "There's something coming to you, too. Something you'll get, by God, or I'm no man!"

He got up, and—silently in his rubber-soled shoes—walked around the porch to the end of it, then stepped down into the grass and crept along by the house. Under the doctor's window he stood, listening acutely. Just what the doctor was doing he must by all means know. Ezra was safe enough. From the kitchen drifted song:

> "Rolling Rio,
> To my rolling Rio Grande!
> Hooray, you rolling Rio!
> So fare ye well, my bonny young girls,
> For I'm bound to the Rio Grande!"

Hal nodded as he heard the springs of the doctor's bed creak, and knew the old man had really laid down for his mid-afternoon nap.

"It's working fine," said he. "Gramp's gone, Ezra's good for half an hour on 'Rio Grande,' and the doc's turned in. Looks like a curse was sticking to me, doesn't it? Not much! Nothing like that can stick to *me*!"

At his feet two or three ants were busy with a grasshopper's leg. Hal smeared them out with a dab of his sole.

"That's the way to do with people that get in your way," he muttered. "Just like that!"

He slouched back to the porch. The resemblance to what Captain Briggs had been in the old days seemed wonderfully striking at just this moment.

Same hang of heavy shoulders, same set of jaw; scowl quite a simulacrum of the other, and even the dark glowering of the eyes almost what once had been.

As Hal Briggs lithely stepped on to the porch again he formed how wonderful an image of that other man who, half a century ago, had swung the poisoned kris upon the decks of the *Silver Fleece*, and, smeared with blood, had hewn his way against all opposition to his will!

"Afraid of an old Malay curse!" sneered Hal. "Poor, piffling fool! Why, Filhiol's loose in the dome, and grandpop's no better. They're a couple of children—ought to be shoved into the nursery. And they think they're going to dictate to *me*?"

He paused a moment at the front door to listen. No sound from within indicated any danger.

"Think they're going to keep me in this graveyard burg!" he gibed. "And stop my having that girl! Well, they've got another think coming. She's mine, that young porpoise. She's mine!"

Into the cabin he made his way, noiselessly, closed the hall door and smiled with exultation.

He needed but a moment to reach the desk, take out the little slip of paper on which the captain had written the combination, and go to the safe.

A few turns of the knob, and the iron door swung wide. Open came the money-compartment. With exultant hands, filled with triumph and evil pride, Hal caught up the sheaf of bills there, quickly counted off five hundred dollars, took a couple more bills for good luck, crammed the money into his pocket, and replaced the pitifully small remnant in the compartment.

"Sorry I've got to leave any," he reflected, "but it'll be safer. It may keep him from noticing. The old man wouldn't let me have a boat, eh? And Laura turned me down, did she? Well now, we'll soon see about all that!"

"Master Hal, sir! What *in* the name o' Tophet are you up to?"

The sound of Ezra's voice swung Hal sharp around. So intent had he been that he had quite failed to notice the cessation of the old cook's chantey. A moment, Hal's eyes, staring, met those of the astonished servitor. Ominous silence filled the room.

"Why, Master Hal!" Ezra quavered. "You—ain't—"

"You sneaking spy!" Hal growled at him, even in his rage and panic careful to keep his voice low, lest he awake the doctor, abovestairs. Toward the old man he advanced, with rowdy oaths of the fo'cs'le.

Ezra stood his ground.

"*I* ain't no spy, Master Hal," he exclaimed, tremblingly. "But I come into the dinin'-saloon, here, an' couldn't help seein'. Tell me it ain't so, Master Hal! Tell me you ain't sunk so low as to be robbin' your own grandpa, while he's to town in all this rain, settlin' up things fer you! Not that, Master Hal—not that!"

"Ezra, you damn son-of-a-sea-cook!" snarled Hal, his face the face of murder. "You call me a thief again, and so help me but I'll wring your neck!" His hand caught Ezra by the throat and closed in a gorilla-grip, shutting off all breath. "You didn't learn your lesson from the club last night, eh? Well, I'll teach you one now, you old gray rat! I'll shut *your* mouth, damn you!"

Viciously he shook the weak old man. Ezra clawed with impotent hands at the vise-clutch strangling him.

"It's my money, my own money, understand?" Hal spat at him. "Every penny of it's mine. He didn't want me to have it just yet, but I'm going to, and you're not going to blow on me! If you *do*—"

He loosed his hold, snatched down from its supporting hooks the Malay kris, and with it gripped in hand confronted the trembling, half-fainting cook.

"See this, Ezra?" And Hal shook the envenomed blade before the poor old fellow's horror-smitten eyes.

"Master—Master Hal!"

"If you breathe so much as one syllable to the captain, I'll split you with this knife, as sure as I'm a foot high! What? Butting in on me, in my own house, are you? Like hell! Take a slant at this knife here, and see how you'd like it through your guts!"

He raised it as if to strike. Ezra cowered, shrinking with the imminent terror of death.

"Master Hal, oh, fer God's sake, now—"

"You're going to keep your jaw-tackle quiet, are you, to the captain?"

"I—I—"

Wickedly Hal slashed at him. Ezra opened his mouth, no doubt to cry aloud, but Hal clapped a sinewed hand over it, and slammed him back against the wall.

"Not a word more!" he commanded, and released the trembling old man. "I've got to turn you loose, Ezra, but if you double-cross me, so help me God —"

"You callin' on God, Master Hal?" quavered Ezra. "You, with your heathen curses an' your Malay sword, an' all the evil seed you're sowin' fer a terrible crop o' misery?"

"Shut up, you!"

"Goin' on this way, Master Hal, after you jest promised the cap'n you was goin' to begin at the bottom o' the ladder an' climb ag'in? This here ain't the bottom; this here is a deep ditch you're diggin', fur below that bottom. Oh, Master Hal," and Ezra's shaking hands went out in passionate appeal, "ef you got any love fer the memory o' your dead mother; ef you got any fer your grandpa, what's been so wonderful good to you; ef you got any little grain o' gratitude to me, fer all these long years—"

"Ezra, you bald-headed old pot-walloper, I'm going to count ten on you," Hal interrupted, terrible with rage. "If, by the end of that time you haven't sworn to keep your mouth shut about this, I'm going to kill you right here in this room! I mean that, Ezra!"

"But ef it's y'r own money, Master Hal, why should you be afeared to let him know?"

Hal struck the old man a staggering blow in the face. "You keep your voice down," he snarled. "If you wake the doctor, and he comes down here, God help the pair of you! Now, Ezra, I'm not going to trifle with you any longer. You're going to swear secrecy, and do it quick, or take the consequences!"

He turned, caught up the captain's well-thumbed Bible from the desk, and with the Bible in one hand, the poisoned kris in the other, confronted Ezra.

"Here! Lay your hand on this book, damn quick!" he ordered. "And repeat what I tell you. Quick, now; *quick!*"

The argument of the raised kris overbore Ezra's resistance. With a look of heart-breaking anguish he laid a trembling, veinous hand on the Bible.

"What is it, Master Hal?" quavered he. "What d'ye want me to say?"

"Say this: 'If I betray this secret—'"

"'If I—if I betray this secret—'"

"'May the black curse of Vishnu fall on me!'"

"'May the'—listen, Master Hal! Please now, jest one minute!"

"Ezra, say it, damn your stiff, obstinate neck! Say it, or you get the knife!"

"'May the black curse o'—o' Vishnoo fall on me!'"

185

"'And may his poisoned kris strike through my heart!'"

"No, no, sir, I can't say that!" pleaded the simple old fellow, ashen to the lips, his forehead lined with deep wrinkles of terror.

"You *will* say it, Ezra, and you'll mean it, or by the powers of darkness I'll butcher you where you stand!" menaced Hal. "And you'll say it quick, too!" Hal was nerving his hand to do cold murder. "One, two, three, four! Say it now before I cut you down! There's blood on this knife, Ezra. See the dark stains? Blood, that my grandfather put on there, fifty years ago—that's what I've heard among old sailors—put on there, because some of his men wouldn't obey him. Well, I can play the same game. What he did, I can do, and will! There'll be more blood on it, fresh blood, your blood, if you don't mind me. Five, six, seven! Say it, you obstinate cur!"

Up rose the kris again, ready to strike. Hal's eyes were glowing. His lips had drawn back, showing the gleam of white teeth.

"Keep your hand on that Bible, Ezra! Take that oath. Say it! Eight, nine, t —"

"I'll say it, Master Hal! I'll say it!" gasped the old man. "Don't kill me— *don't!*"

"Say it, then: 'May this poisoned kris strike through my heart!'"

"'M-m-may this poisoned kris—strike through—my—heart!' There now! Oh! Now I've said it. Let me go—let me go!"

"Go, and be damned to you! Get out o' here, you spying *surka-batcha*— you son-of-a-pig!"

Hal dropped the Bible back on to the desk, swung Ezra 'round, and pitched him, staggering, into the dining-saloon. Ezra dragged himself away, quaking, ghastly, to his own room, there to lock himself in. Spent, terrified, he threw himself upon his bunk, and lay there, half dead.

Well satisfied, Hal reviewed the situation.

"I guess I've kept *him* quiet for a while," he muttered. "Long enough, anyhow. I won't need much more time now."

Back to the fireplace he turned, hung up the kris again on its hooks, glanced around to assure himself he had left no traces of his robbery. He closed the door of the safe, spun the knob, and in the desk-drawer replaced the slip of paper bearing the combination.

"I guess I've fixed things so they'll hold a while now," judged he. "God, what a place—what people! Spies, all spies! They're all spying on me here.

186

And Laura's giving me the laugh, too. Maybe I won't show them all a thing or two!"

He listened a moment, and, satisfied, opened the door into the front hall. To all appearances the coast was free. He snatched a cap, jammed it upon his head, and, hunching into an old raincoat, quietly left the house.

The Airedale would have followed him, but with the menace of an upraised fist he sent it back. Through the gate he went, and turned toward the right, in the direction of Hadlock's Cove, where dwelt Jim Gordon, owner of the *Kittiwink*.

In his ears the wind, ever-rising, and the shouting of the quick-lashed surf along the rocks joined with the slash of the rain to make a chorus glad and mighty, to which his heart expanded. On and on he strode, exultant, filled with evil devisings of a mind half mad in the lusts of strength and passion. And as he went he held communion with himself:

"I'll beat 'em to it—and devil take anything that stands in my way! To hell with them—to hell with everything that goes against me!"

CHAPTER XXXIV

SELF-SACRIFICE

The rapidly increasing northeast storm, that meant so little to Hal Briggs, thoroughly drenched and chilled the old captain long before he reached home.

By the time he had navigated back to Snug Haven, he was wet to the bone, and was shivering with the drive of the gale now piling gray lines of breakers along the shore. Dr. Filhiol, his face very hard, met the old captain at the front door; while Ezra—silent, dejected, with acute misery and fear—took the ancient horse away up the puddled lane.

"This is outrageous, captain!" the doctor expostulated. "The idea of your exposing yourself this way at your age!"

"Where's Hal?" shivered the captain. "I've got to see Hal! G-g-got to tell him all his debts are paid, and he's a free man again!"

"You're hoarse as a frog, sir; you've got a thundering cold!" chided the doctor. "I order you to bed, sir, where I'll give you a stiff glass of whisky and lemon, and sweat you properly."

"Nonsense!" chattered the captain. "I'll j-j-just change my clothes, and sit by the fire, and I'll be all r-r-right. Where's Hal? I want Hal!"

"Hal? How do *I* know?" demanded Filhiol. "He's gone. Where's he bound for? No good, I'll warrant, in this storm. It shows how much *he* cares, what you do for him, the way he—"

"By the Judas priest, sir!" interrupted Briggs. "I'm not going to have anything said against Hal, now he's free. I know you're my guest, doctor, but don't drive me too far!"

"Well, I'll say no more. But now, into your bunk! There's no argument about *that*, anyhow. Bathrobe and hot water-bottle now, and a good tot of rum!"

The captain had to yield. A quarter-hour later the doctor had him safely tucked into his berth in the cabin, with whisky and lemon aboard him. "There, that's better," approved Filhiol. "You'll do now, unless you get up, and take another chill. I want you to stay right there till to-morrow at the very least. Understand me? Now, I prescribe a nap for you. And a good sweat, and by to-morrow you'll be fine as silk."

"All right, doctor," agreed Briggs, though Hal's absence troubled him sore. "There's only one thing I want you to do. Put my receipts in the safe."

"What receipts?"

"For the cash I paid Squire Bean and for the money-order I sent the college."

"Where are they?"

"In my wallet, there, in that inside coat-pocket," answered Briggs, pointing to the big blue coat hung over a chair by the fire. "The combination of the safe is in that top drawer, on a slip of paper. You can open the safe easy enough."

"All right, anything to please you," grumbled the old doctor. "Where shall I put the receipts, captain?"

"In the cash-drawer. Inner drawer, top, right."

Filhiol located the drawer and dropped the precious receipts into it. His eyes, that could still see quite plainly by the fading, gray light of the stormy late afternoon, descried a few bills in the drawer.

"It's been a terrible expense to you, captain," said he with the license of long years of acquaintanceship. "Down a bit on the cash now, eh?"

"Yes, doctor, down a bit. Plims'l-mark's under water this time. But I'm not foundering just yet. There's still seven hundred and fifty or so."

"Seven fifty?" asked the doctor, squinting. A sudden suspicion laid hold of him as he eyed the slender pile of bills. With crooked fingers he ran them over. "Why, there's not—*h-m! h-m!*" he checked himself.

"Eh? What's that, sir?" asked the captain, drowsy already.

"Nothing, sir," answered Filhiol. "I was just going to say there's not many as well fixed as you are, captain. Even though your cash *is* low, you've got a pretty comfortable place here."

"Yes, yes, it's pretty snug," sleepily assented Briggs. "And now that Hal's coming back, I'm happy. A few dollars—they don't matter, eh?"

Hastily Filhiol counted the bills. Only a matter of about two hundred and twenty-five dollars remained. As in a flash the old doctor comprehended everything.

"*Tss! Tss!*" clucked the doctor, going a shade paler. But he said no more.

He closed the safe and put the combination back into the desk-drawer. For a moment he stood leaning on his cane, peering down at the captain, who was already going to sleep. Then he shook his head, grief and rage on his face.

"God!" he was thinking. "Robbery! On top of everything else, downright robbery! This will certainly kill the old man! What black devil is in that boy anyhow? What devil out of hell?"

He paused a moment, looking with profound compassion at the tired old captain. Then he limped out of the room, and made his way to the galley, bent on having speech with Ezra.

Down the walk from the barn Ezra was at this moment coming, shoulders bent against the storm, hat-brim trickling water. The rain was now slashing viciously, in pelting ribbons of gray water that drummed on the tin roof of the kitchen and danced in spatters on the walk.

Filhiol opened the door for Ezra, who peeled off his coat, and shook his wet hands.

"Great, creepin' clams!" he puffed. "But this is some tidy wind, sir! These here Massachusetts storms can't be beat, the way they pounce. An' rain! Say! Must be a picnic somewhere nigh. Never rains like this unless there *is* one!"

The old man tried to smile, but joviality was lacking. He closed the door and came over to the stove. The doctor followed him.

"Ezra," said he, "you don't like me. No matter. You *do* like Captain Briggs, don't you?"

"That ain't a question as needs answerin'," returned Ezra, with suspicious eyes.

"I like the captain, too," continued Filhiol. "We've got to join hands to help him. And he's in very, very serious trouble now."

"Well, what is it?" The old servitor sensed what was in the wind, and braced himself to meet it.

"If it came to choosing between Hal and the captain, which would you stand by?"

"That's another question that ain't needed!" retorted Ezra defiantly.

"It's got to be answered, though. Something critical has happened, Ezra, and we've got to take the bull by the horns."

"Better take the bull by the tail, doctor. Then you can let go without hollerin' fer help."

"This is no time for joking, Ezra! Something has happened that, if the captain finds it out, will have terrible consequences. If he discovers what's happened, I can't answer for the consequences. It might even kill him, the shock might."

"Wha—what d' you mean, sir?" demanded Ezra, going white. "What *are* you gammin' about, anyhow?"

"I might as well tell you, directly. Captain Briggs has just been robbed of more than five hundred dollars."

"Robbed! No! Holy haddock! You—don't—"

"Robbed," asserted Filhiol. "More than five hundred dollars are gone from the safe, and—Hal's gone, too."

"Dr. Filhiol, sir!" exclaimed the old man passionately, but in a low voice that could not reach the cabin. "That wun't go here. You're company, I know, but there's some things that goes too doggone fur. Ef you mean to let on that Master Hal—"

"The money's gone, I tell you, and so is Hal. I know *that!*"

"Yes, an' I know Master Hal, too!" asseverated Ezra, manfully standing by his guns, not through any fear of Hal's vengeance, but only for the honor of the house and of the boy he worshipped. "Ef you mean to accuse him of bein' a *thief*, well then, me an' you has nothin' more to say. We're docked, an' crew an' cargo is discharged right now. All done!"

"Hold on, Ezra!" commanded Filhiol. "I'm not making any direct accusation. All I'm saying is that the money and Hal are both gone."

"How d' *you* know the money's gone? How come *you* to be at the cap'n's safe an' money-drawer?"

"I—why—" stammered Filhiol, taken aback. "Why, the captain had me open it, to put in some receipts, and he told me how much he thought was there. I saw he was mistaken, by more than five hundred."

"Oh, you counted the cap'n's money, did ye?" Ezra demanded boldly. "Well, that's some nerve! In case it comes to a showdown, where would *you* fit? Looks like *your* fingers might git burned, don't it?"

"Mine? What do you mean, sir?"

"Well, you was there, wa'n't ye? An' Master Hal wa'n't, that's all!" Swiftly Ezra was thinking. The loss, he knew, could not be kept from Captain Briggs. And Hal must be protected. Sudden inspiration dawned on him.

"How much d' you say is gone?" demanded he.

"Five hundred and some odd dollars."

"Yes, that's right," said the old man, nodding. "Them's the correct figgers, all right enough."

"How do *you* know?" exclaimed the doctor, staring.

"Why hadn't I ought to, when I took that there money myself?"

"*You?*"

"Me, sir! I'm the one as stole it, an' what's more, I got it now, up-stairs in my trunk!"

Silence a moment while the doctor peered at him with wrinkled brow.

"That's not true, Ezra," said he at last, meeting the old man's defiant look. "You're lying now to shield that boy!"

"Lyin', am I?" And Ezra reddened dully. "Dr. Filhiol, sir, ef you wa'n't an old man, an' hobblin' on a cane, them ain't the words you'd use to me, an' go clear!"

"I—I beg your pardon, Ezra," stammered the doctor. "I'm not saying it in a derogatory sense."

"Rogatory or hogatory, don't make a damn's odds! You called me a liar!"

"A noble liar. That kind of a lie is noble, Ezra, but very foolish. I understand you, all right. When I say you're trying to shield Hal, I've hit the mark."

"You ain't half the shot you think you be, sir! There's lots o' marksmen in this world can't even make a gun go off, an' yet they can't miss fire in the next world. You're one of 'em. I took the money, I tell ye, an' I can prove it by showin' it to you, in two minutes!"

The old man, turning, started for the stairs.

"Where are you going now?" demanded Filhiol.

"To git that there money!"

"Your own savings, no doubt? To shield Hal with?"

"The money I stole, an' don't ye fergit it neither!" retorted Ezra with a look so menacing that the doctor ventured no reply. In silence he watched the old man, wet clothes still clinging to him, plod up the stairs and disappear.

"Lord, if this isn't a tangled web," thought Filhiol, "what is? I ought never to have come. And yet I'm needed every minute, if a terrible catastrophe is to be turned aside!"

His heart contracted at thought of the inevitable shock to Captain Briggs if he should discover the theft. Could Ezra conceal it, even with his savings? And, if he could, would it not be best to let him? Would not anything be

192

preferable to having the captain's soul wrung out of him? Sudden hate against the cause of all this misery flared up in him.

"Great God!" he muttered. "If I only had that Hal for a patient, just one hour!"

The footsteps of Ezra, descending again, roused him. In Ezra's hand was gripped a roll of bills, old and tattered for the most part—a roll that counted up to some five hundred and thirty dollars, or to within about forty dollars of every cent Ezra had in the world. More than fifteen years of hard-earned savings lay in that roll. This money Ezra had hastily dug from under a lot of old clothes in his trunk. And now he shook it before the eyes of Filhiol, eager to sacrifice it.

"Is *that* proof enough fer you now, or ain't it?" Ezra exultantly demanded. "Dollar fer dollar, about, what the cap'n said had oughta be in the safe, an' ain't? Well, does that satisfy ye now?"

Filhiol had no answer. His brain was whirling. Ezra laughed in his face.

"I got *your* goat all right, old feller!" gibed he.

"Ezra," said the doctor slowly, "I don't understand this at all. I'm no detective. This is too much for me. Either you're a monumental fool or a sublime hero. Maybe both. I can't judge. All I want to do is look out for Captain Briggs. I was his medical officer in the old days. Now I seem to be back on the job again. That's all."

"Yes, an' I'm on the job, too, an' you'd better keep out o' what don't consarn ye," menaced Ezra. "Every man to his job, an' yours ain't ratin' down Master Hal an' makin' a thief of him!"

"All right, Ezra. Put the money in the safe. Whether it's yours or not, doesn't matter now. It will protect the captain's peace of mind a little longer, and that's the main thing now."

Ezra nodded. Together they went quietly into the cabin. Watchfully they observed the captain. Face to the wall, he was profoundly sleeping.

"It's all right," said Filhiol. "You can open the safe and put the money in."

Ezra advanced to it, on tiptoe. But Ezra did not open the safe. Puzzled, he stopped and whispered:

"I—doggone it, I've fergot the combination now!"

"Have, eh?" asked Filhiol with a sharp look. "Well then, all you've got to do is look at the paper."

"The—h-m!"

"Of course you know he keeps it on a paper?" said the doctor shrewdly.

"Oh, sure, sure! But just now I disremember where that paper is!"

Filhiol retreated to the dining-room, and beckoned Ezra to him.

"See here," said he in a low tone, "this game of yours is pitifully thin. Why don't you own up to the truth? Your loyalty to Hal is wonderful. The recording angel is writing it all down in his big book; but you can't fool anybody. Why, not even a child would believe you, Ezra, and how can I—a hard-shelled old man who's knocked up and down the seven seas? You know perfectly well Hal Briggs stole that money. Own up now!"

The old cook fixed a look of ire on him, and with clenched fist confronted Filhiol.

"Doctor," said he, "there's two things makes most o' the trouble in this here world. One is evil tongues, to speak ill o' folks, an' the other is evil ears, to listen. There's jest two things you can't do here—speak ill o' the cap'n, an' talk ag'in' Master Hal. Ef you do, doc—it don't signify ef you *be* old, I'll make it damn good an' hot fer you! Now, then, I've warned you proper. That's all—an' that's enough!"

"You don't understand—" the doctor was just going to retort, when a trample of feet on the front porch brought him to silence.

"There's Master Hal now!" exclaimed the old cook, with an expression of dismay. "An' the money ain't back in the safe yit—an' Master Hal's li'ble to wake the cap'n up!"

"He *mustn't* wake him up!" said Filhiol. He turned, and, hobbling on his cane, started for the front door to head him off. Too late! Already Hal had flung off his cap and, stamping wet feet, had entered the cabin. The voice of the captain sounded:

"Oh, that you, Hal? God above! but I'm glad to see you! Come here, boy, come here. I've got news for you. Great, good news!"

CHAPTER XXXV

TREACHERY

Still in his dripping raincoat, Hal approached the berth.

"Whew, but it's hot and stifling in here, gramp!" said he. He turned and opened a window, letting the damp, chill wind draw through. "There, that's better now. Well, what's the big news, eh?"

The old captain regarded him a moment, deeply moved. In the dining-room, Ezra had hastily stuffed the bills into his pocket. Now he was retreating to his galley. Filhiol, undecided what to do, did nothing; but remained in the front hall.

"What's the news?" repeated Hal. He looked disheveled, excited. "And what are *you* in bed for, this time of day?"

His voice betrayed nothing save curiosity. No sympathy softened it.

"The doctor made me turn in," Briggs explained. "I got wet through, going to town. But it was all for you, boy. So why should *I* mind?"

"For me, eh?" demanded Hal. "More trouble? Enough storm outside, without kicking up any more rows inside. Some weather, gramp! Some sailing weather, once a boat got out past the breakwater, where she could make her manners to the nor'east blow!" His tongue seemed a trifle thick, but the captain perceived nothing. "Well, gramp, what was the idea of going to town an afternoon like this?"

"To set you on the right road again, boy." The captain raised himself on one elbow, and peered at his beloved Hal. "To open up a better career for you than *I* had. No more sea-life, Hal. There's been far too much salt in our blood for generations. It's time the Briggs family came ashore. You've got better things ahead of you, now, than fighting the sea. Peel your wet coat off, Hal, and sit down. You'll take cold, I'm afraid."

"Cold, nothing! This is the kind of weather I like!"

He pulled up a chair by the berth, and flung himself down into it, hulking, rude, flushed. In the dim light old Captain Briggs did not see that telltale flush of drink. He did not note the sinister exultation in his grandson's voice. Nor did he understand the look of Hal's searching eyes that tried to fathom whether the old man as yet had any suspicions of the robbery.

The captain reached out from the bedclothes he should have kept well over him, and laid his hand on Hal's.

"Listen," said he, weak and shaken. His forehead glistened, damp with sweat. "It's good news. I've been down to see Squire Bean. I've paid him the money for McLaughlin, and got a receipt for it, and the case against you is all settled. Ended!"

"Is, eh?" demanded Hal, with calculating eyes. "Great! And the apology stuff is all off, too?"

"Well, no, not that. Of course you've still got to apologize to him so all the crew can hear it. But that's only a little detail. Any time will do. I know that after what I've sacrificed for you, boy, you'll be glad to play the part of a man and go down there and apologize, won't you?"

"Surest little thing you know!" Filhiol heard him answer, with malice and deceit which Captain Briggs could not fathom. "The crew will hear from me, all right. Some of 'em already. Yes, that's a fact. I've already apologized to three of 'em. I'll square everything, gramp. So that's all settled. Anything more?"

"You're true metal, at heart!" murmured Briggs, shivering as the draft from the open window struck him. "Thank God for it! Yes, there's one more thing. I've sent the money to the college. Sent a money-order, and got a receipt for that, too. Both receipts are in the money-drawer, in the safe."

"They *are*?" Hal could not dissemble his sudden anxiety. How much, now, did his grandfather know? Everything? Suspiciously he blinked at the old man. "So you put 'em in the safe, did you?" asked he, determined to force the issue.

"The doctor did for me."

"Oh, *he* did, did he? H-m! Well, all right. What next?" Hal stiffened for the blow, but the captain only said:

"It's fine to have the whole thing cleaned up, so you can start on another tack!" The old man smiled with pitiful affection. "Everything's coming out right, after all. You don't know how wonderfully happy I am to-day. It won't be long before I have you back in some other college again."

"The devil it won't!" thought Hal. The doctor, at the rear of the hallway, felt a clutch on his arm. There stood old Ezra.

"Doctor," he whispered in a way that meant business, "you ain't goin' to stand here listenin' to 'em, this way!"

"I'm not, eh?" And Filhiol blinked astonishment. "Why not?"

"There's ten reasons. One is, because I ain't goin' to let you, an' the other nine is because I ain't goin' to let you! I wouldn't do it myself, an' *you* ain't goin' to, neither. Will you clear out o' here, peaceful, or be you goin' to make me matt onta you an' carry you out?"

The doctor hesitated. Ezra added:

"Now, doc, don't you git me harr'd up, or there'll be stormy times!"

Filhiol yielded. He followed Ezra to the galley, where the old man practically interned him. Inwardly he cursed this development. What might not happen, were the captain now to discover the loss of the money while Hal was there? But to argue with Ezra was hopeless. Filhiol settled down by the stove and resigned himself to moody ponderings.

"This summer, take things easy," the captain was saying, with indulgence. "In the fall you'll enter some other college and win honors as we all expect you to. So you'll be glad to go, won't you, Hal?"

"I'll be glad to *go*, all right!"

"That's fine!" smiled the captain. He got out of bed in his bathrobe, slid his feet into slippers, and stood there a moment, looking at Hal.

"Boy," said he, "on the way back from town I made up my mind to do the right thing by you, to give you something every young fellow along the coast ought to have. You were asking me for a boat, and I refused you. I was wrong. Nothing finer, after all, than a little cruising up and down the shore. I've changed my mind, Hal." He laid an affectionate hand on the boy's shoulder. "I'm going to give you the money for Gordon's *Kittiwink*."

"Huh?" grunted Hal, standing up in vast astonishment and anxiety.

"Take the money, Hal, and buy your heart's dearest wish," said the old captain. "It'll maybe pinch me, for a while, but you're all I've got to love and some way I can rub along. If I can give you a happy summer the few hundred dollars won't mean much, after all. So, boy, get yourself the boat. Why, what's the matter? You look kind of flabbergasted, Hal. Aren't you glad and thankful?"

"Surest thing you know, I am!" the boy rallied with a strong effort. "It's great of you, gramp! But—can you afford it?"

"That's for me to judge, Hal," smiled the captain, shivering as the draft struck him. He turned towards the safe. Hal detained him with a hand upon his arm.

"Don't give it to me just yet," said he, anxiously. "Wait a little!"

"No, no, that wouldn't be the same at all," insisted Briggs. "I want you to have this present now, to-day, to make you always remember your fresh start in life."

"Not to-day, gramp!" exclaimed Hal. "I don't feel right about it, and—and I can't accept it. I want to make a really new start. To make my own way—be a man, not a dependent! Please don't spoil everything the first minute by doing this!"

"But, Hal—"

"I know how you feel," said the boy, with feverish energy. "But I've got feelings, too, and now you're hurting them. Please don't, grandfather! Please let me stand on my own feet, and be a man!"

Old Briggs, who had with feeble steps made his way half across the floor, turned and looked at Hal with eyes of profound affection.

"God bless you, boy!" said he with deep emotion. "Do you really mean that?"

"Of course I do! Come, get back into bed now. You're taking cold there. Get back before you have another chill!"

Anxiously he led the captain back towards the berth. His touch was complete betrayal. Into his voice he forced a tone of caressing sincerity, music to the old man's ears.

"I've learned a great deal the last day or two," said he, as with traitor solicitude he put the captain into his berth, and covered him up. "I've been learning some great lessons. What you said to me up there among the graves, has opened my eyes."

"Bless God for that!" And in the captain's eyes tears glistened. "That's wonderful for me to hear, in this room where all those relics of the past—that kris and everything—can't help reminding me of other and worse days. A wonderful, blessèd thing to hear!"

"Well, I'm glad it is, gramp," said Hal, "and it's every bit true. On my honor as a gentleman, it is! From to-day I'm going to stand on my own feet and be a man. You don't know what I've been doing already to give myself a start in life, but if you did, you'd be wonderfully surprised. What I'm still going to do will certainly surprise you more!"

"Lord above, Hal, but you're the right stuff after all!" exclaimed Captain Briggs, the tears now coursing freely. "Oh, if you could only realize what all this means for me after all the years of sacrifice and hopes and fears. We came pretty nigh shipwreck on the reefs, didn't we, boy? But it's all right. It's all right now at last!"

"It surely is. And I'm certainly going to surprise you and Laura and everybody."

"Kneel down beside me, just a minute, boy, and then I'll go to sleep again."

Hal, making a wry face to himself, knelt by the bedside. Old Briggs, with one arm, drew him close. The other hand stroked back Hal's thick, wet hair with a touch that love made gentle as a woman's.

"This is a day of days to me," he whispered. "A wonderful blessèd day! God guide and keep you, forever and ever. Amen!"

He sighed deeply and relaxed. His eyes drooped shut. Hal pulled the blankets up and got to his feet, peering down with eyes of malice.

A moment he stood there while the wind gusted against the house, the rain sprayed along the porch, and branches whipped the roof.

Then, with a smile of infernal triumph, he turned.

"Cinch!" he muttered, as he left the cabin and made his way up-stairs. "Why, it's like taking candy from a baby. He'll sleep for hours now. But won't it jar the old geezer when his pipe goes out, to-night? Just won't it, though?"

With silent laughter Hal reached his room, where, without delay, he started on his final preparations for events now swiftly impending.

Over all the heavens—a blind, gray face of wrath—seemed peering down. But on that face was now no laughter.

Even for Vishnu the Avenger some things must be too terrible.

CHAPTER XXXVI

THE DOCTOR SPEAKS

Hal had been at work five minutes when he was startled by a sharp knock. The door was flung open in no gentle manner.

Dr. Filhiol, leaning on his cane, confronted him. Hal knew trouble lay dead ahead. Standing there in shirt-sleeves, with litter and confusion of packing all about, and two half-filled suit-cases on a couple of chairs, Hal frowned angrily.

"You've got a nerve to butt in like this!" he growled. "What d' you want now?"

"I want to talk to you, sir."

"I've got no time to waste on nonsense!"

"You've got time to talk to me, and talk to me you're going to," returned the doctor. "This is no nonsense." He came in and shut the door. The scent of liquor met his nostrils. "A young man who's been responsible for the things you have, has certainly got time to answer me!"

Awed by the physician's cold determination, and with fear at heart—for might not Filhiol know about the stolen money?—Hal moderated his defiance. This old man must be kept quiet for a few hours yet; Hal must have a few hours.

"You're assuming too much authority for a stranger," said Hal, sullenly. "I never knew before that a gentleman would interfere in this way."

"Probably not, when dealing *with* a gentleman," retorted Filhiol, "but this case is different. My acquaintance with your grandfather dates back more than half a century, and when my duty requires me to speak, no young bully like you is going to stop me. No, you needn't double your fist, or look daggers, because I'm not in the least afraid of you, sir. And I'm not going to mince matters with you. What did you do with the captain's five hundred dollars?"

Hal felt himself lost. He had effectually closed Ezra's mouth, but now here stood the doctor, accusing him. One moment he had the impulse to do murder; but now that all things were in readiness for his flight, he realized violence would be a fatal error. His only hope lay in diplomacy.

"What five hundred dollars?"

"You know very well what five hundred! Come, what did you do with it?"

"Really, Dr. Filhiol, this is a most astonishing accusation!" said Hal. "*I* don't know anything about any five hundred. Is that amount gone?"

"You know very well it's gone!"

"I know nothing of the kind! How should I?"

"You can't fool me, young man!" exclaimed the doctor hotly. He raised his cane in menace.

"Put that stick down, sir," said Hal in a wicked voice. "No man living can threaten me with a stick and get way with it. I tell you I don't know anything about the money! I've been out of this house for some time, and you and Ezra have been here. Now you tell me there's five hundred dollars gone. By God, if you weren't an old man and a guest, you'd eat your words damned quick!"

"I—you—" stammered the doctor, outgeneralled.

"I've wasted enough time on you now!" Hal flung at him. "It's time for you to be going." He gripped Filhiol by the wrist with a vise-pressure that bruised. "And one thing more, you!" he growled. "You'd just better not go stirring up gramp against me, or accusing me to Ezra. It won't be healthy for you to go accusing me of what you can't prove, you prying gray ferret!"

"Ezra knows all about it already!" retorted the doctor, tempted to smash at that insolent, evil face with his cane.

"Knows it, does he?" Hal could not repress a start.

"Yes, he does. He's already sworn to a falsehood to me, to save your worthless hide!"

"What d'you mean?"

"I mean he's accused himself of the theft, you scoundrel!"

"Let him, then! If the shoe fits him, let him put it on!"

"Oh, let him, eh? Yes, and let him beggar himself. Let him try to get his pitiful life-savings back into the safe in time to save you! A man who'll stand by and let a poor old servant, more faithful than a dog, bankrupt himself to cover up a sneaking crime—a man who'll pack up and run away—"

"I've had enough o' you!" snarled Hal. He pushed the doctor out into the hall. "Ezra's admitted it, and gramp wouldn't believe I did it, even if he saw the money in my hand. Get out now, and if you cross my path again, look out!"

The doctor met his threat unflinchingly.

"Young man," said he, "I sailed harder seas, in the old times, than any seas to-day. I sailed with your grandfather when he was a bucko of the old school, and though we didn't usually agree and once I nearly shot him, I never knuckled under. Maybe the bullet that just missed cutting off your grandfather's life is still waiting for its billet. Maybe that's part of the curse on *you*!"

His eyes were cold steel as he peered at the menacing, huge figure of Hal.

"Be careful, sir," he added. "Be very careful how you raise your hand against a man like me!"

"If I ever *do* raise my hand, there'll be no more threats of shooting left in you!" Hal flung at him. With a sudden flare of rage he pushed old Filhiol through the door and turned the lock. The doctor stumbled, dropped his cane and fetched up against the balustrade of the stairs. Ashen and trembling he clung there a moment. Then he raised his shaking fist to heaven.

"Oh, God," he prayed, "God, give me power to stamp this viper's head before it poisons the captain—before it poisons Laura and old Ezra—the town, the very air, the world! God, give me strength to stamp it in the dust!"

Within the room sounded the tread of Hal, going, coming as he growled to himself, packed up his things for flight.

"Aye, go!" thought the doctor. "Go, and devil take you! Go, and if there's any curse, carry it with you to the end of the world!"

The doctor realized that nothing better than this departure could happen. The boy would undoubtedly come to his end before long in some drunken brawl. Sooner or later he would meet his match; would get killed, or would do murder and would finish on the gallows or in the chair. That over-mastering physical strength, backed by the arrogance of conscious power, could not fail to ruin him.

"The world will soon settle with you, Hal Briggs," said he, as he made his way down-stairs. "Soon settle, and for good. It will break the captain's heart to have you go, but it would break it worse to have you stay. This is best."

Calmer now, he stopped a moment at the cabin door to assure himself Captain Briggs was sleeping.

"Lord!" he thought. "I hope Hal gets away before the old man wakes up. It will spare us a terrible scene—a scene that might cost the captain his life!"

His eye caught a glint of red. Oddly enough, firelight, reflected from one of the captain's brass instruments, ticked just a tiny point of crimson on the blade of the old kris.

The doctor shuddered and passed on, failing to notice the open window in the room. He felt oppressed and stifling. Air! he must have air! He got into a coat hanging on the rack, put on his hat and limped out upon the porch.

Up and down walked Dr. Filhiol a few times, trying to shake off heavy bodings of evil. A curious little figure he made, withered, bent, but with the fires of invincible determination burning in his eyes. The time he had passed at Snug Haven had brought back his fighting spirit. Dr. Filhiol seemed quite other from the meek and inoffensive old man who had so short a time ago driven up to the captain's gate. Even the grip of his hand on his cane was different. Hal Briggs might well look out for him now, if any turn of chance should put him into Filhiol's power.

The doctor paused at last on the sheltered side of the porch, near the captain's windows and away from that side of the house where Hal's room was located. More heavily than ever the rain was sheeting down, and from the shore a long thunder told of sea charges broken against the impenetrable defenses of the rocks.

All at once the doctor saw a figure coming along the road, head down to wind and rain—a figure in a mackintosh, with a little white hat drawn down over thick hair—the figure of a woman.

Astonished that a woman should be abroad in such weather, he peered more closely. The woman came to the side gate, stopped there, and, holding her hat and flying hair with one hand, looked anxiously over the hedge at Snug Haven.

Then Dr. Filhiol recognized her.

"Laura! What the devil now?" said he.

The doctor seemed to read her thought, that she was afraid of being seen by Hal, but that she greatly desired speech of some one else. With raised hand he beckoned her; and she, perceiving him, came quickly through the gate to the porch.

Wild-tossed and disheveled she was with frightened eyes and wistful, pleading face. Filhiol's heart yearned to her, filled with pity.

"You're Laura, aren't you?" asked the doctor, taking her hand and steadying her a little. "Laura Maynard? Yes? I'm Dr. Filhiol, a very old and confidential friend of the captain's. What can I do to help you?"

"The captain!" she panted, almost spent with exertion and chill. "I've got to—see the captain right away!"

"My dear, that's quite impossible," said Filhiol, drawing her more into shelter. "He's asleep, worn out with exertions concerning Hal. You've come to see him about Hal. Yes, I thought so. Well, the captain can't be disturbed now, for any reason whatever. But you can tell me, Laura. Perhaps I may do quite as well."

She pondered a moment, then asked with a strong effort: "Where is Hal now?"

"Up-stairs. Do you want to see him?"

"No, no, no!" she shuddered. "God forbid! But—oh, doctor, please let me see the captain, if only for a minute!"

"He's ill, I tell you, Laura."

"Not seriously?" she asked with sudden anxiety.

"Perhaps not yet, but we can't take any chances."

The girl took his hand in a trembling clasp.

"Don't let anything happen to the captain!" she exclaimed, her rain-wet face very beautiful in its anxiety. "Oh, doctor, he's the most wonderful old man in the world, the finest, the noblest! Nothing, nothing must happen to *him*!"

"Nothing shall, if I can help it. If I can stand between him and—and—"

"And Hal?" she queried. "Yes, I understand. What a terrible curse to love a man like that!"

"The captain must soon find it so," said Filhiol. "Every one who loves that boy has got to suffer grievously. You, too, Laura," he added. "You must steel your heart to many things. The captain will soon need all your strength and consolation."

"You know the bad news, too?"

"I know much bad news. But if you've got any more, tell me!"

"You know about the fight he had this afternoon and about his buying Gordon's boat, the *Kittiwink*?"

"No. Nothing about that. But I know Hal's packing some things now to make what they call a getaway. And—"

"And you're not going to stop him?" exclaimed the girl, clutching his arm. "You're *not*?"

"Shhh, my dear!" warned Filhiol. "We mustn't wake the captain in there! Stop Hal? No, no! Nothing better could happen than to have him go before he does murder in this town."

"He almost did murder this afternoon! He ran into three of McLaughlin's men down at Hadlock's Cove, and they twitted him about apologizing to McLaughlin. Then—"

"Say no more," interrupted the doctor, raising his hand. "I understand."

"Yes, doctor, but the news has spread, and the rest of the crew have sworn vengeance on Hal. They'll surely kill him, doctor!"

"God grant they may!" the doctor thought, but what he said was:

"The quicker he goes, then, the better."

"But isn't there any way to bring him to reason, doctor? To make him like other men? To save him?"

"I see none," Filhiol answered. He pondered a moment while the rain-drums rolled their tattoos on the roof of the porch and the sea thundered. "The curse, the real curse on that boy, is his unbridled temper, his gorilla-like strength. His strength has unsettled his judgment and his will. Ordinary men rely on their brains, and have to be decent. Hal, with those battering-ram fists, thinks he can smash down everything, and win, like one of Nietzsche's supermen. If something could drain him of strength, and weaken and humble him, it might be the salvation of him yet."

"God grant it might!"

"You still love him, girl?" asked Filhiol, tenderly as a father. "In spite of everything?"

"I love the good in him, and there's so wonderfully much!"

"I understand, my dear. Just now, the bad is all predominant. There's nothing to do but let him go, Laura. Because—he's determined to go, at all costs. Where, I don't know, or how."

"*I* know how!" exclaimed the girl. "He's bought the *Kittiwink* and laid in supplies. My father's in the boat-brokerage business, and he's got word of it."

"Bought it?" interrupted the doctor. "How? On credit?"

"No, cash. He paid four hundred and seventy-five dollars for it, in bills."

"He did? By—h-m!"

"What is it, doctor? Where could Hal get all that money? Do you know?"

"I know only too well, my dear."

"Tell me!" she exclaimed eagerly, and took him by the hand.

So absorbed were they that neither heard a slight sound from the captain's window, like the quick intake of a breath. How could they know the old man had wakened, had heard their voices; how could they know he had arisen, and, all trembling and weak, was now standing hidden inside the window, listening to words that tore the heart clean out of him?

CHAPTER XXXVII

THE CAPTAIN SEES

Anguished the captain listened. He heard Laura question:

"Where did Hal get that money? Where's he going, and what does it all mean?" Her trembling voice echoed its woe in the captain's tortured soul.

"Where Hal's going I don't know, Laura," the doctor answered, "except it's evident he's planning to escape from here for good. He may be bound for the South Seas with some crazy, wild notion of a free-and-easy buccaneering life. Hal's going, and it's evident he doesn't intend to come back. The best thing we can do is just *let* him go. It seems hard, but there's no other way. As for where he got the money—well—Why not speak plainly to you? It's the best way now."

"Tell me, then!"

Within his cabin, old Captain Briggs clutched his hands together in agony. But still he held himself that he might stand there and hear this revelation to the end.

"I *will* tell you, Laura. The money—there's only one place where it could have come from."

"The captain? He gave it to him?"

"It came from the captain, but not as a gift." "You—

don't mean—"

"It's terribly hard to speak that word, Laura, isn't it?" pitied the old doctor. "Yet the money's gone from the captain's safe. Ezra accuses himself, but that's mere nonsense. Every finger of certainty points to Hal Briggs as a thief. And not only an ordinary thief, but one who's taken advantage of every bond of confidence and affection, most brutally to betray the man who loves him better than life itself!"

"Oh, you—you can't mean *that*—"

"I'm afraid I can't mean anything else. Hal's up-stairs now, unless he's already gone. He's trying to escape before the captain wakes up."

"And you're not going to stop him?"

"Never! You mustn't, either!"

"But this will break the old man's heart—the biggest, most loving heart in the world! This will kill him!"

"Even that would be less cruel than to have Hal stay, and have him torture the old captain."

"And there's nothing you can do? Nothing you'll let *me* do?"

"There's nothing any one can do now, but God. And God holds aloof, these days."

For a minute Laura peered up at him, letting the full import of his words sink into her dazed brain. Then, sensing the tragic inevitability of what must be, she turned, ran down the steps and along the rain-swept path.

He dared not call after her, to bid her take no desperate measures, for fear of waking the captain—the captain, at that very moment shivering inside the window, transfixed by spikes of suffering that nailed him to his cross of Calvary. In silence he watched her, storm-driven like a wraith, grow dim through the rain till she vanished from his sight.

Alone, Dr. Filhiol sank heavily into a wet chair. There he remained, thinking deep and terrible things that wring the heart of man.

And the captain, what of him?

Dazed, staggered, he groped toward the desk. From the drawer he took the slip of paper bearing the combination. With an effort that taxed all his strength he opened the safe, opened the money-compartment. His trembling fingers caught up the few remaining bills there.

"God above!" he gulped.

Then all at once a change, a swift metamorphosis of wrath and outraged love swept over him. He seemed to freeze into a stern, avenging figure, huge of shoulder, hard of fist. The bulk of him loomed vast, in that enfolding bathrobe like a Roman patrician's toga, as he strode through the door and up the stairs.

Silent and grim, he struck Hal's door with his fist. The door resisted. One lunge of the shoulder, and the lock burst.

Hal stood there in corduroy trousers, heavy gray reefer and oilskin hat. Two strapped suit-cases stood by the bureau. Over the floor, the bed, lay a litter of discarded clothes and papers.

"What the hell!" cried the thief, clenching angry fists.

"You, sir!" exclaimed old Captain Briggs, in a voice the boy had never yet heard. "Stand where you are! I have to speak with you!"

Not even the effrontery of Hal's bold eyes could quite meet that blue, piercing look. Had the old man, he wondered, a revolver? Was he minded now to kill? In that terrible and accusing face, he saw what Alpheus Briggs had been in the old, barbarous days. The brute in him recognized the dormant passions of his grandfather, now rekindling. And, though he tried to mask his soul, the fear in it spied through his glance.

"You snake!" the captain flung at him. "You lying Judas!"

"Go easy there!" Hal menaced. That he had been drinking was obvious. The scent of liquor filled the room, abomination in the old man's nostrils. "Go easy! I'm not taking any such talk from any man, even if he is my grandfather!"

"You'll take all I have to say, and you can lay to that, sir!" retorted the old man. Toward Hal he advanced, fists doubled. The boy cast about him for some weapon. Not for all his strength did he dare stand against this overpowering old man.

Below, on the porch, the doctor had heard sounds of war, and had pegged into the hall at his best speed. There he met Ezra, who had just come from the cabin.

"Great gulls! The safe's open—the cap'n—knows! Hell's loose now!" Ezra gasped.

He made for the stairs. The doctor tried to clutch him back.

"No use, Ezra! Too late—you can't stop it now with all that nonsense about your being the thief!"

"Let me up them stairs, damn you!"

"Never! They've got to settle this themselves. You'll only make things worse!"

With an oath, a violent wrench, Ezra tore himself away, and scrambled up the stairs.

"Cap'n Briggs! Hal!" he shouted, torn by conflicting loves. "Wait on, both o' ye. *I* done it—*nobody but me*—"

"There now, how does *that* strike you?" sneered Hal, respited by the shock of this self-accusation that dropped the captain's fists. "The son-of-a-sea-cook owns up to it, himself!"

"Me, me, nobody but me!" vociferated Ezra, who had now reached the room. He clawed at the captain's arm. "Not him, cap'n! *Me!*"

"If that's true, Ezra, how the devil does Hal, here, know what you're talking about, so slick?"

"Ezra lent me five hundred, when it comes to that," put in Hal, "and told me it was his savings. But I see now—he stole it, the damned, black-hearted thief! Didn't you, Ezra?"

"Sure, sure! Cap'n, you listen to me now. Hal, he never—"

"Ezra," said old Briggs, holding his rage in check, "you're wonderful!" He laid a hand of affection on the shoulder of the trembling old man. "It's your heart and soul that's speaking falsehood—falsehood more white and shining than God's truth. But I can't take your word, given to shield this serpent we've been nursing in our bosom. I know all about everything now. I know why Hal robbed me."

"Like hell you do!" the boy blared out.

"Yes, even the name of the very boat he's bought with my hard-saved money. Money that was meant to help him up and on again. It's no use your lying to me, Ezra." He pointed a steady, accusing finger. "There's the thief, Ezra, standing right before you—standing there for the last time he'll ever stand under this roof of mine, so help me God!"

"Cap'n, cap'n," implored the old man sinking to his knees, hands clasped, face streaming tears. "Don't say that! Oh, Lord, don't, don't say that!"

"I don't give a damn *what* the old stiff says now," sneered Hal, picking up his baggage. His red face was brutalized with rage and drink. "Let him go to it. He said a mouthful when he said I grabbed the coin. Sure I did—and I'm only sorry it wasn't more. Wish I'd grabbed it all! I'd like to have cleaned the old tightwad for a decent roll, while I was at it!"

"Hal! Master Hal!"

The doctor, listening from below, quivered with rage, but held himself in check. What, after all, could his weak body accomplish? And as for speech, that was not needed now.

"Get out o' my way, the pair o' you, and let me blow out o' this namby-pamby, Sunday-school dump!" snarled Hal, shouldering forward. "I'm quitting. I told you yesterday I was sick of all this grandpa's-darling stuff. If I can't get out and *live*, I'll cash in my checks. College—apologies—white flannels—*urrgh!*"

The growl in his deep chest and sinewed throat was that of a wolf. Silent, cold, unmoved now, the old captain studied him.

"None o' that for mine, thanks!" Hal threw at him with insolence supreme. "Wait till I catch McLaughlin! *I'll* apologize to him! Say! I've already apologized to three of his men, and Mac'll get it, triple-extract. And then I'll blow. I've got a classy boat that can walk *some*, and let 'em try to stop me, if they want to. I'm not afraid of you, or any man in this town, or in the world!"

He dropped one of the suit-cases, raised his right arm and swelled the formidable biceps, glorying in the brute power of his arm, his trip-hammer fist.

"Afraid? Not while I've got this! Go ahead and try to get me arrested, if you think fit. It'll take more than Albert Mills to pinch me, or Squire Bean to hold me for trial—it'll take more than any jail in this town to keep *me*!

"Now I've said all I'm going to, except that I took the coin. Yes, I took it. And I'll take more wherever I find it. Money, booze, women—I'll take 'em all. They're mine, if I can get 'em. That's all. To hell with everything that stands in my way! You two get out of it now before I throw you out!"

He brutally struck the kneeling old Ezra down and picked up the suit-cases. The captain quivered with the strain of holding his hand from slaughter, and stood aside. Not one word did he speak.

Hal blundered out into the passageway, and, panting with rage, started to descend the stairs.

Old Ezra, crawling on hands and knees, tried to follow.

"Hal! Master Hal, come back! I got money! *I'll—I'll pay!*"

The captain lifted him, held him with an arm of steel.

"Silence, Ezra! Remember, we're not children. We're old deep-water sailormen, you and I. This is mutiny. The boy has chosen. It's all over."

Ezra sank into a chair, covered his face and burst into convulsive sobs, rocking himself to and fro in the excess of his grief.

Alpheus Briggs walked to the top of the stairs, and silently watched Hal descend. At the bottom, Dr. Filhiol confronted the swearing, murderous fellow. He, too, kept silence. Only he stood back a little, avoiding Hal as if the very breath of him were poison.

Hal flung a sneer at him with bared teeth, and paused a moment at the door leading into the cabin. A thought came to his brain, crazed with whisky, rage and the obscure hereditary curse that lay upon him. Something seemed whispering a command to him, irrational enough, yet wholly compelling.

To the fireplace Hal strode, snatched down the kris, opened one of the suit-cases, and threw the weapon in. He locked the case again, and slouched out on to the piazza, defiantly and viciously.

"Might come handy, that knife, if the fists didn't get away with the goods," he muttered. "Take it along, anyhow!"

The Airedale, hearing Hal's step, got up and fawned against him. Hal, with an obscene oath, kicked the animal.

"*Get* out o' my way, you—" he growled. The dog, yelping, still cringed after him as he descended the steps. Mad with the blind passion that kills, Hal flung down his suit-cases, snatched up the dog and dashed it down on the steps with horrible force.

"Damn you, don't you touch that dog again!" shouted old Dr. Filhiol, hobbling out the door.

He brandished his cane. In his pale face flamed holy rage. With a boisterous, horrible laugh, Hal snatched the cane from him, snapped it with one flirt of his huge hands, and threw the pieces into the doctor's face.

The dog, still crying out with the pain of a broken leg, tried to drag himself to Hal. Another oath, a kick, and Ruddy sprawled along the porch.

"I've fixed *you* a while, you fossil quack!" gibed Hal at the doctor. "Maybe you'll butt in again where you're not wanted! Lucky for you I'm in a hurry now, or I'd do a better job!"

Again Hal picked up his cases, and strode down the walk, against the rain and gale. At the gate he paused, triumphant.

"To hell with this place!" he cried. "To hell with the whole business and with all o' you!"

Then he passed through the gate, along the hedge, and vanished in the boisterous storm.

Up in Hal's room, old Ezra was still convulsed with senile grief. The captain, his face white and lined, had sunk down on the bed and with vacant eyes was staring at the books and papers strewn there in confusion.

All at once his attention focused on a sheet of paper whereon a few words seemed vividly to stand out. He advanced a shaking hand, picked up the paper and read:

> The curse must be fulfilled, to the last breath, for by Shiva and the Trimurthi, what is written is written. But if he through whom the curse descendeth on another is stricken to horror and to death, then the Almighty Vishnu, merciful, closes that page. And he who through another's sin was accursed, is cleansed. Thus may the curse be fulfilled. But always one of two must die. *Tuan Allah poonia krajah!* It is the work of the Almighty One! One of two must die!

Carefully the old man read the words. Once more he read them. Then, with a smile of strange comprehension and great joy, he nodded.

"One of two—one of two must die!" said he. "Thank God, I understand! *At last—thank God!*"

CHAPTER XXXVIII

CAPTAIN BRIGGS FINDS THE WAY

The full significance of the curse burning deep into his brain, old Captain Briggs sat there on the bed a moment longer, his eyes fixed on the slip of paper. Then, with a new and very strange expression, as of a man who suddenly has understood, has chosen and is determined, he carefully folded the paper and thrust it into the pocket of his bathrobe. He stood up, peered at Ezra, advanced and laid a hand upon the old man's shoulder.

"Ezra," said he in a deep voice, "there's times when men have got to *be* men, and this is one of 'em. You and I have gone some pretty rough voyages in years past. I don't recall that either of us was ever afraid or refused duty in any wind or weather. We aren't going to now. Whatever's duty, that's what we're going to do. It'll maybe lead me to a terribly dark port, but if that's where I've got to go, as a good seaman, so be it.

"And now," he added in another tone, "now that's all settled, and no more to be said about it." Affectionately he patted the shoulder of the broken-hearted Ezra. "Come, brace up now; brace up!"

"Cap'n Briggs, sir," choked Ezra, distraught with grief, "you ain't goin' to believe what Master Hal said, be you? He accused himself o' stealin' that there money, to pertect me. It was really *me* as done it, sir, not *him*!"

"We won't discuss that any more, Ezra," the captain answered, with a smile of deep affection. "It doesn't much signify. There's so much more to all this than just one particular case of theft. You don't understand, Ezra. Come now, sir; pull yourself together! No more of this!"

"But ain't you goin' to do anythin' to bring him back, cap'n?" asked the old man. He got up and faced the captain with a look of grief and pain. "That there boy of ourn, oh, he can't be let go to the devil this way! Ain't there nothin' you can do to save him?"

"Yes, Ezra, there is."

"Praise God fer that, cap'n! You hadn't ought to be too hard on Hal. You an' me, we're old, but we'd oughta try an' understand a young un. Young folks is always stickin' up the circus-bills along the road o' life, an' old uns is always comin' along an' tearin' 'em down; an' that ain't right, cap'n. You an' me has got to understand!"

"I understand perfectly," smiled the captain, his eyes steady and calm. "I

214

know exactly what I've got to do."

"An' you'll do it?" Ezra's trembling eagerness was pitiful. "You're going' to do it, cap'n?"

Alpheus Briggs nodded. His voice blended with a sudden furious gust of wind as he answered:

"I'm going to do it, Ezra. I'm surely going to."

"An' what *is* it?" insisted Ezra. "Run after him an' bring him back?"

"Bring him back. That's just it."

"Praise the Lord!" The old man's eyes were wet. "When? When you goin' to do it?"

"Very soon, now."

"You got to hurry, cap'n. We mustn't let anythin' happen to our Hal. He's run kinda wild, mebbe, but he's everythin' we got to love. Ef you can git him back agin, we'll be so doggone good to him he'll *hafta* do better. But you mustn't lose no time. Ef he gits aboard that there *Kittiwink* an' tries to make sail out through the Narrers, he's like as not to git stove up on Geyser."

The captain smiled as he made answer:

"I sha'n't lose any unnecessary time, Ezra. But I can't do it all in a moment. And you must let me do this in my own way."

The old man peered up at him through tears.

"You know best how to chart this course, now."

"Yes, I believe I do. To save that boy, I've got to make a journey, and I'll need a little time to get ready. But just the minute I *am* ready, I'll go. You can depend on that!"

"A journey? I'll go too!"

"No, Ezra, this is a journey I must take all alone."

"Well, you know best, cap'n," the old fellow assented. "But ef you need any help, call on!"

"I will, Ezra. Now go to your room and rest. You're badly used up. There's nothing you can do to help, just now."

"But won't you be wantin' me to pack y'r duffel? An' rig Bucephalus?"

"When I want you, I'll let you know," smiled Briggs. With one hand still on the old man's shoulder, his other hand took Ezra's in a strong clasp.

"Ezra," said he, "you've always stood by, through thick and thin, and I know you will now. You've been the most loyal soul in this whole world. No needle ever pointed north half as constant as you've pointed toward your duty by Hal and me. You're a man, Ezra, *a man*—and I'm not ashamed to say I love you for it!"

His grip tightened on the old man's hand. For a moment he looked square into Ezra's wondering, half-frightened eyes. Then he loosened his grasp, turned and walked from the room.

Along the hall he went, and down the stairs. His face, calm, beatified, seemed shining with an inner light that ennobled its patriarchal features.

"Thank God," he whispered, "for light to see my duty, and for strength to do it!"

As he reached the bottom of the stairs, the front door opened, and Dr. Filhiol staggered in, admitting a furious gust of wind and rain. With great difficulty he was managing himself, holding the injured dog. Ruddy was yelping; one leg hung limp and useless.

For a tense moment the doctor confronted Briggs. He pushed the door shut, with rage and bitterness.

"And you, sir," he suddenly exclaimed, "you go against my orders; you leave your bed and expose yourself to serious consequences, for the sake of a beast—who will do a thing like *this*!"

Furiously he nodded downward at the dog.

The captain advanced and, with a hand that trembled, caressed the rough muzzle.

"Hal?" asked he, under his breath. "This, too?"

"Yes, this! Nearly killed the poor creature, sir! Kicked him. And that wasn't enough. When the dog still tried to follow him, grabbed him up and dashed him down on the steps. This leg's broken. Ribs, too, I think. A miracle the dog wasn't killed. Your grandson's intention was to kill him, all right enough, but I guess he didn't want to take time for it!" Filhiol's lips were trembling with passion, so that he could hardly articulate. "This is horrible! Injury to a man is bad enough, but a man can defend himself, and will. But injury to a defenseless, trusting animal—my God, sir, if I'd been anything but a cripple, and if I'd had a weapon handy, I'd have had your grandson's blood, so help me!"

The captain made no answer, but set his teeth into his bearded lip. He patted the dog's head. Ruddy licked his hand.

"Well, sir?" demanded Filhiol. "What have you to say now?"

"Nothing. Hal's gone, and words have no value. Can you repair this damage?"

"Yes, if the internal injuries aren't too bad. But that's not the point. Hal, there, goes scot free and—"

Alpheus Briggs raised his hand for silence.

"Please, no more!" he begged. "I can't stand it, doctor. You've got to spare me now!"

Filhiol looked at him with understanding.

"Forgive me," said he. "But help me with poor old Ruddy, here!"

"Ezra can help you. On a pinch, call in Dr. Marsh, if you like."

"Oh, I think my professional skill is still adequate to set a dog's leg," Filhiol retorted.

"And you don't know how grateful I am to you for doing it," said the captain. "I'm grateful, too, for your not insisting on any more talk about Hal. You're good as gold! I wish you knew how much I thank you!"

The doctor growled something inarticulate and fondled the whimpering animal. Alpheus Briggs forced himself to speak again.

"Please excuse me now. I've got something very important to do." His hand slid into the pocket of his bathrobe, closed on the paper there, and crumpled it. "Will you give me a little time to myself? I want an hour or two undisturbed."

The temptation was strong on the captain to take the hand of Filhiol and say some words that might perhaps serve as a good-by, but he restrained himself. Where poor old Ezra had understood nothing, Filhiol would very swiftly comprehend. So Alpheus Briggs, even in this supreme moment of leave-taking, held his peace.

The doctor, however, appeared suddenly suspicious.

"Captain," he asked, "before I promise you the privacy you ask, I've got one question for you. Have you overheard any of Hal's reading lately, or have you seen any of his translations from the Malay?"

By no slightest quiver of a muscle did the old man betray himself.

"No," he answered. "What do you mean, doctor? Why do you ask?"

"That's something I can't tell you," said Filhiol, thankful that no hint had reached Briggs concerning the curse. Swiftly he thought. Yes, it would well suit his purpose now to get the captain out of the way. That would give Filhiol time to run through the litter of papers in Hal's room, and to destroy the translation that might have such fatal consequences if it should come into the captain's hands.

"Very well, sir," said he. "Take whatever time you need to settle matters relative to Hal's leaving. By rights I ought to order you back to bed; but I know you wouldn't obey me now, anyhow, so what's the use? Only, be reasonably sensible, captain. Even though Hal *has* made a fearful mess of everything, your life is worth a very great deal to lots of people!"

The captain nodded. Filhiol's admonitions suddenly seemed very trivial, just as the world and life itself had all at once become. Already these were retreating from his soul, leaving it alone, with the one imperative of duty. At the last page of the book of life, Alpheus Briggs realized with swift insight how slight the value really was of that poor volume, and how gladly—when love and duty bade him—he could forever close it.

"We'll talk this all over in the morning, doctor," said he. "But till then, no more of it. I've got to get my bearings and answer my helm better before I'll know exactly what to do. You understand?"

"Yes, captain, I think I do," answered the doctor, with compassion. He said no more, but hobbled towards the kitchen, there to summon Ezra and do what could be done for Ruddy.

Thus Captain Briggs was left alone. Alone with the stern consummation of his duty, as he saw it.

CHAPTER XXXIX

"ONE MUST DIE"

Briggs entered his cabin, and locked both doors; then fastened the window giving on the porch. He went to the fireplace, overhung with all that savage arsenal, and put a couple of birch-logs on the glowing coals.

He sat down in his big chair by the fire, pondered a moment with the fireglow on his deep-wrinkled, bearded face, then from the pocket of his bathrobe drew the crumpled bit of paper. Again he studied it, reading it over two or three times. In a low voice he slowly pronounced the words, as if to grave them on his consciousness:

"The curse must be fulfilled, to the last breath, for by Shiva and the Trimurthi, what is written is written. But if he through whom the curse descendeth on another is stricken to horror and to death, then the Almighty Vishnu, merciful, closes that page. And he who through another's sin was cursed, is cleansed. Thus may the curse be fulfilled. But always one of two must die. *Tuan Allah poonia krajah!* It is the work of the Almighty One! One of two must die!"

For some minutes he pondered all this. Before him rose visions—the miasmatic Malay town; the battle in the Straits; the yellow and ghostlike presence of the witch-woman, shrilling her curse at him; the death of Scurlock and the boy, of Mahmud Baba, of Kuala Pahang, of the *amok* Malay who, shot through the spine and half paralyzed, still had writhed forward, horribly, to kill.

"No wonder the curse has followed me," murmured the old man. "I haven't suffered yet as any one would have to suffer to pay for all that. For all that, and so much more—God, how much more! It's justice, that's all; and who can complain about justice? Poor Hal, poor boy of mine! No justice about *his* having to bear it, is there? Why should *he* suffer for what *I* did fifty years ago? Thank God! Oh, thank God!" he exclaimed with passionate fervor, "that I can pay it all, and make him free!"

He relapsed into silence a little while, his face not at all marked with grief or pain, but haloed with a high and steadfast calm. The drumming rain on the porch roof, the shuddering impact of the wind as the storm set its shoulders against Snug Haven, saddened him with thoughts of the fugitive, bearing the curse that was not his, out there somewhere in the tumult and the on-drawing night, trying to flee the whips of atavism. But through that sadness rose happier thoughts.

"It's only for a little while now," said the captain. "The curse is nearly ended. When I've paid the score, it will lift, and he'll come back again. Poor Hal—how little he knew, when he was writing this paper, that he was giving me the chart to steer my right course! If the hand of some divine Providence isn't in this, then there's no Providence to rule this world!"

Another thought struck him. Hal knew nothing of the fact that his grandfather had found the curse. He must never know. In the life of better things that soon was to open out for him, no embittering self-accusation must intrude. All proof must be destroyed.

Captain Briggs tossed the curse of Dengan Jouga into the flames just beginning to flicker upward from the curling birch-bark. The paper browned and puffed into flame. It shriveled to a crisp black shell, on which, for a moment or two, the writing glowed in angry lines of crimson. Captain Briggs caught one last glimpse of a word or two, grotesquely distorted—"*The curse —horror and death—one—must die—*"

Despite himself he shuddered. The hate and malice of the old witch-woman seemed visibly glaring out at him from the flames, after half a century. From the other side of the world, even from "beyond the Silken Sea," words of vengeance blinked at him, then suddenly vanished; and with a gust of the storm-wind, up the chimney whirled the feather bit of ash. The captain drew his bath robe a little closer round him, and glanced behind him into the dark corners of the cabin.

"This—is very strange!" he whispered.

Still he sat pondering. Especially he recalled the Malay he had shot through the spine. That lithe, strong man, suddenly paralyzed into a thing half dead and yet alive, was particularly horrible to remember. Helplessness, death that still did not die....

A spark snapped out upon the floor. He set his foot on it.

"That's the only way to deal with evil," said he. "Stamp it out! And if we're the evil ourselves, if we're the spark of devil-fire, out we must go! What misery I could have saved for Hal, if I'd understood before—and what a cheap price! An old, used-up life for a new, strong, fresh one."

His mind, seeking what way of death would be most fitting, reverted to the poisoned kris, symbol of the evil he had done and of the old, terrible days. He peered up at the mantelpiece; but, look as he would, failed to discover the kris. He rose to his feet, and explored the brickwork with his hands in the half-light reflected from the fire. Nothing there. The hooks, empty, showed where the Malay blade had been taken down, but of the blade itself no trace remained.

The old captain shivered, amazed and wondering. In this event there seemed more than the hand of mere coincidence. Hal was gone; the kris had vanished. The captain could not keep cold tentacles of fear from reaching for his heart. To him it seemed as if he could almost see the eyeless face looming above him, could almost hear the implacable mockery of its far, mirthless laughter.

"God!" he whispered. "This won't do! I—I'll lose my nerve if I keep on this way, and nerve is what I've got to have now!"

Why had Hal taken that knife? What wild notion had inspired the boy? Alpheus Briggs could not imagine. But something predestined, terrible, seemed closing in. The captain felt the urge of swift measures. If Hal were to be rescued, it must be at once.

Turning from the fireplace of such evil associations, he lighted the ship's lamp that hung above it. He sat down at the desk, opened a drawer and took out two photographs. These he studied a few minutes, with the lamp-light on his white hair, his venerable beard, his heavy features. Closely he inspected the photographs.

One was a group, showing himself with the family that once had been, but now had almost ceased to be. The other was a portrait of Hal. Carefully the old man observed this picture, taken but a year ago, noting the fine, broad forehead, the powerful shoulders, the strength of the face that looked out so frankly at him. For the first time he perceived a quality in this face he had never seen before—the undertone of arrogant power, born of unbeaten physical strength.

The captain shook his head with infinite sadness.

"That's the real curse that lay on me," he murmured. "That's what I've got to pay for now. Well, so be it."

He kissed both pictures tenderly, and put them back into the drawer. From it he took a box, and from the box a revolver—an old revolver, the very same that he had carried in the *Silver Fleece* fifty long years ago.

"You've done very great evil," said Alpheus Briggs slowly. "Now you're going to pay for it by doing at least one good act. That's justice. God is being very good to me, showing me the way."

He broke open the revolver, spun the cylinder and snapped the hammer two or three times.

"It's all right," judged he. "This is an important job. It mustn't be made a mess of."

He looked for and found a few cartridges, and carefully loaded the weapon, then snapped it shut, and laid it on the desk. The sound of Dr. Filhiol, coming with another cane along the hall, caused him to slide the gun into the drawer. Filhiol knocked at the door, and Briggs arose to open it. He showed no signs of perturbation. A calm serenity glowed in his eyes.

"Isn't it time you got your writing finished and went to bed?" the doctor demanded tartly.

"Almost time. I'm just finishing up. I sha'n't be long now. Tell me, how's Ruddy?"

"We've made a fair job of it, and Ezra's gone to his room. He's taking everything terribly to heart. Anything I can do for you?"

"Nothing, thank you. Good night."

The captain's hand enfolded Filhiol's. Neither by any undue pressure nor by word did he give the doctor any hint of the fact that this good-by was final. The old doctor turned and very wearily stumped away up-stairs. Briggs turned back into his cabin.

"A good, true friend," said he. "Another one I'm sorry to leave, just as I'm sorry to leave the girl and Ezra. But—well—"

At his task once more, he fetched from the safe his black metal cash-box, and set himself to looking over a few deeds, mortgages and other papers, making sure that all was in order for the welfare of Hal. He reread his will, assuring himself that nothing could prevent Hal from coming into the property, and also that a bequest to Ezra was in correct form. This done, he replaced the papers in the safe.

On his desk a little clock was ticking, each motion of its balance-wheel bringing nearer the tragedy impending. The captain glanced at it.

"Getting late," said he. "Only one more thing to do now, and then I'm ready."

He set himself to write a letter that should make all things clear to Hal. But first he brought out the revolver once more, and laid it on the desk as a kind of *memento mori*, lest in the writing his soul should weaken.

The lamp, shining down upon the old man's gnarled fingers as they painfully traced the words of explanation and farewell, also struck high-lights from the revolver.

The captain's eyes, now and then leaving the written pages as he paused to think, rested upon the gun. At sight of it he smiled; and once he reached out, caressed it and smiled.

CHAPTER XL

ON THE *KITTIWINK*

When Hal left Snug Haven, he bent his shoulders to the storm and with his suit-cases plowed through the gathering dusk toward Hadlock's Cove.

Cold, slashing rain and boistering gusts left his wrath uncooled. Ugly, brutalized, he kept his way past the smithy—past Laura's house, and so with glowering eyes on into the evening that caught and ravened at him.

The sight of Laura's house filled him with an access of rage. That calm security of shaded windows behind the rain-scourged hedge seemed to typify the girl's protection against him. He twisted his mouth into an ugly grin.

"Think you're safe, don't you?" he growled, pausing a moment to glower at the house. "Think I can't get you, eh? I haven't even begun yet!"

In the turmoil of his mind, no clear plan had as yet taken form. He knew only that he had a boat and full supplies, that from him the ocean held no secrets, that his muscles and his will had never yet known defeat, and that the girl was his if he could take her.

"She'll turn me down cold and get away with it, will she?" he snarled. "She will—like hell!"

Forward he pushed again, meeting no one, and so passed Geyser Rock, now booming under the charges of the surf. He skirted a patch of woods, flailed by the wind, and beyond this turned through a stone wall, to follow a path that led down to the cove. On either side of the path stretched a rolling field, rich with tall grasses, with daisies, buttercups, milfoil and devil's paint-brush, drenched and beaten down in the dusk by the sweep of the storm.

Louder and more loud rose, fell, the thunders of the sea, as Hal approached the rocky dune at the far side of the field—a dune that on its other edge sank to a shingle beach that bordered the cove.

To eastward, this beach consolidated itself into the rocky headland of Barberry Point, around which the breakers were curving to hurl themselves on the shingle. The wind, however, was at this point almost parallel with the shore. Hal reckoned, as he tramped across the field, that with good judgment and stiff work he could get the *Kittiwink* to sea at once.

And after that, what? He did not know. No definite idea existed in that half-crazed, passion-scourged brain. The driving power of his strength accursed, took no heed of anything but flight. Away, away, only to be away!

"God!" he panted, stumbling up the dune to its top, where salt spray and stinging rain skirled upon him in skittering drives. He dropped his burdens, and flung out both huge arms toward the dark, tumbling void of waters, streaked with crawling lines of white. "God! that's what I want! That's what they're trying to keep me away from! I'm going to have it now—by God, I am!"

He stood there a moment, his oilskin hat slapping about his face. At his right, three hundred yards away or so, he could just glimpse the dark outlines of Jim Gordon's little store that supplied rough needs of lobstermen and fishers. Hal's lip curled with scorn of the men he knew were gathered in that dingy, smoky place, swapping yarns and smoking pipes. They preferred that to the freedom of the night, the storm, the sea! At them he shook his fist.

"There's not one of you that's half the man I am!" he shouted. "You sit in there and run me down. I know! You're doing it now—telling how gramp had to pay because I licked a bully, and how I've got to apologize! But you don't dare come out into a night like this. I can outsail you and outfight you all—and to hell with you!"

His rage somehow a little eased, he turned to the task immediately confronting him. The beach sloped sharply to the surf. A litter of driftwood, kelp and mulched rubbish was swirling back and forth among the churning pebbles that with each refluent wave went clattering down in a mad chorus. Here, there, drawn up out of harm's way, lay lobster-pots and dories. Just visible as a white blur tossing on the obscure waters, the *Kittiwink* rode at her buoy.

"Great little boat!" cried Hal. A vast longing swept over him to be aboard, and away. The sea was calling his youth, strength, daring.

Laura? And would he go without the girl? Yes. Sometime, soon perhaps, he would come back, would seize her, carry her away; but for now that plan had grown as vaguely formless as his destination. Fumes of liquor in his brain, of passion in his heart, blent with the roaring confusion of the tempest. All was confusion, all a kind of wild and orgiastic dream, culmination of heredity, of a spirit run *amok*.

Night, storm and wind shouted to the savage in this man. And, standing erect there in the dark, arms up to fleeing cloud and ravening gale, he howled back with mad laughter:

"Coming now! By God, I'm coming now!"

There was foam on his lips as he strode down the beach, flung the suit-cases into a dory—and with a run and a huge-shouldered shove across the shingle fairly flung the boat into the surf.

Waist-deep in chilling smothers of brine, he floundered, dragged himself into the dory that shipped heavy seas, and flung the oars on to the thole-pins. He steadied her nose into the surf, and with a few strong pulls got her through the tumble. A matter of two or three minutes, with such strength as lay in his arms of steel, brought him to the lee of the *Kittiwink's* stern. He hove the suit-cases to the deck of the dancing craft, then scrambled aboard and made the painter fast.

Again he laughed, exultingly. Now for the first time in his life his will could be made law. Now he stood on his own deck, with plenty of supplies below, and—above, about him—the unlimited power of the gale to drive him any whither he should choose.

He strode to the companionway, his feet sure on the swaying deck, his body lithely meeting every plunge, and slid back the hatch-cover. Down into the cabin he pitched the cases and followed them. He struck a match. It died. He cursed bitterly, tried again, and lighted the cabin-lamp. His eyes, with the affection of ownership, roved around the little place, taking in the berths, the folding-table, the stools. He threw the suit-cases into a berth, opened one and took out a square-face, which he uncorked and tipped high.

"Ah!" he sighed. "Some class!" He set the bottle in the rack and breathed deeply. "Nice little berths, eh? Laura—she'd look fine here. She'd fit great, as crew. And if she gave me any of her lip, then—"

His fist, doubled, swayed under the lamp-shine as he surveyed it proudly.

"Great little boat," judged Hal. "She'll outsail 'em all, and I'm the boy to make her walk!"

Huge, heavy, evil-faced, he stood there, swaying as the *Kittiwink* rode the swells. He cast open his reefer, took out pipe and tobacco, and lighted up. As he sucked at the stem, his hard lips, corded throat and great jaws gave an impression of brutal power, in no wise differing from that of old Alpheus Briggs, half a hundred years ago.

"Make me go to school and wear a blue ribbon," he gibed, his voice a contrabass to the shrilling of the wind aloft in the rig, the groaning and creaking of the timbers. "Make me go round apologizing to drunken bums. Like—hell!"

A gleam of metal from the opened suit-case attracted his eyes. He took up the kris, and with vast approval studied it. The feel of the lotus-bud handle seemed grateful to his palm. Its balance joyed him. The keen, wavy blade, maculated with the rust of blood and brine, and with the groove where lay another stain whose meaning he knew not, held for him a singular fascination. Back, forth he slashed the weapon, whistling it through the air, flashing it under the lamp-light.

"Fine!" he approved, with thickened speech. "Glad I got it—might come handy in a pinch, what?"

He stopped swinging the kris, and once more observed it, more closely still. Tentatively he ran his thumb along the edge, testing it, then scratched with some inchoate curiosity at the poison crystallized in the groove.

"Wonder what that stuff is, anyhow?" said he. "Doesn't look like the rest. Maybe it's the blood of some P. I., like McLaughlin. *That* ought to make a dirty-looking stain, same as this. Maybe it will, some of these days, if he crosses my bows. Maybe it will at that!"

CHAPTER XLI

FATE STRIKES

Hal tossed the kris into the berth, and was just about to reach for the bottle again when a *thump-thump-thumping* along the hull startled his attention.

"What the devil's that, now?" he growled, stiffening. The sound of voices, then a scramble of feet on deck, flung him toward the companion-ladder. "*Who's there?*"

"He's here, boys, all right!" exulted a voice above. "We got him this time, the—"

Have you seen a bulldog bristle to the attack with bared teeth and throaty growl? So, now, Hal Briggs.

"Got me, have you?" he flung up at the invaders. "More o' that rotten gurry-bucket's crew, eh? More o' Bucko McLaughlin's plug-uglies!"

"Easy there," sounded a caution, as if holding some one back from advancing on Hal. "He's mebbe got a gun."

"T' hell wid it!" shouted another. "He ain't gonna lambaste half our crew an' the ole man, an' git away wid it! Come on, if there's one o' ye wid the guts of a man. We'll rush the son of a pup!"

Heavy sea-boots appeared on the ladder. Hal leaped, grabbed, flung his muscles into a backward haul—and before the first attacker realized what had happened, he landed on his back. One pile-driver fist to the jaw, and the invader quivered into oblivion, blood welling from a lip split to the teeth.

"There's one o' you!" shouted Hal. "One more!" He laughed uproariously, half drunk with alcohol, wholly drunk with the strong waters of battle. "Looks like I'd have to make a job of it, and clean the bunch! Who's next?"

Only silence answered a moment. This swift attack and sudden loss seemed to have disconcerted Mac's men. Hal kicked the fallen enemy into a corner, and faced the companionway. His strategic position, he realized, was almost impregnable. Only a madman would have ventured up to that narrow and slippery deck in the night, with an undetermined number of men armed, perhaps, with murderous weapons, awaiting him. Hal was no madman. A steady fighter, he, and of good generalship. In his heart he meant, as he stood there, to kill or cripple every one of those now arrayed against him. He dared take no chances. Tense as a taut spring, he crouched and waited.

Then as he heard whisperings, furious gusts of mumbled words, oaths at the very top of the companion, an idea took him. He snatched up the unconscious man, thrust him up the ladder and struggled behind him with titanic force. His legs, massive pillars, braced themselves against the sides of the companion. Like a battle-ax he swung the vanquished enemy, beating about him with this human flail. With fortune, might he not sweep one or two assailants off into the running seas?

He saw vague forms, felt the impact of blows, as his weapon struck. Came a rush. Overborne, he fell backward to the floor. Up he leaped, as feet clattered down the ladder, and snatched the kris.

But he could not drive it home in the bulky, dark form leaping down at him. For, lightning-swift, sinewed arms of another man behind him whipped round his neck, jerked his head back, bore him downward.

He realized that he was lost. He had forgotten the forward hatch, opening down into the galley; he had forgotten the little passageway behind him. Now one of McLaughlin's men, familiar with the build of the *Kittiwink*, had got a strangling grip on him. A wild yell of triumph racketed through the cabin, as three more men dropped into that little space.

Hal knew he must use strategy. Backward he fell: and as he fell, he twisted. His right hand still held the kris; his left got a grip on the other's throat.

That other man immediately grew dumb, and ceased to breathe, as the terrible fingers closed. Volleys of blows and kicks rained on Hal ineffectively. Still the fingers tightened; the man's face grew horribly dusky, slaty-blue under the lamp-light, while his tongue protruded and his staring eyes injected themselves with blood.

The arm round Hal's neck loosened, fell limp. Hal flung the man from him, groveled up under the cross-cutting slash of blows, and bored in.

The crash of a stool on his right wrist numbed his arm to the elbow; the stool, shattered, fell apart, and one leg made smithereens of the lamp-globe. The smoky flare redly lighted a horrible, fantastic war. Hal fought to snatch up the knife again; the others to keep him from it, to trample him, bash him in, smear his brains and blood on the floor. Scientific fighting went to pot. This was just jungle war, the war of gouge and bite, confused, unreal.

All the boy knew was that he swayed, bent and recovered in the midst of terrible blows, and that one arm would not serve him. The other fist landed here, there; and now it had grown red, though whether from its own blood or from the wounds of foemen, who could tell? Strange fires spangled outward before Hal's eyes; he tasted blood, and, clacking his jaws, set his teeth into a hand and through it.

Something wrenched, cracked dully. Blasphemy howled through the smoky air, voicing the anguish of a broken arm. A rolling, swaying, tumbling mass, the men trampled the fallen one, pulping his face. Broken glass gritted under hammering bootheels, as the shards of lamp-chimney were ground fine.

Back, forth, strained the fighters, with each heave and wallow of the boat. The floor grew slippery. The folding-table, torn from its hinges, collapsed into kindling; and one of these sticks, aimed at Hal's head, missed him, but struck the square-face.

Liquor gurgled down; the smell of whisky added its fetor to the stench of oil, bilge, sweat and blood. The floor grew slippery, and crimson splashes blotched the cabin walls.

"Kill—the son—of—" strainingly grunted some one.

Hal choked out a gasping, husky laugh. Only one eye was doing duty now; but that one still knew the kris was lying in the corner by the starboard berth.

He tugged, bucked, burst through, fell on the kris, grappled its knob and writhed up, crouching.

He flung the blade aloft to strike. Everything was whirling in a haze of dust and dancing confusion, lurid under the flare. Grinning, bleeding faces, rage-distorted, gyrated before him. He swirled the kris at the nearest.

A hand, vising his wrist, snapped the blade downward, drove it back. Hal felt a swift sting, a burning, lancinating pain in his right pectoral muscle. It seemed to pierce the chest, the lung itself.

He dropped his arm, staring. The kris, smeared brightly red, thumped to the floor.

"Got 'im, b' God!" wheezed somebody.

"Got him—yes, an' now it won't be healthy fer us, if we're caught here, neither!" panted another.

The men stood away from him, peering curiously. Hal confronted them, one arm limp. The other hand rested against the cabin bulkhead. He swayed, with the swaying of the boat; his head, sagging forward, seemed all at once very heavy. He felt a hot trickle down his breast.

"You—you've got me, you—" he coughed, and, leaning his back against the bulkhead, got his free hand feebly to the wound. It came away horribly red. By the smoky, feeble flare, he blinked at it. The three hulking men still on foot—vague figures, with black shadows on bearded faces, with eyes of fear and dying anger—found no answer. One sopped at a cut cheek with his sleeve; another rubbed his elbow and growled a curse. On the cabin floor two lay inert, amid the trample of débris.

"*Now* you've done it, Coombs," suddenly spat the smallest of McLaughlin's men. He shook a violent forefinger at the blood-smeared kris that had fallen near the ladder. "Now we got murder on our hands, you damn fool! We didn't come here to kill the son of a dog. We only come to give him a damn good beatin'-up, an' now see what you've went an' done! We got to clear out, all of us! An' stick, too; we got to fix this story right!"

"What—what d'you mean?" stammered Coombs, he of the bleeding cheek. He had gone ashy pale. The whiteness of his skin make startling contrast with the oozing blood. "What story? What we gotta do?"

"Get ashore an' all chew it over an' agree on how we wasn't within a mile o' here to-night. Fix it, an' git ready to swear to it! If we don't, we'll all go up! Come along out o' here! Quick!"

"Aw, hell! If he dies, serves him right!" spoke up the third man. "They can't touch us fer killin' a skunk!"

"You'll soon find out if they can or not!" retorted the small man, livid with fear. "Out o' here now!"

"An' not fix him up none? Not bandage him ner nothing?" put in Coombs. "Gosh!"

"Bandage nothin'!" cried the small man. "Tully's right. We got to be clearin'. But *I* say, set fire to her an' burn her where she lays, an' him in her, an'—"

"Yes, an' have the whole damn town here, an' everythin'! You got a head on you like a capstan. Come on, beat it!"

"We can't go an' leave our fellers here, can we?" demanded Coombs, while Hal, sliding down along the bulkhead, collapsed upon the blood-stained floor. He felt his life oozing out hotly, but now had no power even to raise a hand. Coombs peered down, his eyes unnaturally big. "We can't leave *them*! That'd be a dead give-away. An' we hadn't oughta leave a man bleed to death that way, neither."

"T' hell with 'im!" shrilled the little man, more and more panic-stricken. "We should worry! Git hold o' Nears an' Dunning here, an' on deck with 'em. We can git 'em ashore, an' the others, too, in the dory. We can all git down to

Hammill's fish-shed an' no one the wiser. Give us a hand here, you!"

"I'm goin' to stay an' fix this here man up," decided Coombs. "I reckon I stuck him, or he stuck himself because I gaffled onta his hand. Anyhow, I done it. You clear out, if you wanta. I ain't goin' to let that feller——"

"You're comin' with us, an' no double-crossin'!" shouted Tully, his bruised face terrible, one eye blackened and swollen. He bored a big-knuckled fist against Coombs's nose. "If you're caught here, we're *all* done. You're comin' now, or, by the jumpin' jews-harps, I'll knock you cold myself, an' lug you straight ashore!"

"An' I'll help ye!" volunteered the little man, with a string of oaths. "Come on now, git busy!"

Overborne, Coombs had to yield. The three men prepared to make good their escape and to cover all tracks. Not even lifting Hal into a berth, but leaving him sprawled face-downward on the floor, with blood more and more soaking his heavy reefer, they dragged the unconscious men to the companion, hauled them up and across the pitching, slippery deck, and dropped them like potato sacks into the dory that had brought them. Then they did likewise with the unconscious man Hal had used as a flail against them. In the dark and storm, all this took minutes and caused great exertion. But at last it was done; and now Tully once more descended to the cabin.

He looked around with great care, blinking his one still serviceable eye, his torn face horrible by the guttering oil-flame that danced as puffs of wind entered the hatch.

"What you doin' down there, Tully?" demanded a voice from above. "Friskin' him fer his watch?"

"I'll frisk *you* when I git you ashore!" Tully flung up at him. Coombs slid down into the cabin.

"That's all right," said he, "but I ain't trustin' you much!"

"Aw, go to hell!" Tully spat. He stooped and began pawing over the ruck on the floor. Here he picked up a cap, there a piece of torn sleeve. He even found a button, and pocketed that. His search was thorough. When it ended, nothing incriminating was left.

"I reckon they won't git much on us *now*," he grinned, and contemplatively worked back and forth a loosened tooth that hardly hung to the gum. "An' if they try to lay it on us, they can't prove nothin'. All of us swearin' together can git by. There ain't no witness except *him*," with a jerk of the thumb at the gasping, unconscious form. "Nobody, unless he gits well, which he ain't noways likely to."

He rolled Hal over, looked down with malice and hate at the pale, battered face, listened a moment to the laboring, slow *râle* of the breath, and nodded with satisfaction. Even the bloody froth on Hal's blue lips gave him joy.

"You got what's comin' to *you*, all right!" he sneered. "Got it proper. Thought you'd git funny with Mac an' his gang, huh? Always butted through everythin', did you? Well, this here was one proposition you couldn't butt through. We was one too many fer *you*, all righto!"

He turned, and saw Coombs with the kris in hand. Fear leaped into his face, but Coombs only gibed:

"You're a great one, ain't you? Coverin' up the story o' what happened here an' leavin' that in a corner!"

Fear gave way to sudden covetousness.

"Gimme that there knife!" demanded Tully. "There *is* a souvenir! That there's a krish. I can hide it O. K. Gimme it!"

Coombs's answer was to stoop, lay the kris down and set his huge sea-boot on it. A quick, upward wrench at the lotus-bud handle and the snaky, poisoned blade, maybe a thousand years old, snapped with a jangle of dissevered steel.

"Here, you!" shouted Tully. But already Coombs had swung to the companion. One toss, and lotus-bud and shattered blade gyrated into the dark. The waves, white-foaming, received them; they vanished forever from the world of men.

"On deck with you now!" commanded Coombs. "If we're goin' to do this at all, we're goin' to make a good job of it. You go first!"

Tully had to obey. Coombs puffed out the light and—leaving Hal Briggs in utter dark, bleeding, poisoned, dying—followed on up the ladder. The dory pushed away, laden with three unconscious men and three others by no means unscathed of battle. Toward the shore it struggled, borne on the hungry surges.

Thus fled the men of McLaughlin's crew—avenged. Thus, brought low by the cursèd thing that had come half-way 'round the world and waited half a hundred years to strike, Hal sank toward the great blackness.

Lotus-bud, symbol of sleep, and poisoned blade—cobra-fang from the dim, mysterious Orient—now with their work well done, lay under waves of storm in a wild, northern sea.

Above, in the black, storm-whipped sky, was the blind face of Destiny peering with laughter down upon the fulfilment of its prophecy?

CHAPTER XLII

IN EXTREMIS

It would be difficult to tell how long the wounded boy lay there, but after a certain time, some vague glimmering of consciousness returned. No light came back. Neither was motion possible to him. His understanding now was merely pain, confusion and a great roaring wind and wave. Utter weakness gripped his body; but more than this seemed to enchain him. By no effort of his reviving will could he move hand or foot; and even the slow breath he took, each respiration a stab of agony, seemed for some reason a mighty effort.

Though Hal knew it not, already the *curaré* was at work, the *curaré* whose terrible effect is this: that it paralyzes every muscle, first the voluntaries, then those of the respiratory centers and of the heart itself. Yet he could think and feel. *Curaré* does not numb sensation or attack the brain. It strikes its victims down by rendering them more helpless than an infant; and then, fingering its way to the breath and to the blood, closes on those a grip that has one outcome only.

Hal Briggs, who had so gloried in the strength and swift control of all his muscles, who had so wrought evil and violent things, trusting to his unbeatable power, now lay there, chained, immobile, paralyzed.

He thought, after a few vain efforts to move:

"I must be badly cut to be as weak as this. I must be bled almost to death. I'm going to die. That's certain!"

Still, he was not afraid. The soul of him confronted death, unterrified. Even while his laboring heart struggled against the slow instillation of the *curaré*, and even while his lungs caught sluggishly at the air, his mind was undaunted.

He wanted light, but there was none. A velvet dark enveloped everything —a dark in which the creaking fabric of the *Kittiwink* heaved, plunged till it rolled his inert body back against the shell of the craft, then forward again.

"I got some of them, anyhow," he reflected, with strange calmness. "They didn't get away without a lot of punishment. If they hadn't knifed me, I'd have cleaned up the whole bunch!"

A certain satisfaction filled his thoughts. If one must die, it is good to know the enemy has taken grievous harm.

Still, what, after all, did it matter? He felt so very languid, so transfixed with that insistent pain in the right lung! Even though he had killed them all, would that have recompensed him for the failure of all his cherished plans, for the loss of the life that was to have meant so wildly much to him?

He felt a warm oozing on his breast, and knew blood was still seeping. His lips tasted salty, but he could not even spit away the blood on them. *Curaré* is of a hundred different types. This, which he had received, had numbed his muscles beyond any possibility of waking them to action. A few vain efforts convinced him he could not move. So there he lay, suffering, wondering how any loss of blood—so long as life remained—could so paralyze him.

His thoughts drifted to Snug Haven, to his grandfather, to Ezra, to Laura, but now in more confusion. He realized that he was fainting and could do nothing to prevent it. A humming, different from the storm-wind, welled up in his ears. He felt that he was sinking down, away. Then all at once he ceased alike to think, to feel.

When next he came to some vague consciousness, he sensed—millions of miles away—a touch on his shoulder, a voice in his ears. He knew that voice; and yet, somehow, he could not tell whose voice it was. He understood that his head was being raised. Very dimly, through closed eyelids that he could not open, he perceived the faint glimmer of a light.

"Hal!" he heard his name. And then again: "Hal!"

The futile effort to move, to answer, spent his last forces. Once more the blackness of oblivion received him mercifully.

"Hal! Oh, God! Hal, speak to me! *Answer me!*" Laura's voice trembled, broke as she pleaded. "Oh—they've killed you! *They've killed you!*"

With eyes of terror she peered down at him. In her shaking hand the little electric search-lamp sent its trembling beam to illuminate the terrible sight there on the cabin floor. The girl could get only broken impressions—a pale, wan face; closed eyes that would not open; a fearful welter of blood on throat and chest.

"Look at me! Speak to me! You aren't dead—look at me! It's Laura! Hal —*Hal!*"

Her words were disjointed. For a moment presence of mind left her. For a moment, she was just a frightened girl, suddenly confronted by this horrible thing, by the broken, dying body of the man she had so loved. And while that moment lasted she cried out; she gathered Hal to her breast; she called to him and called again, and got no answer.

But soon her first anguish passed. She whipped back her reason and forced herself to think. The prescience she had felt of evil had indeed come true. The furtive, dark figures that from her window she had seen slinking toward Hadlock's Cove, had indeed sought Hal just as she had felt that they were seeking him. And the numb grief that, after she had seen Hal passing down the road, had still chained her at that upper window peering out into the darkening storm, had all at once given place to action.

What strategies she had had to employ to escape from the house! What a battle with the tempest she had fought, with wind and rain tearing at her long coat, the pocket of which had held the flashlight! Ay, and that battle had been only a skirmish compared to the launching of a dory, the mad struggle through the surf. All thought of danger flung to the wings of heaven, all fear of Hal abandoned, and of losing her good name in case of being seen by any one, so she had battled her way to him—to warn him, to save him.

Laura, suddenly grown calm with that heroic resolution which inspires every true woman in the moment of need, let the boy's head fall back and mustered her thoughts. She realized the essential thing was go for help, at once. Strong as she was, and nerved with desperation, she knew the task of dragging Hal up the companionway, of getting him into her dory, of carrying him ashore in the gale-beaten surf surpassed her powers.

So she must leave him, even though he should die alone there.

But, first, she could at least give him some aid. She peered about her, flicking the electric beam over the trampled confusion. What could she use for bandages? A smashed suit-case yawned wide, its contents slewed about. She caught up a shirt, tore it into broad strips and, laying the flashlight in the berth, bent to her work.

"Oh, God!" she whispered, as she laid bare the wound; but though she felt giddy, she kept on. The sagging dead weight of Hal's body almost overbore her strength. She held it up, however, and very tightly bound him, up around the massive neck, over the back, across the high-arched, muscular chest. She knotted her bandages, and let Hal sink down again.

Then she smoothed back his drabbled hair. She bent and kissed him; snatched the light, turned and fled up the companion, clambered down into the dory, and cast loose.

All the strength of her young arms had to strain their uttermost. Passionately she labored. The wounded man no longer was the brute who had so cruelly sought to wrong her. He was no longer the untamed savage, the bully, the thief. No, in his helplessness he had gone swiftly back to the boy she had known and loved—just Hal, her boy.

The storm-devils, snatching at her, seemed incarnate things that fought her for his life. The wind that drove her away from the shingle-beach and toward the rocks below Jim Gordon's store, the lathering crests that spewed their cold surges into the dory as it heaved high and swung far down, seemed shouting: "Death to Hal!"

Laura, her hair down and flying wild, pulled till wrists and arms seemed breaking. For a few minutes she thought herself lost; but presently, when breath and strength were at the ragged edge, she began to hear the loud, rattling clamor of pebbles on the shingle. A breaker caught the dory, flung it half round, upset it. Into the water, strangling, struggling, Laura plunged. The backwash caught her, tugged at her. She found footing, lost it, fell and choked a cry in cold brine.

The next breaker heaved her up. She crawled through wrack and weed, over jagged stones, and fell exhausted on a sodden windrow of drift.

For a minute she could move no further, but had to lie under the pelting rain, with the dark hands of ocean clutching to drag her back. But presently a little strength revived. She crawled forward once more, staggered to her feet, and, falling, getting up again, won to the top of the dune.

Off to her left, dim through the shouting night, the vague light-blurs of old man Gordon's windows were fronting the tempest. The girl struggled forward, sobbing for breath. Not all the fury of the North Atlantic, flung against that shore, had turned her from her task.

Astonished beyond words, the lobstermen and fishers eyed her with blank faces as she burst in the door. Under the light of tin reflectors, quids remained unchewed, pipes unsmoked. Bearded jaws fell. Eyes blinked.

The girl's wet, draggled hair, her bloodless face and burning eyes stunned them all.

"Quick, quick!" she implored. "Hal Briggs—"

"What's he done now, girl?" cried old Sy Whittaker, starting up. "He ain't hurt *you*, has he? If he *has*—"

"He's been stabbed, aboard the *Kittiwink*! He's bleeding to death there!"

Chairs scraped. Excitement blazed.

"What's that, Laura?" cried Gordon. "Stabbed? Who done it?"

"Oh, no matter—go, quick—go, *go*!"

"Damn funny!" growled a voice from behind the stove. "Gal goin' aboard night like this, an' him stabbed. Looks mighty bad!"

"You'll look a damn sight wuss if you say that agin, or anythin' like it!" shouted the old storekeeper with doubled fist. "Hal Briggs ain't worryin' me none, but this here is Laura, old man Maynard's gal, an' by the Jeeruzlem nobody ain't goin' to say nothin' about her! Tell me, gal," he added, "is he hurt bad?"

She caught him by the arm. He had to hold her up.

"Dying, Jim! Bleeding to death! Oh, for the love of God—hurry, *hurry!*"

Around them the rough, bearded men jostled in pea-coats, slickers, sou'westers. The tin reflectors struck harsh lights and shadows from rugged faces of astonishment.

"Who could o' done it?" began Shorrocks, the blacksmith. "They'd oughta be ketched, an'—"

"Never you mind about that!" cried Gordon. He caught from a nail a formless old felt hat and jammed it on his head; he snatched up a lighted lantern standing on the counter, and with a hobnailed clatter ran for the door.

"Everybody out!" he bellowed. "Everybody out now, to help Laura!"

Into the storm he flung himself. All hands cascaded toward the door.

"You stay here, gal!" advised Asahel Calkins, lobsterman. "Ain't no night fer you!"

"I can't stay! Let me go, too!" she pleaded. They made way for her. With the men she ran. Two or three others had lanterns, but these made no more than tiny dancing blurs of light in the drenching dark. Along a path, then into the field and up to the storm-scourged dune they stumbled, pantingly, bucking the gale. The lanterns set giant legs of shadows striding up against the curtain of the rain-drive, as the men pressed onward. Snapping, Laura's skirts flailed.

Over the dune they charged, and scuffled down to the dories. Disjointed words, cries, commands whipped away. Strong hands hustled a dory down. Laura was clambering in already, but Jim Gordon pulled her back.

"No, gal, no!" he ordered sternly. His voice flared on the wind as he shoved her into the arms of Shorrocks. "You, Henry, look out for her. Don't let her do nothin' foolish!"

He set his lantern in the dory, impressed Calkins and another into his service, and scrambled aboard. A dozen hands ran the dory out through the first breakers. Oars caught; and as the men came up the beach, dripping in the vague lantern-light, the dory pulled away.

To Laura, waiting with distracted fear among the fishermen, it seemed an hour; yet at the most hardly fifteen minutes had passed before the little boat came leaping shoreward in white smothers. Out jumped Gordon. Laura ran to him, knee-deep in a breaker.

"Is he—*dead?*" she shivered, with clacking teeth.

"Nope. Ain't much time to lose, though, an' that's a fact. He's cut *some*, looks like! Goddy mighty, but there must o' been some fight out there!"

He turned to the dory. With others, he lifted out a heavy body, wrapped in sailcloth, horribly suggestive of a burial at sea. Laura gripped her hands together for self-mastery.

"Oh, hurry, hurry!" she entreated.

"We'll do all we kin, gal," some one answered, "but we ain't no real amb'lance-corpse. It's goin' to be a slow job, gittin' him home."

"Here, Laura, you carry a lantern an' go ahead, 'cross the field," commanded Gordon, with deep wisdom. Only to give her something to do, something to occupy her mind, was kindness of the deepest. Into her hand old Calkins thrust a lantern.

"All ready!" cried he. "H'ist anchor, an' away!"

Seven or eight men got hold, round the edges of the sailcloth, and so, swinging the inert Hal as in a cradle, they stumbled to the road, with Laura going on ahead.

To the right they turned, toward Snug Haven. Now Laura walked beside them. Once in a while she looked at the white face half seen in its white cradle, now beginning to be mottled with crimson stains.

But she said no other word. Strong with the calm that had reasserted itself, she walked that night road of storm and agony.

Thus was Hal Briggs borne back to his grandfather's house.

In the cabin at Snug Haven old Captain Briggs—having finished his letter to Hal and put that, too, in the safe—had now come to the last task of all, the sacrifice that, so he faithfully believed, was to remove the curse of Dengan Jouga from his boy.

A strange lassitude weighed down upon the old man, the weariness that comes when a long journey is almost done and the lights of home begin to shine out through "the evening dews and damps." The captain felt that he had come at last to journey's end. He sat there at his desk, eying the revolver, a sturdy, resolute figure; an heroic figure, unflinchingly determined; a figure ennobled by impending sacrifice, thoughtful, quiet, strong. His face, that had been lined with grief, had grown quite calm. The light upon it seemed less from his old-time cabin-lamp than from some inner flame. With a new kind of happiness, more blessed than any he had ever known, he smiled.

"Thank God!" he murmured, with devout earnestness. "It won't be long now afore I'm with the others that have waited for me all this time up there on Croft Hill. I'm glad to go. It isn't everybody than can save the person they love best of anything in the world, by dying. I thought God was hard with me, but after all I find He's very good. He'll understand. He'd ought to know, Himself, what dying means to save something that must be saved!"

Once more he looked at Hal's picture. Earnestly and simply, he kissed it. Then he laid it on the desk again.

"Good-by," said he. "Maybe you won't ever understand. Maybe you'll blame me. Lots will. I'll be called a coward. You'll have to bear some burden on account of me, but this is the only way."

His expression reflected the calm happiness which comes with realization that to die for one beloved is a better and more blessèd thing than life. Never had old Captain Briggs felt such joy. Not only was he opening the ways of life to Hal, but he was cleansing his own soul. And all at once he felt the horror of this brooding curse was lifting—this curse which, during fifty years, had been reaching out from the dark and violent past.

He breathed deeply and picked up the revolver.

"God, Thou art very good to me," he said quietly. "I couldn't understand the way till it was shown me. But now I understand."

Toward his berth he turned, to lie down there for the last time. As he advanced toward it he became vaguely conscious of some confusion outside. A sound of voices, gusty and faint through the wind, reached him. These came nearer, grew louder.

Listening, he paused, with a frown. Of a sudden, feet clumped on the front steps. Heavily they thudded across the porch. And with sharp insistence his electric door-bell trilled its musical *brrr!*

"What's that, now?" said the captain. Premonitions of evil pierced his heart. As he hesitated, not knowing what to do, the front door boomed with the thudding of stout fists. A heavy boot kicked the panels. A voice bawled hoarsely:

"Briggs! Ahoy, there, cap'n! Let us in! Fer God's sake, let us in!"

CHAPTER XLIII

CURARÉ

"Who's there?" cried Alpheus Briggs, astonished and afraid. He faced toward the front hall. "What's wanted?"

A tapping at his window-pane, with eager knuckles, drew his attention. He heard a woman's voice—the voice of Laura Maynard:

"Here's Hal! Let us in; quick, *quick!*"

"Hal?" cried the old man, turning very white. That evil had indeed come to him was certain now. He strode to his desk, dropped the revolver into the top drawer and closed it, then crossed over to the window and raised the shade. The face of Laura, with disheveled hair and fear-widened eyes, was peering in at him. Briggs flung the window up.

"Where is he, Laura? What's happened? Who's here with him?"

"Oh, I can't tell you, captain!" she whispered. He saw her trembling; he noted those big, terror-stricken eyes, and thrilled with panic. From the front door sounded a confused bass murmur; and again the bell sounded. "Men from the store," she gulped, "Jim Gordon and others. They're—"

"They're what, Laura? Bringing Hal back home?"

She nodded silently. He thought he had never seen a woman so pale.

"Captain, let them in!" she cried. "I've got to tell you. Hal—is injured. Open the door, quick! Get Dr. Filhiol!"

Everything else forgotten now, the captain turned, precipitated himself into the hall and snatched open the front door. Gusts of rain and wind tugged at him, flapping his bath robe. For a moment, not understanding anything, he stood peering out at what was all a blur of perfectly incomprehensible confusion. His fear-stricken eyes and brain failed to register any clear perception. A second or two, he neither heard nor saw. Then he became aware that some one—Jim Gordon, yes—was saying:

"We done the best we could, cap'n. Got him here as fast as we could. We'll bring him right in."

The captain saw something white out there on the dark, wet porch. In the midst of this whiteness a form was visible—and now the old man perceived a face; Hal's face—and what, for God's sake, was all this crimson stain?

He plunged forward, thrusting the men aside. A lantern swung, and he saw clearly.

"God above! They've—they've murdered him!"

"No, cap'n, he ain't dead yit," said some one, "but you'd better git him 'tended to, right snug off."

Old Briggs was on his knees now gathering the lax figure to his arms.

"Hal! Hal!"

"Shhh!" exclaimed Gordon. "No use makin' a touse, cap'n. He's cut some, that's a fact, but—"

"Who killed my boy?" cried the old man, terrible to look upon. "Who did this thing?"

"Captain Briggs," said Laura tremulously, as she pulled at his sleeve, "you mustn't waste a minute! Not a second! He's got to be put right to bed. We've got to get a doctor now!"

"Here, cap'n, we'll carry him in, fer ye," spoke up Shorrocks. "Git up, cap'n, an' we'll lug him right in the front room."

"Nobody shall carry my boy into this house but just his grandfather!" cried the captain in a loud, strange voice.

The old-time strength of Alpheus Briggs surged back. His arms, that felt no weakness now, gathered up Hal as in the old days they had caught him when a child. Into the house he bore him, with the others following; into the cabin, and so to the berth. The boy's head, hanging limp, rested against the old man's arm, tensed with supreme effort. The crimson stain from the grandson's breast tinged the grandsire's. Down in the berth the captain laid him, and, raising his head, entreated:

"Hal, boy! Speak to me—speak!"

Gordon laid a hand on his shoulder.

"It ain't no use, cap'n," said he. "He's too fur gone." With a muffled clumping of feet the others, dripping, awed, silent, trickled into the room. Laura had already run up-stairs, swift-footed, in quest of Dr. Filhiol. "It ain't no use. Though mebbe if we was to git a little whisky into him—"

"Hal! Master Hal!" wailed a voice of agony. Old Ezra, ghastly and disheveled, appeared in the doorway. He would have run to the berth, but Shorrocks held him back.

"You can't do no good, Ez!" he growled. "He's gotta have air—don't you go crowdin' now!"

The shuffling of lame feet announced Dr. Filhiol. Laura, still in her drenched long coat, helped him move swiftly. Calkins shoved up a chair for him beside the berth, and the old doctor dropped into it.

"A light here!" commanded he, with sudden return of professional instinct and authority. Laura threw off her coat, seized the lamp from its swinging-ring over the desk, and held it close. Its shine revealed the pallor of her face, the great beauty of her eyes, the soul of her that seemed made visible in their compassionate depths, where dwelt an infinite forgiveness.

"You'll have to stand back, captain," ordered the doctor succinctly. "You're only smothering him that way, holding him in your arms; and you must *not* kiss him! Lay him down—so! Ezra, stop that noise! Give me scissors or a knife, quick!"

Speaking, the doctor was already at work. With the sharp blade that Calkins passed him he cut away the blood-soaked bandage and threw it to the floor. His old hands did not tremble now; the call of duty had steeled his muscles with instinctive reactions. His eyes, narrowed behind their spectacles, made careful appraisal.

"Deep stab-wound," said he. "How did he get this? Any one know anything about it?"

"He got it in the cabin of the *Kittiwink*," answered Laura. "Everything was smashed up there. It looked to me as if Hal had fought three or four men."

"McLaughlin's!" cried the captain. His fists clenched passionately. "Oh, God! They've murdered my boy! Is he going to die, Filhiol? Is he?"

"That's impossible to say. We'll need plenty of hot water here, and soap and peroxide. Towels, lots of them! Ezra, you hear me? Get your local doctor at once. And have him bring his surgical kit as well as his medical. Tell him it's a deep stab, with great loss of blood. Get a move on, somebody!"

Ezra, Gordon and Calkins departed. The front door slammed, feet ran across the porch, then down the steps and away.

"Everybody else go, too," directed Filhiol. "We can't have outsiders messing round here. Get out, all the rest of you—and mind now you don't go making any loose talk about who did it!"

Silently the fishermen obeyed. A minute, and no one was left in the cabin save old Briggs, Filhiol and Laura, gathered beside the wounded, immobile figure in the berth.

"How long will it take to get your local doctor?" demanded Filhiol, inspecting the wound that still oozed bright, frothy blood, showing the lung to be involved in the injury.

"Ten minutes, perhaps," said Laura.

"H-m! There's no time to lose here."

"Is he going to die?" asked the old captain, his voice now firm. He had grown calm again; only his lips were very tight, and under the lamp-glow his forehead gleamed with myriad tiny drops. "Is this boy of mine going to die?"

"How can I tell? Why ask?"

"If he does, I won't survive him! That's the simple truth."

"H-m!" grunted Filhiol, once more. He cast an oblique glance at the captain. And in that second he realized that the thought, which had been germinating in his brain, could lead him nowhere; the thought that now his wish had really come to pass—that Hal was really now his patient, as he had wished the boy might be. He knew, now, that even though he could so far forget his ethics as to fail in his whole duty toward Hal Briggs, the captain held an unconscious whip-hand over him. Just those few simple words, spoken from the soul—"I won't survive him"—had closed the doors of possibility for a great crime.

Ezra came in with a steaming basin, with soap and many towels.

"Put those on this chair here," commanded Filhiol. "And then either keep perfectly quiet, or get out and stay out!"

Cowed, the old man tremblingly obliterated himself in the shadow behind the desk. The doctor began a little superficial cleaning up of his patient. Hal had still shown no signs of consciousness, nor had he opened his eyes. Yet the fact was, he remained entirely conscious. Everything that was said he heard and understood. But the paralysis gripping him had made of him a thing wherein no slightest power lay to indicate his thought, or understanding. Alive, yet dead, he lay there, much as the *amok* Malay of fifty years before had lain upon the deck of the *Silver Fleece*. And all his vital forces now had narrowed to just one effort—to keep heart and lungs in laboring action.

Little by little the invading poison was attacking even this last citadel of his life. Little by little, heart and lungs were failing, as the *curaré* fingered its way into the last, inner nerve-centers. But still life fought. And as the doctor bent above Hal, washing away the blood from lips and throat and chest, a half-instinctive analysis of the situation forced itself upon him. This wound, these symptoms—well, what other diagnosis would apply?

"There's something more at work here," thought he, "than just loss of blood. This man could stand a deal of that and still not be in any such collapse. There's poison of some kind at work. And if this wound isn't the cut of a kris, I never saw one!"

He raised one eyelid, and peered at the pupil. Then he closed the eye again.

"By the Almighty!" he whispered.

"What is it, doctor?" demanded the captain. "Don't keep anything from me!"

"I hate to tell you!"

The old man caught his breath, but never flinched.

"Tell me!" he commanded. Laura peered in silence, very white. "I can stand it. Tell me all there is to tell!"

"Well, captain, from what I find here—there can be no doubt—"

"No doubt of what?"

"The blade that stabbed Hal was—"

"That poisoned kris?"

Filhiol nodded silently.

"God above! The curse—retribution!"

"Oh, for heaven's sake, captain, drop all that nonsense!" flared out the doctor from taut nerves. "This is no time for your infernal superstitions! We've got all we can handle without cluttering things up with a mess of rubbish. We've got a long, hard fight on our hands."

"I know. But you can save him, doctor! You must!"

"I'll do all in human power. This wound here I'm not in a position to deal with. Your local doctor can attend to that. It isn't the vital feature of this case. The poison is!"

"You've got a remedy for that, haven't you? You said you had!"

"Do you realize it's been an hour, perhaps, since this wound was made? If the *curaré* had been fresh and new—" He finished with an expressive gesture. "It's old and dried, and some of it must have been worn off the blade. Perhaps, not a great deal got into the cut. There's a chance, a fighting chance —perhaps."

"Then the remedy! Quick, doctor! Get it, make it!"

"I've got to wait till the physician comes. I've got no drugs with me."

"Will he have the right ones?"

"They're common enough. It all depends on the formula, the exact mixture."

"You remember them?"

"Maybe I can, if you don't disturb my mind too much."

"I'll be quiet, doctor. You just order me, and I'll do anything you say," the old man promised abjectly. His eyes were cavernous with suffering. "Lord God! why don't Dr. Marsh come?"

"Hal here is suffering from a general paralysis," said Filhiol. "This *curaré* is peculiar stuff." He laid his ear to Hal's chest, listened a moment, then raised his head. "There's some heart-action yet," said he. "Our problem is to keep it going, and the respiration, till the effects pass. It's quite possible Hal isn't unconscious. He may know what's going on. With this poison the victim feels and knows and understands, and yet can't move hand or foot. In fact, he's reduced to complete helplessness."

"And yet you call me superstitious when I talk retribution!" the captain whispered tensely. "I lived by force in the old days. He, poor boy, put all his faith and trust in it; he made it his God, and worshipped it. And now—he's struck down, helpless—"

"It *is* strange," Filhiol had to admit. "I don't believe in anything like that. But certainly this is very, very strange. Yes, your grandson is more helpless now than any child. Even if he lives, he'll be helpless for a long time, and very weak for months and months. This kind of *curaré* used by the upper Malay people is the most diabolical stuff ever concocted. Its effects are swift and far-reaching; they last a long, long time, in case they don't kill at once. Hal can never be the same man he used to be, captain. You've got to make up your mind to that, anyhow."

"Thank the Lord for it!" the old man fervently ejaculated. "Thank the good Lord above!"

"If he lives, he may sometime get back a fair amount of strength. He may be as well as an average man, but the days of his unbridled power and his terrific force are all over. His fighting heart and arrogant soul are gone, never to return."

"God is being very good to me!" cried Briggs, tears starting down his wrinkled cheeks.

"Amen to that!" said Laura. "I don't care what he'll be, doctor. Only give him back to me!"

"He'll be an invalid a very long time, girl."

"And all that time I can nurse him and love him back to health!"

Footsteps suddenly clattered on the porch. The front door flung open.

"Laura! Are you all right? Are you safe?" cried a new voice.

"There's my father!" exclaimed the girl. "And there's Dr. Marsh, with him!"

Into the cabin penetrated two men. Nathaniel Maynard—thin, gray, wiry —stood staring. The physician, brisk and competent, set his bag on a chair and peeled off his coat, dripping rain.

"Laura! Tell me—"

"Not now, father! Shhh! I'm all right, every way. But Hal here—"

"We won't have any unnecessary conversation, Mr. Maynard," directed Dr. Marsh. He approached the berth. "What is this, now? Stab-wound? Ah, yes. Well, I'll wash right up and get to work."

"Do, please," answered Filhiol. "You can handle it alone, all right. I've got a job of my own. There's poisoning present, too. *Curaré.*"

"*Curaré!*" exclaimed Marsh, amazed. "That's most unusual! Are you sure?"

"I didn't serve on ships in the Orient, for nothing," answered Filhiol with asperity. "My diagnosis is absolute. There was dried *curaré* on the blade that stabbed this man. It's a very complex poison—either $C_{18}H_{35}N$, or $C_{10}H_{35}N$. Only one man, Sir Robert Schomburg, ever found out how the natives make it, and only one man—myself—ever learned the secret of the antidote."

"So, so?" commented Marsh, rolling up his shirt-sleeve. He set out antiseptics, dressings, pads, drainage, and proceeded to scrub up. "We can't do this work here in the berth. Clear the desk, Ezra," he directed. "It's long enough for an operating-table. Make up a bed there—a few blankets and a clean sheet. Then we can lift him over. We'll strip his chest as he lies—cut the clothes off. Lively, every one! *Curaré*, eh? I never came in contact with it, Dr. Filhiol. I'm not above asking its physiological effects."

"It's unique," answered Filhiol. He got up from beside the wounded man and approached the chair on which stood the doctor's bag. "It produces a type of pure motor-paralysis, acting on the end plates of the muscles and the peripheral end-organs of the motor-nerves. First it attacks the voluntary muscles, and then those of respiration. It doesn't cause unconsciousness, however. The patient here may know all that's going on, but he can't make a sign. Don't trust to this apparent unconsciousness in exploring the wound. Give plenty of anesthetic, just as if he seemed fully conscious."

"Glad you told me that," said Marsh, nodding. "How about stimulants, or even a little nitroglycerine for the heart?"

"Useless. There's just one remedy."

"And you've got it?"

"I can compound it, I think. It's a secret, given me fifty years ago by a Parsee in Bombay. He'd have lost his life for having given it, if it had been known. Let me have some of your drugs, will you?"

"Help yourself," answered Marsh, drying his hands.

While Laura and the captain watched in silence, Filhiol opened the bag, and after some deliberation chose three vials.

"All right," said he. "Now you to your work, and I to mine!"

"Got everything you need?"

"I'll want a hypodermic when I come back—if I succeed in compounding the formula."

"How long will you be?"

"If I'm *very* long—" His look finished the phrase. Laura came close to Filhiol.

"Doctor," she whispered, her face tense with terrible earnestness. "You *must* remember the formula. You can't fail! There's more than Hal's life at stake, now. The captain—you've got to save him!"

"And you, too! Your happiness—that is to say, your life!" the old man answered, laying a hand on hers. "I understand it all, dear. All, perfectly. I needn't tell you more than that!"

He turned toward the door.

"Captain Briggs, sir," said he, "I was with you in the old days, and I'm with you now—all the way through. Courage, and don't give up the ship!"

CHAPTER XLIV

NEW DAWN

Twenty minutes later, anxious fingers tapped at Filhiol's door.

"Come!" bade the doctor. Laura entered.

"Forgive me," she begged. "I—I couldn't stay away. Dr. Marsh has got the wound closed. He says that, in itself, isn't fatal. But—"

She could not finish. From the hallway, through the open door, penetrated the smell of ether.

"The captain's been just splendid!" said she. "And Ezra's got his nerve back. I've helped as much as I could. Hal's in the berth again."

"What's his condition?"

"Dr. Marsh says the heart action is very weak and slow."

"Respiration?" And Filhiol peered over his glasses at her as he sat there before his washstand, on which he had spread a newspaper, now covered with various little piles of powder.

"Hardly ten to the minute. For God's sake, doctor, do something! Haven't you got the formula yet?"

"Not yet, Laura. It's a very delicate compound, and I have no means here for making proper analyses, or even for weighing out minute quantities. I don't suppose a man ever tried to work under such fearful handicaps."

"I know," she answered. "But—oh, there must be *some* way you can get it!"

Their eyes met and silence came. On the porch roof, below the doctor's window, the rain was ruffling all its drums. The window, rattled in its sash, seemed in the grip of some jinnee that sought to force entrance. Filhiol glanced down at his little powders and said:

"Here's what I'm up against, Laura. I'm positively sure one of these two nearest me is correct. But I can't tell which."

"Why not test them?"

"One or the other is fearfully poisonous. My old brain doesn't work as well as it used to, and after fifty years—But, yes, one of these two here," and he pointed at the little conical heaps nearest him with the point of the knife wherewith he had been mixing them, "one of these two must be the correct formula. The other—well, it's deadly. I don't know which is which."

"If you knew definitely which one was poisonous," asked she, "would that make you certain of the other?"

"Yes," he answered, not at all understanding. "But without the means of making qualitative analyses, or the time for them, how can I find out?"

She had come close, and now stood at his left side. Before he could advance a hand to stop her, she had caught up, between thumb and finger, a little of the powder nearest her and had put it into her mouth.

"Holy Lord, girl!" shouted the old man, springing up. His chair clashed to the floor. "How do you know which—"

"I'll know in a few moments, won't I?" she asked. "And then you'll be able to give the right one to Hal?"

The old doctor could only stare at her. Then he groaned, and began to cry. The tears that had not flowed in years were flowing now. For the first time in all that long and lonesome life, without the love of woman to soften it, he had realized what manner of thing a woman's love can be.

She remained there, smiling a little, untroubled, calm. The doctor blinked away his tears, ashamed.

"Laura," said he, "I didn't think there was anything like that in the world. I didn't think there was any woman anywhere like you. It's too wonderful for any words. So I won't talk about it. But tell me, now, what sensations do you get?" His face grew anxious with a very great fear. He came close to her, took her hand, closely watched her. "Do you feel anything yet?"

"There's a kind of stinging sensation on my tongue," she answered, with complete quietude, as though the scales of life and death for her had not an even balance. "And—well, my mouth feels a little numb and cold. Is that the poison?"

"Do you experience any dizziness?" His voice was hardly audible. By the lamp-light his pale face and widened eyes looked very strange. "Does your heart begin to accelerate? Here, let me see!"

He took her wrist, carefully observing the pulse.

"No, doctor," she answered, "I don't feel anything except just what I've already told you."

"Thank the good God for that!" he exclaimed, letting her hand fall. "You're all right. You got the harmless powder. Laura, you're—you're too wonderful for me even to try to express it. You're—"

"We're wasting time here!" she exclaimed. "Every second's precious. You know which powder to use, now. Come along!"

"Yes, you're right. I'll come at once." He turned, took up the knife, and with its blade scraped on to a bit of paper the powder that the girl had tested. This he wrapped up carefully and tucked into his waistcoat-pocket.

"Dow-nstairs, Laura!" said he. "If we can pull him through, it's you that have saved him—it's *you!*"

The thud of the old doctor's feet seemed to echo in the captain's heart like thunders of doom. He got up from beside the berth and faced the door, like a man who waits the summons to walk forth at dawn and face the firing-squad. Dr. Marsh, still seated by the berth, frowned and shook his head. Evidently he had no faith in this old man, relic of a school past and gone, who claimed to know strange secrets of the Orient.

"This boy is dying," thought Marsh. "I don't believe in all this talk about *curaré*. He's dying of hemorrhage and shock. His pulse and respiration are practically *nil*—his skin is dusky with suffocation already. Even if the old chap has a remedy, he's too late. Hal's gone—and it will kill the captain, too. What a curse seems to have hung to this family! Wiped out, all wiped out!"

In the doorway appeared Laura and old Filhiol. The girl's face was burning with excitement. The doctor's eyes shone strangely.

"Still alive, is he?" demanded Filhiol.

"Yes," answered Marsh. "But you've got no time for more than one experiment."

"Got it, Filhiol?" choked the captain. His hands twitched with appeal. "Tell me you've—got it!"

"Water! The hypodermic needle!" directed Filhiol, his voice a whiplash.

He mixed the powder in a quarter-glass of water, and drew the solution up into the glass barrel of the syringe. Ezra, unable to bear any further strain, sank down in a chair, buried his face in both hands and remained there, motionless. Dr. Marsh, frankly skeptical, watched in silence. The girl, her arm about the captain, was whispering something to him. Through the room sounded a hollow roaring, blent of surf and tempest and wind-buffetings of the great chimney.

Filhiol handed the hypodermic to Marsh.

"Administer this," he commanded. "Your hands have been sterilized, and mine haven't. We mustn't even waste the time for me to scrub up, and I'm taking no chances at all with any non-surgical conditions."

Marsh nodded. The old man was undoubtedly a little cracked, but it could do no harm to humor him. Marsh quickly prepared an area of Hal's arm, rubbing it with alcohol. He tossed away the pledget of cotton, pinched up the bloodless skin, and jabbed the needle home.

"All of it?" asked he, as he pushed down the ring.

"All!" answered Filhiol. "It's a thundering dosage, but this is no time for half measures!"

The ring came wholly down. Marsh withdrew the needle, took more cotton and again rubbed the puncture. Then he felt Hal's pulse, and very grimly shook his head.

"Laura," said he, "I think you'd better go. Your father, when he left, told me to tell you he wanted you to go home."

"I'm not afraid to see Hal die, if he's got to die, any more than I'm afraid to have him live. He's mine, either way." Her eyes were wonderful. "I'm going to stay!"

"Well, as you wish." Dr. Marsh turned back to his observation of the patient.

Filhiol stood beside him. Wan and haggard he was, with deep lines of exhaustion in his face. The old captain, seated now at the head of the berth, was leaning close, listening to each slow gasp. Now and again he passed a hand over his forehead, but always the sweat dampened it once more.

"Any change?" he whispered hoarsely.

"Not yet," Marsh answered.

"It couldn't take effect so soon, anyhow," cut in Filhiol. "It'll be ten minutes before it's noticeable."

Marsh curled a lip of scorn. What did this superannuated relic know? What, save folly, could be expected of him?

The seconds dragged to minutes, and still Marsh kept his hold on the boy's wrist. A gust of wind puffed ashes out upon the hearth. Somewhere at the back of the house a loose blind slammed. The tumult of the surf shuddered the air.

"Oh, God! Can't you tell yet?" whispered the captain. "Can't you tell?"

"*Shhh!*" cautioned Filhiol. "Remember, you're captain of this clipper.

252

You've got to hold your nerve!"

The clock on the mantel gave a little preliminary click, then began striking. One by one it tolled out twelve musical notes, startlingly loud in that tense silence.

Marsh shifted his feet, pursed his lips and leaned a little forward. He drew out his watch.

"Humph!" he grunted.

"Better?" gulped Alpheus Briggs. "Better—or worse?"

"I'll be damned!" exclaimed Marsh.

"What *is* it?"

"Dr. Filhiol, you've done it!"

"Is he—dead?" breathed Laura.

"Two more beats per minute already!" Marsh answered. "And greater amplitude. Captain Briggs, if nothing happens now, your boy will live!"

The old man tried to speak, but the words died on his white lips. His eyes closed, his head dropped forward as he sat there, and his arms fell limp. In his excess of joy, Captain Alpheus Briggs had fainted.

By early dawn the tempest, blowing itself clean away with all its wrack of cloud and rain, left a pure-washed sky of rose and blue over-arching the wild-tossing sea. The sun burned its way in gold and crimson up into a morning sprayed with spindrift from the surf-charges against the granite coast. All along the north shore that wave army charged; and the bell-buoy, wildly clanging, seemed to revel in furious exultation over the departed storm.

The early rays flashed out billions of jewels from drops of water trembling on the captain's lawn. Through the eastward-looking portholes of the cabin, long spears of sunlight penetrated, paling the flames on the hearth. Those flames had been fed with wood surpassing strange—with all the captain's barbarous collection of bows and arrows, blowpipes, spears and clubs, even to the brutal "Penang lawyer" itself.

Before the fire, in a big chair, Ezra slept in absolute exhaustion. Dr. Marsh was gone. By the berth Filhiol was still on guard with Laura and the captain. All three were spent with the terrible vigil, but happiness brooded over them, and none thought of rest or sleep.

In the berth, now with open eyes, lay Hal, his face white as the pillow. With the conquering of the paralysis, some slight power of motion had returned to him; but the extreme exhaustion of that heavy loss of blood still gripped him. His eyes, though, moved from face to face of the three watchers, and his blue lips were smiling.

A different look lay in those eyes than any that had ever been there, even in the boy's moments of greatest good humor. No longer was there visible that latent expression of arrogance, of power, cruelty and pride that at any moment had been wont to leap like a trapped beast tearing its cage asunder. Hal's look was now not merely weakness; it took hold on gentleness and on humanity; it was the look of one who, having always gloried in the right of might, had found it swiftly turn to the bursting bubble of illusion.

This Hal now lying bandaged and inert in the old captain's berth was no longer the Hal of yesterday. That personality had died; another had replaced it. Something had departed from the boy's face, never to return again. One would almost have said the eyes were those of madness that had become suddenly sane—eyes from which a curse had all at once been lifted, leaving them rational and calm.

Hal's eyes drifted from the old doctor's face to the captain's, rested a moment on Laura, and then wandered to the fireplace. Surprise came, at sight of the bare bricks. The captain understood.

"They're gone, Hal," said he. "Burned up—they were all part and parcel of the old life; and now that *that's* gone they can't have any place here. I know you'll understand."

Hal made an effort. His lips formed the words soundlessly: "I understand."

"He'll do now," said Filhiol. "I'm pretty far gone. I've got to get a little rest or you'll have two sick men on your hands. If you need anything, call me, though. And don't let him talk! That punctured lung of his has got to rest!"

He got up heavily, patted Hal's hand that lay outside the spread, and hobbled toward the door.

The captain followed him, laid a hand on his shoulder.

"Doctor," said he in a low tone, "if you knew what you've done for me— if you could only understand—"

"None of that, sir!" interrupted the old man sternly. "A professional duty, sir, nothing more!"

"A million times more than that! You've opened up a new heaven and a new earth. You've given Hal back to me! I can see the change. It's real! The old book's closed. The new one's opened. You've saved a thing infinitely more than life to me. You've saved my boy!"

Filhiol nodded.

"And you, too," he murmured. "Yes, facts are facts. Still, it was all in the line of duty. We're neither of us too old to stand up to duty, captain. I hope we'll never be. Hal's cured. There can't be any manner of doubt about *that*. The curse of unbridled strength is lifted from him. He's another man now. The powers of darkness have defeated themselves. And the new dawn is breaking."

He paused a moment, looking intently into the old captain's face, then turned again toward the door.

"I'm very tired now," said he. "There's nothing more I can do. Let me go, captain."

Alpheus Briggs clasped his hand in silence. For a long minute the hands of the two old men gripped each other with eloquent force. Then Filhiol hobbled through the door and disappeared.

The captain turned back to Laura. There were tears in his eyes as he said:

"If there were more like Filhiol, what a different world this would be!"

"It *is* a different world to-day, anyhow, from what it was yesterday," smiled Laura. She bent over Hal and smoothed back the heavy black hair from his white forehead. "A different world for all of us, Hal!"

His hand moved slightly, but could not go to hers. She took it, clasped it against her full, warm breast, and raised it to her mouth and kissed it. She felt a slight, almost imperceptible pressure of his fingers. Her smile grew deep with meaning, for in that instant visions of the future were revealed.

The sunlight, strengthening, moved slowly across the wall whence now the kris had been torn down. A ray touched the old captain's white hair, englorifying it. He laid his hand on Laura's hand and Hal's; and in his eyes were tears, but now glad tears that washed away all bitter memories.

From without, through a half-opened window that let sweet June drift in, echoed sounds of life. Voices of village children sounded along the hedge. Cartwheels rattled. The anvil, early at work, sent up its musical *clank-clank-clank* to Snug Haven.

From an elm near the broad porch, the sudden melody of a robin, greeting the new day after the night of storm, echoed in hearts now infinitely glad.

THE END

Lightning Source UK Ltd.
Milton Keynes UK
UKHW010721130722
405793UK00001B/235